SCRIBBLING THE ETERNAL

For Ashley Vargas,
Meet me in the Oblivion.

And in memory of my friend Ian Williamson,
I wrote my sequel as promised.

ONE

Berthold Leitz returned from his walk around the observation deck of the Tokyo Skytree and took his place beside me and remained silent as I continued to stare beyond the glass windows at the circuitry of lights below that stretched in all directions, defining the boundaries of this great metropolis where we had spent our past six years. Including my mortal birthdays, today was my twenty-second. But to anyone else observing us on this observation deck, I was still only twelve, and the tall man accompanying me was my father, even though, in truth, my immortality began years before his. As far as anyone was concerned, we were but American tourists with lots of money to spend. No one saw us for what we really were—nocturnal predators who lived on human blood.

"Orly, is there anything you'd like for your birthday?" Berthold asked.

As had become my habit, my right hand went to the diamond pendant that hung from my neck over my heart. When I realized I was holding it, I let go and continued to stare at the lights below. Neither of us could fly to this height in our relatively youthful immortalities. We had taken the elevator up, like all the mortals around us.

I recalled how relieved I had been when we first arrived in Japan. The visual overstimulation of lights and the constant movement of crowds worked as a distraction to the memories of what I had left behind in Los Angeles. The overwhelming confusion that came with the full and immediate immersion into a culture and language I did not comprehend was an even greater comfort as it impaired my understanding of my surroundings. My mind went gray and I became purely visceral. I was no longer in my headspace dwelling on naming the things that hurt, not even in my own language. I felt only nameless pain, and for me, that was easier to live with. And so that is how I survived in the beginning, after Berthold and I retreated to the other side of the world. Every night, I roamed the streets of Tokyo, feeding, and giving no thought to my broken heart.

But as the months passed and we became accustomed to this new way of life and our proficiencies in this new language grew, I regained the consciousness that displacement and alienation had formerly allowed me to discard. When that happened, harrowing thoughts returned and haunted memories were replenished in my mind's eye. It was beyond doubt—torment had found its way back to me here—here, in the Land of the Rising Sun.

Berthold suspected my feelings and suggested we go elsewhere, again someplace where we didn't know the language—where we could stop thinking so much and thereby stop feeling as much. But it wasn't as easy as throwing a dart at a map to find a place to run to. In too many countries, too many people spoke English as a second or third language. And in many of the countries where English was not spoken, we would not be welcome as Americans, so we would likely have to remain in Asia.

The elevator door opened behind me and with the exception of the uniformed operator, the car was empty. I did not need to turn to know he was a young man with a youthful haircut. He stood waiting for someone who wanted to descend. I turned and headed straight for him. Berthold followed.

"Matano okoshiwo omachi shiteorimasu." he said when I entered the car.

"Tanoshikatta desuyo," I replied, and he smiled. The fluency of a twelve-year-old foreigner surprised him.

The elevator door closed and our descent began. No one said a word, but it was an expected silence rather than an uncomfortable one. My eyes glanced at the throat of the elevator operator. His Adam's apple hardly protruded, making his throat appear soft, feminine, delicate, and delicious. I turned to Berthold. "There is something I would like for my birthday."

He looked at me and his eyes flashed at the operator.

I shook my head and Berthold waited for me to reveal my birthday wish. I had decided right there, during the descent inside that elevator car that I would no longer distance myself from the place of origin of my grief.

"I want to go home. To Los Angeles."

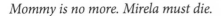

Mommy is no more. Mirela must die.

Six years have passed since I said those words to myself the night I found Yelena dead, a pile of ashes on her bed—killed by the sunlight she allowed to enter her bedroom and lay in wait for. My mother had been driven to suicide by a promise made by Mirela Cobălcescu, our bloodline's empress, a promise that she would kill me if Yelena did not first kill herself. As mementos from that morning I have only the lab created diamond I wear around my neck—made of my mother's remains—and the black scar on my wrist that never healed since the sunlight seared my skin when I tried to save her. Though I no longer feel the physical pain of the burn, the scar serves as a constant reminder of the sacrifice Yelena had made out of love for me and how terribly cruel I had been to her before she gave up her life in order to preserve mine.

Six years have passed and I never took my revenge. I never even attempted it. I never even saw Mirela again. My heart may still be reckless, but my mind was slowly becoming cautious as I matured, and I had Berthold's counsel telling me that no one so young as I could challenge one who has roamed the Earth for more than five thousand years. I would need powerful allies, ancient allies, Berthold advised in the weeks following Yelena's death when my anger toward Mirela still raged beyond my control. I had no such allies. And in my limited exposure to our Cobălcescu bloodline, I had never met a Cobălcescu who had lived even a tenth of Mirela's five millennia, save for Alexi Pavlovich, and he was her consort.

And even if I had a band of ancient vampires by my side, would the sum total of their years, even if in excess of Mirela's, be enough to murder the source of our bloodline? And what would happen to us, her descendants, when the brightest light of the Cobălcescu was snuffed out?

It was fated. I was doomed to endure my mother's murderer forever. The true forever. I would never avenge Yelena.

After descending the Skytree, Berthold and I fed in Shinjuku, close to where we lived when we first arrived. For our first residence we rented a "mansion" which in Tokyo basically meant a two bedroom apartment. We chose Shinjuku because we read it was where the most nightlife was. For the most part, it was true. It was easy to disappear in the throngs of people excitedly roaming the streets at night. Finding desirable victims took no effort at all. The vitality and ecstasy the blood gave me kept me as merciless as ever and I fed regularly without conscience.

Berthold and I loved Shinjuku, but in my perennial sadness over the loss of Yelena and my inability to find romantic love, living amongst constant crowds eventually became too much for me to deal with once I had fed, and so, a couple years later, we leased a new upscale and expensive apartment in Azabu. It was still Tokyo, but the wealth required to live there also meant it was quieter. We would still venture into Shinjuku and Shibuya to feed, but after our thirsts were satiated we had the luxury to retreat to someplace tranquil.

We thought of moving to Kyoto but were advised to stay in Tokyo by the Ketsuen coven of vampires who presided over all the islands of Japan. Their bloodline, like all of the eleven bloodlines, had spread across the globe, but the Ketsuen origins were here, and it was said that the eldest of them, Hisashi and Konomi—known as the Eternal Lovers— remained here as well, but were rarely seen by any of the Ketsuen, and certainly never by us.

The Ketsuen were very hospitable. We had been given an introduction through Yelena's best friend Hisato, who was also part of the Ketsuen bloodline. The Ketsuen treated us like family and always invited us to their blood parties which were lavish and bordered on ostentatious. They all had the same theme—feeding, drinking, and sex. It made things clear for me in how Hisato had cultivated his flamboyance. The first blood party we attended was actually thrown in our honor to celebrate our arrival. We fed, got drunk, but only Berthold had sex. I was still a virgin, according to Yelena at least—the rapes by my foster brother when I was seven didn't count. We were given many gifts. I was given mostly clothing and jewelry and Berthold was given an expensive watch and a black Porsche Turbo Cabriolet. He loved driving that car through the Tokyo streets at night with the top down when it wasn't raining. But the greatest gifts we received that night weren't exactly gifts—they were on loan to us. They were humans. Servants to do our bidding, to procure things for us in the hours of daylight, and most importantly, of course, they were tasked with disposing of all the corpses our unquenchable thirsts would stack up. Their names were Arliss Bloch and Mayuko Mochizuki. They were chosen for us as they were fluent in both Japanese and English.

Arliss did not look Japanese as he was not. He came from Belgium. Besides Japanese and English, he also spoke Dutch, French, German, and Hebrew. He was on loan to Berthold from a senior vampire named Eizo. And when I say senior, I don't only mean in terms of seniority amongst the Ketsuen, but also because he was already elderly when first given his immortal blood, which, as far as I had seen, was not common among the vampire race as physical beauty was always sought first, except in a case like mine. I was noticed by Yelena Solodnikova due to my ability to scribble portraits of people and see their pasts within the scribbles. Through the scribbles I found evildoers for her to feed upon guiltlessly. Yelena's love quickly followed, but it still stands that I wasn't discovered for my beauty, and therefore I would always appear plain in the presence of other vampires. But perhaps my lack of a striking appearance is what made my looks remarkable amongst them. Arliss, on the other hand, was very good looking. He was in his mid-twenties, slightly shorter than Berthold, but still tall, especially in Japan. He had dark brown hair but stunningly bright blue eyes. He was already pale, but not vampire pale, as was evidenced by his ruddy cheeks whenever it rained.

With Arliss serving Berthold, this meant Mayuko would be serving me. Unlike Arliss, however, Mayuko did not belong to any one of the Ketsuen—she was acquired in anticipation of my arrival. She was beautiful, with irises that were like black pearls and her skin was without wrinkle or blemish. Like many young Japanese women, her hair was lightened, Mayuko's dyed a milk tea brown. It hung nearly to her shoulders and on one side she always wore a hair clip, which helped show off her prepossessing face.

Mayuko was quiet, but not timid, and she had the most tranquil smile I had ever known. At five foot three, she was taller than I was, but unlike me, she appeared delicate, like the fronds of a fern—far more feminine than I was, stuck within my undeveloped child's body. With a slight frame and a grace that reminded me of Yelena, Mayuko, with her nimble steps, seemed already to move with the elegance of a vampire. But a vampire she was not—the scent of her blood gave her mortality away. But what always caught my attention were Mayuko's legs. Despite being in proportion with the rest of her, her legs appeared remarkably thin. Upon first sight, I was perplexed, wondering how the Ketsuen believed this frail tendril of a woman could possibly ever carry a corpse.

But to my surprise, she managed with ease. Her appearance was deceiving—she was quite strong. Though I was still sixteen and she was already nineteen when we met, we became fast friends, and because of that, I often spent my nights hunting with her at my side. Early on, Mayuko told me she was interested in watching me kill. She wasn't sadistic, she just wanted to know what her own future would look like when her period of servitude for the Ketsuen ended and she would be made immortal herself.

I never scribbled while I was in Japan as I had never adopted Yelena's guilt for killing the innocent, and scribbling would have brought back too many memories from my own past with her. So instead, I fed on anonymous victims, not caring what they had done or not done. I don't know why, and I don't believe it was intentional, but I certainly had more male victims than female. Maybe it meant I didn't like men, or maybe it meant that I liked them more. Because even though I was killing them, there was still something inherently intimate about placing my teeth on a man's throat. Regardless of the reason, my eyes naturally selected men, but something trivial like an annoying laugh was enough for me to prey upon a woman instead.

As we prowled the crowded city together, something else that always caught my attention when it came to Mayuko was the way men would look at her. Even though they were not subtle in the way they would turn their heads to follow her with their eyes, Mayuko never seemed to notice. But I did. She was obviously beautiful to look at and her presence was enhanced by her grace, which I have already mentioned. Both of these qualities drew notice, but what held their admiration beyond a glance was the way she dressed. It wasn't revealing or vivacious. If anything, it was subdued. It stated that she wasn't an attention seeker, an aspiring celebrity, or internet famous. I think it made her more desirable as it gave the impression of her being within reach. She adorned herself with simple blouses covered with soft cardigans. Her stylish skirts were modest and neatly pressed, and to complete her ensemble, Mayuko always wore black stockings. When the weather grew colder I made her trade in her stockings for warmer thigh high socks, and the contrast between the black woven fabric and the porcelain skin of her thighs made her admirers gawk even more shamelessly. Whether it was love or lust, I could never be sure, but she certainly held their interest, and this made me jealous. And because of my jealousy, it occurred to me on more than one occasion to kill her, but each time I relented, and instead only smiled at her, after remembering how much I enjoyed her company. I then killed her admirers instead.

Mayuko was wearing thigh high socks this night we encountered a sharply dressed young salaryman coming out of a bar. He immediately had eyes for Mayuko, and for the first time, Mayuko also glanced at him. But as we were already engaged in a conversation about the sacrificial murder of a child in the kabuki play Shinrei Yaguchi No Watashi, she said nothing of the young salaryman to me, and we kept walking. From behind, I heard him turn his head to watch Mayuko go, but something must have sparked inside him and given him courage because, soon after, his footsteps began to pursue us.

As he didn't know he was following us to his own death, he stayed with us for nearly ten minutes when I turned down an empty alley and Mayuko followed. When we were near a metal staircase that ran up the side of a building and I could hear his footsteps getting close to the mouth of the alley, I hid in the shadows, leaving Mayuko alone under the staircase. The man entered the alley and saw Mayuko in the distance. As he approached, his gait remained even, never pausing in his steps, even when he noticed the little American who had been with Mayuko was no longer there. He was probably glad I was gone.

From the shadows, I watched as he neared her. He smiled and then so did she. He asked her name. He asked why she was in this alley alone, but he never asked about where I had gone. The small talk didn't last long before he placed his hands around her waist and leaned forward and kissed Mayuko gently. She didn't kiss him back at first, but as he continued to kiss her she finally responded—kissing him and placing her dainty hands on his firm upper arms. It was a beautiful moment between them and I would have savored it longer had it not flashed in my mind that I would never know such a moment myself. No stranger would ever kiss me in a lonely alleyway on a chilly night like this. My jealousy embraced my hate and my soul screamed that I had seen enough. I sprung from the cover of shadow and pulled the young salaryman down to the pavement by the hair on the back of his head. Mayuko stumbled a couple of steps backward and our eyes locked as I bit into his throat. Though the bloody drama unfolding was, by that night, routine, it was also extraordinary. There was something new in Mayuko's countenance, something I had never seen in her face—remorse.

I released my bite. Although I had not bled him dry, he was dead. While drinking, I had felt his heart stop. Mayuko also knew her newfound lover was dead. She had seen so many dead versions of my victims that she now recognized them on sight. She stared at me mournfully.

Though I knew the answer, I asked her, "What's wrong?"

"Nothing."

"You look upset, Button." Button was my nickname for her.

She shook her head. "I'm fine, Cricket." Cricket was her nickname for me.

"You should have told me not to kill him."

"But why?"

"Because you loved him," I said, showing my inexperience in matters of the heart.

"I knew him only a minute." Her eyes were fixed upon his corpse.

"Maybe it was love at first sight."

She looked at me when I said that. "You are my master, Orly. I am here to serve you, and you must feed. My feelings are unimportant."

Even though I knew she meant what she said about her feelings not being important, I didn't know how true it was. They were important to me and I became frightened. Mayuko was my closest girlfriend. I didn't want to lose her friendship and affection or have her hating me. I told myself I would make it up to her.

I would have preferred to watch the men, potential boyfriends for Mayuko, go by from the vantage point of a rooftop, above the crowds, rather than down on the sidewalk, in the midst of them, but Mayuko's eyes were not yet vampiric, so she couldn't recognize attraction at that distance. We stood in front of the plate glass window of a storefront, looking into the faces of the men who passed. Most of them looked at Mayuko as they walked by, but she was skilled at observing without making eye contact. Mayuko was very picky indeed, and I was hungry. But finally, she allowed herself to look one in the eye, and he stopped when she smiled. As I vanished within the crowd, she asked him if he knew of a good teppanyaki restaurant nearby and he did. I watched them go, before departing in the opposite direction, hungry and alone.

Since I was still so young as an immortal, it was difficult not to feed. Without human blood, I would become ill pretty quickly. I could only go two nights without it, and with the weakness that came without feeding, that second night had to be spent shut inside the coffin I traveled with as coffins were generally lighter than caskets. Besides that practicality, I had left the casket Yelena had given me in Los Angeles to remind me where my true home was.

At that time I still didn't know Tokyo well enough to be able to dispose of victims myself, so I would have needed Mayuko if I killed. But I wanted her to be happy, dining with her sweetheart over teppanyaki. I wanted her to find as much romantic love as she could so I killed a man without her anyway. After I drank all his blood, I weighted his corpse and after a long, fast walk over the water's surface, I dropped him into Tokyo Bay.

Mayuko and I spent our nights like this for over a month. Me watching her attract men, and her going off with them. Me killing in the city alone, and then gliding over the small moonlit waves like a phantom, laying to rest bodies that were eagerly swallowed by the darkness of the bay.

Often Mayuko would protest, telling me that she wasn't fulfilling her duties, especially with the disposal of the bodies, but I reminded her that she was there to serve me and until I said otherwise, her primary job duty was to find love every night.

When evening came, Mayuko would wake me, simply by placing her hand on the lid of my coffin. I could feel the warmth of her mortality emanating through the dark wood, and I would gently slide the lid open, letting her know I was awake. As the coffin I traveled with was too large for me, I would rise and sit in it like a bathtub, pulling my knees into my chest and invite Mayuko to remove the lid completely and come in and sit at the foot end of the coffin and tell me about her adventure on the previous night.

I loved hearing what the men would say to try to seduce her. Sometimes she was receptive, but usually she wasn't, which meant sometimes she had sex, but usually she didn't. She would tell me about the dinners, the drinks, the long midnight strolls, and the slow dances where their bodies pressed together. As she related the amorous details to me I often stopped seeing Mayuko's face in the story and replaced it with my own. I wanted these romances myself, but was resigned to live vicariously through my servant.

Everything was fine until, by freak accident, an unmanned university submarine came across the remains of two of my victims at the bottom of Tokyo Bay. The police were alerted and whatever the university had been researching had to be put on hold while the bay was dragged for more bodies. For a couple of weeks, body after body made news headlines, causing a panic throughout Tokyo. In truth, the police didn't find half the bodies I had deposited in the bay but they recovered sixteen corpses. At first, all eyes looked upon different factions of the Yakuza gangs, but as bodies were identified through DNA records and were matched up with missing person reports, doubt was cast on the organized crime theory as only one of my victims fished out of the sea had a criminal record. The next theory was more accurate and more terrifying to the public—there was a serial killer on the loose.

But the Ketsuen knew it was neither the Yakuza nor an ordinary serial killer. They knew the truth. They knew it was a vampire. They also knew it was a vampire who, through the sloppy disposal of a body at the bottom of a bay that had a depth of only forty meters, risked exposure of their existence.

And their theory was confirmed when that sixteenth body was recovered. It belonged to a subway packer named Joji Kishimoto. The fish at the bottom of the bay had not chewed on his corpse long enough before he was dragged to the surface. My tiny bite marks were still plainly visible on his throat.

TWO

Mayuko and I immediately went back to the roles expected of us when the first body was discovered. I hunted and she disposed of the remains according to the secret customs of the Ketsuen. Together, we decided to pretend we had never done anything but what tradition demanded and hope for the best. But when that sixteenth corpse of Joji Kishimoto was found with two punctures along his jugular and the headline that day was Kyūketsuki!, meaning Vampire!, we really panicked. Though I had no expectation of what the Ketsuen response would be, I expected one and was fearful of it. But I was not nearly as frightened as Mayuko.

Trembling as she sat opposite me in my coffin Mayuko whispered, "If they find out it's us, they might be lenient with you, Orly, but they will never pity a mortal. And they will give me a bad death."

I hugged her because I didn't know what to say. I knew she was right. And vampires can be so clever in their methods of killing. I squeezed her so tightly to stop her anxious quivering that I almost killed her.

But as the nights passed, the strangest thing happened—nothing. Nothing at all. Eventually the body count stopped climbing and the headlines moved on to more mundane things. New months replaced former months and I began to feel we were in the clear, and by the time of the cherry blossoms, Mayuko was her old self again.

But I missed hearing of her romances. Mayuko recognized this and for a few weeks she attempted to date during the day, while I slept, so she would have stories to tell when she woke me, but after spending night after night ridding the world of my kills, she was usually too tired to be anything more than listless on her dates, and despite her beauty, it seemed to be a turn off to most men. I wanted love so badly that I needed it, and no longer having Mayuko as a firsthand source to satisfy me, I decided to go out looking for it for myself. I didn't tell Mayuko or Berthold though. I didn't tell anybody. I didn't think they would laugh at me, but I thought they would express too much concern and want to chaperone me or give me advice I didn't want to hear. For even though I was in my late teens, everyone still treated me like the child I appeared to be.

When I would venture out alone after a feeding, I would scan the nightlife until I found a group of twenty year olds and follow them. Often these pursuits led me to bars or dance clubs where I was either not permitted inside or I was removed once discovered. But during the minutes I was inside among them it was never difficult for me to gain the attention of whomever I desired—I was a vampire after all. Our gaze is naturally meant to attract, and mine did too. But when man or woman would answer the call of my eyes and approach, they wouldn't embrace me as they would have Yelena or Berthold. Instead, they would kneel to my height, or worse—pat me on the head. The seduction in my eyes made them love me, just not in the way I longed for. Their blood pumping hearts would beat for me affectionately as a child they wanted to care for and protect, but not throb for me as a lover they wanted to fondle and abuse. In the end it usually made me wish they hadn't seen me at all.

I didn't think it would be this difficult to find a guy to have sex with me in Japan. It's pretty apparent that contemporary Japanese society sexualizes young girls. Just look at the manga and the maid bars. But as an American white girl, maybe I looked too out of place to sexualize. And being a child wandering the streets late at night only made me more conspicuous. I wanted to disappear.

I never forgot how Yelena could walk amongst mortals unseen. That's how she would walk right past the nurses outside of visiting hours and stay with me in the hospital when I was still dying of cancer. "It's in the way you look back at them," she said. "They no longer register you're there." I tried with great effort to find meaning and instruction in those two sentences that made the feat seem so simple, but it was far from easy.

As it should already be clear, there were always people out and about I could look back at, hoping to disappear before them. In order to practice, I began walking through Ueno Park nightly. The later the hour the more stares I would receive, which told me I wasn't succeeding in my quest for invisibility amongst mortals. I looked right back at them, staring into their faces, but they still saw me, and now, with this different type of gaze, never once did I see desire in their eyes. The repeated lack of desire in their eyes hurt me enough that at times I thought of scribbling for pedophiles, but I wanted love, not rape.

Yelena used to marvel at my ability to see the innermost secrets people held just by looking into the scribbled renditions I would create of them. I wondered, had I put into words how I did it, could I have passed on my talent to my mother? I doubted it. My scribbling was not a vampiric power. It was a skill I possessed before she used immortality to save me from my leukemia.

But I knew it was possible to force the learning of vampiric powers. Through practice and determination I learned to open locks and doors with my mind years before most fledgling vampires could accomplish such a task. But after months of wandering amongst the crowds, still unsuccessful and fully visible, I concluded that not all vampiric powers could be gained through sheer will—it seemed this one I would have to wait for.

It was around the time I quit trying to disappear that I stumbled upon Harajuku. The clothing and styles I found worn and sold there fascinated me. The dress patterns seemed to be from a former century. I loved all the soft colors and all the lace. I admired the designs imprinted on the fabric—carousel horses and cupcakes—the cuteness of it all—kawaii as they called it.

Many of the girls who wore these dresses were in their twenties, just like I nearly was, but they were purposely made to look younger, like the age I naturally appeared to be. It was a revelation. I decided to change my image and embody the style of this subculture which embraced childlike youth, thinking I might finally fit in here and find someone to love me.

I had more than enough money to buy a whole new wardrobe, and during my first night in Harajuku, I went into a shopping frenzy. In the first store I entered, I grabbed dress after dress off the racks. The piles of designer clothing I stacked up branched out like a pastel rainbow. What a new look this would be for me!

But the rainbow evaporated while I was in the dressing room. The dress I put on first was white and lilac and looked as happy as a birthday cake. It was all wrong. I stood before the mirror looking like an effigy made by a sculptor who never knew me. I held up more dresses, without putting them on, thinking I just needed a new color. I tried sky blue, mint green, carnation pink. They were a spectrum of mistakes.

By that year, I was so accustomed to wearing black exclusively, just like Yelena had, that I couldn't see myself in anything else.

I beheld myself in the first dress again and reasoned that maybe it was only a case of too much change too quickly, and that I would grow accustomed to it and find my place, my inconspicuous place, amongst the other girls of Harajuku. But the longer I stared in the mirror the more sure I became that even if I blended in, like milk in coffee, I would still feel conspicuous, and not in a way that would allow me to feel good about myself.

There was a knock on the door frame and the curtain opened. The sales girl looked at me in the mirror and exclaimed how kawaii I appeared, but then I turned to her and she saw the expression on my face. My Japanese still wasn't great back then so it was difficult for me to explain to the girls running the shop that I couldn't stand to wear all those colors. But eventually they nodded. They understood. I knew they understood because they appeared disappointed. They would have to put back all the dresses I insisted trying on. But then, in one of those eureka moments, one of the girls cried out in English, "Gothic Lolita!" and suddenly everyone was smiling again.

They tried to make me understand, but I couldn't be made to, and eventually one of them, Shiori, walked me out of the little store and down the alley to another store that renewed all my hopes. The styles inside were similar, with the ruffles and lace, but the colors were absent. The dresses were black. Well, mostly black. Many incorporated white opposite the black and a few used color accents, but the primary color was definitely black. I thanked Shiori and expected her to go back to her shop, but she insisted on staying with me, helping me try on black dresses.

As Shiori buttoned the back of the first black dress, I looked at myself again in the mirror, and it's hard to say what I felt, but I was smiling. It was a brand new me that I still recognized. I didn't exactly feel like a princess, but I felt like I could walk into the pages of a fairy tale. I felt stuck in time, like a porcelain doll who would never grow up. And with that being my own personal truth, I realized that this look, this Gothic Lolita as they had called it, was quite fitting for me. In both reality and illusion, I was a blossoming adult in the guise of a child. Shiori was so ecstatic that it was easy for me to feel excited about my transformation.

We had already put seven dresses, four pairs of shoes, three pairs of boots, and a number of accessories aside, when I found myself in the dressing room alone, trying on an eighth dress. Shiori was in another section of the store, looking for parasols. By then blind exhilaration had transformed into acute scrutiny, as I examined the details and accents of the dress and paid particular attention to how it hung on my body. The dress was exquisite, but as I caught my first glimpse of myself in it I thought absentmindedly, "You look like a nineteenth century child going to her mother's funeral."

Her mother's funeral.

I paused and stared so deeply into the mirror that I saw beyond myself.

Yelena.

I closed my eyes and, with a struggle, I kept a blood tear from falling.

I sensed someone's hand on the knob of the door behind me. I opened my eyes and looked above my head in the mirror to see who was coming in behind me. I expected Shiori, but it wasn't anyone I recognized. It was another young woman. She was pretty. Prettier than I was, and I stared, looking at her deeply until she began to flatten in my vision, as if losing her third dimension and no longer standing out before her background, as if she were trapped inside the mirror she came to see herself in.

She stepped into the tiny dressing room and bumped into me as she tried to close the door. I blinked my eyes and refocused upon her eyes. She saw me then and began apologizing and bowing, and I realized then she had not seen me at all until I allowed it. I had done it. If only for an instant, I had become invisible.

Shiori helped me carry all the things I purchased back to the first shop. The two other shop girls were surprised at how much I purchased as these fashions were far from inexpensive. I felt so grateful to the three of them, Shiori especially, that in my broken Japanese I told them I'd like to buy each of them a new dress, but none of them accepted.

I took a cab back to Shinjuku as to not appear conspicuous to the girls in the shop. In the cab, all I could think about was that young woman not seeing me. I stared forward into the rear view mirror, noticing the cab driver watching me now and then. I practiced looking back at him, trying to remember and recreate the gaze I had inadvertently perfected in the dressing room. It took multiple glances, but once he slammed on the brakes when he no longer saw me in the mirror, I knew with certainty I had acquired the vampiric skill. He quickly turned around in his seat and saw me smiling back at him. My fangs horrified him.

Mayuko was late arriving the next evening. I assumed it was because she had to get rid of a second body the night before. When she had been late in the past, I would simply slide open the coffin lid myself, rise, and listen to music, often dancing alone until she showed up to dance with me. But as I was wearing one of my new dress ensembles, I lay there in my coffin waiting impatiently for her to touch the lid and wake me.

The quarter of an hour she was late felt like half an eternity, but eventually I heard her enter the apartment. She stepped into my room, knelt, and placed her hand on the lid of my coffin. I shut my eyes. Not receiving a response, she knocked lightly, but it wasn't enough to rouse me from my pretended sleep. Slowly, she slid open the coffin lid, and stared down at my lifeless body.

She gasped at the sight of me. "Look at your clothes!" she exclaimed happily. "Orly," she called. But I did not answer.

She leaned close to my right ear. "Orly," she whispered. "Good morning, sunshine."

I struggled not to smile as that phrase she often used to wake me seemed so odd to say to a vampire. She shook me gently, but I still wouldn't wake. Instinctively, as a living and breathing human, Mayuko touched my face to see if I was warm, but of course I was cold, and my frigidity quickly reminded her that I was undead.

"Orly," she said sternly, and shook me harder, but still I lay dead. "Orly," she said again, this time louder and with a trace of panic in her voice. She turned her head toward the open doorway. "Berthold!" she cried. "Come quick! It's Orly!"

In an instant, Berthold was in the doorway. There would be no fooling him. He would know I was alive and just playing dead. He assessed the situation immediately and played along. "What is it?" he asked in an irritated voice that made it clear he did not appreciate being disturbed.

"I'm sorry," Mayuko said. "But she won't wake."

"No? That's perplexing," Berthold said flatly. "Perhaps she lost track of time."

Mayuko looked at him, confused.

"I suggest you sit her up," he said.

Mayuko grabbed both of my wrists and began pulling me into a seated position in my coffin. When I reached ninety degrees I let my eyes pop open, the way a doll would open its glass eyes, and startled her. Stupefied, Mayuko screamed, and in reaction to the fright I gave her and in what appeared to be a single motion, she let go of my wrists and slapped me across the face. I fell back and my head softly hit the satin pillow inside my coffin. Mayuko brought her hands to her mouth, horrified that she had struck me. Immediately, she bowed lowly, placing her hands flat on the floor and resting her forehead upon her fingers. She began gushing apologies, to me, her mistress, begging for forgiveness.

I lay still just to savor the moment a little longer, and then began to laugh, and so did Berthold. I sat up, still laughing, and watched as Mayuko lifted her head just enough to look at me and gauge my temperament. I extended my arms to her. "I'm sorry, Button," I said. "It was only a joke. I let it go too far."

She rose to her knees and bowed her head, a little embarrassed, but then she too began to giggle and allowed me to take her in my arms.

I released her and stepped out of my coffin and twirled in my new dress for Mayuko to see. Berthold took his leave, probably to go read something boring, as Mayuko raved over my new look. I opened my closet and showed her the other dresses one by one.

After I fed, I returned to Ueno Park again, alone. Mayuko had asked to accompany me once the body was taken care of, but I declined and instructed her to go home. I strolled down the many paved paths looking for groups of people I could approach and walk amongst without them ever seeing me. Invisibility became more natural with every person I passed. But there was more to this trick, I remembered. When Yelena would disappear, it wasn't like watching a magician vanish in a puff of smoke, leaving an audience mystified and wondering where he would reappear. When Yelena would disappear, those who had been looking at her would forget they ever saw her. It was as if she had never been there. How had she done it? If only Yelena were here to teach me. But as that was hopeless, I knew I would have to learn this part of the trick on my own just as I had with the invisibility itself.

I was standing before a shrine when I heard a couple approaching. I turned and looked at them, but didn't allow my gaze to flatten. It was two women, probably in their thirties. Startled, they stopped in their tracks when they saw me—this pale little girl, this pallid, colorless Gothic Lolita. I adjusted my gaze and vanished before their eyes. They screamed, looked around for me briefly before turning and running away. I had failed, or rather, I had only half succeeded. I disappeared but they saw me disappear and were able to remember that I had once been there. Dejected, I left the shrine and walked on. I came upon more people, this time a group of teens. They saw me coming but then also saw me disappear, dematerializing before their eyes. Some of them screamed and all of them ran.

Berthold was out when I got home. I assumed he was feeding. Around three o'clock he entered the apartment. He asked me how my evening had been and I told him I had learned to disappear. I hadn't told him the night before when I had actually discovered how, and I didn't know why. I sensed he was envious, so I did my best to describe to him how I had done it, and we began practicing together. It was difficult to gauge our success as we could not disappear in this way to another vampire. He used his cell phone to call Arliss and told him to come to the apartment immediately. Arliss arrived no more than ten minutes later.

"How may I be of service?" Arliss asked after he had shut the door.

"Just stand there, please," Berthold answered.

I did not attempt to disappear, but Berthold was doing his best to follow the instructions I had given him. Arliss looked at us both bewildered, wondering what we were trying to prove by standing before him silently, and why it was necessary for him to come over at this late hour to witness our odd behavior. Neither Berthold nor I revealed our goal to Arliss. Again, I don't know why we didn't tell him; it just felt unnatural to be forthcoming just as it was unnecessary to provide an explanation to a servant.

About an hour passed like this, with all three of us standing before each other, when Berthold finally said, "Arliss, go home please."

"As you wish," his servant replied, more confused than ever as he left.

"Thank you for not disappearing before him," Berthold said.

I nodded my head. He didn't need to say more. I knew not to disappear as it would reveal to Arliss what Berthold was trying to do and thereby highlight what he, his master, was unable to accomplish. I sensed his envy again.

"It just takes practice," I said, trying to console him.

He pursed his lips and muttered something unintelligible.

"I haven't perfected it myself," I said. "I can't do it like Yelena did."

"What do you mean?"

"Well, like, if I disappear in front of someone they see me disappear. Or no, that's not it. They remember that I was just standing there and then freak out when I'm suddenly gone. You know what I mean?"

"I understand."

"Yelena somehow made them forget. Like she was never there in the first place. Do you remember?"

Even though he hadn't been saying much, the mention of Yelena seemed to make Berthold grow quiet. He responded to my question merely with a nod.

"Did she ever tell you how she did it?" I asked, knowing it was unlikely that he would be able to answer in the affirmative, as by the time Berthold first rose from the earth as a vampire, Yelena was already dead.

He shook his head slightly. Of course, he was telling the truth, but I began to wonder if he would tell me a lie if she had shared the secret with him. I don't know what I would have said in his place.

I persevered in practicing every night in Ueno Park, but I made no progress. All that was accomplished was the origination of a rumor regarding the ghost of a little girl haunting the park. People would get a glimpse of her and suddenly she would be gone. I had been seen at various shrines, on various paths, beside Shinobazu Pond, and inside and outside the museum. I didn't care though. Let them think I was a ghost. What was important was that I needed to figure out how to make them forget me.

I began to worry that my specter was causing more attention than the Ketsuen would tolerate. So I decided to move my studies to Chikurin Park instead. I had just vanished in a bamboo grove, causing a passerby to point and shriek in horror, when there was suddenly a hand on my shoulder. I turned quickly.

"Oh Amy, you scared the shit out of me," I laughed, relieved to see a friendly face.

Amy was an American but was part of the Ketsuen. She was short, but I was still shorter, and her brown hair was long and wavy. Like the scarves she always wore, there was always something warm about her, despite the fact that her skin, like mine, was always cold.

"Orly," she said. "Take a walk with me."

We wandered further into the bamboo, distancing ourselves from the path.

"Forgive me," she began, "but I must ask you to stop roaming these places. People are already saying Ueno Park is haunted by a little girl. I see now that Chikurin Park will soon carry the same myth."

"Why?" I asked stupidly.

She smiled pleasantly. "I know you're trying to learn and gain powers, but you must be patient. These things will all come in time. Trust me."

"But if you practice you can gain powers faster. I know. I've done it."

"Orly, you're not understanding. I'm asking you to stop, but the Ketsuen are demanding it. You're drawing too much attention again."

"Again?"

"We know it was you dumping bodies in the bay."

My mind immediately went to Mayuko. The Ketsuen knew it was me. Would Mayuko be safe?

Amy told me no one was going to stop me from wandering Tokyo invisibly, but my disappearing act before onlookers had to stop, and it had to stop that night. There was nothing I could do but agree. As we walked on, I thought again of Mayuko and wondered if she was alone in bed that night.

THREE

I continued to prowl the streets unseen by those around me. Invisible, I walked right into bars and nightclubs. I stood beside groups of girls and waited with them for men to approach and ask them to dance. I stood at the edge of the dance floor eyeing them closely as their dancing became more intimate. I stayed near when they retreated to booths, sitting close together over drinks. And when they left together I would follow them, sometimes ending up at a love hotel. Inside these hourly rooms, when the man was on top of the woman, I would get in bed beside them, and lie on my back, trying to fathom what it felt like to be loved for a night.

But my voyeuristic nights didn't last long. The more I partook in them, even when laying beside them, the more excluded and unloved I felt. I knew Berthold loved me. I knew Mayuko loved me. But it wasn't the same. And it was then that the crowds in Tokyo began to overwhelm me with loneliness, finally driving us out of Shinjuku. And in the relative silence of Azabu, when I finally took pause in my search for romantic love, I realized all that was left in my heart was the void Yelena created when she willingly went to her own death.

Nearly four more years passed before I found myself at the Tokyo Skytree telling Berthold it was time to return to Los Angeles. I had run to the edge of the world in order to avoid feeling Yelena's absence and finally recognized I had to go home to face her where I had left her—where I had known her best, where I knew I would see traces of her in the places we had spent together, bonded as mother and child.

When I made my announcement to the Ketsuen that Berthold and I were leaving for America, it took great effort to convince them that it wasn't due to a lack of hospitality. And then it wasn't long before I learned that they were planning a farewell blood party for us.

Mayuko did my hair the night of the party. As she brushed it, I was frustrated with hunger. Ordinarily I would have already fed by that hour. Mayuko reminded me to be patient, telling me I would feed at the blood party. I knew she was right and I began to imagine what the victims would look like and how they would behave once they realized they were caught in the spider's web. Yelena couldn't have stomached one of these parties. She would have pitied those being caroused into attendance before being escorted into a cage. In truth, most went willingly into the cages, mesmerized by the beauty of their escorts and thinking it was the beginning of some kinky game. Once the cages were locked the party would really begin—bottles and bottles of champagnes and whiskies were opened and consumed. Inebriation often led to sexual advances which, in turn, led to sexual adventures between vampires, all out in the open, but never with me—the sole vampire child. The mortals would look on from the cages, eagerly waiting for their release so they too could participate. But it was during the animalistic passions of vampiric lovemaking that fangs would first appear, and bloodletting would take place in orgies of undead paramours. Then the screaming would begin. I loved that moment. It fascinated me. My attentions would turn to the cages kept in the corners of the banquet hall, where the mortals locked within would first realize what we were and that they were awaiting slaughter. The behaviors that followed ranged widely: panic, aggression, confusion, denial, and despair.

Even though I was very hungry, we were purposely late to our party. By the time we arrived to the banquet hall, everything was in full swing. The music was loud. The room brightly lit by candlelight. A large banner hung from the ceiling wishing Berthold and me a safe trip home. Many bottles had already been opened and emptied.

Berthold was immediately grabbed by Natsumi, a vampire he had made love to many times and I believe he truly loved but was unwilling to give himself completely to her because of the torch he still carried for Yelena. They went to a table and sat beside each other over a glass of champagne. Arliss, who had followed Berthold into the hall, became a wallflower, turning his head slightly away from Berthold's direction, but still watching him out of the corner of his eye, waiting for any command on this last night of service to his American master. Arliss was fond of Berthold and earlier in the evening, Berthold gave him a gift of ten million yen for his years of faithful service. At that time it was about a hundred thousand American dollars. Arliss tried to refuse, as was expected, but Berthold insisted.

I held Mayuko's hand as we entered the banquet hall. I was happy to see Mayuko was already wearing the bracelet I had given her earlier in the evening. It was platinum and alternated between diamonds and deep blue sapphires all the way around her slim wrist. I took a seat at a table and Mayuko sat beside me. Drinks were brought to us. We declined the champagne and took whiskies instead. As we drank, I stared at my servant, marveling once again at her natural beauty but also wondering if her milk tea hair color would revert to black the night she finally became immortal like us. It was difficult to know. When I was turned, my hair grew back in after having fallen out from the chemotherapy. It grew in the color I remembered it to have been before it had fallen out. It made me believe vampirism simply healed our wounds. Yet this theory was dispelled by my friend Darcy who was still covered in the tattoos she had received as a mortal. She told me she tried to get another once she became a vampire, but it had disappeared by the time she woke next in her casket. Yet I heard of other vampires whose mortal tattoos did vanish. There seemed to be no pattern, but one thing I was certain of—the wound that would never heal was the one the sunlight had burned into my wrist.

As I finished my first drink, I was still looking at Mayuko when a blood tear escaped from my eye and began to slide down my cheek. Mayuko immediately grabbed a cloth napkin and wiped it before it might fall onto my newest Lolita dress.

"What's the matter, Cricket?" she asked, but I think she knew. She too looked like she wanted to cry.

I shrugged, trying to pretend it was nothing, but then it spilled out of me anyway, "I'm going to miss you so much, Button."

Even though Mayuko had no prior master, and was acquired only for my sake, she did not belong to me. She belonged to the Ketsuen and bringing her to America wasn't possible unless they gave her to me as a gift, but this was unlikely to happen. Among the Ketsuen and perhaps other covens as well it was considered shameful behavior to have an emotional attachment to your mortal servant. Certainly it was considered bad manners to display that attachment, but I didn't care. I hugged her anyway in front of everyone, just as we naturally did when in private and, in our long embrace, I felt her warm saline tears fall upon my shoulder.

"I hope my new master will be as kind as you have been to me," she whispered in my ear.

"If he's not I'll kill him and drop him in the bay," I whispered back.

We laughed and released each other, but seeing I still had tears in my eyes, Mayuko said, "It's going to be okay, Cricket. We can still message and I'll tell you all about my boyfriends."

I nodded, holding back my tears. At that moment she removed the hair clip she was wearing and clipped it into my hair. As I smiled at her, knowing my fangs were visible but not frightening to her, I realized something wasn't right. Something was different about this party but I couldn't figure out what it was. I scanned the room. There was no one I didn't know. Another round of whiskies was brought to us. The taste was familiar. I knew the song playing. It was one that Mayuko and I would often dance to. The room was lit by candlelight as it always was. I felt the pangs of hunger again, and then it occurred to me what the difference was—the cages were missing. The dance floor was thereby more spacious. A blood party without victims. That wasn't like the Ketsuen. I sat there, puzzled.

"Where are the cages?" I asked Mayuko.

Mayuko looked in the direction of the dance floor. She hadn't noticed either, until I mentioned it, and she said she did not know.

Amy was on the dance floor, dancing with Junko and Daisuke near to where the cages ordinarily were.

"I'll be right back," I said to Mayuko.

As I made my way to the dance floor, I realized I was being watched. I turned and was met by the gaze of the elder vampire, Eizo. He bowed slightly and gave me a soft smile. I stopped, turned, and bowed to him, lower than he had bowed to me, out of respect for his age. But when I was again standing erect, he was gone. I turned back toward the dance floor and was startled to see Amy standing before me, adjusting her scarf. She hugged me and began leading me onto the dance floor.

"Oh, Orly, how we are all going to miss you."

I told her I would miss her as well and we engaged briefly in small talk as we strode onto the dance floor, before I stopped her and asked, "Why are there no victims?"

"I'm not sure," she answered. "But I think there will be. I heard Eizo brought a special victim for the occasion. But your guess is as good as mine as to what that means."

We began to dance, but my mind was elsewhere, pondering what kind of special victim it would be. But then I heard the scream. A mortal scream. Overcome with a thirst for blood, I spun quickly in the direction of the scream only to see Mayuko being held aloft by the back of her neck in the grip of Eizo.

I immediately tried to rush to her, but Amy was too quick, and held me back with only one firm hand on my shoulder.

"Orly, wait!" she said. "The elder speaks."

Eizo spoke in English as Mayuko kicked fruitlessly in the air. Eizo had no trouble holding her. It was as though Mayuko were as light as a feather.

"Berthold Leitz and Orly Solodnikova, you are our honored guests tonight," he began. "These past six years have been our pleasure to spend with you. Tonight we say our goodbyes, but know that we, the Ketsuen, hope our paths will converge again. You are always welcome amongst us and we would like to present each of you with a small token of our affection, so that you always remember the hospitality of the Ketsuen. However, before that, it is time for you to return to us what is rightfully ours, the servants we have lent you. Arliss Bloch, tonight you resume your place with me."

Arliss stepped forward from the wall, bowed a final time to Berthold, and walked quietly toward Eizo and stood behind him. In turn, Eizo, still holding Mayuko aloft, slowly stepped forward to the center of the room.

"As for this one," he said, giving Mayuko a shake, "she has no master. Which of you Ketsuen will claim her?"

At the terminus of his question, Eizo threw Mayuko over twenty feet without effort, the trajectory avoiding all tables and chairs. She landed hard near the edge of the dance floor, at my feet. Mayuko whimpered as she cowered in pain. I tried to go to her, but again, Amy held me in place.

"Before you answer, you will recall it was this faithless servant who neglected her responsibilities to her mistress which ultimately resulted in the discovery of many corpses in the bay. Speak now if you would foolishly trust a mortal so treacherous, and she is yours. Speak not, and she remains masterless."

The room remained silent, save for Mayuko who wept on the floor.

"Please," she begged. "Forgive."

"I claim her!" I shouted.

Amy released me.

Eizo shook his head. "You are our guest, but you are not Ketsuen. You may not have her."

I looked at Berthold. He was standing now, appearing gravely concerned, but he said nothing.

Eizo looked around the room. It was all for show. The silent audience had already spoken.

"Very well," the elder said. "This masterless mortal has seen too much of our coven, she must die."

"No!" I exclaimed.

Mayuko burst forth with a new flood of tears.

Eizo looked at me, "I offer her throat first to you, Miss Solodnikova."

I knelt and cradled Mayuko. This time no one stopped me. Mayuko gripped me tightly as she wept. I looked up at the elder.

"If you will not give her to me, then please allow me to buy her."

"She is not for sale," he replied calmly.

"I'll pay anything you want."

Without emotion, he stared down at me, saying nothing but allowing his fangs to show.

I looked around the room for a friend to come to my aid, but all I saw were the solemn expressions on a couple of friends and exposed fangs on the rest. I didn't know what to say. I didn't know what more I could do to try to save my best friend's life. I looked again at Berthold. He was staring at me directly. When our eyes met, his eyes flashed toward the ceiling, and then back to me. He was trying to convey something, but I didn't understand. Was he telling me to pray to God? There was no time for that. But then I understood. He was looking above. Even above Eizo. He was telling me to beseech those above the elder.

"Then I wanna talk to your boss!" I blurted out, realizing after the fact that my choice of words made it sound like I was lodging a complaint against an employee who provided poor customer service.

Laughter immediately swept over the Ketsuen, but I held firm. "The Eternal Lovers," I cried out, struggling to remember their names. "Hisashi and Konomi," I finally recalled. "Let me speak to them."

The laughter increased in volume. This time even Eizo laughed.

"No one speaks with them," he replied, still laughing.

I knew he was right. The Eternal Lovers never attended these gatherings. I had never even seen them and they had certainly never heard of me. For all I knew, they were only legends and didn't exist at all. I gripped Mayuko more tightly, but in my heart it was like hugging a statue made of warm sand. I felt her slipping through my fingers.

"You have to let go now," Amy said softly behind me.

More voices came from the crowd as the laughter continued.

"She's just a mortal!"

"Worthless!"

"You can't trust her!"

"Bleed her already!"

Mayuko continued to weep in my arms.

"Please," was all I could find in my lexicon to say to those surrounding us.

"Miss Solodnikova, you must forget about this servant now. You will find a new one in America. Come, it is time to feed."

"Please," I said again, finally weeping myself. "Yoroshiku onegaishimasu."

Perhaps my pleading in Japanese finally allowed Eizo to sympathize with me, for his laughter ceased and he spoke to me gently.

"Orly, even I have not seen the Eternal Lovers in over four centuries."

The laughter died and the most silent whispers traveled through the crowd. All knew it was likely that if anyone had seen or spoken to the Eternal Lovers, it would have been Eizo, but no one knew for sure how long it had been.

The murmur was broken by Isamu, the constant comedian in the coven. "Yeah, for four centuries they've been too busy eternally loving themselves!" Isamu laughed and grabbed Itsumi, who had been his mortal sister, and tossed her on a table, knocking glasses to the floor, and pretended to fornicate with her. Itsumi played along, moaning wildly, again increasing the laughter in the room.

I was truly at a loss for what to do. I didn't know how to save Mayuko. But a million times faster than the laughter had started, it stopped. I looked up into their faces to see what had occurred, and then saw that the throats of both Isamu and Itsumi had been sliced open and were bleeding. They were still alive but, by the looks of the wounds, whatever had cut into their throats had been razor sharp and could have easily severed their heads from their spines. This had been a warning.

Everyone in the room went to their knees and bowed lowly. Having appeared from nothing and having come from nowhere, in the center of the room stood a beautiful, youthful Japanese woman, with porcelain skin and calm black eyes. Her black hair was worn up but wispy tendrils escaped at her temples and at the back of her neck. She wore a pristine pale pink silk kimono, decorated with cherry blossoms. She slowly sheathed her sword in the weathered black scabbard she carried in her left hand. I knew it was Konomi, one of the Eternal Lovers.

"Rise," she commanded phlegmatically to all who remained on their knees, bowing.

FOUR

The room came to its feet. Many appeared apprehensive, some were plainly afraid. Isamu and Itsumi hung their heads and I saw that their wounds were already healing. I remained on the floor, holding Mayuko whose eyes quickly glanced upon the immortal woman wearing the kimono and then looked away. She did not dare raise her head.

"Orly," Konomi said tenderly, "come with me, please."

I was in awe of her presence and astonished she was summoning me to go with her. How did she know my name? Where were we going? What was her purpose? Had she appeared because of Isamu and Itsumi's insult? Or had she come here for me?

"Please forgive me, Lady Konomi, but I can't leave this mortal girl here alone."

"I see. Then she may accompany us, at least part of the way. Her fate shall be decided upon our return."

Gently, I unlocked Mayuko's fingers from where they gripped my arms. I rose to my feet and bowed lowly, to Konomi. She gave a slight nod. I reached out to Mayuko.

She took my hand and I pulled her to her feet. She too bowed lowly to Konomi.

"Please, continue your party. Be happy. Be at peace," Konomi said, looking at all of the Ketsuen, but most specifically at Eizo.

Konomi turned and headed to a rear exit of the banquet hall. Through a door that opened on its own at Konomi's approach, we stepped out into a dimly lit courtyard paved in stone and fenced in with tall redwood planks. The courtyard was furnished with chairs and a few tables, also made of redwood.

"Your servant may sit there," Konomi said to me.

I bowed and turned and looked at Mayuko and she took a seat on one of the chairs, struggling to compose herself, still visibly shaken by what had occurred inside, and still uncertain of her future.

In the center of the courtyard was a large koi pond, surrounded by a low stone ledge. Konomi walked us over to it. As we neared, a group of koi inside the pond began to gather to the surface. Konomi dropped her sword, surprising me that she could be clumsy, but when it landed on the ledge it made no sound. It was as if she had placed it there with the most gentle care. With the moon overhead, our reflections in the water undulated in the ripples caused by the fish competing for the front. I glanced at Konomi in the reflection and she turned her head to me. I looked up at her.

"I want to be your friend, Orly," she said plainly.

I wondered what possible interest she could have in me and wanted to ask her, but I hesitated as I did not know if it was permissible to question one so ancient. But my youth caught up to me and I did ask. "Forgive me, Lady Konomi, but why? Why would you want to be my friend?"

"Because I pity you, Orly. You were made so young."

I looked down at her small feet, feeling something close to shame.

"But besides that," she continued, "you also have a talent."

I looked up again at her face.

"Your scribbles."

I didn't know she knew about my scribbles.

"They are well known, Orly."

I wasn't sure if she had guessed my thoughts or had read them. "You want me to scribble for you?" I asked, and felt like I was back in time with Yelena.

"Presently, I do not. But I recognize their potential and see how they would be useful, especially to an elder."

I didn't know why they would be especially useful to an elder. Did Konomi feel guilty for her centuries of killing? Is that where eternity would lead us all?

"You learned to disappear, but haven't learned how to make people forget. Am I correct?"

I nodded.

"You have a counterpart who is at once both older and younger than you."

"Berthold," I answered.

"When you learned to disappear, it was a difficult decision whether to pass the knowledge onto him."

"You're right. I didn't tell him at first, and I didn't know why. But Lady Konomi, how did you know that?"

"It is unnatural for us to share our powers with each other, Orly. It goes against our instincts of self-preservation, as betrayal is commonplace amongst our kind."

I looked down at the fish. They were still waiting to be fed.

"As you age you'll learn you must choose wisely with whom you will share."

"But I trust Berthold," I said.

"I mean no insult, but your youth shows. Trust is not something to be given away carelessly, Orly, even to those within your bloodline, and especially to those without."

I thought again of Yelena. Her best friend, Hisato, was not part of her bloodline, yet they were so close. Was Konomi being overly paranoid?

"That being said, someday, I hope we will trust each other, Orly."

"I hope that too," I said, even though I felt like I already trusted her, mostly because she stole Mayuko from the crowd who wanted to bleed her dry. But perhaps in the end, at the terminus of this conversation, she would return Mayuko to their gang of gnashing fangs, or behead my best friend herself.

"Then, will you be my friend?" Konomi asked.

"Lady Konomi, I would be honored," I answered quickly, mostly out of fear as to what would happen if I refused.

"Shall we make a pact of our friendship?" she asked.

I nodded eagerly, wondering what the pact would be like. Konomi reached into the sleeve of her kimono and removed a small tanto—a dagger—unsheathed it and handed it to me. I looked at her for instructions.

"Open your right wrist," she said.

I looked at my right wrist. It held the scar where I had been burned by the sunlight. Was the right wrist a tradition or was it her intention to cut into my sun-kissed discoloration? Would this heal my wound? I didn't ask for an explanation, and brought the blade to my wrist. It was so sharp that it cut deeply into my skin with the least amount of pressure. My blood dripped quickly from my wrist into the pond. The koi attempted to feed upon the deep red drops as they hit the surface, but once they realized it was not food, or realized it tasted like death, they left the surface and scattered, swimming away. I handed the dagger back to Konomi. She took it, and as she had with her sword, she dropped it, and it fell vertically, blade downward into the pond. The blade dipped into the the water, just far enough to wash my blood away, the handle never getting wet, before rising again, as if retracted on an elastic string until it was again in Konomi's hand. She brought the dagger to her own wrist and sliced it open. Her blood too dripped into the pond, and within seconds, all the koi in the pond floated to the surface on their backs, dead.

"Press your wrist to mine," she said, and I did, our blood mingling upon our wrists.

Would any of her blood enter my artery and give me powers that belonged to her or was this all symbolic? I didn't ask.

"Repeat after me, please," she continued. "By my blood I swear eternal affinity and friendship."

"By my blood I swear eternal affinity and friendship."

We held our wrists together until we felt them heal. I again wondered if her blood had entered my body.

"Thank you, Orly. I will forever treasure our pact."

I didn't know how to answer her, so I merely bowed and said, "Thank you, Lady Konomi."

"You may call me Konomi, for you are now my blood sister."

"Thank you, Konomi," I said, addressing her for the first time without "Lady" preceding her name.

Now that our pact has been made, I would like to take you someplace, she said.

"Where?"

A secret place nearby.

"What about Mayuko?"

She will be safe, until our return, and you will give her something to read.

"Something to read? I didn't bring anything."

Give her this, she said, and from beneath her kimono,

Konomi produced a small sheet of fine handmade paper, folded in half.

She handed it to me. I opened it and saw a poem written in kanji, in thick strokes of the blackest ink.

Ask her to read it to us in English. Perhaps it will give us more time together.

I took the five or six steps needed to reach Mayuko who remained sitting quietly. She still appeared unsettled. I handed the sheet of paper to her. Her hands trembled as she took it and looked at me, puzzled. She had been within earshot. Was she so frightened she had not heard Konomi wanted her to read it in English? Had she purposely avoided eavesdropping? But then it occurred to me, as I reflected upon what Konomi had last said, that her lips never moved and that I never heard the words of her request uttered. I had heard her only in my mind. She had communicated her wishes to me telepathically. How much of our conversation had been conveyed in such a fashion? From Mayuko's perspective had we stood by the pond silently all that time? Had our pact also been similarly noiseless? Surely my words at least would have been audible, as I was no telepath, or had they somehow been silent as well?

"Button, will you please recite this poem to us in English?"

Mayuko looked at the poem, scanning its vertical lines, and then looked back up at me, nervous, as if her life depended on her success. "I will do my best."

I smiled and touched her hair gently. "Everything is going to be okay," I said to her reassuringly.

Mayuko nodded quickly, wanting to believe me. I then returned to Konomi. She was now sitting beside the pond, with her legs tucked under her. "Please sit with me, Orly," she said warmly. Her lips definitely moved that time. She had spoken vocally.

I sat as she sat, tucking my dress under my knees as she had done with her kimono.

She held out her hands to me, palms facing upward. "Place your hands in mine and close your eyes."

I did as she said.

"Ask your servant to recite the poem," Konomi said, but with my eyes closed I wasn't completely sure she had said it aloud.

I spoke. "Mayuko, please read the poem."

Mayuko began at once, but read slowly as she was translating.

> Here in the shadow of death it is hard
> To utter the final word.
> I'll only say, then,
> "Without saying."
> Nothing more.
> Nothing more.

The poem ended.

There is no magic in those words. It is not an incantation, merely the death poem of a sixteenth century monk, Konomi said.

It was difficult to separate what my ears heard versus what my mind understood, but I believed Konomi had not spoken aloud. "Can she hear you too?" I asked, meaning Mayuko.

Don't speak, Orly. She cannot hear me. No one shall hear. Open your thoughts to me and allow our minds to be one. With your eyes closed, look at your surroundings. What do you see?

I didn't know how to speak back to her in silence. But I did my best to open my mind to her so she would know my thoughts.

In my mind's eye I saw Mayuko sitting with the poem. I saw the moon and the lights of the city. I saw three stars and then a fourth and fifth and…I saw the dead fish in the pond. I wondered if Konomi knew her blood would kill them.

Yes, I knew. Listen for the river.

I wondered what river she meant. I heard nothing.

You will hear it. Now without rising, take a walk around the courtyard and show me what you see.

I obeyed and, in my mind, I toured the courtyard. I saw the furniture. I saw Mayuko again. I could see over her shoulder at us sitting. My hands were in Konomi's. I saw candlelights through the glass. The party was still going on inside. I saw the high fence that ran along the edge of the courtyard. The wood was reddish like the wood of the furniture. Then most strangely, I felt as if Konomi was walking beside me.

Yes. I am with you. Go closer to the fence. Touch the plank in front of you.

I reached out. The plank was rough like it hadn't been sanded. Then, to my surprise, I heard it. I heard the river.

Good. You're almost there. Now look at the wood plank closely. Count the grains. Go closer until your vision begins to blur and you can't count them anymore. Now touch the plank again. Push it gently.

It opened. I wondered how she knew there was a door here.

There is no door, Orly. Not to others at least.

I hesitated, pondering what could possibly be behind this door that did not truly exist.

You will see. Have your servant recite the poem once more, but not more than once.

I tried to concentrate, willing Mayuko to read the poem again.

She cannot hear you. You must use your voice to instruct her.

Again, I hesitated, thinking if I broke the silence, this place, with its secret door, would disappear.

It will remain. Ask her.

"Mayuko," I said aloud, "read the poem again, but only one time."

I looked back over my shoulder. Mayuko stared at the sheet of paper. Konomi and I were still sitting by the pond facing each other, our hands touching. Mayuko began again.

Here in the shadow of death…

I turned to the opening in the fence, at the blackness beyond it, and then at Konomi. She smiled, took me by my hand, and stepped through the entrance.

FIVE

The quality of darkness was different beyond the doorway. It was thicker, richer. Konomi and I stood side by side in tall grass. The blades grazed my skin as a gentle night breeze whispered through them. I heard the sound of water flowing. The night sky was at once blacker and brighter; it held more stars than I had ever known were visible from Earth.

"It's magical," I said.

"No, Orly. It is not. It is the way the world once looked, before the beauty faded beneath the beacon of industrialization."

I turned to Konomi, and was startled to see that she held a long staff, as tall as she was. It was made even taller as it was tipped with the blade of a sword.

"This is called a naginata," she said. "It is the first weapon I learned to use."

The new weapon wasn't the only thing that was different about her. Her clothing had changed as well. She was no longer robed in the elegant silk kimono she had worn when she appeared at the party. The fabric of her clothing was coarser and styled similarly to what samurai once wore, but if I had to guess, her costume was of an earlier age than what we envision when we think of feudal Japan. Her shitagi shirt, the type worn beneath armor, was a dark gray with an intricate line work pattern in white. Her hakama trousers were black and showed wear and parts were caked with dried mud. The sword I saw her leave at the edge of the koi pond hung at her waist.

I looked at my own appearance. Nothing had changed. I was still wearing the Lolita dress I had bought for my farewell party. I turned and looked back from where we had come, expecting to see the opening in the fence and Mayuko reading beyond it. But I saw neither. Behind us, I saw only tall grass beneath the star-filled sky.

Although in masculine dress, Konomi was scented lightly with a floral perfume. But beneath the fragrance was something I had not noticed before. She carried the scent of mortal human blood.

I looked away and ran my tongue along my top row of teeth. My vampiric fangs were still there, sharp as ever.

"You smell my blood," Konomi said.

"I do."

"As my new blood sister, I am already placing a deep level of trust in you by bringing you to this place, Orly. Here, as you can sense, I am mortal and vulnerable. However, I assure you I am still a formidable opponent, even to you, and I can leave you behind in this place without a way out."

"Then I am trusting you too. Is that right?"

"It is."

I looked at her again. "What is this place?"

"It is called Bokyaku," she answered.

"The Oblivion?" I asked, unsure of my translation.

"Yes. The Oblivion. Let us walk. There is more to see."

As we walked through the grass Konomi used her naginata as a walking stick. With each step we ascended. It felt as if we were approaching the moon, which hung full, and that soon its celestial body would be within reach. Eventually we were met with forest, and we continued to climb, making our way through the trees until at last we were at the top of a hill.

Down below, on the other side of the foliage-lined hill was a river and, in a clearing along it was an encampment lit by torchlight and peopled with hundreds of male warriors who, like Konomi, wore swords at their waists. On the other side of the river lay another encampment, ten times the size of the one nearest us.

"When daylight comes, The Battle Beside the Mogami River will begin," Konomi said.

I looked at her.

"It is the battle where I am finally cut down."

"You died here?"

"Yes. Here, let us sit and I will tell you."

Konomi laid her weapon on the ground and sat with her back against a tree. I sat beside her.

"I was born at the dawning of the Kofun Period, the period of the burial mounds. I don't know my exact birth year but history books tell us that the Kofun Period began around the year two hundred and fifty.

"As men in our village were often off at war, we lacked protection, so in my youth, like many women, I learned the ways of the warrior. I was trained in the arts of the dagger and the naginata I have already shown you. Without being boastful, my skills in both far exceeded the women in my village as well as most of the male warriors I had come in contact with. As a result, my elevated proficiencies led to learning the ways of my preferred weapon, a weapon reserved for men—the sword.

"I defended my village for many seasons, but eventually I went off to war myself. I lived through many of the hostile campaigns led by warlords before I finally died on the battlefield. But by then my name was known in many provinces. I had slain countless men in combat and taken over two hundred heads. The violence sometimes overwhelmed me and threatened what femininity I had left, but that was because blood didn't mean the same thing to me then.

"My final battle happened here, beside the Mogami River. As I said, it began at dawn, but it still raged on into the night. Once the moon rose, my lover and maker, Hisashi—he had no surname but was Lord of the Ketsuen—one of the surviving eleven bloodlines—observed me from afar, atop this very hill where we are sitting, far out of range of the arrows and of notice. But of course, with his vampiric powers, even from this distance and through the darkness, he watched me as closely as if he were by my side. The slaughter at the edge of my sword was substantial and Hisashi's eyes followed me as I cut through the ranks of my enemies, my valor causing his heart to tremble. But as you've seen, the enemy numbers were too great, and I and my allies, including two of my brothers, were soon surrounded and I fell when a spear was thrust through my back. I was left for dead as the rest met their own deaths. As the battle ended, the surviving victors left the field and the night grew quiet. I lay there in my blood, looking at the starlit sky and listening to the cries of the birds that flew at night.

"Hisashi came to me and cradled my head in his lap. The moon shone like a halo behind his head. I looked into his eyes; they were completely black, including what would otherwise be the whites of his eyes. I had never seen such eyes and thought I had already passed on to the world of the gods. Never had I felt such peace than when I first looked into those obsidian orbs. He smiled and I saw his white teeth and elongated canines for the first time. Without a word he lifted my throat to his mouth and bit into me. I felt very little as I was already dying from the blood I had lost, but I could feel he was drinking from me. He did not indulge himself, he drank just enough to mix my blood with his. As he released me I watched as his eyes closed, my blood still on his lips. He was savoring me. When his eyes opened again he lifted his wrist to his mouth and bit into it until the blood began to flow in rushes. He brought his wrist to my mouth and told me to drink. I turned my head away, but he grabbed it with his other hand and forced my mouth open. "Live forever," he whispered. I still struggled, but as the first drops from his wrist fell into my mouth, I felt an awakening, as if the whole world was expanding beyond this battlefield, beyond the provinces, beyond the entire island itself. And then I coughed violently, gasping for breath, feeling I would suffocate. He removed his wrist from my lips and watched me die as his poisoned blood took my life.

"I woke in the ground, covered in earth, not needing to breathe, and lay there still, until I was dug up and lifted out and embraced by Hisashi for the first time in our eternity. He took me to feed and after I experienced the ecstasy of human blood, we made love for the first time. I have remained by his side and he by mine ever since."

"The Eternal Lovers," I said.

"Yes. We are called that by others."

"It is a beautiful story."

Konomi didn't respond. I thought maybe she did not appreciate my calling her history a story. I changed the subject.

"Is the Oblivion always here? At this battlefield?"

"For me it is."

"So each time you enter the Oblivion you relive your own death?"

"No. As I said, the battle begins at dawn, but in the Oblivion, it is forever night. The sun never rises in the Bokyaku."

"So why do you come here?" I asked.

"This place is peaceful in a way the material world is not for a vampire."

"What do you mean?"

"Here, in the Oblivion, I can age."

"And that makes you feel better?"

"There is a certain insanity that comes with immortality. One day you will know it. It is not easy to exist with no end. But here, in the Oblivion, if I stay long enough, I can feel the approach of my own end."

"How long do you stay here?"

"Sometimes long enough for me to wrinkle and develop liver spots."

"And so you can just walk away from the world for seventy years or whatever it would be?"

"The minutes pass differently here because the Oblivion is a place of the mind and thoughts move much more quickly than time. I could sit on this hill for a hundred years and when I returned to the true world, not even a night will have passed."

"Then life here is even longer than what we're used to? It seems strange that something would be able to make eternity even longer."

"I understand your meaning. I too have made that observation."

"Have you ever stayed so long that you died of old age?"

"No. I've never dared stay that long because I don't know if doing so would mean dying in the true world and leaving Hisashi alone for the rest of time."

"Since you're mortal here, do you have to eat food?"

"Yes, and I sleep and dream the way a mortal sleeps."

"And you can be killed?"

"By you and by them."

Konomi pointed across the river.

"Have they ever tried to kill you?"

"Yes. And it is quite thrilling. But fortunately all have failed."

"How come I am still immortal here?"

"Because this is my Oblivion, not yours."

I looked at her curiously. "Do I have an Oblivion?"

"You will have to find that out for yourself. But let me tell you something, Orly," she said, looking back at me, "You'll find that a large part of gaining powers is knowing what is possible. Does that make sense?"

"I think so," I answered.

"Just as it is unlikely that you would think disappearing was possible had you not seen Yelena do it first, it is highly unlikely that you could find the Oblivion if you did not first know it existed."

I was surprised she knew of Yelena, but I didn't remark upon it as I assumed her knowledge was vast. "And do all vampires know the Oblivion exists?"

"Quite the contrary. Hardly any know and that's why so many of them go insane."

"What do you mean, they go insane?"

"Orly, how many vampires have you met that are older than a thousand years?"

I thought for a moment before answering. "I guess three. You, Eizo, and Mirela."

"Ah. Mirela Cobălcescu."

"Do you know her?"

"We have met on occasion over the millennia."

There was a change in pitch in Konomi's voice when she said that. I didn't know for sure, but I didn't get the sense that they were on the best of terms, not that they should be, being Ancients of opposing bloodlines.

"A thousand years is a long time, Orly, and too long for most of our kind. Eventually, the monotony of living night after night with little to no variation overwhelms us. It's then that they to put an end to it, most by walking into the sunlight."

"That's how Marcel died. Well, he ran to it."

"Your mother's beloved?"

She did know a lot about Yelena's life. I nodded my head in assent to her question. "But I don't think he did so because he went crazy over living for eternity."

"Perhaps not."

"How come you don't tell the other vampires about this place? Or why not at least tell all the Ketsuen? You could keep them from going insane and your coven would grow even stronger with the more ancient vampires you have."

"As I said, Orly, betrayal amongst our kind is commonplace. Our desire for power naturally leads us to treachery. But also understand this. The rate at which your strength grows decreases as you age."

"What do you mean?"

"Think of how fast you have grown since you were made. Think of the powers you have already mastered so quickly. As you age your powers will enhance—you will fly higher, your mind will quicken, you will be able to remain out of your coffin longer, you will heal faster. But also as you age, the number of new powers unfolding before you, becoming within reach, diminishes. The powers you already possess strengthen at a slower pace. Therefore the difference between a vampire who is ten years old and a hundred years old is great while the difference between one who is a thousand years old versus one who is two thousand years old is scant."

"Meaning we will eventually become as strong as the source of our bloodline?" I asked, hiding my excitement, as this meant if I waited long enough, one day I would be as powerful as Mirela. I would avenge Yelena. I would have my revenge at last. I was so preoccupied in this thought that I didn't realize until later that Konomi didn't answer my question.

"Wisdom is what distinguishes the Eternal," she said instead. "And it is wisdom that a coven lord must depend on to find the balance between maintaining power while not excessively weakening the coven."

I left my thoughts of vengeance and reflected for a moment about what Konomi had just revealed to me.

"The leader of a coven will kill the elders who don't go insane?"

"That is often the case, and often a necessity. But a coven lord will also reward and rely on the loyal," Konomi replied.

"But that means the elders will always act the most loyal since they're the ones who will probably get killed."

"It's not always an act, Orly, but yes, as they are the most likely to threaten the coven lord, they are the most likely to be eliminated. To preserve themselves, they must show the greatest loyalty, whether they mean it or not."

"We're talking about trust again."

"Yes."

"Lord Hisashi must trust you," I said.

"I would give my life for his and he knows that, not in his heart, but in his mind. In the end, trust, not love, is the paramount thing."

I sat quietly, thinking that over.

"I understand your need for love, Orly. And I know it consumes you. But when it comes to love, if you will permit me, I would like to caution you."

"Please, tell me everything," I said, eager to learn whatever someone so ancient could tell me about love, and hoping what she said would help me find it.

"That would take more than a lifetime," she smiled and then asked, "Do you know how sake is made?"

"No," I answered, perplexed.

"It is the mixture of two ingredients that stay apart, but when when they sit together long enough, they fuse. They become one, and you cannot separate them again. Do you understand what I'm telling you?"

"I don't know."

"There is great risk when you love so deeply. When you are with a lover whom you love truly, century after century, you become fused, just like the sake. Once that happens, you cannot go on separated. If you lose them, you lose yourself. Yelena Solodnikova discovered this too late."

I sat thinking of Yelena and wondering of the truth of what Konomi had just said. Instinctively, I thought she was wrong, that Yelena's love for me replaced her love for Marcel. But the more consideration I gave it, the more I questioned whether I could've ever been enough to put Yelena back together after she lost Marcel.

After a moment, I noticed Konomi was staring at the night sky.

"The beauty of stars never fades," she said aloud, but I believe she was speaking more to herself.

I paused, not wanting to interrupt her reverie, and joined her in looking up at the night sky, but my head lowered before hers did.

"Besides you and Lord Hisashi, is Eizo the only Ketsuen who is over a thousand years old?"

She remained staring at stars. "He is the only one in residing in Tokyo. But there are others." She lowered her head and looked me in the face. "I won't tell you how many."

She doesn't trust me, I thought to myself.

She continued. "The smart ones go into hiding, burying themselves for centuries, waiting for the right time to rise and resurface into the world. Likely when there is a new war. Certainly, you know of our great war that took place over five thousand years ago."

"Yes. It left only eleven vampires alive. They are the sources of the eleven bloodlines."

"Did you know that not all of those original eleven were the eldest of their coven?"

"No. I didn't know that."

"Just as not all of today's coven lords are of the original eleven."

I hadn't known that either.

"As I've said more than once tonight, treachery is great amongst our kind."

"Is Hisashi one of the original eleven?"

"Yes. He is."

"Is Mirela Cobălcescu?"

"Yes. She is as well."

"Do you think Mirela knows of the Oblivion?"

"I don't know. Her age would suggest that she must, but her temperament would suggest otherwise."

What did she mean by Mirela's temperament? All I knew of Mirela's temperament was the behavior of a jilted lover of Marcel's who took her revenge upon my mother, but I didn't ask Konomi to explain. The more I talked to her the more I sensed what she would and wouldn't answer plainly.

"Was Mirela the oldest of her bloodline, before the war started?" I asked, almost afraid of the answer I expected.

Konomi didn't answer as quickly as she usually did, but finally she uttered a simple, "No."

She grabbed the naginata and rose to her feet.

"Come, we must head back."

Konomi began the descent through the forest. I rose and took one last long look at the battlefield, before easily catching up to her with my vampiric speed. We didn't speak as we walked. I wondered if Konomi thought she had told me too much, but then, upon reflection, I concluded she wasn't, with all her years, one who made mistakes.

Faster than we had come, we neared the exit which was now visible and open. I saw Mayuko, still sitting, still holding the poem. Before we arrived at the opening, I reached for Konomi and gently tugged at the sleeve of her shitagi. She stopped and turned to me.

"What would you like to ask, Orly?"

She had expected a question.

"Why did you bring me here? I mean, why show *me* the Oblivion?"

"Because I believe it will save you from thousands of years of torment."

"Because I'm a child?"

"Your childhood is a coincidence," she said. "I mean because of your scribbles."

I tried to understand her meaning, but before I could speak again, she spoke.

"I feel for you, Orly."

I remembered Mirela had uttered those same words before she betrayed me.

The tall grass bowed gently. The breeze carried the scent of Konomi's mortal blood.

"As you would probably guess, Hisashi first showed me the Oblivion. But can you guess who showed him?"

"His maker?" I asked.

"Hisashi had no maker. No vampiric maker, that is."

"Then a vampire from another bloodline."

"No. It was his progeny who showed him. A powerful vampire named Gaku, who died in the great war. He found the Oblivion on his own, without instruction. He happened upon it during a long period of meditation in the earth."

"But how could one younger than him know about it first?"

"It has happened more than once that progeny discovers a power before their maker. We Eternal don't know everything that is possible, Orly. We can only know what presents itself before us."

I understood at last. "That's why you mentioned my scribbles. I've shown that it's possible."

"That is precisely what I am saying. And having a strength that no one else possesses only makes its power greater."

"And now that my power is known, others will want it?"

"I am certain others already do."

"Do you want it? Is that why you brought me here?"

"You would be wise to think that, Orly."

But what else could I think?

"Strength is gained by time and by the sharing of blood. Had you been made by a vampire older than Yelena Solodnikova, you would have awakened in the earth more powerful than you are. Skills would come easier to you, and the magnitude of your strength and speed would be greater— nearly equal to that of your maker. This is why you will witness very few elders sharing their blood or making new vampires. The recipient of the blood would become too powerful before the elder knew whether or not to trust them."

Yet she had shared her blood with me.

"When we put our wrists together, that was an exchange, but a symbolic one. You would need to drink more to gain any part of my strength, just as I would need more of your blood to gain the power of your scribbles."

"But I had this power as a mortal. Maybe it wouldn't even work for a vampire, even if you drank all of my blood."

"I have no intention of drinking any of your blood, Orly. What I am trying to tell you is this: Fear your elders, but know your elders are also afraid of you."

As we stepped back through the opening in the fence, I realized that Mayuko was still reading the poem even though she had been instructed to read it only once.

…it is hard

To utter the final word.

I'll only say, then,

"Without saying."

Nothing more.

Nothing more.

In reality, that is, outside of the Oblivion, Konomi and I were still sitting opposite each other beside the koi pond.

"I have enjoyed meeting you, Orly."

This meant our journey was over. What would happen to Mayuko now?

"I have enjoyed meeting you too, Konomi. Immensely. I am grateful for the wisdom you have imparted to me."

Konomi bowed her head slightly.

There was a slight pause.

"About my servant," I asked irresolutely, and I could feel Mayuko listening, "what is to become of her?"

"What do you think should become of her? When you consider your answer, remember, she is only a mortal, one of millions."

"Yes, but I would like her to live."

"Despite her failure in her duties to you?"

"That was my fault."

"No. The fault belongs to her."

"I love her, Konomi."

"I already know that. Do you trust her? As I've said, that is paramount."

"I do. I trust her with all my heart."

Konomi smiled, her fangs showing.

I realized my mistake. I said I trusted with my heart. But it was too late to take back.

"May you have many ages ahead of you to learn what the Eternal already know, Miss Orly Solodnikova."

She rose to her feet and we followed suit.

She must have sensed that I still did not understand Mayuko's fate, and thus she spoke. "I have just ordered Eizo to release your servant to you and issued an edict that no Ketsuen shall harm her. Are you satisfied?"

I bowed lowly, and Mayuko even lower. "Thank you, Konomi," I said. "I am forever grateful."

"Until we meet again, my blood sister," and she took her leave, heading back toward the blood party, taking small steps due to the restriction of her kimono. But before she reached the door she vanished, evaporating into the night air, leaving Mayuko and me alone, beside the pond of dead koi.

SIX

We returned to America in a private jet loaned to us by the Ketsuen. Even though Berthold and I flew in our funerary boxes as cargo, it was just like flying first class in the sense that we could sleep the entire way. But even in the comfort and security of my coffin, I didn't sleep at all. I was preoccupied with the knowledge that the six years I spent in Tokyo had come to a close and not once during that time had I found anyone to love me. As I said, Berthold and Mayuko loved me. I knew they did. But their love wasn't enough. Their hugs and their kisses were simply the wrong kind. My soul was twenty-two years old and I needed more. I needed adult love and I needed it reciprocated. And now I was on my way to Los Angeles, six years older than I had been when I left. Very likely the new surroundings would be just as lonely and cold as they had been in Tokyo. And the lack of love I would find there was only going to be compounded by Yelena's absence.

We used a service to pre-clear our flight with customs, but to avoid any potential difficulties, we landed at a small airport where customs and immigration did not typically meet incoming flights. As it was not completely dark when our plane landed, Mayuko instructed the pilot to drive the plane into a hangar she had arranged in advance. As Konomi forbade any of the Ketsuen to kill Mayuko, they released her from her obligations to them and she agreed to follow me to the United States partially out of fear that the Ketsuen would eventually defy Konomi's order. Mayuko would be in America as a tourist but I liked to tease her that we would soon get her a fiancée visa once I found a dreamy American man for her. I said I would marry her myself if I weren't stuck being a child and she liked the idea, but Berthold advised that we not worry too much about visas as Immigration didn't hunt down Japanese tourists, and because a death certificate was easy enough to forge that Mayuko could live with us as long as I liked, with no true identity at all.

A fresh wave of anxiety washed over me before our plane even landed, and I remained intently awake within my traveling coffin the entire time we were in the hangar, but I would not rise until Mayuko woke us. I knew I had to come back to Los Angeles, but now that I was here I wish I hadn't insisted on returning so soon. I wondered if Berthold was awake and how he was feeling about being back. I hadn't given him much say in whether or not we should return and on what timeline. Maybe he wasn't ready. Maybe he would have to leave me and go back abroad. My anxiety worsened.

Eventually, Mayuko did wake me as she always did. I stepped out of my coffin and knocked on Berthold's coffin.

He slid off the lid himself and sat up and looked at me but didn't say anything. In the hangar, a limousine with blacked out windows was waiting for us. A van was also waiting that would transport all of our luggage.

Berthold and I didn't say much on the drive back to Hollywood. Instead we stared out opposite windows, observing the freeways, streets, and buildings that were still familiar to us. It looked largely as I remembered it, but being there felt different than it had before, and certainly that was because Yelena was no longer beside me.

I shut my eyes when we turned off Sunset Boulevard and began our ascent into the hills. I could still anticipate the curves in the road, and with each turn, I felt myself closer to the place I had once called home.

"Not much longer now," Berthold said. Small talk was uncharacteristic of Berthold. Perhaps he too was ill at ease and didn't fully understand what he was feeling either. I didn't answer him.

We reached the driveway and the driver killed the engine. I opened my eyes. Yelena's mansion. The exterior looked as it had when we left. It didn't appear the hedges or cypress trees had grown even an inch. Sylvia, the woman we employed to run the house in our absence had done a good job of overseeing our gardeners. When we entered the house I saw it was the same inside as it was on the outside—just as we had left it. Yelena's collection of art was everywhere, paintings and sculptures, her minimalist furniture, and the scribbles of mine she had purchased so many years ago at the Clover Gallery. Half of me wished I hadn't instructed Sylvia to keep things exactly as they were and the other half of me wished she wasn't so meticulous in her work. It was like viewing a painting I had a long standing sentimental attachment to and suddenly realizing some important element in the foreground was now missing. Yelena.

Before I could take it all in and settle my thoughts, I heard the van pull into the driveway and shortly after, our luggage was being carried inside.

"What time…" I cleared my throat, "What time is it?"

"Just after nine-thirty," Mayuko answered.

"It's early still, let me show you your room."

There were four other bedrooms I could have put Mayuko in, but I brought her to the room Yelena had Berthold decorate for me when I was still a child and still mortal and still dying, when Yelena so desperately wanted to adopt me legally. We sat on the bed together, holding hands, and I looked around, allowing memories to envelop me. The first scribble I did of Yelena, when I met her in the hospital cafeteria, still hung on the wall. Why hadn't I taken it to Japan with us? I don't know. I was just running away, I guess. Running in denial. Before morning, I would take it off the wall and bring it with me down to the secret subterranean chamber, accessible through Yelena's closet, where I would again be sleeping. It would be the first of many changes I knew I needed to make to the house, in order to recreate it as ours so that we could move on in this eternity we were left behind with.

Mayuko's luggage was brought to her room and I left her so she could unpack and went to go find Berthold, to see if he had gone below yet. I found him sitting at the dining room table with a tumbler and a bottle of Japanese scotch he brought back with us. I was about to ask him if he was ready to see our old caskets when I heard the rattling of an old pickup truck pull into the driveway. I immediately went to the front door and just as the men who had carried in our luggage were descending the steps in departure, a tall man with long black hair and sharp green eyes, who wore old-fashioned clothing, glided up the long steps.

"Zacharias!" I called out and he ran up the remaining steps and, in the doorway, he lifted me off my feet to hug me firmly. I rested my head on his shoulder, happy to see him. It was the first glimpse of happiness since our return. Berthold was soon in the doorway and Zacharias put me down and greeted Berthold warmly.

"That truck is as old as you are," Berthold said affectionately.

Zacharias smiled, and though his fangs were sharp, it appeared friendly.

We went inside the house and Zacharias and I sat in the living room while Berthold diverted himself to the kitchen to fetch the bottle of Japanese scotch and three tumblers. He joined us and poured drinks which we all sipped before speaking.

"So now tell me, if you will, how was your stay in Tokyo? Delightful I hope," Zacharias began.

"It was unimaginable," Berthold answered, and for nearly an hour, Berthold and I spoke of our experiences abroad, the multitude of lifestyle adjustments we were forced to make, and the lavish hospitality of the Ketsuen. I wanted to scream how lonely it was for me there, but instead I called for Mayuko and when she entered, I introduced her to Zacharias and related to her the story of the night I met him, when I was only two nights old and had mistaken him for Yelena's beloved Marcel, and how he had helped me dispose of the body of the first man I had killed alone. At the mention of Marcel, Berthold winced. Hearing Marcel's name reminded him of the years he endured hoping for Yelena's love and watching her give it to another man even long after he was dead.

Mayuko sat beside me and I handed her my tumbler so she could drink with us.

"I too traveled abroad during your absence. Did you know?" Zacharias asked.

"I didn't," Berthold replied. "Where did you go?"

"I wandered mostly on foot through Northern Africa, spending a significant time in Tunisia before crossing the Mediterranean into Greece and then north by way of Macedonia, Kosovo, and Serbia."

"And did your journey stop there?" Berthold asked. Something changed in his voice, something subtle; there was a note of consternation.

"No," Zacharias continued, "I did not stop there. I made my way to Romania."

And then I understood Berthold's dismay. Romania, I thought. Where Mirela still lives. I looked at Berthold; his jaw was clenched.

"Please forgive me, Mayuko," Zacharias said pleasantly. "Would you be a dear and leave us for a moment? We must speak in private."

Mayuko rose to her feet. Zacharias rose as well and thanked her politely, and she headed back to her bedroom.

In a quieter tone, Zacharias asked, "Have you heard? There is to be a Communion of the Ancients."

"I don't know what that is," I responded quickly.

"Nor do I," Berthold followed.

"It is a tradition that dates back thousands of years in which the Ancients gather together and offer their blood to the empress. In exchange she may bestow her blood upon them. A Communion has not taken place in over three hundred years."

"Why is it happening now?" Berthold asked.

"That I do not know. On my life, I do not know," Zacharias responded.

I thought of what Konomi said about being cautious with whom you share your blood. "Why would they give their blood to her? And why would she give her blood to them?"

"They do it to prove their loyalty," Zacharias answered.

"In what way?" Berthold inquired.

"If they are living, they must come before her, even if it means coming out of hiding, and even if one has gone to ground. They must appear before her and make themselves vulnerable by allowing her to feed upon their throats. In this ceremony she could kill any of them she chooses, and it is said that she has always taken life."

"Then why go?" Berthold asked.

"For the reward of her blood?" I asked animatedly.

"The empress takes much, but gives little. She will drink until the Ancient is near death, uncertain of his fate, and if allowed to live she will give back a drop of her own blood. Obviously, it's more symbolic than useful."

"I ask again," Berthold interrupted, "why go at all?"

"Those who do not will be branded as traitors and hunted down by the brood. Once caught they will be brought before her for execution, and the method then is always horrific and languishing."

"Yeah, but if I was close enough to her for her to feed on me, that'd mean I'd also be close enough to—"

"Orly!" Berthold said sternly. I turned to him and he shook his head. "You must not even think such things, let alone say them."

"He is right, Orly," Zacharias concurred. "Besides, there is no need to think of it, as you are not an Ancient."

"I'm immortal," I said, impetuously.

"In the old counting system one was considered an Ancient when roughly five hundred eighty years. But in the modern system it has been brought down to half a millennia. Just like you, I am not yet old enough to attend myself. Vampires as young as us are not yet enough of a threat to where we would have to prove our loyalty. Our short lives mean nothing to them."

Berthold nodded his head gravely.

I thought again of what I was not supposed to think. If I were that close, with Mirela's fangs sunk into my throat, somehow I could drive a stake through her heart or behead her once and for all. But half a millennia. Would I have to wait five hundred years to avenge my mother?

I must have spent too much time plotting my revenge, because I soon felt eyes upon me. I blinked and saw both Berthold and Zacharias eyeing me suspiciously. It annoyed me.

"If you're not old enough and we're not old enough, then why are you even telling us this?" I snapped.

"Calm down, Orly," Berthold said softly and then turned to Zacharias. It seemed Berthold also wanted to know the answer to my question.

But before Zacharias could answer, our conversation was cut short by the low rumble of a sports car pulling into our driveway. Shortly after the front door of our house was opened and we were greeted by a familiar boisterous voice.

"Welcome home, bitches!" the voice called.

I jumped up from my seat and saw Hisato and Corinne entering the living room. I ran up and gave Hisato a hug and he lifted me in the air and spun me in circles before putting me down, slightly dizzy.

"Damn girl, you haven't aged a bit," Hisato said with a laugh. I laughed too as I knew his sense of humor by now.

"She hasn't grown an inch either," Corinne said sharply. I stopped laughing. She was still as bitchy as ever, and I wondered if my six years in Tokyo was long enough for her to forget we had become friends.

Berthold came over and greeted both of them in earnest.

"You're late," Zacharias said sharply.

"I didn't want to help unpack," Hisato answered playfully.

"Where are Darcy and Grace?" I asked, puzzled by their absence.

"Here we are!" Grace called excitedly from the doorway.

"Ever since he bought his Ferrari we've had to drive ourselves," Darcy said dryly.

We all exchanged our own greetings, including Zacharias. And as I looked at Hisato and his three girls, I was reminded that they were all Ketsuen, so I called for Mayuko. She came out of her room quickly and bowed to them.

"Ah yes, the rule breaker," Hisato said roughly.

Mayuko looked at me nervously and I looked at Hisato.

"Ha ha!" Hisato laughed. "I'm just fucking with you! Fuck them and their rules! We'll be great friends being disobedient!"

As we all headed into the living room, I heard yet another vehicle.

"Did you invite someone else?" I asked Corinne.

"Ask him," she answered, rolling her eyes. "It was his idea."

But before I could ask Hisato, he quickly said, "Everyone act somber, all gloomy and shit."

The front door opened a crack. "Knock knock!" a peppy voice said. "We're here!"

In walked six conservatively dressed women and men, ranging from their mid-twenties to their early fifties. A woman in her thirties named Tisha seemed to be the group's spokesperson. She immediately went to Hisato who looked glum for the first time I had ever known.

"Hisato, it's good to see you again, and thank you for inviting us."

"Yeah," Hisato replied. "Come in everyone. Let's sit down. These are my friends I told you about. Like me, they're unsaved and feel a terrible emptiness in their lives."

"That emptiness will be filled once you accept Our Savior Jesus Christ into your hearts," an elderly man said with a reassuring smile.

"Oh my god, you didn't," I muttered loudly.

"Hush, blasphemer!" Hisato barked at me and then turned to Tisha, "I'm sorry, she may be too young for saving."

"Nonsense, we are all God's children, no matter what age," Tisha said cheerfully.

"Even two hundred and nineteen?" Zacharias asked flatly.

"You have a sense of humor," Tisha replied. "But to answer your question, yes. Even two hundred and nineteen. Look at Methuselah. He was nine hundred and sixty-nine years, and God loved him too."

"I wonder if he knows Mirela." I said aloud and Zacharias and Berthold smiled but were careful not to show their fangs.

Tisha knelt to my level. "And what is your name, little girl?"

"Orly."

"And how old are you, Orly?"

"Twelve, going on twenty-three."

"I was about your age when I was saved, Orly. I was thirteen and didn't have God in my life. I remember thinking to myself all the time, 'If there is a God then why do I want to kill myself when I'm only thirteen?'"

"What'd he say?"

"Well, at that point, he didn't say anything. I only learned the answer to that question when I became reborn."

"Can I kill her already?" I looked up at Hisato, who in turn looked at the ceiling and let out a howl of laughter.

In an instant, I stuck a finger in each of Tisha's eyes and, like talons, clawed my fingers into her sockets and pulled her throat to my mouth. The blood from her eyes gushed onto the floor, while the blood that pumped from her artery flowed into my mouth. She thrashed and screamed, but my hold upon her was too strong.

Just as quickly, the rest of the vampiric party, Ketsuen and Cobălcescu, descended upon the other missionaries.

Hisato moved in on the youngest male in the group, taking him with one hand by the throat. He lifted him off the ground and they flew upward until the boy's head slammed against the high ceiling. Hisato bit into his neck and drank but released his bite early and let out a loud sinister laugh. The boy's blood, still pumping from his neck, showered like rain upon us below.

Corinne, Darcy, and Grace all took their victims in an instant as well. Corinne drank her fill, and as per her usual, she did not drink her victim dry. As the woman continued to struggle with the small amount of strength she had left, Corinne broke her neck, and she became still. Darcy pinned her man to the ground and as she fed, his legs instinctively tried to run one way, and then the other, his kicking smearing the blood that had already spilled across the floor. Grace squealed with delight as she took her mouth away from the elderly man's throat and held her mouth open, catching whatever blood she could as it sprayed like a sprinkler over her angelic face.

This left only one victim and he was shared by Berthold and Zacharias. The two of them devoured him fiercely, biting both at the jugular and the wrist.

When Tisha died in my mouth, I released my jaw's grip on her throat and looked up at those around me. Most were still feeding, hunched over their prey, but Berthold was sitting erect, with blood on his lips, watching me. He reached for my hand and I gave it to him. He brought it to his lips and kissed it, leaving freshly spilled blood upon my skin.

"Welcome home, Orly," he said and smiled tenderly.

SEVEN

We placed the six corpses in three bathtubs, but in the foyer there was still quite a mess to clean up. Hisato phoned his servants, stunning Vietnamese twin brothers—Bao and Dao—to help Mayuko with the cleaning and disposal of the bodies.

Though we had a couple of hours before daybreak, Berthold announced he hadn't slept on the plane and would need to retire early. Zacharias took his leave shortly after. I offered a bedroom to Hisato and his girls but he said they needed to get back before sunrise as well. I saw them to the door and then locked it and headed back into the house. When I reached Yelena's bedroom, I saw that the closet door was already open. Berthold had already passed through and headed below to where we would sleep.

The closet was still full of Yelena's clothes. A wall of expensive black garments. I stepped inside and shut the closet door behind me, but I didn't open the secret passage and make my way below ground. I touched the fabrics with my fingers and pulled them to my face and inhaled, trying to smell Yelena on them, but she wasn't there. I put my back to the wall and lowered myself to a seated position. The hems of her dresses brushed upon my face. How I missed her. And how much I wished she were still here with me. I thought about how much she loved me and how she kept me in the dark when she was knowingly going to her death in order to keep me alive. And whenever the knowledge of Yelena's awareness of her forthcoming immolation returned to me, it always pierced my heart to remember that she was smiling while lovingly caressing my bratty face. At the time, I hadn't known she was telling me goodbye. Sitting in her closet, I began to cry, my tears blood.

As I wept, the closet door opened from the outside. In my sorrow, I was taken by surprise. Berthold had already gone below, so it couldn't be him. From behind Yelena's wardrobe all I saw were a pair of black designer jeans below the knees capped off with a pair of blue Maison Corthay oxfords. It was Hisato. He had returned.

"May I join you?" he asked softly, quite out of character.

Instinctively I would have nodded as my tears had given me the sniffles, but as I couldn't see his face, he couldn't see mine. I cleared my throat and then said, "You may, but shut the door behind you."

Hisato stepped into the closet and slid the door to its closed position. He too put his back to the wall and then slid down until he was seated. Yelena's clothes hung like drapery between us, but I could see part of his face.

"Where are the girls?" I asked.

"I sent them home."

"And you came back. Why?"

"I don't know. I guess seeing you here tonight, reminded me so much of her. She really loved you, Orly, I hope you know that. She told me all the time and I'm sure I was probably like 'yeah yeah yeah,' but even if she didn't say anything, I could tell. I know how I come across, besides being beyond beautiful, I mean. Flamboyant, obnoxious, whatever you want to call it. But I want you to know, these six years without her haven't been easy for me either. The title of *best friend* is too simple. *Sister* isn't even enough. Even though we were so different from each other, Yelena was like my lover on a mental level. Yeah. My mental lover who knew it was more important for me to hear her say, 'I understand you' than 'I love you.'"

I didn't know if he was waiting for a response. Regardless, I didn't have one I was willing to share. The truth was, I was happy he was hurting. This seriousness of his was something I'd never seen in him. He was right about the impression he gives. Before this conversation, I thought nothing ever touched him deeply and that his eternal life was just a series of shallow parties.

He sighed loudly. "I'm babbling and I'm not even drunk anymore."

"It's okay," I said at last.

I heard him unscrew the cap of a flask and drink.

"I'd like to stay drunk forever. That's basically how I've been dealing with her being gone. But I learned that's the problem with being a vampire. You can't even become an alcoholic."

He screwed the cap back on the flask and with his right arm, Hisato parted the clothing that hung between us. I could see his whole face now. Even though he had just made a joke, he wasn't smiling.

"We have to kill her, Orly."

"Who?" I asked, but I knew he meant Mirela.

"That cunt."

I nodded my head.

He opened the flask again and held it out to me. "Let's drink on it."

I took the flask and brought it to my lips. It was bourbon. I swallowed and handed it back to him. As he brought it to his mouth, the clothing fell back into place, and I heard him take a long pull from the flask.

"You should rest," he said.

I nodded this time even though I knew he couldn't see me.

"You mind if I sleep here?" he asked.

"In the closet?"

"Yeah."

"No," I said. "I understand."

I pressed my back against the wall and rose to my feet. I made my way toward him through the black dresses.

With my left hand, I messed up Hisato's hair before opening the secret doorway to the chamber below.

It was dark, but I didn't need light to see. Two caskets and a coffin. Berthold asleep in the casket on the right, my casket in the middle, and Yelena's coffin to the left, now forever empty. The button beneath her coffin that depressed by her body weight would never again trigger the audio recording of the Malibu shoreline where her beloved Marcel had perished in the sunlight.

I slipped into my casket and pulled the lid shut, and once inside I began to reacquaint myself with the casket Yelena had given me when she first made me a vampire. I lay still, struggling to fall asleep, listening to the worms burrowing through the earth beneath our flagstone floor.

As my eyes closed, my nose twitched. My eyes reopened wide. I smelled fresh blood. Vampiric blood. Berthold's blood. Though he remained silent within his casket, not making a whimper, I could smell his tears. They were falling for Yelena.

What a mournful coterie we made—Berthold, Hisato, and myself. We had all loved Yelena in different ways and we had all lost her forever.

I continued to smell Berthold's fresh blood. His tears kept replenishing. My thoughts dwelt upon the way he had loved Yelena so purely during his mortal life. What it must feel like to be loved like that. Did Yelena feel any of it in her heart? No. She did not. Her romantic heart belonged to Marcel and to Marcel alone. But had she lived centuries longer, would Yelena have finally let Berthold in? Would she have eventually healed from heartache and allowed her romantic heart to reopen? And now that she was gone, where would that leave Berthold? Would he ever love like that again? I had hopes that he would. Having been reborn in the shadow of death, Berthold now had endless nights to find new love. My nights would also be endless, but unlike Berthold's, they would be spent adrift in a darkness in which no one was within reach, a darkness devoid of romantic love, because of the permanence of my childhood.

It was not unusual that Berthold kissed my hand tonight. He kissed me often. My hands. My head. My cheek. But the way he looked at me after we had fed—he had been watching me feed. What did that mean? Did it mean anything? Was he just happy to be back in Los Angeles? Was he happy that we were back in Los Angeles together? If it was because we were here together, was his kissing me entirely innocent? In my heart of hearts, I admit, I hoped it wasn't.

Berthold and me. Me and Berthold. Could we ever be? Berthold knows I'm not really a child. He knows I'm truly a woman. Couldn't he look past my prepubescent body and touch my flesh and love the woman who resided beneath my skin? Couldn't he save me from this doom? Was that asking too much? Yes, it probably was. But why had he been looking at me like that? What was in his eyes as he watched me feed?

Could it be desire? Could he ever love me half as much as he loved Yelena? If he does already love me and he were to become my lover, what would Yelena think? Would she have stopped us? And if she did would she be stopping it for my sake or her own? Did any of that even matter now? She was never coming back to mother me. And even if she did, would she or could she do anything about it if I were already nested within Berthold's heart?

How had I been so blind? Why had I never seen him in this light in Tokyo? Was it because I was in mourning? We were mourning the same person. We could have comforted each other. We should comfort each other now.

As a vampire, he would understand me. He would understand that my youth is in body alone. He would look past it and see within me. He would long to be fused with my soul so fiercely that he would eventually lust for my body and become my lover. And then I would know his skin on mine. He would envelop me and crush me under his weight. He would penetrate and ejaculate inside me the way he always wanted to inside of Yelena.

The smell of fresh blood began to evaporate. His sanguine tears had dried. What was he thinking now inside his casket? Was he dreaming? Was he dreaming of Yelena or of me?

But my pondering and yearning were cut short when I recalled what Hisato had said to me.

We have to kill her.

EIGHT

When we awoke the next night, the house was spotless. All traces of the missionaries had been cleaned until they no longer existed. Mayuko was in her bed, sound asleep. She had had a long night with Bao and Dao, burying the six bodies out in the desert, on the property Yelena had willed to me before her death. Though I was dying to ask Mayuko what she would think of me and Berthold being together, I decided not to wake her. If I had the strength, I would give her a night off and not feed, but unfortunately, Berthold and I were still too young to go without blood for a night without becoming sick. Consequently, when she awoke, Mayuko would have to dispose of bodies for both of us, just like Berthold had to dispose of the bodies discarded by both me and Yelena when he was still mortal. I remember how tiring that was for him and I had felt guilty, suddenly being another mouth to feed. I hated thinking of Mayuko working so much.

"We have to find you a servant," I said to Berthold as I walked down the hallway toward him.

"That's already in the works," he replied.

Of course it was. Berthold was always so efficient.

"I have tickets to the theatre tonight. Would you like to go?" Berthold asked as we finished inspecting the house.

I stood close to him and rested my head upon his arm. "Of course, my love."

"Good. We'll feed after the show."

Berthold didn't remark on me calling him "my love" though I'd never called him that before. I concluded he didn't mind.

I dressed up for the theatre as best as I could, wearing a Lolita dress Berthold had never seen me in, making every effort to appear beautiful. That was also the night I finally had the courage to wear the silicone breast forms I secretly purchased in Tokyo in front of anyone else besides the mirror. Before we left, I checked in again to see if Mayuko was still asleep, and she was. I went to the living room where Berthold was waiting, looking divinely handsome and masculine in one of his dark Ermenegildo Zegna suits. His eyes glanced across my larger bust and then back to my eyes, but he didn't say a word.

The night sky was clear and the air crisp. Parked on the driveway was a deep blue Maserati Gran Turismo. Hisato had loaned it to him. Berthold opened my door and I stepped inside. Soon we were speeding down the winding road, descending upon the Los Angeles nightlife.

I did not know the play we saw, but one of the characters was a young girl from a former century who fell in love with her tutor. It was a period piece of sorts, where the present day collided with the past. At one point both times exist on the stage simultaneously. It caused me to reflect upon our immortality and how Berthold and I would live together through many eras, eras that would only become distinct from each other as enough time passed. In the end of the play we learn the girl perished in a fire, but on stage, she waltzes in the arms of her tutor until the lights go down. A young girl and an older man. It could have been us dancing. Had Berthold purposely taken me to this play? I asked if he had seen it before, but he replied that he had only read it.

Our thirsts for blood were strong by the end of the play and so we followed a couple, who had rudely talked through most of the performance, to their house in Encino. I was happy we would kill them somewhere so private as it would make the disposal for Mayuko easier.

"We'll bleed them dry and be careful not to spill a drop, okay?" I asked Berthold. He smiled as we exited the freeway, following the BMW belonging to the doomed couple from a distance.

We entered their house easily and noiselessly and we said nothing as I took the man and Berthold took the woman. I drank slowly, so that Berthold might finish first. While my head was buried in the man's throat, I looked up with my eyes and saw that Berthold had already laid the woman's desiccated corpse to rest on the floor and was again looking at me as I finished feeding. Once my victim was bloodless I released his throat and sat up and smiled at Berthold.

"Where would you like to go now?" he asked.

"Take me to a nice restaurant," I answered. "A candlelit one."

Berthold asked that we be seated in a quiet corner, away from the other late night patrons. Our table was square and covered with fine linen. We sat adjacently rather than across from each other so the two lit candles on the table did not burn between us. What we ordered didn't matter. We would only pick at it just to experience tastes other than blood. I asked Berthold to order a bottle of white wine, and despite my childlike appearance, the waiter poured a glass for both of us, as Berthold had requested.

We mostly talked about our first night back in Los Angeles. I related to him my conversation with Hisato inside Yelena's closet and Berthold remarked that it was not easy for him to pass through her clothing. He wanted them to remain untouched, hanging as closely as possible to how she had left them. I placed my right hand on his left and after a moment, he placed his other hand on top of mine and patted it a couple of times before signaling our waiter for a third bottle of wine.

As we polished off glass after glass of wine, Berthold remained largely composed, but spoke a little louder than usual. As for myself, weighing under one hundred pounds, I was pretty drunk.

"Tell me, my love, what are we gonna do about this Communion of the Ancients thing Zacharias was talking about?" I asked sloppily.

"What can we do about it?"

"We can go, is what we can do."

"We're not Ancients. You heard what Zacharais said, to be invited you must be at least five hundred years old."

"So I gotta wait five hundred years to kill her?"

"Orly. I caution you. Please mind your words. You never know who's listening. It could be Mirela herself."

"Fuck her. That bitch is dead."

Berthold stood up.

"Come on, it's time we left," he said and helped me up.

I looked around the restaurant and saw there were no patrons left and the remaining staff sat at tables waiting for us to leave.

"Leave a big tip," I mumbled.

"It's already taken care of."

"Let's go dancing. Teach me to waltz!" I shouted as he escorted me out of the restaurant.

Though it was not nearly sunrise, Berthold drove us home because I was so intoxicated. By that time, I was so sloppy that he had to carry me from the car, inside the house. As we passed through Yelena's closet and descended the stone staircase, I tried to kiss his face, but couldn't reach and so I did my best to press my silicone breasts into his chest.

"I want to sleep in your coffin tonight."

"Casket."

"Whatevs. So okay? You'll let me?"

"Orly."

"What?"

"You're drunk."

"I am not. Well not much. I'm immortal. And Hisato said we can't become alcoholics."

"Being an alcoholic and being drunk are two separate things."

"Huh?"

He held me aloft with one arm as he opened the lid of my casket.

"Let me sleep with you," I said again. "I won't do anything. I promise."

But it was as if he were no longer listening. He laid me to rest in my casket and then told me to close my eyes. Frustrated, I didn't obey and looked right at him as he leaned forward and kissed my forehead before shutting the lid on me.

Berthold went back upstairs and had another drink.

Because I was shut inside my casket, I began to sober quickly. And as that happened, I was overcome with humiliation. I had made such a fool of myself, getting drunk and throwing myself at him, and he hadn't responded at all.

I wanted to rush upstairs and try to explain myself, but I was embarrassed and didn't know what I could say that wouldn't be a lie. I couldn't tell him I didn't mean it and only said those things because I was drunk. I wanted him to love me mentally and emotionally, or at the very least, physically.

A couple of hours passed before I heard Berthold closing the closet door and descending the stairs. I wondered if he was going to come talk to me, but he didn't. He got into his own casket and shut the lid. I lay in silence, wondering what he was thinking. Was he thinking of me and all my foolishness? Was he considering my offer or thinking of a way to let me down easy while still maintaining a firm boundary between us? But then I smelled his blood again. His eyes leaked only a drop or two, but it was enough for me to know he wasn't thinking of me at all.

NINE

Mayuko was waiting for me at the kitchen table when I came upstairs the next night. She looked well rested and was sipping a cappuccino she bought from Starbucks. I took the seat across from her.

"Can I have some of that?" I asked, as I enjoyed the taste of coffee.

Rather than pushing the cup across the table, Mayuko stood and carried the coffee to my side of the table and then took her seat once more. I thanked her and, as I was about to bring the paper coffee cup to my lips, I noticed the writing on the cup. There was a lot of it, all in black felt pen. Her name was written, spelled correctly. Beside it was a flower that resembled a daisy whose central disc was transformed into a happy face. Beside that was a phone number. Below that was the name Seth. Though I registered all of these details in the mere blink of an eye and did my best not to react, I know Mayuko noticed the soured expression pass quickly over my face before I feigned a smile. She tilted her head, looking at me, waiting for me to speak.

"Someone named Seth gave you his number?" I asked.

"Yeah. He was kinda cute and he told me he would remember my double tall nonfat dry vanilla cappuccino forever."

"He doesn't know what forever is," I said bitterly, but again forced my smile which must have been convincing because Mayuko smiled in return.

Mayuko longed to be immortal and hoped it would happen while she was still in the prime of her beauty. Ten years of servitude was customary as far as I knew, but I loved having Mayuko as my girlfriend so much that I wanted to make her a vampire already. Unfortunately, Zacharias told me my blood was not yet strong enough to bring Mayuko back from the dead and into immortality if I took her life.

I put the paper cup down without drinking. "You can have this back now."

"What's wrong, Cricket?"

"Nothing. It's just that nobody has ever given me their phone number. It sucks."

Mayuko again rose from her seat and picked up the cup.

"Fuck Seth," she said and poured the coffee out in the sink and disposed of the cup.

"I tried to have sex with Berthold last night."

Mayuko's eyes grew wide and she sat down quickly. "And did you?" she asked, stunned.

"No. He totally rejected me."

She appeared relieved.

"What's that look for?" I asked curtly.

"Nothing. I mean, I think it would have been bad if you had done that with Berthold."

"Why? I'm old enough."

"Yes, I know. I know that Orly. And I know it is difficult for you, to be a young woman in the body of a girl, but…"

"You don't know," I answered sharply and I could tell that I frightened her.

Mayuko bowed her head in shame and stared down at the table instead of looking directly at me. "I apologize, Orly. I did not mean to upset you."

Her apology softened my flash of anger, and my fondness for her was remembered and I was able to admit to myself that I was taking the pain of Berthold's rejection out on her.

"I'm sorry," I said softly and I stood up and walked around the table and lifted her chin with my fingers. "I'm not mad at you. I'm mad at myself. Please. I think I already know, but tell me why it would be bad between me and Berthold."

Mayuko took my hand and kissed it in nearly the exact same place Berthold had two nights earlier, and as she held my hand in her hands she said, "I think he sees you as a daughter, not as a lover."

I nodded my head. They were the words I didn't want to hear but knew were true.

"I'm stuck in the fucking daughter zone."

Mayuko knew it was a joke and she laughed, and I laughed with her until I heard Berthold's casket cover open.

"Come on, get your keys," I said.

And even though I was still wearing the same dress as the night before, the dress I had worn for the father figure I failed to seduce, we rushed out the front door and got into Mayuko's car and quickly pulled out of the driveway.

"Find me someone to kill," I said flatly as we raced through the canyon in Mayuko's black Cadillac XTS. She picked that model of car because of the extra large trunk.

"You want me to pick someone for you?"

"No, I want you to call Seth."

"I threw the cup away."

"I remember the number."

"Are you serious? The barista?"

I was serious until I saw her hesitation. "Of course not. He's probably a child." I was going to let it go and let Seth, who draws daisies, live. But then Mayuko surprised me.

"He doesn't mean anything to me," she said.

Because I tended to be selfish, Seth not meaning anything to her made me want to kill him less.

The moment we stepped inside Starbucks, and without reading name tags, I saw that Seth's shift hadn't ended. I knew immediately which barista he was as his face brightened like a searchlight when he saw Mayuko enter the cafe. Had my appearance ever induced such a smile on anyone other than Yelena?

We went up to the counter. Seth immediately grabbed a cup and wrote *Mayuko* on it. He was older than I imagined when we were still in my kitchen. His handwriting looked immature.

"Let me guess," he said. "Double tall nonfat dry hazelnut cappuccino?"

"Vanilla, actually," Mayuko replied.

"Oh that's right. Sorry, it's been a long shift."

"It's okay."

"Who's your little friend?" Seth asked, meaning me even though I was still wearing my silicone breasts from the night before. Maybe I would kill him after all.

Mayuko answered, "This is my cousin Ashley."

"Really? You're cousins?" He laughed. He couldn't tell if Mayuko was joking as we looked nothing alike. "And what would she like?" he asked Mayuko.

"Same as me. Thank you."

Seth reached for another cup, paused with pen in hand, and then wrote *Mayuko* on that cup as well. Mayuko looked at me in a way that told me she knew I noted that he had already forgotten my fake name. He was doomed.

"What time are you off?" Mayuko asked, trying to deflect.

"Depends who's asking," Seth answered flirtatiously.

"I'm asking," I interrupted stoically.

Seth's smile faded when he looked down into my cold gaze. He seemed suddenly afraid and I enjoyed that.

"Eleven," he finally spit out.

"Great," Mayuko said, "maybe we'll still be here."

We waited for our identical drinks and when they arrived we looked for a table. The cafe was crowded, but a couple just happened to be leaving and Mayuko claimed the table for us. Again we sat across from each other as we sipped our cappuccinos.

"So how do you like America so far?" I asked.

"It's only been three nights!"

"So?"

"Well, I don't know. It's good. It's not as crowded, but I thought everyone would dress more stylishly like on *Sex and the City*. But I still like it."

"You don't regret leaving everything behind?"

"Nothing was left behind. I had no family. No boyfriend. No dog. Everything that matters to me is here with you. Orly, I'm happy the Ketsuen released me."

"You need to stop looking for Mr. Right and instead manifest the man of your dreams," a woman with an abundance of optimism said to a sullen looking woman at the table behind Mayuko. "Do you understand what I'm saying?" she continued.

"Um, I think so?" the sullen woman replied.

"I'm saying that your time is now. The universe is listening, but it will only give you what you want when you are ready to receive it. Are you ready to receive it?"

"I've been ready."

"Great! So let's run through it. What will you do, to manifest the man of your dreams, Becky? Close your eyes and tell me the five steps."

Becky closed her eyes and somewhat dejectedly began to speak as if it were a recital. "I will quiet myself and focus within. I will embrace my vibrational energies. I will envision whatever I want more of. I will claim what I want."

"Are you listening to this shit?" Mayuko whispered to me.

I nodded my head.

"What the hell is she talking about?" Mayuko whispered again.

I shrugged my shoulders, pretty much writing these mantras off as nonsense, but then thought about Berthold. Wasn't he the man I would choose to manifest?

Becky finished by saying, "I will be the goddess I truly am and actualize the type of man I deserve."

"Perfect. Now open your eyes."

Becky opened her eyes.

"How do you feel?"

"I feel good."

"As you should. When you truly believe something will happen and you set your intentions toward that thing happening, it will happen."

Mayuko rolled her eyes. I rolled my eyes with her. Even though Berthold was still in the back of my mind, I knew everything I had overheard was bullshit. Nothing in life was that easy. Especially not love.

"Well, I guess that's our time for this week. Good work!"

"Thank you so much, Parvin," Becky said and then reached in her purse and counted out ten twenty dollar bills and handed it to Parvin.

"Can I get a hug?" Parvin asked.

They pushed their seats back, Parvin bumping Mayuko's chair and not apologizing, and stood and hugged each other. Parvin left the cafe with a smile on her face and Becky sat back down, and after a moment buried her head in her hands.

I got up from my chair and went to Becky. I placed my hand on her forearm and she flinched at my cold touch. As she looked up, she appeared surprised I was a child.

"I'm sorry," I said. "I was just wondering if you were okay."

"Oh yes, I'm fine."

Mayuko swiveled in her seat to join the conversation.

"Was she your therapist?" Mayuko asked.

"Sort of. She's my life coach."

"Life coach?" I asked. I had not heard of a life coach before.

"Yeah, she's there to offer guidance in many different aspects of my life."

"Does it work?" I questioned her again.

"I don't know. It was only my second session."

"It sounds interesting," Mayuko replied. "Maybe she could help me."

"Oh really?" Becky asked. "I think I have one of her cards. One sec. Let me look."

Becky opened her purse again and dug through it until she found a slightly bent business card. She handed it to Mayuko who thanked her earnestly. We said our goodbyes and left the cafe. Seth would live to see another shift.

Outside, Mayuko handed me the card. There was only a phone number and email address. No physical address.

"Don't worry," Mayuko said, "I'll call and make an appointment for tonight."

"And if she says not tonight?"

"Double her rate?"

I nodded my head. "Manifesting the death of a life coach. Is that irony?"

Mayuko shrugged her shoulders just as Parvin answered her phone.

For the next two weeks, I snuck out of the house before Berthold woke, hunted, mostly alone, and returned perilously close to daybreak to ensure Berthold was already secure inside his casket. In other words, I avoided seeing Berthold altogether.

I don't really know why I did it for as long as I did. At first it was out of embarrassment at being rejected, but that embarrassment quickly turned to the despair of love unrequited, and I longed for comfort from him more than anyone else.

The despair affected the way I killed. Despite my vampiric strengths, it was like I became lethargic, feeding because I had to, but no longer taking pleasure in the euphoria the blood could give me. Maybe I was depressed. A couple of times, my prey almost escaped because I was so inattentive and withdrawn as I was extinguishing their lives.

On the fifteenth night of avoiding Berthold completely, Mayuko asked to have a girls' night out as she wanted to take me somewhere after I fed. She would not reveal to me where.

My victim that night was an older man who wore a red cap that said "Make America Great Again." Again, my killing that night was without enthusiasm, but I did drink him dry because Mayuko was watching. Mayuko put the corpse in the trunk and I threw the cap in the gutter and we got into her Cadillac and headed north until streetlights became farther and farther spaced apart. I didn't press Mayuko to tell me where we were going. In accordance with my listlessness, I didn't care.

By the time she killed the engine, I had no idea where we were.

"Buhi buhi," Mayuko said.

"You mean, 'oink oink,'" I replied.

We got out of the car. It was dark out and we were standing on packed earth. There were wooden buildings and fences with wooden posts.

"Is this a farm or something?" I asked.

"It's an animal sanctuary."

That made sense. Mayuko always loved animals. She pressed a button on her key fob and the trunk of her Cadillac opened. With the remarkable strength I have already mentioned, Mayuko easily slung the wrapped corpse over her shoulder. We walked up a slight incline for nearly fifty yards and when we came to a low fence, she threw the body over and it landed in the dirt with a thud. She hopped over the fence with ease. I simply levitated over it and landed, not disturbing the dust.

Beyond the fence, the animals began to stir. It smelled like a zoo. In stables there were eleven horses and four donkeys. Fenced in another section were at least twenty-five cows. Elsewhere in smaller pens were goats and sheep. There was even a peacock. Mayuko picked up the corpse again and walked with a determined gait. It was clear she had been here before. The smell had changed slightly when we stopped at the pens where eighteen pigs lived.

"They're big and hairy," I said. Before that moment I had only ever seen pigs on children's shows and a pink rubber eraser I had in the hospital that was shaped like a pig. They were all small and smooth and cute. These pigs were much larger and had coarse hair, but were still cute in their own way. "This is what you wanted to show me?"

"Not exactly. Just watch."

Mayuko unwrapped the body and threw the corpse into the pen. The ground wasn't as muddy as I expected for pigs. One of the pigs came up and sniffed the corpse and then another. Soon enough, the first one bit into it. And then the second. The pigs squealed with excitement, causing a commotion amongst the other pigs who also rushed over. Within moments, they were all upon the body, gnawing at it.

"How long's this gonna take?"

"Couple hours. It would've helped if I made the body moist by pouring milk over it."

"Will the other animals eat dead bodies too? They have a lot of cows here."

"No. A cow's digestive system is meant to eat roughage. A pig's digestive system is like a human's. It can handle eating proteins like muscle."

"How do you know all this?"

"The Ketsuen taught me. It's a very clean disposal. You just pick up the bones afterwards and crush them to dust. We'll need more pigs than this though with the way you and Berthold feed."

"You want to do this instead of driving out to the desert?"

"It's easier."

"I love you," I said excitedly. "But where are we going to get pigs from?"

"That's the best part!" she said with a big smile. "We'll rescue them from being eaten!"

"We'll have to buy new land. A farm or something so that it's not suspicious."

"Yes, and hopefully somewhere closer than the desert."

"Well this place is close to the middle of nowhere where Zacharias lives. Maybe he'd let us have a farm on his land."

We watched for over two hours as the pigs picked the bones clean. We hopped over the fence and petted some of the pigs before Mayuko shooed them away so she could collect the bones. She wrapped them and put them back in the trunk. She would have to find a way to crush them to dust later. It had been a good girls' night out.

As planned, I got home close to sunrise. I could feel the weakness brought by the approaching daylight begin to overcome me. I entered the house and everything was still. All the window coverings were shut. I opened Yelena's closet, stepped inside, and shut the door behind me. I moved through the secret door and began to descend the stairs. Though it was silent below, I was taken by surprise when I saw Berthold standing near his casket, his back to the wall, with his hands behind him, palms pressed to the stone surface. He had waited up for me.

"You're awake," I said as I finished descending the staircase.

"You can't avoid me forever, Orly. We're going to have to talk about it sometime."

"Talk about what?"

"The feelings you expressed for me."

"What's there to talk about? I love you and you don't love me."

"You know that's not true. You know I love you. Maybe not in the way you had hoped, but I love you."

"Like a father, right?"

"Something like that."

I nodded my head in resignation. He stepped away from the wall toward me.

"Believe me, Orly, you wouldn't want my love anyway. It isn't mine to give. My heart loves a ghost."

"Then don't give me your heart. Give me everything else."

"I can't do that."

"Why not? You made love to Natsumi."

"I don't know if I would call that love."

"Then call it something else. Something worse. Something ugly even. And give me whatever that is."

He shook his head.

"You think I'm a child."

"No. I know you are not. You are young, but you are no child."

"Then what then?"

He didn't respond.

"Do you see me as a woman?"

Hesitantly, he shook his head. "No. I do not. I'm sorry, Orly."

"So what do we do now?"

"We go back to how things were when we were in Tokyo."

"But we're not in Tokyo."

"We cannot be lovers, Orly."

He wasn't going to give in and I knew it, so as best as I could I showed that I accepted it, and nodded my head, but inside I was crushed. He stepped toward me again and put his hands on my upper arms. I closed my eyes as he kissed my forehead.

It was time to retire. We shut ourselves in our own caskets. But that morning, as I lay upon dark purple satin, it was my eyes that leaked blood.

TEN

To my surprise, things did go back to how they were in Tokyo with relative ease, externally at least. All it took was for me not to say anything about loving Berthold in ways that were not welcome.

When Berthold's black Porsche Cabriolet arrived from Japan, courtesy of the Ketsuen, it felt like being in Tokyo with him again, as we prowled the night at high speeds in and around Los Angeles. I was happy as I could be riding beside him, despite my silent yearning, as I at least had him all to myself.

January came and Mayuko's double duty ended as Berthold secured himself a new servant. His name was Khalil Walker. He was a recent and distinguished law school graduate, but the prospect of immortality appealed to him more than a future partnership in a large law firm. He was not quite as tall as Berthold, nor did he have Berthold's breadth, but he was incredibly handsome, with his ebony skin and dark corkscrew coiled hair that fell to the top of his collared shirts. He had a short and neatly trimmed goatee and wore dark framed glasses whenever he read or used a computer. He and Mayuko took a platonic liking to each other immediately.

By February Mayuko's pig sanctuary occupied nearly a third of Zacharias' ranch. Thirty-five pigs destined for slaughter were easily purchased and housed in pens. A barn was erected to hide two large meat grinders that, in the beginning, were used to pulverize the bones, although the process was laborious. Shortly thereafter, Zacharias suggested placing the bones in the kiln he had used for decades to burn his corpses. Fired in the kiln, the bones would become brittle and could be more easily crushed into bone meal, which Zacharias then used to fertilize his acres of gardens and foliage. With the body count provided by Zacharias, Berthold, and me, our rescued pigs were well fed.

On a chilly night in March, after Berthold and I had fed on a drunk driver and his passenger, we found ourselves sitting together at a secluded table in the back of a Thai restaurant in Hollywood with two bottles of Pinot Gris that were supposed to pair well with the mee krob neither of us touched. As we had been wandering the streets of Hollywood on foot, we hadn't intended to dine at this restaurant in particular. Therefore, when we left, Berthold's car was not with the valet parkers, but was instead parked many blocks away in a parking lot that had a flat rate of twenty dollars for the night. I didn't mind the long walk as the crisp air felt good on my skin and Berthold didn't prevent us from walking arm in arm.

As we neared an area that was swarming with nightlife, club goers mostly, I gripped Berthold's arm more tightly. We passed through the throngs of revelers and they parted at our approach, perhaps sensing our undead auras. There was a dreamlike quality to everything, as though Berthold and I were the only characters in focus in an old black and white film. But the focus deepened when Berthold suddenly stopped and didn't take another step.

"What is it?" I asked, but he didn't answer.

He stood as though contemplating something that perplexed him, as if there were a sudden fork in the road and he had to choose a direction quickly. After a moment, he spoke.

"Come on," he said. "Let's go this way."

And he turned us round and we began to retrace our steps, heading back to whence we came.

"Where are we going? The car's back there."

"I know. It'll be fine. There's just something I need to see."

We walked two blocks and stopped in front of a music hall. I looked at the marquee. It said a band named Deafheaven was playing and that the show was sold out. I let go of him as he stepped up to the ticket window and confirmed there were no other tickets.

He stepped away, disappointed. A young couple moved to the window after Berthold cleared the way.

"They should be under the name Ben Porter," the man said. "They're VIP seats, if that helps."

The will call attendant found their tickets and slid them through the opening at the bottom of the window. The couple was about to step inside the venue when Berthold unexpectedly put his hand on the man's shoulder, causing him to turn around suddenly.

"Excuse me, but don't I know you?" Berthold asked.

The man searched Berthold's face for a moment and then said, "I'm sorry, I don't believe so."

"Look at me again. I have met you both," he said, this time including the woman.

He was charming them. I stepped forward and took Berthold's side.

"You want to give me your tickets."

"Yes, of course."

"Babe, give him the tickets."

The man handed Berthold the tickets and Berthold reached into his pants pocket, pulled out some bills and stuffed them into the man's inner coat pocket. It was at least a thousand dollars.

"Enjoy your night," Berthold said, and they left.

"Do you know this band?" I asked.

Berthold shook his head as he guided me into the venue. This time I had to charm the security guard as to him I was clearly underage.

An opening band was already on stage, their guitars wailing. The dance floor was nearly full of people, mostly in their twenties and early thirties, hardly paying attention to the band. The VIP section was on the second level and had rows of seats. Berthold led me up the staircase. Our seats were in the front row of the balcony overlooking the large dance floor below. By the time we were seated, the band performing was thanking everyone for being a great audience and announced that Deafheaven would be on shortly.

"Should we get drinks?" I asked.

"I'm okay."

His eyes were scanning the crowd.

"Who are you looking for?"

"I beg your pardon? What did you say?"

"Who are you looking for?

"No one. It's no one."

As I knew he didn't know the band I knew he was lying. His eyes eventually stopped roaming over the crowd on the dance floor below and I followed his gaze and saw who he had been looking for. A small cluster of people, clad in black, had gathered near the edge of the floor. Among them was a svelte young woman with platinum hair. Her hair was long like Yelena's.

"I see who you're looking at," I said softly, but I knew he could hear me over the noise of the crowd.

"Do you?"

"Do you know her?"

"No. We passed her on the street."

"And you want to kill her?"

"No."

Berthold continued to watch her silently while roadies set the stage for the next band. I scrutinized her myself and decided that although she was willowy like Yelena and had the platinum hair, the similarities ended there. This woman's eyes were lighter than Yelena's and softer in their gaze. Her smile was beautiful and wide as she animatedly spoke to her friends and she threw her head back when she laughed. Yelena rarely smiled and almost never laughed. Yelena was taller than she was and more graceful in her movements.

Berthold suddenly stood as she and her girlfriend broke away from the group of friends and disappeared below the edge of the balcony. His impulsive action quickly made me jealous. He moved as if he were going to scoot down the aisle past me and head back downstairs.

"Let her go," I said and grabbed the sleeve of his coat.

Berthold looked at me, unsure of what I had said.

"She's not Yelena."

"Of course she's not," he said, appearing puzzled.

Had he not noticed the similarities? Was he drawn to her instinctively without any cognizance whatsoever?

"She's not going to leave the show before the headliner. Sit back down, please."

Berthold resumed his seat and sat looking both anxious and bored at the same time. But just as Deafheaven took the stage the woman with the platinum hair appeared in the VIP section with her girlfriend. Their seats were to our right, many rows behind us, but with our extended peripheral vision, we had only to turn slightly to gain full view of the pair and it was as if we were facing them head on.

I liked the band a lot and told Berthold I wanted a Deafheaven t-shirt and any CDs they were selling, but he wasn't listening. He was staring at her so intensely that I was surprised she didn't notice. At the end of the second song, the woman with the platinum hair stood up and made her way to the stairs, leaving her friend behind. As she disappeared down the staircase, Berthold stood up as well.

"Are you serious?" I asked.

"I'm sorry. I must speak with her," he responded.

My jealousy felt like a bee sting. I watched him make his way to the end of our aisle, but to my surprise, Berthold did not head for the staircase in pursuit of the woman with platinum hair. Instead he made his way to the friend she left behind.

How childish, I thought, Berthold asking the friend who remained if her friend who had left had a boyfriend. Even if she did, we could just kill him.

I used my vampiric senses to listen to their conversation over the noise of the concert.

"Good evening," he said.

"Hi."

"My name is Berthold Leitz. I don't mean to disturb you, but I couldn't help but notice you were sitting alone."

"Oh, I'm here with a friend actually, but she went downstairs to look for her boyfriend. You can sit, until she comes back if you want. Knowing her, she might not even come back," she said and laughed.

Berthold sat beside her.

"Since you remained up here, I'm hoping that means you don't also have a boyfriend to look for."

The woman blushed. "No. I don't have a boyfriend."

It was her Berthold wanted, not the other. And his asking if she had a boyfriend told me he was interested in her romantically rather than as only someone beautiful to feed upon. My eyes shifted from him to her.

"What's your name?" Berthold asked.

"Kristy," she answered.

"Kristy…?" Berthold asked.

"Oh, sorry. Kristy Amare."

"Kristy Amare," Berthold repeated and sat down beside her.

She was more beautiful than I was and not just because she was a woman and I was not. Her features had made her a beautiful child as well. I was sure of it. Her hair was dark brown and hung more than halfway down her back, and in the front it cascaded gently about her heart shaped face. As her complexion was fair, her blushes were emphasized upon her pronounced cheekbones. And her eyes. What eyes she had. Her irises were a pale green and they glistened like abalone shells in sunlight whenever they caught the white beams of light spinning from the ceiling. The darker limbal rings that bordered the circumferences of her irises had a bluish tint so softly defined that they made her eyes appear as gentle as the ephemeral and hemispherical bubbles that are born on the sidewalk during a hard rain. Her smile was bright and radiated the spark of mortal life, and when her lips closed, they naturally pressed together as if she were anticipating a kiss.

Out of pure jealousy, I hated her.

Berthold asked for her phone number and permission to call her, and she gave it to him and said she hoped he would call her soon. It was clear she was taken with him. When he told her he should return to his seat beside his friend, she didn't see the friend he mentioned and assumed she misheard him because of the loud music and didn't inquire further. I had disappeared to her of course. Looking at her and knowing my own appearance, how could I allow her to see me? When he rose, she stood as well and with sylphlike arms she hugged my Berthold goodbye. Her stature, due to her long shapely legs, placed her head at the height of his broad chest. Her full breasts, fuller than the phony pair I had stuffed into the bra I didn't need, pressed firmly upon him.

I remained invisible to her even after Berthold resumed his seat beside me. I remained invisible to everyone.

"So you like her? This Kristy?"

"You listened to our conversation?"

"What do you think?"

"Please don't be upset, Orly."

"I'm not upset, but why her?"

"In truth, I don't know why. We passed her on the street and I felt my blood stir and it was as if all of my senses magnetically reached out in an attempt to embrace her. I felt my heart leap in a way it had not since…"

He didn't finish his sentence so I finished it for him.

"Since Yelena?"

"Yes. Look, I didn't want or expect this to happen, but it has. I feel things for her that…"

I interrupted him. "You just fucking met her!"

"Please calm yourself, Orly. I already know. Believe me. I am just as perplexed. I can only think that, as a vampire, my feelings, they've intensified to extremes I never knew as a mortal."

"You didn't feel this way about Natsumi or any of the other lovers you took as a vampire."

"I realize that. But I just know she is different. I cannot explain my draw to her but it feels like she is meant to be with me. No. It is the opposite. I am meant to be with her. I must know her, Orly. And I am sorry. I know this is terrible timing with everything we discussed last December, about your feelings for me."

"It seems like she already has strong feelings for you too."

He didn't reply, but he knew I was right. Vampiric charm always drew many mortals to us. It often rendered them helpless, making it so easy for us to beguile lovers and victims. Well, for me at least, it helped bring me victims.

I knew this was bound to happen someday—Berthold falling in love. I had hoped it would happen after I had fallen in love with someone else. I felt so alone and unwanted as Deafheaven continued to play the rest of their set.

"Please, Orly. Please don't be angry."

"I already told you I'm not angry."

"Then promise me something."

"What?"

"That you won't kill her."

The next night Berthold and I hunted together and then walked along the Santa Monica pier where we rode the Ferris wheel twice and the roller coaster once. We then watched the waves for over an hour.

The night after that we hunted together again but Berthold had a date with Kristy later and so we would have to separate. He offered to drive me back to our house before his date, but I told him I'd rather wander around Hollywood. We parted at Sunset and Ivar, outside Amoeba Records. I felt a mixture of anger and sorrow as I entered the record store, searching for vinyl records or compact discs by Deafheaven.

After I left the record store, I phoned Mayuko to ask her to hang out, but she too was on a date. She readily offered to ditch her companion, but I told her it was fine and to have a good time. Somehow, sounding like I was happy for her on the phone made me feel better about feeling sorry for myself. Just as I hung up, an old homeless man approached and asked me for spare change. I told him I didn't have any cash on me and asked him to accompany me. I held his hand as we walked together and at an ATM at Sunset and Vine I withdrew five hundred dollars, as that was all the machine would give me in a twenty-four hour period. I handed it to him and walked off before he could say anything or count the money.

I wondered what Berthold was doing. Where would he take Kristy on their first date? Would they dine at a restaurant we had dined at? Would they hold hands or even kiss? What would they talk about? Would he tell the truth about him being a vampire? Would she run away in fear or not believe him and laugh? How many dates would it be before they had sex? It could easily happen tonight if Berthold were to seduce her with his vampiric gaze, but I knew he wouldn't. He would want her to fall for him all on her own.

I wondered when it would be that someone would try to seduce me. I walked all the way home alone.

Our nights continued in this way for a couple of weeks. Hunting and then going our separate ways. Eventually, we even stopped hunting together because it hurt me too much to watch him go, but I didn't tell him that was my reason.

Instead, I told him I would be going out with Hisato, and sometimes that was true, but most of the time it wasn't. Berthold stayed out with Kristy later and later each night, but was still always careful to come home before sunrise. Whenever he entered our subterranean chamber, and even while in my casket, I could smell the faint and sweet scent of her perfume on his skin.

I felt like I had lost him. I had believed before that he was here in this house and in my life, for me. Maybe I felt that way because at one time he had been our servant. I thought of hurting myself to get his attention, but I didn't know how to do that except by burning my skin with sunlight, and that had hurt so much before and was permanently scarring that I didn't have the courage to do it.

What I assumed was depression extended the hours I remained inside my casket to the point where I no longer saw Berthold at all. Night would come and he would rise while I remained shut inside. He would be gone before my hunger got the best of me, forcing me to get up, get ready, and go out to kill someone. And after I fed, I would come straight home and lay myself to rest again. A couple of times, my depression was strong enough that I elected to suffer the hunger, the weakness, and the illness, that came with not feeding at all.

Eventually, I came to realize that this was no way to live and decided that I had to accept that Berthold found someone to love who was not me, and that if I wanted love, I would have to find it someplace else, as a potential paramour wouldn't be found within my casket. When I accepted this, I felt like I had finally behaved maturely. Or rather, I saw that all my previous actions had been immature. So after I fed that night, I decided I would not dwell on Berthold's relationship with Kristy and have fun with him instead by hiding inside his casket so I could scare the shit out of him when he returned home weary from the approaching sunrise.

I lay in his casket for nearly an hour before I heard him upstairs. I tried to keep myself from laughing as I waited for him to come downstairs into our sleeping chamber, but he didn't come. Thirty minutes passed since he had come home and he still had not descended the staircase. What was he doing up there?

I pushed opened the lid of his casket and stepped out. I walked as silently as I could up the stairs and opened the secret door and then the closet door noiselessly. I smelled Kristy's perfume more strongly than when it had been left on his skin. I made myself invisible and didn't make a sound as I walked across the cherrywood floor into the bedroom.

There they were, in Yelena's bed, making love. Kristy was on top of my Berthold, her hips gyrating in a slow circular motion. Berthold's hands roamed over her flesh—the bend where her hips met her thighs, her waist, her stomach, and of course her large breasts. With admirable envy I stared at her bare breasts and the curves of her behind. I saw just how much more of a woman she was than I would ever be.

She didn't see me of course; that was to be expected. But Berthold didn't see me either. He didn't even sense my presence as another vampire in his midst, as he should have for his own safety. But by that age, I had already learned that our emotions could subdue our vampiric senses, and in that moment, that knowledge devastated me because I knew it meant he loved her.

They rolled over and she was engulfed by all his masculinity. Their lovemaking was not only sensual, but beautiful in that they were so overcome and absorbed in their shared moment. As their nether regions rhythmically pulsed together, they kissed each other's faces, necks, and shoulders. And when they moved to kiss on the lips they stared deeply into each other's eyes.

In an instant, I could have torn her to shreds. I could deliver more pain than she had ever felt or would ever feel in her relatively short existence. I wanted to make her scream so loudly that she would expel whatever life she had left in her. I would rip her throat wide open and not drink a single drop. I would allow her blood to fountain all over Berthold and spill off his naked body onto Yelena's bedsheets, and have every single sanguine ounce wasted. But of course, I didn't do anything of the sort. I knew murdering her would only hurt him and still not make him love me, and that knowledge made me too sad to kill anyone at all.

I didn't wait for them to finish before I slipped back through the closet. Kristy must have asked to see where he lived and wanted to finally spend the entire night with him. Though the bedroom would remain dark throughout the day because of the heavy window coverings, Berthold would not have his full strength when he woke, having spent the hours of daylight outside of his casket. But in a heartbeat, I too would abandon my casket if it meant dreaming while intertwined in the arms of someone I loved.

I never made it to my casket by morning. I too would wake in a weakened state as I remained inside Yelena's closet, laying on the floor staring up at the hanging wardrobe that had made her appear so elegant and chic. And as I lay there, I wondered whether Kristy now knew Berthold was a vampire. What lie could he have invented to explain having to remain in absolute darkness during the diurnal existence she was accustomed to? If there was no lie, then he must have told her the truth, and if she still loved him despite his being a vampire, it could only mean one thing—she wanted an immortal existence with him.

The path to becoming a vampire generally happened in one of two ways. The first would be Berthold's and Mayuko's path—a defined period of absolute servitude to a vampire that was eventually rewarded with immortality. The second was Yelena's path, and now seemingly Kristy's path—a vampire would fall in love and could not bear the thought of their beloved passing away from sickness, violence, or old age. Neither applied to me as I was an anomaly because of my scribbles.

But just as I was not old enough for my blood to have the strength to turn Mayuko into a vampire, Berthold was similarly too weak to give Kristy everlasting life. And by the time he was strong enough, she would have hopefully already rotted away in the earth, or at the very least, withered into a crone. He would have to ask an older vampire to share his blood in order to turn her, and that would be an impolite request as vampires are notoriously stingy about shedding and offering their own blood, especially when it does not serve them personally.

I reached up and felt the hem of one of Yelena's dresses. How fine the material was. Why had Berthold chosen to make love in Yelena's bed? My guess was that he had to appear to Kristy as the master of the house, and Yelena's bedroom was obviously the master bedroom. But it was a bed I had often shared with Yelena, snuggling before descending below to our real places of rest. Berthold had slept with his beloved Yelena once in that bed as well. They did not have sex, but they were partially clothed and he had spooned her. Didn't that make the bed sacred to him? Didn't Yelena's memory matter to Berthold any longer? Is this what eternity is like? Does time keep pushing you further and further away from what was until everything that once mattered so deeply becomes too distant to recognize? Is this what is meant by healing?

Maybe he was healing but I was not. My heart remained here, beneath these black fabric ghosts of the woman who had loved me like no one else.

ELEVEN

The following night was difficult. I woke in a haze and somewhat weak, but I was able to stand and step out of the closet with relative ease. My condition was not nearly as bad as the first time I slept outside of my casket. That time I had only been two nights old. I woke so debilitated that I needed Yelena to carry me to my casket. But that was now a decade ago. I was obviously getting stronger. It is said some of the Ancients do not need their coffins at all.

The window coverings had already risen on their automatic timers and the stars were plentiful that night. The bed where Berthold and Kristy made love was unmade and vacant. I passed through the secret door and went below but Berthold's casket was empty. I returned upstairs and entered the living room and then the kitchen looking for a note from Berthold, but there wasn't one to be found. He was out with her again. Would they again spend the night together in Yelena's bed? Did Berthold have the strength to do that for a second night in a row? Had he cultivated the power to not need his casket nightly and not shared that knowledge with me? Perhaps. Regardless, right now he needed to feed and if he were with Kristy that meant she knew what he truly was. She did want to be with him forever.

Though I was hungry and needed to go out and feed, I drew myself a bath. But I had difficulty relaxing and I stepped out of the tub prematurely when I heard the front door open and close and smelled mortal blood in the house. I wrapped a towel around me and exited the bathroom.

In the bedroom Khalil was pulling the sheets off of the unmade bed. He looked too well dressed to be making beds. He hadn't heard me approach and was startled when he looked up while pulling a pillow from a pillowcase.

"Hello, Miss Bialek. I'm sorry. Is it Miss Solodnikova? Mr. Leitz has used both names."

"Please call me Orly."

"Orly. Okay. I didn't mean to intrude, Orly, Mr. Leitz just asked that I straighten up."

"Please leave it alone."

"But Mr. Leitz said…"

"Mr. Leitz is not here and I am the lady of the house. Do as I say, please. Put the sheets and pillows back as they were, and when you're done with that, as there is nothing else in the house that needs straightening, you may leave."

"Yes, madam."

"Orly," I reminded him.

"Yes, Orly."

After Khalil left, I dressed while standing over the unmade bed. I could smell their sex on Yelena's satin sheets.

I love you, madam. I have loved you for so long.

Those were the words Berthold whispered to Yelena the night she bit into his neck and made him immortal. And as she gave him her own blood from her wrist, he knew more of what was happening than I did. He knew she was planning to die. In that beautiful and long awaited embrace Berthold knew he would never see her again.

I was unrested and hungry, but despondent, and so I still decided not to hunt. I opened the three sets of French doors that led into the backyard and allowed the gelid air to rush in, and barefoot, I stepped out into the night. I dipped my toe in the swimming pool and the water was cold as winter as it was still March. It would take a long time to warm, but I turned the pool heater on anyway. I walked across the lawn and felt the blades of grass poke between my toes. I pressed a button to ignite the fire pit and I sat myself in a chair, extending my legs onto the brick ledge of the pit and warmed my feet.

The night became darker and the glow of the flames intensified. I sat beside the fire thinking for more than two hours of what I knew I was going to do. A cloud covered the brightest star in the sky and I made that my signal to rise.

I reentered the house through the French doors and headed straight for Yelena's closet. I slid the door open and slowly, I removed a dress from a hanger. I dropped it on the floor. I removed another and another. A black fashionable mountain grew at my feet. I stopped and then stooped over and picked up as much of it as my twelve-year-old arms would allow. I headed back out to the backyard, a garment slipping from my grasp now and then. At the fire pit, I lifted the clothing to my face and tried again to smell Yelena, but she was still not there. I dropped the clothing into the flames and watched them smoke and burn to ash, just as Yelena had in her bed. The same bed that Berthold had desecrated with his new love.

As Yelena's wardrobe was large, it required many trips back into the house to retrieve more garments that I would let go of over the fire. Eventually, my hands held the overbust corset Yelena had been wearing the night I first saw her in the hospital cafeteria. I hugged it tightly and thought of keeping it, but with sorrow I relinquished it into the fire and watched it burn. In the end, the closet was empty, save for the hangers that hung like skeletons.

Outside, I turned off the fuel line of the fire pit and sat and watched as the embers died. I was so tired and malnourished that I knew I needed to either lay in my casket or go out and hunt, but again I chose to do neither. Instead, I reentered the house and lay on Yelena's unmade bed. I closed my eyes and explored the soiled sheets beneath me with my olfactory senses. Kristy's perfume and Berthold's cologne were easy to identify. I smelled sweat. One I recognized as Berthold's so the other distinct sweat had to belong to Kristy. I knew the scent of Kristy's vaginal fluid as I had smelled similar warm aromas when I had been in the presence of Hisato's girls having sex. I was cognizant of the smell of semen, not only from the sexual encounters of Hisato's girls, and the love hotels I had visited in Tokyo, but first and foremost from the memory of my foster brother when he raped me twice in my foster mom's garage. In this bouquet of lust, I didn't smell a trace of Yelena at all.

I lay there for over an hour, and when it was just past one o'clock, I heard a key inserted in the lock of the front door.

"Hello?" a meek voice called out.

It was Mayuko. I didn't answer. I knew she would find me on her own. But I smelled another mortal with her. It smelled like a man.

"Why don't you just sit over here," she said to him.

I heard her heels on the hardwood floors and soon enough Mayuko was standing over me as I lay in Yelena's bed.

"Hi Button," I said gently.

"You didn't feed tonight, did you? Normally you would have called by now. You must be starving."

"I didn't sleep in my casket last night either."

"Oh my dear. Cricket, you must feel so sick."

"I'm fine. I'm just going to lie here until Berthold gets home."

"How do you say it? No way José?"

"Yeah, fucking José and his no way."

"I'll carry you."

She scooped me out of the bed with ease. I expected her to bring me down to the secret chamber to lay me to rest, but instead she brought me to the living room. Seated on the sofa was a muscularly bulging man wearing a tight gray t-shirt. It looked unnatural the way he was overdeveloped.

"Who's this?" he asked, referring to me.

"This is Orly. I told you about Orly."

"Yeah, but she's just a little girl. You said we'd have a threesome, but you didn't say anything about kids. I ain't into no kid shit."

Mayuko placed me on the sofa beside him and he scooted away from me.

"This shit's weird. I better get going," he said and moved to get up but as he was still off balance, Mayuko deftly pushed him back onto the sofa and got on her knees between his legs, which he opened a little wider as she undid his canvas belt and pulled his pants down. He wasn't wearing any underwear. His dick was hard and looked even more veiny than his biceps. He made it move on its own, like a teetering bowling pin, beckoning Mayuko to touch it with her hands or mouth, but when she did neither, he glanced in my direction, annoyed.

"Can't you just send her to bed or something?"

"No way José!" Mayuko exclaimed cheerfully and pushed him over. With his pants still around his ankles he toppled over easily, his head falling into my lap. Enfeebled as I was,

I mustered up the strength to plunge upon his throat. He shouted expletives at first but they were quickly reduced to guttural agony. His struggle was great because of his physical strength and my current weakened state. But as I sucked his blood into my mouth I began to feel myself strengthen and soon he had no chance at all. My hands held him in place like a vise as I drank until I killed him.

I sat up knowing I had blood smeared across my lips.

"Feel any better?" Mayuko asked.

I nodded. "I love you, Button."

She smiled wide and then laughed.

"Oh my god, Orly! I'm so sorry you had to see his ding dong. I had no idea he was a commando guy. Now I have to clean his bare ass off the sofa!"

Mayuko stood and pulled on the corpse and let it roll off of my knees. It hit the wood floor with a thud.

"Well, that's all I came for. I got a date with some pigs now," Mayuko said. "You should go to your casket, Orly."

I told her I would but I waited until she got the body out of the living room.

My slumber was not deep and therefore I felt my whole being reviving as I lay in the darkness of my casket. It must have been past four o'clock when I heard Berthold enter the house. He had come home alone. I heard his footsteps and the closet door slide open, and then no further movement. He was staring at the barrenness of a closet that was no longer filled with bittersweet memories.

He opened the secret door and descended the stairs. He knelt beside my casket and knocked.

"Please talk to me, Orly," he said.

I pushed the lid of my casket open and looked into his eyes.

"What did you do with her clothing?"

Slowly, I sat up, never taking my eyes off of his. "I burned them."

He stared for a moment before he finally asked, "But why?"

"Why did you have sex in her bed?"

"It's no longer her bed, Orly."

"Maybe to you it's not. But just because you fuck on it doesn't make it yours. I can smell your cum on it."

He flushed.

"I'm sorry. I told Khalil to change the sheets."

"I know. I sent him away."

"All of her clothes. You burned all of it?"

I nodded.

He shook his head. "You shouldn't have done it."

I shot back at him. "How come it's not her bed but it's still her clothes? Who says you get to pick what's sacred?"

"You did this to punish me for meeting Kristy."

"And for fucking her. You don't even love Yelena anymore."

"That's not fair, Orly. Do you think Yelena wants us to be mourning her forever?"

"Yelena doesn't want anything. I want it. I want you to mourn her."

"I do mourn her."

"Why Kristy?" I screamed.

"I don't know how to put this love into words, Orly. I've tried because I wanted to explain it to you."

"So now you love her?"

He nodded. "I do."

"You know, I didn't say shit when you told me to promise not to kill her."

"I know you didn't. But I'm asking you again. Give me this, Orly. Yelena would want us both to find love again."

"Stop saying what Yelena would want! She didn't even love you!"

Those words knocked the wind out of him. I knew it wasn't true and that I had gone too far but in some irrational and maniacal way I was fighting with everything I had not to lose him.

He staggered when he first rose to his feet, but when he regained his footing, he went to his casket without another word. I slammed my casket shut.

We lay apart in dead silence, knowing we were caught in our own whirlpools of anguish and no longer had each other as a lifeline. I was too angry with him to cry, and as I did not smell his tears, I assumed he was just as furious with me.

But then there was something else. Something that broke the silence between us. Some other sign of suffering. It was vocal but stifled, gagged, like a murmur of grief, and it echoed throughout our chamber. I shivered as I had never heard such a sound before. I had wounded him profoundly, deeply.

Listening to his smothered cry, I took a deep breath as regret washed over me. I knew I had to give in and apologize for my cruelty. I pushed open the lid of my casket and stepped out. His suffocated outcry still resounded. I rested my hand on Berthold's casket, but he did not open it for me. I knocked and knocked again but was given no response. Finally, I lifted the lid myself and to my horror, I saw that he was not within.

TWELVE

Hotbod27: a/s/l?
Vampkid: how old r u?
Hotbod27: asked you 1st
Vampkid: 12/f/losangeles
Hotbod27: 29/m/canada
[Vampkid has left chat.]

Eros_in_Cali: Hey
Vampkid: hi
Eros_in_Cali: How are you tonight?
Eros_in_Cali: Hello?
Eros_in_Cali: How old are you?
Vampkid: im 12
Eros_in_Cali: You're a little too young
for me
Vampkid: ur in teenchat dont u know?
Vampkid: how old r u?
Eros_in_Cali: Too old for you sweetheart.
Eros_in_Cali: Take care.
[Eros_in_Cali has left chat.]

BallerzzWorldWide: hey vamp
BallerzzWorldWide: a/s/l?
Vampkid: 15/f/los angels

BallerzzWorldWide: coo
Vampkid: u?
BallerzzWorldWide: 22/m/$imi
Vampkid: is tht far from me?
BallerzzWorldWide: nah
Vampkid: send me ur pic
BallerzzWorldWide: u first
[Vampkid would like to send you an image file.]
BallerzzWorldWide: kinda plainjane tbh but it coo
BallerzzWorldWide: u look yung for 15 tho
BallerzzWorldWide: u aint even got yo titties uyet
Vampkid: show me u
BallerzzWorldWide: k
[BallerzzWorldWide would like to send you an image file.]
Vampkid: I cant even see ur face
BallerzzWorldWide: u seen one that big b4?
Vampkid: dunno
BallerzzWorldWide: u like it
Vampkid: show me ur face
BallerzzWorldWide: what 4
Vampkid: cuz ill hnag up if u dont
BallerzzWorldWide: ?????
BallerzzWorldWide: fine
[BallerzzWorldWide would like to send you an image file.]
[Vampkid has left chat.]

SideArmGuy45: hi there
Vampkid: hey
SideArmGuy45: home on a saturday night?

Vampkid: arent u 2?
SideArmGuy45: lol
SideArmGuy45: I guess
SideArmGuy45: you got me
Vampkid: r u 45?
SideArmGuy45: no LOL that's a kind of gun
Vampkid: oh
Vampkid: how old r u then?
SideArmGuy45: me?
Vampkid: yeah
SideArmGuy45: 24 but I look a little older
because I have a beard
SideArmGuy45: what about you?
SideArmGuy45: a/s/l?
Vampkid: 12/F/losangeles
SideArmGuy45: wow!
Vampkid: what?
SideArmGuy45: cha ching!
SideArmGuy45: lol!
SideArmGuy45: jk
Vampkid: what?
SideArmGuy45: you're young
Vampkid: :(I know
SideArmGuy45: no! its okay
SideArmGuy45: I like young girls
SideArmGuy45: like really young
SideArmGuy45: send me a pic?
Vampkid: u first
[SideArmGuy45 would like to send you an
image file.]
Vampkid: u look alright
SideArmGuy45: just alright
SideArmGuy45: lmao
Vampkid: uou look older

SideArmGuy45: its becaus e of the beard
SideArmGuy45: like I told you
SideArmGuy45: send me youur pic now
Vampkid: uh I dunno
SideArmGuy45: come on baby
SideArmGuy45: I just know your pretty
SideArmGuy45: I want to see if I'm right
SideArmGuy45: just your face
SideArmGuy45: unless you want to show more
SideArmGuy45: lol
[Vampkid would like to send you an image file.]
SideArmGuy45: see? Told you!
SideArmGuy45: your cute!
SideArmGuy45: you got small little tits
SideArmGuy45: you go9t topless shots? :)
Vampkid: uh uh
SideArmGuy45: but you got small baby tits
SideArmGuy45: dont you
Vampkid: yeah
SideArmGuy45: small nips too?
Vampkid: I guess so
SideArmGuy45: picnh them for me
Vampkid: huh
SideArmGuy45: pinch your nips
SideArmGuy45: pinch them hard
Vampkid: k
SideArmGuy45: did you do it?
Vampkid: yeah
SideArmGuy45: hard?
SideArmGuy45: did you twist them?
Vampkid: kinda
SideArmGuy45: hot
SideArmGuy45: your making my dick haRD

SideArmGuy45: are you still clean?
Vampkid: huh?
SideArmGuy45: you had sex yet?
Vampkid: no
SideArmGuy45: no oral?
Vampkid: no im 12!
SideArmGuy45: you knever know lots of girls your age have
SideArmGuy45: your pussy must be so tightt
SideArmGuy45: love to be your first
SideArmGuy45: you ever seen a hard cock?
Vampkid: lmao yes!
SideArmGuy45: yeah? Where?
Vampkid: just like 5 min ago
SideArmGuy45: WAT!!!!
Vampkid: not irl just on here
Vampkid: some perv sent me a pic of his dick
SideArmGuy45: oh lmao!
SideArmGuy45: what about in real life?
SideArmGuy45: you ever touch one
Vampkid: nuh uh
SideArmGuy45: you ever watch porn?
Vampkid: yeh
SideArmGuy45: what kind did you watch?
Vampkid: dunno?
Vampkid: the regular kind?
SideArmGuy45: http://underteenxtreme.com/s245leix3
Vampkid: k hold on
Vampkid: is that u?
SideArmGuy45: no its just a vid
SideArmGuy45: did you watch it?
Vampkid: yeah

SideArmGuy45: and?
Vampkid: it was okay
SideArmGuy45: did you like it?
SideArmGuy45: what he was doing to her?
Vampkid: yeah I guess
SideArmGuy45: want to do that with me?
Vampkid: LMAO
Vampkid: srsly?
SideArmGuy45: it would feel really good
SideArmGuy45: for you I mean.
Vampkid: it kinda looked like it hurt
SideArmGuy45: no not when the guy knows
what hes doing
SideArmGuy45: I would never hurt you baby
Vampkid: really?
SideArmGuy45: of course baby
SideArmGuy45: I like you
SideArmGuy45: I care about you
Vampkid: wait where r u?
SideArmGuy45: close by baby
SideArmGuy45: rpV
Vampkid: wheres that?
SideArmGuy45: rancho palos verde
Vampkid: you can drive here then?
SideArmGuy45: of course baby
Vampkid: tonight?
Vampkid: hello?
SideArmGuy45: tonight?
Vampkid: yeah
SideArmGuy45: are you being for real?
Vampkid: yeah aren't u?
SideArmGuy45: are you alone?
Vampkid: yeah my dads at his girlfriends

Vampkid: he won't b back 2nite
SideArmGuy45: he just leaves you home all
by yourself?
Vampkid: all the time
Vampkid: like almost every night
[SideArmGuy45 would like to video chat.]
[Vampkid declined video chat.]
SideArmGuy45: why did you reject me?
Vampkid: I dont wanna do video
SideArmGuy45: I knew you were fake
Vampkid: whatever
SideArmGuy45: hello
Vampkid: what
SideArmGuy45: you really wont go on video?
Vampkid: I dont even know your name
SideArmGuy45: I don't know yours either
Vampkid: Orly
SideArmGuy45: Orly?
SideArmGuy45: thats your name or
SideArmGuy45: are you saying o really?
Vampkid: its my name
SideArmGuy45: huh never heard that one
SideArmGuy45: are you making it up?
Vampkid: whats your name then
SideArmGuy45: joe
SideArmGuy45: so now that you know my
name
SideArmGuy45: will you do video?
Vampkid: if I do youll come over?
SideArmGuy45: of course baby orly
Vampkid: tonight?
SideArmGuy45: yeah ba by
[SideArmGuy45 would like to video chat.]

Joe didn't actually come over that night. He was worried I was part of a police sting operation arresting pedophiles. We chatted the following four nights, mostly on video. He had me take my clothes off and touch myself so he could watch while he masturbated. He finally believed I really was just a lonely twelve-year-old girl at home alone, and agreed to come over. By that time he had described to me over and over again the things he wanted to do with me sexually—orally, vaginally, anally. He said he wanted to be my teacher. He said he loved me.

I never believed his name was really Joe, but I didn't care. I knew he had reason to lie, and I just wanted something to call him so I could project the fantasies of love I consciously created upon him. In truth, I never fully believed the fantasies, but in momentary lapses of forgetfulness, Joe became my first love who loved me back.

The more we talked the more I allowed my fantasies to be substantiated. Joe cared for me and cherished the complexity of my personality that resided within the naked body of the child he jerked off to via webcam. And in that way, I began to see him as a man who liked me for me and not only as a little girl he could baby talk and sexualize. However, our conversations were only permitted to go so far, as Joe was often hesitant to answer, acting like I was changing the subject whenever I would ask him things about his nonsexual life—his job, his friends, and what sports he liked to watch.

On the night Joe was to come over, it was Saturday, and it had been nine nights since my fight with Berthold. In that time I hadn't received any word or seen any sign of him. I assumed he was with Kristy, but I didn't know where she lived and I didn't want to hunt her down and I wouldn't have gone over there even if I were invited.

I didn't know where Berthold slept, but I didn't doubt he was alive. Perhaps he procured a new casket and stored it wherever Kristy lived. Perhaps he went to ground every night. On three of those nine days apart, I heard the murmurs again. I could not discover their source. The first two times I knew I was absolutely alone and the sound only emanated within our subterranean chamber. I searched every inch of the room without success. On the third occasion, I was awakened by the murmurs, but this time I had Mayuko with me. She had brought an inflatable mattress and bedding downstairs and laid it at the foot of my casket. At the sound, I slowly opened my casket and sat up and saw Mayuko still sleeping quietly. I got out and awoke her.

"There! Do you hear it?"

"Hear what?"

"That muffled sound. Like someone buried in the ground."

"I don't hear anything."

I considered that perhaps it took vampiric ears to hear it, but since I couldn't prove that in the moment, I concluded I was the only one hearing it. But I worried less about whether or not I was going crazy, and concerned myself more with what the sound meant. For the last time I had an experience that felt similar to this one was six years ago when I experienced dreams where I heard the name Mirela whispered over and over. Those dreams foreshadowed Mirela's arrival and that was what eventually led to Yelena's death. What could these murmurs possibly predict was coming now? I wished Berthold were here.

On the Saturday night I arranged to have Joe come over, I went to the backyard again, barefoot, and tested the temperature of the swimming pool with my toes. It was warm. I rolled up my pajama pants and sat at the edge of the pool, allowing my legs to dangle in the water. I looked at the stars in the sky. In my heart of hearts, I didn't really want what was coming, but I didn't see any other way to experience the semblance of love. I was doomed for all eternity to wear the body of a child, despite how old I truly was. At twenty-two years old, I wasn't going to romantically fall in love with a child who was the age I appeared to be. To feel loved, I only had one choice—someone who craved the body of a child.

Joe texted when he was near and I waited outside, in the dark, on our balcony that overlooked the street. He said he would be driving a yellow Ford Mustang. It was nearly nine-thirty when the car came up our street, but it passed the house slowly and disappeared. Minutes later, it came again from the other direction, again driving slowly, and again passed the house. Ten minutes elapsed without any sign of the car again and I texted Joe to ask why he had driven by and not parked. He told me he just parked, and he had, but on another street. He was now walking to the house, and I went downstairs and opened the front door and stood under the porch light.

He stood at the edge of the driveway for a moment and then walked up.

"What took you so long?" I asked, knowing he was just being cautious.

"No one's home, right?"

"Just me," I replied and tried to hug him, but he shrugged me off.

"Let's go inside," he said.

He followed me in and I shut the front door. He glanced about the house.

"Damn. Your dad must be rich."

"Yeah."

"What does he do?"

"He's a lawyer."

"Of course he is."

He walked around the house a bit more to ensure we really were alone. He took note of Yelena's many paintings and sculptures.

"He's an art collector too?"

"Uh uh. My mom was."

"Your mom? Where is she?"

"She died."

"Oh. I'm sorry, baby."

And at that, he finally gave me a long hug that led to a kiss. I walked him over to the bar and poured two whiskies.

"Really?" he smiled.

"I like it."

I handed him his glass and as we drank he noticed my four framed scribbles hanging on the wall and stared at them, trying to understand them.

"They're people just like you," I explained.

"I don't get abstract stuff, I guess."

He downed his drink in a gulp and then began to caress my body. I was only wearing a black tank top and pajama pants. Very quickly, he began to pinch my nipples as he kissed me with too much tongue. I fended him off and told him we should go swimming, but he resisted. He said he'd rather stay inside. He said it was too cold. He said he didn't bring anything to swim in. And when I began to head to the backyard anyway, he tried to hold me and I accidentally surprised him with my strength when I playfully pushed him off too forcefully.

As I walked away from him, I lifted my tank top over my head and dropped it on the floor. I turned to him so he could see my small breasts which I knew he lusted after so much. As he stepped toward me, I stepped out of my pajamas and then let my panties fall to the floor.

I flipped a switch to turn off all the lights in the backyard, so that it was quite dark, save the blue glow of the pool.

"Can you turn that off too?" he asked, as he removed his shirt.

I shut the pool light off, and all that was left were the stars in the sky above and the lights of the city below. I walked outside, fully nude, and stepped down into the pool. I watched Joe remove the rest of his clothing and hurry outside and into the pool quickly after me, rushing mostly in the hope of not being seen by neighbors, rather than out of excitement.

But once he was in the warm water, he moved toward me and I dog paddled backwards so that he would have to pursue me, which he did. Eventually, I was in the deep end, backed up against a wall and he had me cornered. He grabbed me and kissed me, his hands roamed beneath the surface of the water, over my bare legs, his fingers lightly grazing over my labia but he was careful not to penetrate me. I was certain he was saving that first insertion for his cock. Since he knew nothing of my true childhood, he believed I had never had one inside me.

He kicked away from the wall and we whirled our way to the center of the pool still kissing. When his feet touched bottom he lifted me out of the water and brought his lips to my nipples and sucked on each of them, one and then the other, very hard. I didn't particularly enjoy his touch—it felt prescribed and more about his pleasure than mine—but I ran my fingers through his wet hair as he did this and then leaned my face forward to kiss him again. I could feel his erection poking against my knees and then further up my thighs, and he eventually guided my right hand to it and showed me with his own hand how to stroke it.

He moved us to the shallow end of the pool and lifted me out of the water and sat me on the ledge. He gave me a gentle nudge, to suggest that I lay on my back. He opened my thin, girlish legs, and placed his head between them. I felt his tongue on me, but again, not in me. I closed my eyes and welcomed pleasure, tightening my slight thighs around his head, but it wasn't as pleasurable as it was when I touched myself. I wanted him to go more slowly, softly and rhythmically, but I didn't know how to tell him without appearing more experienced than he knew. So instead I let out a soft moan and let him keep going. But after a few seconds more, he stopped on his own.

"Is it too cold?" he whispered, meaning the chilled concrete against my back.

I shook my head, and waited to feel his tongue again between my legs, but instead, he pulled me up and back into the warm water of the pool.

"Let's go inside," he said. "I want to fuck you."

I nodded my head and led him to the steps out of the pool. Although the night air felt wonderful on my wet skin, I could see him shivering, so I pretended to be cold as well, and hurried into the house. He couldn't follow fast enough and I lost him.

"Hey, where did you go?" he called out, once inside the house.

But I didn't need to answer, as I reappeared quickly with two large towels and handed one to him. We dried ourselves off and then he approached me, cock still erect, with his towel around his back and outstretched in his hands like the cape of Dracula. He wrapped his arms around me.

"Oh my god, you're so cold," he said.

"I'm fine."

"Let's go to your bedroom."

I hadn't thought ahead where I would take him when this moment came, but I decided to take him to Mayuko's room, my childhood bedroom, as it appeared occupied. Once inside, he dropped the towel and placed one of his arms at the bend of my knees and scooped me up into a cradle and laid me down on the queen sized bed. He climbed on the bed and hovered over me on his knees, his cock extending toward me. He reached forward and caressed my breasts, again pinching my nipples. Unintentionally, as he did this, my eyes caught the sight of the bare spot on the wall where my first scribble of Yelena had once hung. My mother was not here to witness my step into womanhood, disguised as the destruction of my childhood, as her scribbled portrait now rested at the head of her empty coffin.

He pulled me by the legs toward him and rubbed the head of his throbbing cock against my lips.

"Are you ready?" he asked.

I looked in his eyes, searching for love within them. I nodded my head and he entered me. I bit my lip and pretended it was painful. After a short while, he turned me on my side and continued to thrust himself inside of me. Through the rapid beating of his heart, I could feel his excitement—to be having sex with one he mistakenly understood to be a child—but again it felt like the entire exchange was about his pleasure alone. It was neither sensual nor passionate and I felt the sensation of my presence disappearing—my sense of self being removed from the act. I was necessary but objectified. He turned me over and took me from behind, and when it was time for him to finish, he pulled out of me and told me to flip over on my back. I looked into his eyes, again looking for love, but he closed them as he stroked himself to orgasm. He opened them again just as he ejaculated on my underdeveloped breasts.

Spent, he lay beside me, once more becoming affectionate, kissing both my face and my right shoulder.

"How did you like it?" he asked.

"I liked it," I answered softly.

"I told you it wouldn't hurt. You didn't even bleed. Damn, baby, your skin is still so cold. We should get under the covers."

Just as I was about to agree, I stopped myself. I sensed someone else in the house. Someone vampiric.

"Shit," I said.

"What is it?"

"My dad's home."

Joe jumped out of the bed.

"My clothes are out there," he whispered in a panic.

"They're right here," Berthold's deep voice said from the doorway. He was holding the pile of Joe's clothing and tossed them to the ground. "And I found this," he continued, and in his hand was a .45 caliber pistol.

I sat up in the bed, still uncovered, and with Joe's semen running down my chest.

"Hey, we didn't do anything, man. We were just talking."

Berthold extended the pistol to Joe with the butt of the gun benignly facing him. "Take it, you're going to need it."

"Berthold," I said. "Don't. I invited him over."

Joe hesitated to take the gun.

"I'm a woman, Berthold!"

But Berthold didn't acknowledge what I had said and shook the pistol gently in Joe's direction until Joe took it from him.

"This wasn't against my will!" I exclaimed.

"I don't care if it wasn't, Orly," Berthold responded calmly. "He dies."

Joe hesitated nervously, but then panicked and fired the gun three times into Berthold's chest, causing blood to splatter, but Berthold didn't drop. In a flash, he knocked the gun out of Joe's hand, grabbed him by the throat and instantly traveled the length of the room until Joe's back hit the wall and he gasped for air. With his free hand, Berthold reached down and tore Joe's penis off from the root and dropped it. Joe let out an asphyxiated scream of agony, but it ended quickly when Berthold broke his neck and let his body fall to the floor.

I jumped out of the bed and flew at Berthold and struck him in the face.

"You don't want anyone to love me!"

"This wasn't love, Orly! He's a sick fucking pedophile!"

I fell to the floor. I thought I might cry but I didn't. I wanted it to be love with Joe, but in my soul, I knew I was willing to accept any illusion of tenderness and pretend it was love.

Berthold left the room.

When I first moved in with Yelena as a mortal child, she gave me this bedroom as it was the only room in the house in which no one had been killed. No such room existed in our home now.

Berthold returned, holding one of his robes along with a large pad of paper and a box of black crayons. He dropped the pad and crayons to the floor and then wrapped the robe around me. I wiggled my arms into the sleeves and pulled the robe over my exposed genitals. Berthold took a seat beside me on the floor.

In front of us, slumped against the wall was Joe with his broken neck, and blood occasionally spurting from where his penis had been.

"Scribble him," he said.

"I don't want to know," I replied.

"You need to know, Orly."

Berthold picked up the pad of paper and opened it to a blank white sheet. He grabbed one of the crayons and began to scribble, trying to imitate me, having seen me do it many times.

I let him go at it for a while, but then shook my head.

"It doesn't look anything like him," I said.

He handed the crayon to me, and I took it. He turned the page and I began scribbling the portrait of Joe's corpse.

It turned out his name wasn't Joe at all. It was Brian. And I wasn't the youngest girl he had had sex with. Two had been younger. He had told other young girls how he loved them, and they weren't lies, but they weren't truths either. Joe's love looked nothing like the love Berthold had for Yelena or the love Yelena had for Marcel. Joe was merely filled with obsessive desires, underdeveloped emotions, and addled lust. He loved me like he loved them. In other words, he didn't love me at all. He didn't have the capacity to.

I dropped the crayon and Berthold put his arm around me. I cried blood tears into his bullet-riddled shirt, our blood likely mixing.

"Who's ever going to love me?" I whimpered into his chest. "No one is ever going to love me, Berthold. Only sickos who want to touch children. Forever it's gonna be like that."

I continued to cry.

He held me tighter, but had no answer.

"My, my. You Americans do have strange customs," a man's voice said from behind us.

Berthold shot up in an instant. I rose more slowly. It was Alexi Pavlovich, consort to Mirela, imparateasa of the Cobălcescu bloodline we both belonged to.

Alexi Pavlovich studied the scene curiously. Berthold was filled with gunshot wounds, I was a child in a man's robe and otherwise naked, and there was a corpse on the floor sans penis.

Berthold bowed and I curtsied to Alexi Pavlovich, wondering if Mirela were with him and if there would be an immediate opportunity to kill her.

Alexi Pavlovich bowed politely in return.

"Please forgive the state of our household," Berthold began, but Alexi Pavlovich cut him short.

"Please do not mention it," he said. "Decorum is unimportant as the imparateasa has not traveled with me."

"What brings you to Los Angeles?" Berthold asked.

"I have the pleasure of personally delivering an invitation to the Communion of the Ancients. You have heard of this before?"

"We have," Berthold again answered for us, "but we are hardly Ancients. Why should we be invited?"

"My apologizes, Mr. Leitz. I should have stated matters more clearly. The invitation is for Miss Bialek alone. She is to be the special guest of the imparateasa."

THIRTEEN

Alexi Pavlovich didn't stay with us. We weren't even sure if he stayed in Los Angeles or went back to Romania, or wherever Mirela currently was. We were very much in the dark, except for what he told us. I was expected to be in Romania by the next night, and as the special guest of the imparateasa, there was nothing I needed to bring, not even clothing, as everything would be provided for me.

While everyone else was in the dining room drinking to my health and safe return, I asked Darcy to help me pack a small bag anyway. As per her usual, Darcy was wearing a top that showcased her large breasts and tattoos, a short skirt with fishnet stockings, and black platform boots.

"So how the fuck long is this Communion of the Ancients anyway?" Darcy asked.

"Traditionally, between six and nine nights according to Zacharias, but he also said that in reality it's for as long as Mirela says it is."

"Queen bitch sounds like a control freak. The Ketsuen have tons of ceremonies and rituals but none of them where you have to give your blood to your leader. I've still never even seen Hisashi or Konomi. I hope you realize how lucky you are to have seen one of them, not to mention making a friend of her. How the hell did you pull that off?"

I shrugged my shoulders without really thinking. Instead I considered what Darcy had said about the Ketsuen not having such a ceremony. It aligned with Konomi's assertion that elders are reluctant to share their own blood. On the contrary, Mirela took a taste from all of the Cobălcescu Ancients, undoubtedly to assess their power. I'm sure she gave them no choice. It was their blood or their death. But what was she hoping to understand from tasting my weak, young blood? No doubt it was my scribbles, but I had that talent as a mortal. Would she be able to taste it if she drank from me? But none of this was why I asked Darcy to help me pack.

"Hey Darcy," I began, "a long time ago, when I was still underage, you told me vampire love can only go one of two ways—death or immortality. Do you remember telling me that?"

"Doesn't sound so profound now, but yes, I remember."

"You were trying to make me understand that since I was too young to create another one of our kind, I was better off killing my lovers rather than watching them die slowly of old age."

"Yeah. I still feel that way."

"I know. But, you see, for me there's a bigger problem with your theory."

"I know what you're going to say. My theory presumes there is a lover in the first place."

"Yeah. Exactly."

"What Berthold did, he did out of love for you. He thought he was protecting you from a child predator, which that fucker was. But what he fails to see is that for you, you only have two realities—another vampire or a pedophile. And I hate to be the one to tell it to you Orly, but you're more likely to find a willing pedophile than a willing vampire. The longest immortality won't ever be long enough for our kind to disassociate your child body with your true age. There's something inherently wrong with amorous or sexual love between a child and adult. That's why we're not supposed to give our blood to kids."

The use of the word *kids* stuck me like a straight pin.

"But Darcy, you see what Berthold does not. If he or you could just get used to me having an adult lover."

"It'll never be normalized, Orly. Even though I understand all about your reality, I would have killed that fucker too. I couldn't have helped it."

Darcy hugged me warmly and then lifted me and sat me on my suitcase to close it.

After it was shut, I hopped off of the suitcase and told Darcy I needed some time alone.

"I'll rejoin the others," she said.

"I think I just need some fresh air."

Darcy opened a bedroom window for me.

"You should go out this way then. If you tried to pass them on your way out, they'd never let you leave," she said and winked at me.

As I wasn't hunting, I didn't use my vampiric speed as I walked along Mullholland Drive. I walked quite slowly in fact, wondering if I could ever find another vampire to fall in love with me, one who could look past my child form because of their firsthand experience of aging mentally and emotionally but not physically during their own immortality. Besides that, the most beautiful were mostly made while in their twenties. That was only eight years my senior. Couldn't a vampire who was hundreds of years old overlook that sliver of eight years? Darcy had said no, and I desperately wanted her to be wrong.

Was Joe a bad guy? Yes. He was. He raped those other children. Yelena would have taken her sweet time killing him. But what if I found a mortal man who had never touched a child who I could somehow make fall in love with only me? That didn't seem likely. It was as Darcy had said—it would never be normalized. And as I was still too young to offer immortality to another, the only dowry I could lay before such a man would be not to kill him.

A child could crush on me, but as I was already an adult, I could not do to a child what I permitted Joe to do to me.

Why was love so necessary to me? Couldn't I be satisfied with immortality alone? You would think so, but not if it meant an eternity of loneliness. Immortality without love was a fatality. But I couldn't dwell on this now. I had something much more pressing in front of me. I would soon be in the presence of Mirela, the woman I needed to kill to avenge Yelena, but who could probably kill me with a mere thought. She must know I aim to kill her, no matter how long it takes. Why has she let me live as long as I have?

A coyote crossed the road in front of me. Happy hunting, friend. And as I heard him disappear in the brush, I noticed that my footsteps now had an echo. There was a vampire with me, but I didn't feel afraid. I took a step forward and heard a step taken behind me. I took three steps and heard three more. I stopped and their steps stopped with me.

"It's only a game, Orly," an untroubled and tranquil voice said.

I recognized it. I turned and bowed to the beautiful woman wearing a pale blue kimono in the middle of the road some twenty yards away.

"Lady Konomi," I said.

"Just Konomi please, my dearest Orly."

We walked to each other.

"What troubles you? What were you thinking about?"

"Love," I said.

"Ah yes. That wound is still open, I see."

"I know I should be past it. You told me trust is the paramount thing."

"You have a good memory, but don't make the mistake of thinking you must adopt things quickly just because you understand them to be true. Heart and mind often lie together in disagreement."

I nodded my head.

"Do you know why I have come?" she asked.

"No, Konomi, I do not. But I am very happy to see you again."

"As I am you. But I came to ask if you have found your Oblivion."

I shook my head. "No. Not yet. But I confess, I haven't devoted much of myself to finding it."

It was as though Konomi's eyes nodded in recognition instead of her head.

"Become mindful of senses which recall memories of your mortal life. Do you understand?"

I thought of what she said, but wasn't sure I understood.

"When I permitted you to enter my Oblivion, what was it you heard that you knew was not part of the material world that surrounded us?"

"Water," I replied.

"Yes. You heard the sound of the Mogami River flowing. I heard it that night as well, which was how I passed through. There are other things I am keen to which will carry me into my Oblivion, but all it takes is one, Orly. You must find one for yourself, a key to your own Oblivion, my blood sister, and you must do this quickly. It will serve you in the ordeal you are about to face."

"What ordeal?" I asked.

"Soon you are to be face to face with Mirela."

"You know about that?"

Konomi smiled gently. She caressed my face in a way that would make a cat purr. I closed my eyes in comfort. Lightly, she kissed my lips. Slowly, I opened my eyes, wanting to ask her what she knew about my coming ordeal, but she was gone. The night had grown silent. Even the coyotes were still.

I arrived home through the front door and everyone was still seated at the dining room table, considerably more drunk since I had seen them last. I resumed the chair I had before I left to pack and no one acknowledged I had been gone, but that was because Darcy had been kind enough to ask them to give me space.

"Fuck it. I don't think she should go," Hisato said while looking at me from across the dining room table.

"She has no choice. Don't you understand that?" Zacharias said with frustration.

"The last time your imparateasa, or whatever you call her, involved herself with us, my best friend died," Hisato argued. "Anybody remember that?"

"We all remember it," Berthold answered.

"But why does she have to go alone?" Grace asked.

"She's not going alone," Mayuko said from where she stood behind my chair. "She's permitted one mortal servant."

"Oh, and like you could protect her," Corinne said to Mayuko sharply without turning in her direction to acknowledge her presence.

"The mortal servant is a formality," Zacharias said.

"Listen to me," Berthold interjected. "She has to go and not even all of us together can protect her. Not against Ancients. If they want Orly dead, she's dead. What matters is the reason Mirela chose for Orly to attend, and that answer is obvious. It's for her scribbles."

"She needs Orly's help," Zacharias agreed.

"Don't help that bitch," Hisato said, raising his voice.

"You would be wise to silence yourself."

"Shut up," Hisato said to Zacharias. "I'm so fucking over you."

Zacharias rose from his chair.

"Do something," Hisato said, smiling and showing his fangs and not bothering to get up.

"Can you both stop?" I said with frustration. "Zacharias, please sit back down. Please. We are all friends here."

Zacharias resumed his seat.

"You should stop smiling now," I continued.

Hisato wiped the grin from his face.

"Now does anyone want to know what I think?" I asked the entire group.

"I'm afraid I already know," Berthold said.

"Well, I'm going to tell you anyway. I'm glad I was invited. I want to go. And if she wants me to scribble her or anyone else, I will, just to get close to her."

Berthold shook his head.

"Berthold and I could be killed just for hearing you say that and not killing you for it," Zacharias said.

Berthold placed his hand on Zacharias' forearm to silence him so that he could speak. "You can't kill her, Orly." He lowered his voice. "As much as I wish you could, you can't. She's five thousand years old. She hasn't lasted this long by accident. There is nothing you or I or anyone here can think of that she won't see coming."

"You said yourself I have to go. What do you expect me to do when I'm there?"

"I expect you to survive and come home."

"Berthold, do you remember that time I made you drive me out to the desert so I could watch you bury those four bodies? Two of them were kids."

Berthold nodded his head.

"You remember how my gums started bleeding and you had to take me to the hospital?"

Berthold nodded again.

"I didn't know at the time I'd never come out of that hospital alive. I thought it would just be another visit. But when I realized I wasn't ever going to leave, that this time I was going to die for real, I remember thinking how stupid I was asking you to bring me to bury bodies. I had liked you so much Berthold that it would have been much better had I made you take me to the beach, so that your last memory of me would be in a happy place."

Berthold placed his elbow on the table and his palm under his chin.

"I was meant to die from my cancer. In the hospital, even when my eyes were closing, I didn't expect Yelena to inject me with her blood. I expected to die. Every single night I've lived since my flatline has been a gift from Yelena. I was twelve when I was in the hospital and now I'm twenty-two. She's already given me ten extra years. So if I die now, killing the woman who killed her, I will be happy. And I think I'll feel at peace with it."

There was a silence in the room until Berthold broke it.

"That's not what Yelena would want, Orly. Like me, like all of us, she would want you to live."

All of our vampire guests left before sunrise. Mayuko was already asleep in her bedroom and Khalil was asleep in the bedroom Berthold offered him. Only Berthold and I remained awake, but we had moved to the living room and Berthold brought a bottle of scotch and two tumblers with him. As this was to be my last night in America, I was tempted to ask again to sleep with Berthold in his casket, but I didn't.

I knew he would refuse, and perhaps partially it would be because of his feelings for Kristy. And perhaps that was part of the reason I didn't tell him I saw Konomi, but it wasn't the only reason. Had I told him, it may have led to talk of the Oblivion, which Berthold still knew nothing about. It was true: as a vampire, it was in my nature to be secretive about powers, even those I did not yet possess myself.

Berthold poured us both a scotch neat.

"Can I scribble you?" I asked as he handed me my tumbler.

"Why? I have no secrets from you."

"I know you don't."

"Besides, it will be sunrise soon."

"Just one more time before I go. That way I can keep you with me when I'm gone."

"Don't say it like that."

"I don't mean gone gone. I just mean gone on my trip."

"I'll give you until I finish my drink," he finally assented.

I ran to get my pad of paper and a new black crayon and returned to where Berthold sat. As I scribbled, a pattern of nearly concentric circles began to form. They were overlaid by lines going in all directions but the circular shapes, one within the next, were definitely there. As one set of circles ended another would begin to develop beside it. Berthold's previous scribbles didn't look anything like this. Is this what love looked like? He said he could not put this love into words, but perhaps I could put it into scribbles and hopefully understand. I'm pretty sure he knew what I was doing.

I could see Kristy within him. On their first date together, they went for a walk along the Third Street Promenade. He tried to buy her things but she wouldn't allow it. They went to a restaurant and Berthold did his best to appear mortal, eating as though he were hungry. When it was time for dessert, Kristy asked if the strawberry cheesecake came with whole strawberries, and the server said that the cheesecake was topped with a strawberry syrup and whole strawberries sliced in halves. Kristy asked that the strawberries be left off. Bemused, Berthold inquired about the strawberries after the server left. If she did not like strawberries why order strawberry cheesecake? Kristy answered that she loved the taste of strawberries, but she was trypophobic, which meant she had a phobia related to irregular patterns of holes or bumps, such as the kind that occurred on the outer flesh of strawberries. The sight of open pores on one's face made her cringe. Even honeycombs disgusted her. Berthold found it fascinating, but he also wondered if her phobia would disappear once he made her a vampire. But of course, Berthold recognized that was only a fantasy; he knew his blood was not yet powerful enough to turn her.

Berthold asked Kristy many questions about herself. Where she had grown up. Whether she had siblings and what her upbringing was like. Where she had studied accounting.

He learned she had just had her birthday in December and was now thirty-four.

"You look younger," he remarked.

She beamed at him with her scintillating smile, and it warmed him. Though Berthold was unable to read her mind, he could see her amorous feelings expressed upon her face and in the subtle movements of her body language. With the directness and sincerity in which he spoke to her, he could feel her become increasingly fond of him and knew she yearned to know the secrets enshrouded in his soul. That wasn't remarkable, however. Berthold had always had that effect on women, even when he was mortal. But now that he was vampiric, he presented much more, and thus, with every passing moment, the fecundity of her libidinous desire for him swelled. There was no stopping or diverting the growth of her feelings. By the time the restaurant closed, Kristy was in love.

I lifted the black crayon off the page and looked up at Berthold, expecting to see the bliss of requited love. But he didn't know what I was seeing in that moment within the scribble and so I saw no expression at all. He was just staring off blankly, holding his tumbler of scotch. I placed the crayon back upon the page and it virtually dragged itself in another circular motion.

Back out in the cold, they sipped on hot coffees and as the hour grew late and the Promenade emptied, Kristy drew close to Berthold for warmth and with confusion she realized she found the opposite. His body was frigid, yet he removed his overcoat and put it over her. She slipped her arms through the sleeves, but her fingertips barely exceeded the cuffs.

"Aren't you cold?" she asked.

Berthold smiled with his lips and shook his head. "Not at all. I feel perfect. I had a nice time tonight with you, Kristy," he said.

"I did too."

"I hope this means I'll get to see you again."

"I was actually going to ask if you'd like to see me tomorrow."

"I would enjoy that very much," Berthold answered.

"Great. I could make us a picnic. I live near a really nice park with a pond."

Berthold's expression soured. Kristy noticed and asked him what was wrong.

"I must confess, I have a phobia as well," Berthold replied.

"Oh really? What's that?" Kristy asked with great interest.

"Heliophobia."

"Fear of the sun?"

"And sunlight."

"Ah, I see. And people don't usually picnic at night."

"Precisely," Berthold responded.

"Well I'm down for a picnic by candlelight if you are."

Berthold adored her answer and was touched by her ardent desire to spend time with him. They continued to walk closely as the shop lights were turned out one by one.

"I take it you're not nyctophobic," she said.

"Are you testing my vocabulary?" he asked.

"Maybe," she said and smiled.

"No. I am not in the least afraid of the dark."

"I'm impressed."

"What about you? Do you have any other phobias?"

"Nope. I'm not acrophobic, agoraphobic, aquaphobic, or arachnophobic."

"Androphobic?" Berthold asked.

"Now you're testing me?"

"That's right."

"Androphobic. Fear of men. Obviously not. Alektorophobia?"

"No. I have no fear of chickens. Globophobia?"

"Nope. I quite love balloons. Okay, here is a serious one. Aphenphosmphobia?"

"Okay, you got me," Berthold answered. "I don't know that one."

"It's the fear of intimacy."

"Oh, no. I don't suffer from that at all," he said and embraced her.

With his chin above the top of her head, Berthold was surprised to feel his fangs forming. He loved her. He didn't want to kill her and wondered why his instincts were preparing him to bite. To turn her obviously, but he couldn't, not at his young age. Kristy moved to pull away, but he held her firmly, not wanting her to see his face. She did not find his gesture unnatural and hugged him more tightly.

"Are you sure you're not cold?"

"I'm fine. I just need to hold you a bit longer."

The hug was becoming awkward and Berthold knew it.

"Is everything okay?" she asked.

"I have one more to ask you. One more phobia."

"Okay. Shoot."

"Sanguivoriphobia. The fear of blood drinkers."

"Fear of vampires, you mean?"

"Yes. That is what I mean."

She laughed softly. "Are you trying to tell me you're some kind of vampire or something?"

Berthold paused for a moment and then said, "Yes. I am telling you that."

She pulled away from him and he let her go. She looked into his face and he showed her his fangs. She smiled brightly.

"Oh my god. You're so funny. I had implants like those for Halloween a couple years ago. Mine didn't look as good as yours though."

"These aren't implants, Kristy."

"Oh no?" she said, still not believing him. "Let me feel them and see."

She rose on her tiptoes for a kiss and Berthold greeted her with both trepidation and desire. During their kiss Kristy ran her tongue along his fangs.

"Wow. Those are sharp."

She smiled but noticed that though his teeth were visible, Berthold was not smiling. There was no fear in telling her the truth. If she reacted poorly, and all her love evaporated, his recently acquired vampiric powers, which he did not tell me he had mastered, allowed him to cloud her memory and make her forget his confession. But Berthold's heart ached at the thought of having to perform such a trick on Kristy. The thought of her loathing him anguished his entire being.

"I won't hurt you," he said, hoping to see no sign of fear in her pale green eyes.

Berthold downed the rest of his scotch and stood. "Time's up," he said to me and began to lead the way to the secret staircase.

"I'll be down soon," I said. "I want to check in on Mayuko."

But I didn't go and check on Mayuko. I stared again at the scribble. The stacks of circles looked like bottomless holes and Kristy did not appear afraid. What kind of woman doesn't run from the revelation that the man standing before her is undead and sustains himself by drinking blood, blood just like the blood pumping through her veins? The kind of woman Berthold loved. That's what kind.

I put the scribble down and headed to where Berthold had already gone. I passed through the secret doorway and stood at the top of the stairs. My traveling coffin had already been placed on the floor below, near my casket, and that was where I would now sleep. I saw that Berthold's casket was already closed, and he was within. I stood looking down at the four funerary boxes for some time as I knew once I laid myself to rest, I would not wake again until I was in Romania. For sometime during the day, as I slept, Mayuko and Khalil would carry my traveling coffin out of our secret chamber and put me on the private plane Mayuko arranged at great expense. As my permitted mortal servant, she would remain on the plane and accompany me on my journey. I hoped with all my heart I could keep her safe for the duration of our trip.

I descended the staircase and before going to my coffin, I went to Berthold's casket. Though I knew he was breathing inside, the scene of his closed casket appeared so lifeless. I kissed my fingertips and pressed them on the lid of his casket and watched as my fingerprints evanesced. I then removed the lid to my own coffin, lay down and shut myself within. In the darkness, I tried to do as Konomi said—to become mindful of senses that recalled my mortal life. My eyes saw only darkness. I smelled the polish used to protect and shine our funerary boxes, Berthold's cologne, and dust that had collected in the corners of the room. I tasted blood and whiskey. My fingers felt the smoothness of the satin lining my coffin. And as always, I heard the faint sound of worms burrowing beneath our chamber. None of it, that I could tell, recalled my mortal life.

How would I find my Oblivion like this? And if I ever did find it, how would it help me with Mirela? And what was the ordeal Konomi mentioned? Did she mean an ordeal in general terms simply because I would be in the presence of the woman who killed my mother? Or did she know something specific Mirela had in mind for me? Mirela had given Yelena a choice—save her own life or mine. Mirela said she hoped Yelena would choose to let me die. Did she still want me dead?

These thoughts raced through my mind and soon I realized I was no longer concentrating on my senses and finding the way to my Oblivion. But just after I realized that, the sound came again—the murmurs. They were louder than ever, a muffled ringing in my ears. Mayuko hadn't heard them when she had slept down here beside me, but she was mortal. Now that Berthold was here, I would know if hearing the murmurs required vampiric senses, or if I was the only one hearing them.

I slid the lid off of my coffin and sat up too quickly as I became dizzy from moving too fast after morning had begun to dawn. I turned and saw Berthold's casket remained closed. Did he not hear it? Or did he remain in repose, concentrating upon the sound to ascertain its source? I waited for a few seconds, as the murmurs continued, but with my usual impatience I soon couldn't wait any longer, and with an exertion, I crawled out of my coffin, crossed the stone floor on my hands and knees and knocked on Berthold's casket.

Slowly the lid of Berthold's casket opened. I had roused him.

"What is it, Orly?" he said softly and sleepily.

I shook my head. "Nothing, I just wanted to say goodbye. I'll be gone in the morning."

"I know you will. I shall miss you very much."

I leaned forward and kissed his cheek.

"Sorry to wake you. Go back to sleep."

"I love you, Orly," he said and smiled with his lips and I slowly shut the lid of his casket for him.

He could not hear it, and I didn't ask him to listen for it because whatever it was, it was obviously meant for me alone to hear, and that meant secrets for me alone to understand. I reentered my coffin and focused on the murmurs. Were these murmurs the way to my Oblivion? If so, I couldn't recall how they pertained to my mortal life, and even as I closed my eyes to listen more closely, I could not find myself in any place other than the material world I was accustomed to.

FOURTEEN

I woke before we reached our destination. The vibrations I felt within my coffin told me we were still traveling. I often awoke early, but since I could not rely on the darkness of our secret chamber, I had to wait for Mayuko to let me know it was safe to rise. Nearly a half hour elapsed when I felt Mayuko's gentle hand placed on the lid of my coffin. I slid open the lid of my coffin and sat up to discover we were riding in a hearse.

"Good morning, sunshine!" Mayuko said cheerfully.

"That's still not funny," I said, smiling.

I expected to see the city lights of Bucharest when I looked out the windows, but I discovered our location was much more rural. Mayuko apprised me that we had been driving for many hours with a driver who spoke very little and only when addressed. She related that point to me in Japanese as to not offend the driver. Mayuko said she enjoyed the natural scenery immensely and told me she was sorry I had to miss so much of it. Forested mountains surrounded us on both sides of the narrow road. We were heading north, in the general direction of Lacul Bicaz. Mayuko informed me that lacul meant lake. But in a valley, just outside the crossroads town of Gheorgheni, Alexi Pavlovich would be waiting for us to take us the rest of the way.

I asked Mayuko how the man she had recently begun seeing reacted when she told him she needed to leave the country. She said he wasn't happy about it, but she didn't care what he thought because she was far from being in love with him.

"If he's not there waiting when I get back, I won't really care," she said and laughed.

Even though Mayuko knew on some level it hurt me to hear how easily men fell in love with her, I was always appreciative that she chose to tell me the truth without sparing my feelings. I loved her for it, and often it felt like I was living her romances vicariously through her, as an attractive young woman that, at best, I only was on the inside.

"Oh, but listen to this," she continued. "When you were sleeping and we were still in Bucharest a man approached me and asked if I spoke Romanian. I told him in English that I did not, but luckily he spoke English anyway. You'll never guess what he said."

"What did he say?" I asked.

"He goes, 'You look exactly like someone I know.' So I say, 'Oh yeah? Who is that?' and he says, 'The girl of my dreams.'"

"Vomit. Did he ask for your number?"

"Of course. But I told him I'm from America and that I was here on my way to Gheorgheni, and I pointed at the hearse, and his face changed. Like he was scared of me all of a sudden. He actually kind of ran off."

The drive continued for a couple more hours and eventually we arrived in Gheorgheni without incident. We drove slightly beyond the city proper, before our driver finally pulled off the road and killed the engine. Mayuko and I stepped out of the hearse and immediately saw Alexi Pavlovich standing beside a covered carriage pulled by four black horses. He approached us immediately and bowed.

"I welcome you both to the land of the imparateasa," he said warmly. "As you can see, we will travel by coach for the remainder of your journey."

"Why use horses when we have a car?" I asked curiously.

"My dear, we must climb many mountains to reach the castle of the imparateasa."

When I considered how many hours it took us to get here by car, and now we were going to travel mountain roads by horse, I was concerned that we would not make it before sunrise.

The driver of the hearse and the coachman, both human, secured our luggage to the back of the coach and my coffin on top of it. Alexi Pavlovich opened the coach door and invited us to step inside first. In a gentlemanly way, he took my hand as I entered the coach and did the same for Mayuko. We sat side by side, facing forward, and Alexi Pavlovich sat opposite us, apparently not minding that he would be traveling backwards.

I heard the crack of the coachman's whip, and the coach lurched forward and gained speed as the clopping of hooves on the pavement increased in rapidity. The sound changed as our pathway turned to a dirt road, and the ride became uneven and increasingly bumpy, making for an uncomfortable trip. I looked out my window and saw in the distance a fog had rolled in and I could no longer see the foot of the mountain, only the dark trees above its base that covered the entirety of the mountain face.

I heard the crack of the whip again and the horses' clip turned to a gallop. I looked out my window a second time and saw that the density of the fog intensified, preventing my ability to view the road ahead, and I wondered how our mortal driver could continue to see the road when even I could not. To make matters worse, the height of the fog continued to climb, as if some sleeping giant were pulling a thick blanket over himself as he lay in his alpine repose. I turned to Alexi Pavlovich, but he appeared at ease.

"Something troubles you, Miss Bialek?" he asked me.

"The fog. It is so thick. I cannot see the road," I answered.

"Do not think of it. You are quite safe. Atanase has made this trip many times," Alexi Pavlovich said, referring to the coachman.

Alexi's confidence assured me little and I continued to wait for the moment when we would slam into the rocky face of the mountain. Mayuko must have thought the same thing because she squeezed my hand tightly. I squeezed hers back gently, trying to appear calm. Just as I was doubting Alexi Pavlovich, I heard the crack of the whip a third time and felt the incline that signaled the beginning of our ascent. What astonished me was that the dirt road, which had been laden with potholes, had suddenly grown smooth. I heard the wagon wheels spinning, but heard no sound that would indicate the type of surface we were currently traveling on. We continued to rise at an accelerated pace. Outside, all I could see was fog.

"There, you see? There was no reason to worry yourself. Our path is quite safe."

"The road is very smooth," I answered.

"There is no road. We are riding upon the fog of the imparateasa."

Mayuko looked at me in disbelief and Alexi Pavlovich smiled at us both, but he was not joking—our horse driven coach was traversing the tree lined mountain range by flying above it on the fog that apparently belonged to Mirela. The powers of the imparateasa seemed limitless.

"Have you been to one of these Communions before?" I asked Alexi Pavlovich.

"Yes. They are great fun."

"What will we do there?"

"A great many things. We shall drink, and dance, and hear tales of adventures around the world."

"And we will feed?"

"Oh yes. We will feed a great deal."

This made me nervous for Mayuko and I knew it made her nervous as well as she squeezed my hand tightly again.

"And the imparateasa, she will drink from each of us?"

"If she chooses to. It is a great honor to be bitten by the lips of our imparateasa. It shows she recognizes your greatness, and in return she will share her own blood, which is all-powerful."

"You've drank her blood."

"Of course. I am her consort."

"You must be very powerful then."

He smiled, but did not answer.

What I expected to take hours took only minutes, for soon, I felt the wagon wheels touch solid ground and heard the hooves of the horses gallop again upon the earth.

"If you will take my advice, my child," Alexi Pavlovich said.

The *my child* perturbed me, but I responded quickly, "Please, I would appreciate anything you might impart to me."

"Don't be so serious here. The Communion of the Ancients is merely a family reunion. It is about one's enjoyment and getting to see those whom you have not seen for centuries."

Outside my window, in a clearing in the woods, I could see an expansive castle made of dark gray rock. The castle had few towers and was much wider than high. It was spectacular but had little ornamentation. It was definitely of an older age, when a castle's primary purpose was to defend against siege during battle, rather than to provide a luxurious abode to a liege lord.

A portcullis was raised and the coach entered the castle grounds. And as we disembarked, the portcullis slowly descended into place, preventing anyone else, anyone mortal at least, from entering behind us. Beyond all the walls was forest—trees that towered over the castle and formed a tight perimeter around its walls.

Who but the Cobălcescu knew this castle existed in these alpine woods? Remote or not, it would certainly be a tourist attraction. I longed for my laptop so I could view the area via satellite to see if it was visible from above.

In the courtyard, I expected to see the carriages of the Ancients who had already arrived, but there were none, and I reflected that they must all have traveled in the same coach that Mayuko and I had. Mortal servants exited quickly from within the castle to retrieve our luggage and my coffin.

"Come. This way," Alexi Pavlovich gestured toward a broad structure of three stories that was illuminated brightly from within. I was nervous. I was about to enter the home of Mirela Cobălcescu. I had no expectation of what her greeting would be like. I could be living my final moments in the here and now.

We ascended four wide stone steps and were met by an imposing pair of oaken doors. The doors opened at our approach, but there was no sign of anyone within who had pulled them open. It was clear that Alexi Pavlovich had opened them merely with his mental faculties. We stepped inside and were overcome with firelight. A large fire roared in a fireplace whose height was greater than that of a man. Tall white candles glowed from sconces mounted throughout the interior. The stone floors were of the same hue of the castle walls and in many places were covered by ornate rugs. Dark tapestries and ancient portraits dimmed by years of smoke hung from the walls. The decor was a far cry from the modern art which decorated Yelena's home.

The mortal servants entered the house behind us, carrying our things. Alexi Pavlovich spoke to them in a commanding tone, in Romanian, which I did not understand and they nodded silently and continued past us, undoubtedly to deposit our belongings in some designated place.

Although I knew the structure was large and contained many rooms yet to be seen, to my astonishment, the place appeared and felt empty.

"Are we alone here?" I asked Alexi Pavlovich.

"But of course not," he replied. "The imparateasa is within and will be down shortly to greet you."

"But the Ancients, where are they?"

"They will come in due time," he said with a smile.

"Due time? When is that?"

"The Communion of the Ancients does not yet begin for another two nights."

"Then why did you tell me that I had to come here so early? You gave me only one night to pack."

"I apologize if you are upset, Miss Bialek, but the imparateasa asked that I summon you early as she wished to spend some time your company."

I didn't like the sound of that nor the smile on his face. I felt I had crossed the globe only to step into a trap and I had led Mayuko the entire way to share in my demise.

"For shame, Alyosha," a pleasant but firm voice called from the far end of the entrance hall. "Why have you not offered our guests a place to sit and libations?"

The voice belonged to Mirela. I remembered its pitch and recalled how she referred to Alexi Pavlovich as *Alyosha*. Without having sensed her descending any staircase or entering the large room in which we three stood, I was taken by surprise and turned just in time to watch Mirela step out of a shadow that seemed to be swallowed by light once she was no longer in it.

As before she wore a violet gown that matched her eyes. The metallic flecks in her irises shimmered in the firelight. Her deep auburn hair cascaded over her pale bare shoulders and led one's eyes to the roundness of her breasts which swelled within the gown, which was clearly tailored to accentuate all the curves of her statuesque and voluptuous body. She appeared only a year or two older than my true age, but even with her youthful appearance she naturally possessed an awe-inspiring regal air to her.

Mirela was not heavily adorned with jewelry. Small strands of diamonds hung from each of her earlobes, but her arms and fingers were bare. The first time I had seen her she wore a necklace of large amethysts, but tonight she wore diamonds around her neck. Diamonds that I recognized. From a platinum chain hung the diamond kaleidoscope key pendant Yelena had given me and that Mirela had taken under the pretense of wanting something to remember me by. This was before I knew she meant to betray us and probably anticipated my death instead of Yelena's.

She wore a friendly smile, but I was certain she knew I would recognize the diamond key. I wanted to tear it from her throat.

"Welcome to Castle Cobălcescu, Orly Bialek."

I curtsied and she extended her hand. I kissed it. Unlike all other immortals I had ever met, Mirela's skin was warm, just as it had been in Los Angeles—the first and only time we had met. I saw it as a sign of her age and power. She could pass for human. I wondered if she warmed her skin at will or if it was always like that. I acknowledged she used the name Bialek instead of my new legal surname of Solodnikova. That wasn't by accident. She would hate Yelena for all eternity for stealing Marcel's heart away from her.

"Thank you, Imparateasa," I replied softly.

"Now, please tell me, what is your servant called?"

"Her name is Mayuko Mochizuki."

Mayuko bowed to Mirela, but unlike she had done with me, Mirela did not welcome Mayuko or extend her hand.

"She is beautiful enough to envy," Mirela said, with a smile that showed her sharp fangs. "Alyosha, show the servant to her quarters. I would like some time alone with Miss Bialek."

"This way please," Alexi Pavlovich said to Mayuko, and she looked back at me as she followed him across the expanse of the great hall before turning down a corridor.

"Permit me to show you my home," Mirela said politely and I followed her as she led the way through Castle Cobălcescu. There was a large formal dining room, with fireplaces at both ends. There was an enormous ballroom with a high ceiling from which hung six crystal chandeliers. Mirela's library contained three levels of exquisitely bound books of varying ages, mixed with the latest literary paperbacks. There were four sitting rooms, a study, and countless quarters for guests. All were heavily decorated with more portraits, pastoral paintings, and tapestries. It occurred to me while we were in her large music room that all the grandeur and spaciousness I was being shown could not possibly all fit in the structure I had seen from the courtyard.

Mirela never showed me her own quarters, which, I learned later, occupied the entirety of the third floor.

To my surprise we ended up in a conservatory with three glass walls and an angled glass roof. It was filled with sweetly fragrant flowers of all colors and varieties. A stone water fountain in the center of the room adorned with spitting gargoyles lent the room a humidity I had not experienced since my arrival in Romania. Though the sound was completely different, the spouting water recalled the flow of the Mogami River.

"Please sit," Mirela said, and gestured to a stone bench.

I sat and she sat beside me. She inhaled deeply, exhaled, and then spoke, her eyes fixed on a cluster of gardenias. "Besides my bedchamber, I spend most of my time here. I had loved flowers even as a girl. It's such a shame I never see this room filled with the sunlight that calls forth the blooming of all my petaled delicacies."

I thought to myself of her sitting here until the sun was high in the sky, turning her to ash, but I didn't say anything.

She took my hand and held it. I thought, if she was going to be this touchy feely with me, it should make it easier for me to kill her.

"Do you know why I brought you here?"

"Yes, Imparateasa, I think I do."

"Please, Orly. Call me Mirela as you once had when we were friends for a night. For it is my sincerest hope we shall be friends again."

I wanted to tell her that was far from fucking possible, but she broached the subject herself.

"I know you want to kill me, Orly. And I understand why you feel that way. You loved Yelena, perhaps as your mother, perhaps as more, but I did not love her. I could not. She rivaled my beauty and took what was mine and killed him."

"No, Mirela, Marcel left you all on his own and he killed himself."

Mirela's pallid cheeks flushed at the sound of his name.

I wasn't afraid of her. I had come to kill her after all, even if it meant dying during the attempt.

"Myshka moya, don't hurt me so."

Myshka moya was the nickname she had given me the night she came to Los Angeles. It meant *my little mouse.*

"Please Orly, do not think anymore of killing me. There is no hope of it. You must accept that. And I promise you, I make a much better friend than enemy."

It was a bitter pill to swallow and I refused to swallow it.

"Believe me when I tell you," she continued, "that when it comes to me, Marcel, and your Yelena, there is more to that story than you know."

"Not from Yelena's perspective," I shot back.

"Yelena's perspective. Do tell me, Orly, of a story you know that has but one side."

"I thought you wanted me to tell you why I think you brought me here."

"Yes, indeed. Please, tell me that instead."

"It's because of my scribbles."

"Quite right, but what else do I desire of you?"

"Besides my scribbles? My blood. You want to drink my blood."

"I will drink your blood, but I don't expect anything from it. You possessed this power as a mortal. But I value your sketches because they allow you to know the secrets held deep within those around you."

"You want me to tell you your secrets?"

"Never. I already know them all." She paused and began again. "My little mouse, there are traitors in our bloodline. I want you to find them for me."

I noted that she referred to it as our bloodline. Perhaps she did not see me only as an appendage of Yelena.

"How do you know there's traitors?"

"Because when you have lived as long as I have, you learn there will always be traitors."

"You want me to scribble the Ancients."

"There will be thirty-eight Ancients in attendance. Though I admit, I am concerned mostly with the six who have aged more than two thousand years. For only they could truly challenge me."

"That still leaves thirty-two other Ancients. They could all band together."

"No, even all of them together would still require at least one of the Eternal."

"The Eternal?" I asked, recalling that Konomi had also used that term when we spoke in the Oblivion.

"It's a distinction given to those who have survived over two thousand years. Though not always true, it is said that those who can mentally live that long will live forever."

My mind hurtled. This is how I would kill her. I would enlist the help of one or all of the Eternal. But why would they help me? I needed time to think.

"But I will have you draw all thirty-eight anyway. For we have all the time you require, and it would be to my advantage to know who have allied with the Eternal instead of allying with me."

"And what will you do with the traitors if I find them for you?" I asked.

"You know the answer to that."

"Yeah, but I don't know how you would do it. I know you are cruel."

"I come from a different lifetime, Orly. Remember that."

"And if I draw them for you, what will you give me?"

"I will give you my blood."

"One drop?"

Mirela smiled.

"I will give you more. More than I have given anyone else."

"Then I would be as strong as you."

"No, little mouse, you would need all of my blood for that."

"Fine. But will you give me more than you have given your beloved Alyosha?" I asked, feeling as if I had begun to bargain with her.

"Do not refer to Alexi Pavlovich as my beloved, despite his station as my consort. But yes, dearest, I will give you even more than I have ever given him."

"And if I refuse to scribble anybody?"

"You will not refuse, Orly."

"How do you know?"

"Moments ago, I told you that besides your sketches, there was something else of yours I desire. Do you remember?"

"I remember. And what is that?"

"I want your love, Orly."

"You said you're from a different lifetime. Are you from a different planet too?"

Mirela laughed genuinely.

"I know you're the empress and everything, but why do you think there is even a chance I would ever give you my love?"

"There are two things that ail you, Orly. The first is that you are still mourning Yelena. The second is that you want love. A love no one can offer you because you are trapped in the body of a child. You know your love with your pedophile was not real love. And now your only hope is to find it in the arms of another vampire who would understand your plight and be capable of looking at you beyond your childish form."

I wasn't expecting our conversation to take this turn.

The diamond kaleidoscope key fell from her neck into her right hand as though the chain had broken, but it had not. The platinum chain was still clasped and intact. She reached over with her left hand and opened my right and then placed the kaleidoscope key Yelena had given me into my hand and then closed my hand over it with both her hands. Again, her touch was warm.

"Please forgive me. I beg you, Orly. Forgive me for allowing my senseless thirst for revenge to take from you the woman you loved so much. I can't change what has already been done, but I ask you to try to forget the past. Eternity is a long time to live with hate in your heart. Yelena would want you to move on and live."

"Don't tell me what Yelena would want."

"Pardon me," Mirela acquiesced. "I have said too much."

Her humility surprised me. It wasn't a side of the imparateasa I expected her to possess.

With my thumb, I felt the diamonds that studded the kaleidoscope key pendant in my hand. It brought back memories, but I did not consider putting it on. I was so suspicious of Mirela that I thought it possible she had cursed it in some way. Furthermore, as it had just come from her hand, I didn't want it touching Yelena's diamond I wore beneath my dress, over my heart.

"You said you wanted my love," I said.

"I do."

"Why?"

"In the simplest terms, I am in love with your youth. Perhaps even the folly of your youth. I mean that as no insult. Though you are an adult, you are still so young, Orly. You are very much like these flowers, just beginning to bloom."

"You want to love me like a mother?"

"You no longer need a mother."

"You want to love me like a friend?"

"I want to love you as my lover."

I didn't expect those words, and even though I hated this woman and had sworn to kill her, I felt the murderous part inside my soul recede at the thought of being loved amorously.

"Orly, in the years since our meeting, you have remained a constant in my mind. My memory of you and what knowledge I have gleaned of your life since has captured my heart and I can no longer hide it."

I turned to her and addressed her sharply. "Six years ago, when you took me higher than I have ever been in the night sky, you told me I would never have love. You said I would always be seen as a child and that romantic love is never truly offered to children. You said others would love me as a child and even those who got to know me well would only love me as a friend. You said Yelena should have let my cancer kill me because with child vampires it always ends under the saddest of circumstances because eventually I would no longer be able to ignore my eternal loneliness. You said what existence I had would be filled with sorrow, but that it wouldn't last forever, because I would finally die from grief, and when I did it would feel like a blessing."

"My darling tragedy, you remember our conversation well."

I looked away, paused, and then spoke more gently, as if speaking aloud to myself rather than to her. "It just feels strange. The woman who told me I would never know love now tells me she loves me."

Mirela reached for my hand, but I pulled away. I turned to look at her again.

"Yelena told me what you just did. She said I would't find love with a mortal but with a vampire anything could happen because they would sense my true age. Are telling me you're that vampire? The one who can forget I have the body of a child?"

"I have already forgotten it as I perceive your true nature as an immortal and know you are already a woman, but this is not what I mean to tell you in this moment."

"Then what are you trying to tell me?"

"Do you think I am beautiful, Orly?"

"You know you're beautiful."

"But do you think I am beautiful, Orly?"

"I think you are the most beautiful woman I have ever seen."

"Thank you. That is always the answer I long to hear, but it was not the answer I had always received. Like you, I was born quite plain to the eye. The body you see beside you is stolen. I took it from a queen and with it I became an empress, and now it is forever mine to keep. Be my lover, Orly. Allow me to love you, and you may forget about being seen as a child ever again. I will give you a new body, a young woman's body that will be coveted all over the world, by men and women alike, for all eternity."

FIFTEEN

Before sunrise, a mortal servant led me to my room where Mayuko was already asleep on a luxurious bed and the coffin I traveled with rested on a dais on the other side of the room. I knew Mayuko would have wanted to put me to bed, but I made certain my movements were silent so I would not wake her.

Inside my coffin, though I lay flat, my mind turned over and over. I had come here with one task—to kill the empress of our bloodline. But now my all-powerful victim was offering me what I thought I could never have during my eternity—a woman's body to live in and wipe away the doom of my everlasting lovelessness.

For the first time in my mortal and immortal life, someone wanted to love me as my lover. Why did that suitor have to be the woman who killed my mother? She asked my forgiveness but how could I ever forgive her? I loved Yelena. I would always love Yelena. But wasn't Mirela right? *Eternity is a long time to live with hate in your heart.* It certainly was, and I imagine Mirela knew the truth of her words. But what she failed to mention was the one thing other than forgiveness that might prevent me from hating her forever, and that was her death. But if she were ever to become my lover, my true vampiric lover, how long could I resist forgiving her once her blood was within me and all the hours of daylight were spent sleeping in her arms?

I gripped the kaleidoscope key tightly. "I'm sorry, Yelena, that I'm even giving this thought. I haven't forgotten your sacrifice or your love for me. I'll accept nothing from her that doesn't include her death." That last sentence was spoken like a decree, but in my mind the words echoed without the resolve they possessed when I had said them aloud. I dropped the kaleidoscope key to my side and placed my hand over my heart and Yelena's diamond. I lay silent, wishing there were some way for Yelena to hear me, and I secretly hoped she would tell me to accept the new body, to accept the blood of the empress, and to accept Mirela's love.

But then something familiar but less memorable than the sound of Yelena's voice resonated. It was the murmurs. They had followed me here, across the globe. I noticed that though they were still muffled they somehow sounded more near. It occurred to me then that perhaps the murmurs had not followed me, but that I had instead closed in on them. That whoever or whatever was making those sounds resided somewhere in this castle. As I lay there listening to them, I wondered if either Mirela or Alexi Pavlovich could hear them as well. If they did, did it not annoy them so that they would put an end to it? Perhaps one of them was the source. But as I pondered that, I noticed there was a faint new smell inside my coffin. Beneath the familiar odor of wood polish was the scent of rubbing alcohol. Mayuko had never used rubbing alcohol to service my funerary boxes before. Had someone here in Castle Cobălcescu tampered with my resting place? But as soon as that suspicion was aroused in me, I noticed I was sniffing the trapped air with increasing vigor, trying to cling to the new smell until I eventually concluded it was no longer present. Had I become accustomed to it or had it actually vanished? I still smelled the wood polish as I finally fell asleep.

Mayuko woke me just after sunset. She was already fully dressed. I sat up and invited her to sit at the opposite end of my coffin, facing me, which she did. Though I knew it was futile to inquire, I asked her if she had heard the murmurs or smelled rubbing alcohol. She looked at me puzzled and said she had experienced neither. I hadn't been given any instructions as to what was expected of me when I woke, and I presumed Alexi Pavlovich would come or Mirela would summon me when either of them desired my presence. Mayuko, on the other hand, related that she had been given a very specific set of instructions. Day and night, she was granted full access to every room on the ground floor and access to my chamber on the second floor. The third floor, however, was limited to the imparateasa, her personal servants, and upon her request, her consort, Alexi Pavlovich. At night, she had the freedom to explore the castle grounds. But the most serious rule laid out for her, that was to be broken under no circumstance, was that during the hours of daylight she must remain within the darkness of the castle, never exiting it, never opening exterior doors, and never drawing open any of the window coverings.

Not opening the window coverings and doors made obvious sense in case a vampire was not at rest and roamed the halls, especially since Ancients did not require the amounts of sleep that a young vampire like myself needed, and it was rumored that those as old as they no longer required their rest to take place inside coffin or casket. But the part that didn't make sense was that Mayuko was not permitted to go outside, or even peek behind the drapes when no one else was around, to look outside, as the sunlight could not possibly hurt her. I asked her if she knew the reason for the rule, but she said Alexi Pavlovich was so forceful in his delivery that she didn't dare question him.

"Do you think he's cute?" I asked.

"Alexi Pavlovich? Of course. He's gorgeous. Don't you think so? Besides, what would you expect of the consort to the imparateasa?"

"Yeah," was all I said, recreating Alexi Pavlovich's face in my mind and seeing how perfect it was. I knew the sick feeling it gave me in my stomach would only multiply when the Ancients arrived. Undoubtably they would all be beautiful, and I would look nothing like them. Yet Mirela wanted to take me as her lover. What would Alexi Pavlovich have to say about that? What would the Ancients? What would Berthold? Would Berthold even care now that he was so wrapped up in Kristy?

I told Mayuko about Mirela's offer to give me a woman's body but not the part about becoming Mirela's lover. I don't know why I left that part out. I think it was out of shame. At any rate, Mayuko's response surprised me.

"How do you know she can really do it?"

I hadn't even considered that, but Mayuko was right. I didn't know she could do it, and I felt foolish for taking Mirela's word for it. But when I considered she had said her own body was stolen, considered the power of the fog she created to allow our carriage to fly to the mountaintop where we now resided, and recalled that when I first met her she had flown me so high that we were no longer in the atmosphere, I felt Mirela's powers were limitless. Of course she could give me a new body.

"Are you hungry?" Mayuko asked, interrupting my thoughts.

"Yeah. Are you?"

"Super hungry."

"Wonder when the hell they're gonna come for us."

"I could brush your hair while we wait."

I nodded and Mayuko went to fetch Yelena's diamond encrusted hairbrush. I loved that Mayuko enjoyed brushing my hair; she could do it for hours and I found it so very relaxing. The feeling it gave me is the closest thing I had to what I imagined my Oblivion to be, except for most of my mortal life I didn't have my hair brushed at all as I was usually bald from the chemotherapy.

"Why do you want to be a vampire, Button?"

"Why did you want to be a vampire?" Mayuko replied.

"I didn't. I just didn't want to die."

"I don't want to die either."

"You don't want to die so much that killing people doesn't bother you?"

"I don't know. I haven't killed anyone yet. But it didn't gross me out or make me feel bad the times I've seen you do it. I'm pretty numb to seeing the dead bodies. Now I mostly just think of it as how we feed our cute little pigs."

I smiled. I loved Mayuko so much.

At that moment a mortal servant knocked on the door and when I answered, she entered carrying boxes tied with ribbons. She bowed and said in a servile tone, "Tonight's garments for Miss Bialek."

Mayuko accepted them on my behalf and set them down on her bed and the servant left.

"Can I open them?" Mayuko asked excitedly.

"Of course," I said, knowing it would make her happy as Mayuko enjoyed new clothes more than I did.

In the largest box was a fuchsia ball gown tailored to my size. It was completely different from the gothic Lolita dresses I had grown accustomed to and similar instead to the gowns that Mirela was known to wear. In another box were matching heels that were not excessively high. A thin box contained lace undergarments. The smallest boxes contained a diamond bracelet and a diamond solitaire necklace. I left those in their boxes and chose to wear my own jewelry. It occurred to me that it may not have been an accident that Mirela sent a diamond solitaire necklace to me as the solitaire diamond that always hung from my neck within its asymmetrical heart was made of Yelena's ashes. Maybe she was trying to replace Yelena's diamond with her own, if she even knew my diamond was a lab creation of her former rival. Perhaps if she did know, she would have not permitted it within her household. But that thought didn't last long, for as her honored guest, and pursued lover, I felt there was little I would not be entitled to do.

Mayuko helped me dress, and as if he knew the moment my high heeled shoes were slipped onto my feet, Alexi Pavlovich knocked on the door to announce that it was time for dinner. We followed him along the corridor and down a wide and curved staircase until we were on the ground floor. He led us to the dining room where at the head of a darkly polished long wooden table sat Mirela. She rose when we we entered. She too was wearing a ball gown, hers a deep emerald green, and she was bedecked in matching jewels. Alexi Pavlovich wore a tuxedo from an older age. Only Mayuko looked underdressed in her her normal clothes, and I saw her flush at this realization.

Alexi took his seat at Mirela's right, and Mirela gestured for me to sit at her left. This left Mayuko standing.

"Your servant shall be permitted to eat with us until the Communion begins," Mirela said.

"Thank you," I said. I wasn't sure why exactly, but I sensed that Mirela permitted Mayuko to join us for my sake alone.

Uninstructed, Mayuko took the seat beside me.

"No." Mirela began, "she may not sit there," addressing me instead of Mayuko. "She shall sit there," and Mirela pointed down the table to one chair further. Mayuko sat where she was indirectly directed, leaving an empty chair between us. I didn't know if Mirela created this gap between us because Mayuko was mortal or if it was out of jealousy as our affection for each other was so apparent. I also wasn't sure if the gap was meant to exclude Mayuko from partaking in any dinner conversation that might take place.

Servants entered with silver covered trays and set them down before us, including Mayuko, and lifted off the lids. We were each served a piece of veal, a grain I didn't recognize, and vegetables. It looked appetizing, but I needed blood. As everyone, including myself, picked up our forks, and began to eat, I only poked at my food, and then noticed Mirela smiling.

"Alyosha," she addressed Alexi Pavlovich, "Where is Miss Bialek's vessel?"

"She is within. She has been bathed and perfumed. She will be brought in shortly."

"I do not want shortly. I want now."

Alexi Pavlovich stood. "As you say, ma chère." And Alexi Pavlovich promptly left the room.

Mirela used a knife to cut into her veal and placed a small piece in her mouth. I wondered what kind of victim they had prepared for me, but whoever it was, I was relieved that I would soon be receiving the blood I craved.

I turned to Mayuko and noticed she had a confused expression on her face as she chewed her food. She noticed me looking at her and I tilted my head slightly as to ask her what happened but she only shook her head.

Minutes later, Alexi Pavlovich returned with a young blonde woman, beautiful, barefoot, and wearing a white silk camisole that barely covered her private parts. Around her neck she wore a thin white scarf, also made of silk. She appeared apprehensive, but not terror stricken as someone who knew she was about to die. I thought she had been given sedatives like Berthold once told me the condemned are given in Saudi Arabia before they are publicly beheaded.

Alexi Pavlovich introduced her as Adela and she gave me a slight bow. Though she was barefoot, she was unlikely cold as a large fire blazed in the fireplace. Alexi Pavlovich pulled the empty chair beside me out for Adela and she sat.

Slowly Adela unwound the thin scarf from around her neck. On the side of her neck that faced me were eight scars, the puncture wounds of four vampire bites. I had never fed on someone who had been fed on before and it was unsightly to me.

"Is something wrong?" Adela asked meekly.

I was surprised she was permitted to speak at the dinner table as it seemed Mayuko was not.

I wanted to tell her she looked like a junkie who shot up in her neck but instead I simply bit into my bottom lip until it bled, wiped my index finger across the bleeding, and then smeared my blood over the puncture marks on Adelas's throat. Within moments the puncture marks began to fade and I licked my own blood off her throat.

Mirela laughed. "Such a blood snob. No hand-me-downs for you, Orly. How I adore thee."

Adela appeared embarrassed.

"With our location being so remote," Alexi Pavlovich began, "it is impractical to hunt nightly. Additionally, because of our age, we do not require live blood as frequently as one as youthful as yourself. All things considered, it made more sense to house them with us, feed and allow them to recover, and eventually allow them to earn their immortality."

So there was another path to immortality. It wasn't limited to love or servitude. Just being a blood vessel, as Mirela had referred to Adela, was enough.

"Please," Alexi Pavlovich gestured and Adela leaned in my direction positioning her throat near my lips. "Her blood is sweet. You shall see."

What I saw was that Adela's breasts were quite large and I held one of them in my hand and squeezed it gently until her eyes closed and then I bit into her neck. Adela's blood was in fact sweet, just like Alexi Pavlovich had said. I turned Adela's body slightly, pulling her closer to my chest, so that I could lay my eyes on Mirela as I fed. I noticed Mirela's mouth opened slightly, perhaps lustfully as she watched me caressing this woman's breast while sucking on her neck.

My hunger was soon satisfied, but I wanted more. I released her throat and turned to Alexi Pavlovich.

"How much may I drink?"

"Enough to satiate yourself, but not so much as to kill her. Do you know how to measure that?"

In truth I did not, but before I could inform him of my ignorance, Mirela interjected.

"Kill her if you like. She makes no difference to me."

The thought of all her sweet blood streaming down my greedy throat excited me and this thrill was enhanced as the expression on Adela's face turned to sheer horror.

I contemplated killing her and licked my lips, but instead of biting again, I spoke. "Her blood is sweet. It is better to have her again and again." I decided I would let Adela live.

Mirela laughed, clearly amused.

I don't know why I made that choice. As my vampiric instincts dictated, I felt no mercy for mortals. Yet Adela was different. In her position it was like she was already half of one of us, similar to the way Mayuko was. She was a woman destined to be a vampire. An aspiring immortal. It would have been counterproductive not to have shown her mercy. Or maybe that wasn't the reason at all. Maybe I just didn't want to do what Mirela said. I don't always know why I do the things I do. Even when I scribble myself, my truths aren't always clear to me like they are when I scribble others.

Adela rose from her seat and left the room slowly, undoubtedly to rest after her loss of blood.

"How many more like her do you have?" I asked Mirela.

"Enough," was all she said with a smile.

After dinner the four of us retired to the music room. Mirela sat on a fainting couch while Alexi Pavlovich and I sat in opposing wing chairs. There were a variety of instruments within the room including a grand piano. For the first time, Mirela spoke directly to Mayuko. She gestured to the piano and said, "Play for us."

Fortunately Mayuko was proficient on the piano, but I wondered how Mirela could have known that. Perhaps she had noticed Mayuko's long slender fingers. They were pianist fingers. I wondered what the penalty would have been had Mayuko not known how to play at all.

Without a word, Mayuko took her seat at the piano bench and began to play Chopin.

"No. Not that," Mirela said tersely. "Something older."

Immediately, Mayuko changed to playing Bach.

Mirela sighed. "Doesn't your servant know what is meant by older?" she asked, annoyed.

"She's not an old lady like you," I said haughtily, defending Mayuko.

It was a risk. I wasn't sure how Mirela would react to my insolence, but she just laughed, and Mayuko continued to play the Bach piece. A servant entered carrying a large pad of paper and a box of multi-colored crayons. I felt my purpose here had come to the forefront at last. Mirela gestured toward me and the servant offered the pad of paper, which I accepted, and then the crayons.

"Do you require an easel?" Alexi Pavlovich said. "One can be brought."

"I don't have to have one, but it is more comfortable when someone is sitting for me."

Alexi Pavlovich nodded to the servant who left the room quickly and returned with an H-frame easel and placed it in front of me.

"Who do you want me to draw? Mayuko?" I asked.

"No," Mirela answered. "That will prove little as you know her intimately."

"And probably you've drawn her many times," Alexi Pavlovich said.

"Not once," I answered, "Right, Button?"

Mayuko nodded her head as she continued to play.

"How can that be?" Alexi Pavlovich asked.

"Because we have no secrets from each other. In truth, I've scribbled very little since Yelena died."

"And why is that?" Mirela questioned sharply.

"Because unlike Yelena, I don't care who I kill."

Mirela and Alexi Pavlovich smiled and I felt a pang of guilt, talking so casually about Yelena with them, especially as I had eluded to her vampiric deficiency of possessing a conscience. It was like I had made a joke and they were laughing at her. I became angry with myself, and shot back at them. "So who am I drawing then?"

"Draw my consort," Mirela replied.

I opened the sketch pad. The first page was blank. I placed it on the easel. I opened the box of crayons, removed the black one, and let the box fall on the floor at my feet, the array of colored crayons scattering and rolling across the carpet.

"So it is true, that you must draw in black." Mirela said.

It wasn't a question so I didn't reply.

"And what is the result if you were to draw in color?" Alexi Pavlovich asked.

"I would only see what you would see. Meaningless unordered lines. Any more questions?"

Neither responded and I looked at Alexi Pavlovich sitting opposite me, and brought the black crayon to the empty sheet and began to scribble. Soon his history began to take shape.

"You were mortally born in the year thirteen thirty-seven. Your father was a scribe for the Imperial Court. You were the youngest of three children. You had a sister and a brother. You joined the army when you were sixteen. You were part of the cavalry. You visited many brothels and in one, you fell in love with a whore named Zoya. You dreamed of deserting the army and taking her out of Moscow, but instead you married the daughter of a small town magistrate. When you could, you continued to visit Zoya and lay with her."

"May we stop here?" Alexi Pavlovich interrupted.

"Why?" Mirela laughed.

"Hasn't she proven her ability enough?"

"Perhaps, but I would like to hear more about this Zoya of yours."

"What color were her eyes?" Alexi Pavlovich asked as if quizzing me.

"Her eyes were blue. They were dark blue, as blue eyes go."

I could see on Alexi Pavlovich's face that I was correct, and I continued, just to show how far I could go beyond his inquiry.

"She always wore white. Her legs were short, a little out of proportion with the rest of her body, but she had a nice figure. She had a birthmark on her upper left arm. Her hair was long and black. Her pussy was really hairy."

Mirela squealed in amusement.

"That was the custom in those days," Alexi Pavlovich said defensively.

"I'm sorry. I was just playing with you."

"Can you recount conversations?" Mirela asked eagerly.

"He once told you you were the only woman he ever truly loved."

"And now we see that was a lie." Mirela answered, but by her smile, it was clear she didn't care.

The expression on Alexi Pavlovich's face was less friendly, however.

I looked away from him and studied the scribble, assessing the overall dullness of his mortal life, and all the bloodshed of his immortal life. But then I saw something I could not have expected in the sliver between those two periods. I looked up at Mirela, who was looking back at me intently.

"I see you know," Mirela said, concentrating on my face.

"What does she know?" Alexi Pavlovich interjected.

"That you were made by Marcel," I answered.

"Oh yes. That is certainly no secret." Alexi Pavlovich responded.

Perhaps it was no secret between them, but it was certainly interesting to me that Mirela's consort was made by the vampire she had been in love with and spurned by. Did she choose Alexi Pavlovich out of some sort of attachment to Marcel?

I immediately realized of how little import there was in the answer to that question and that instead, I should take advantage of the pause in conversation of Alexi Pavlovich's scribble. Not foolish enough to turn to a blank page, I began to quickly scribble Mirela in an unused corner of Alexi Pavlovich's scribble, but just as I began to see the formation of tears slipping from a pair of violet eyes that reflected fire, the entire pad of paper burst into flames. I threw it to the floor and watched it burn unnaturally quick to cinders, strangely without the ancient carpet igniting, or anything else in the room catching fire. Mayuko stopped playing the Bach piece. I looked at Mirela.

"The next time you attempt to draw me, both art and artist will be burned to ash. Have I made myself understood?"

I nodded my head.

"Answer me with words," Mirela commanded.

"Yes, Imparateasa. I understand." How had she known I was scribbling her? Could she read my thoughts? Was it intuition or just a logical conclusion? If she had begun to trust me in the slightest, I was sure that had just gone up in smoke. If I still planned to kill her, it would only be harder now.

"Tell me, Orly," she said calmly, "can you sketch people from memory?"

It was true, she did not trust me and feared my gift.

"No, Imparateasa, I cannot scribble from memory, not even from a photograph. I have tried and it's never been accurate and usually it's completely wrong."

"Can you scribble the people you see in your scribbles of others?" she asked.

I noticed she adopted the use of the word *scribble* instead of referring to them as sketches.

"No, Imparateasa, I cannot."

"Do I believe you?"

"I've tried to scribble Marcel from Yelena's scribbles and have never found out a single thing about him, except for how beautiful he looked through Yelena's eyes and her feelings for him."

At this, Mirela stood. "Alyosha, have the ashes swept away," she said and abruptly left the room. Her gait was brisk as I heard her ascend two flights of stairs.

As Mayuko and I walked along the castle walls, stopping to take in the view at each parapet, it seemed the sky was exceedingly dark that night, despite the moon's waxing. There wasn't a single cloud, and down each forested mountain face there was no sign of fog. I supposed the fog only came when Mirela summoned it to be traveled upon.

The grounds on the interior of the wall looked even more plain than ordinary. It was mostly dirt, with dried patches of grasses here and there. I wondered again what could be so special about Mayuko seeing such an unremarkable place during the day.

As no torches lined the castle walls, Mayuko took my arm as we walked the perimeter. Many of the castle windows were dark, but the majority of them were still well lit by candlelight. As we continued along the walls to the rear of the house, there were many large windows on the third floor with their curtains already drawn. These had to be Mirela's rooms.

"Do you think I actually hurt her?"

"I think you mentioning Yelena loving Marcel probably did."

"How do you think she knew I was drawing her?"

"She's smart, Orly. It's like Berthold said. It's not an accident that she's been alive for five thousand years. She knows you don't trust her and that you want to find out any weakness she might have."

"Yeah. And I think me starting to scribble faster gave it away."

"She probably realized what a bore her consort's life was and figured if you were still scribbling at all you had to be scribbling somebody more interesting, and that had to be her."

I didn't laugh aloud, but I squeezed Mayuko's hand to let her know I recognized her jest. "Mirela knew I'd discover that Marcel made Alexi Pavlovich. She wanted me to know it. She knew it would lead to talk of Marcel with Yelena. She expected to get hurt."

"Was Marcel really that beautiful?"

"Yes, he was," I answered.

"But?"

"But nothing."

"Oh, I thought you were gonna say something else."

"I think Berthold is more beautiful, but my heart probably affects what I see. Marcel had to be more beautiful though, otherwise Yelena would have eventually loved Berthold over Marcel's memory."

"That's not necessarily true. There have to be feelings. Beautiful or not. But maybe there were feelings. How do you know she didn't love Berthold?"

"Because I've scribbled Yelena many times. She cared for him, but it wasn't like what she felt for Marcel."

"I guess there's nothing more telling than your scribbles."

A few more steps and I changed the subject.

"It's daytime in America. Berthold must be sleeping. I wonder if she's sharing his casket with him already," I said, referring to Kristy.

"Can she do that?"

"No one's ever told me any rule against sharing your funerary box with a mortal. I would do it but I can't find anyone short enough."

Although I meant that as a joke, my heart hurt at the thought of Kristy in the arms of Berthold beneath the cover of his darkly stained casket, and so I changed the subject again.

"What was with you at dinner?"

"What do you mean?"

"You made a strange face when you tasted the food."

"Oh, that. It's nothing. I can't really describe it as it's not really a taste, but it's like the food felt powdery somehow."

We reached the next parapet and and began to walk along the eastern wall.

"So what will your new body look like?" Mayuko asked.

"I have no idea. But I hope it won't come from one of the vessels."

"You want someone new."

"Yeah. Don't you think that makes sense?"

"I'd be the same way. Maybe you could pick that supermodel you love so much."

"Jazzelle Zanaughtti."

"Yeah, Jazzelle Zanaughtti. Her beauty would be immortalized forever and ever."

"It already is, there's so many photos of her. But it wouldn't work. She's too much in the public eye. People would notice after a thousand magazine covers that she isn't aging. Since you're not famous, maybe Mirela should give me your body, then your beauty could be immortalized instead," I said and Mayuko slightly lost her footing at the next step. "I'm only kidding, Button, but what if you could trade bodies with me and become immortal this very minute, would you?"

Mayuko didn't take another step forward. She turned to me.

"You don't have to answer that," I said.

"I don't want to hurt your feelings. I love you, Orly. Maybe more than you even know, but I see how difficult it is for you to forever be a child."

I squeezed her hand again. "I wouldn't take your body from you anyway."

At that moment, I noticed movement in one of the windows. The room was dark, but slightly illuminated by candlelight from the hallway outside the chamber. It was a woman. She was vampiric, but she was not Mirela. She was fair to look at but not exceedingly beautiful as vampires usually were. I could sense she was much older than I was. Was she an early arrived Ancient? She was watching me, only me, as if Mayuko were not even there. She knew I was aware of her presence, but it didn't seem to affect her, and as we walked on, I felt her eyes following me through the night.

I wished we could remain on the castle walls until daybreak, or that at least Mayuko could. But well before dawn, we reentered the house and retired to our chamber, Mayuko upon her bed, me inside my coffin. Both of us were nervous and sleeping fitfully knowing that when we woke, we could expect to see the the remainder of the Cobălcescu Ancients, including the six Eternals Mirela suspected of treachery and expected me to scribble to prove their innocence or guilt. Primarily guilt. Within my coffin, I had the uneasy feeling I would not be well received as a Cobălcescu debutante.

I didn't notice when the murmurs began. When I heard them, I had the sense they had been echoing in my ears for some time. But there was something different. They were softer. Gentler. They almost hummed like a lullaby. I fell asleep.

SIXTEEN

Again, Mayuko was already dressed when she woke me. She was wearing a dark copper colored gown she had brought that contrasted well with her pale skin.

I arose from my coffin and was surprised to see a headless dress mold had been placed in the center of our room. I had not sensed anyone enter while I slept, but I was not alarmed as the intrusion was benign in nature. For upon the mold hung a new dress that appeared to be my size. It was black and made of satin with a chiffon sash. There were more wrapped boxes, containing black heels, black undergarments, and jewelry—all black diamonds. I realized everything was the color of the crayons I used and this made me suspect I would be expected to scribble tonight. I decided to wear the black diamond jewelry around my left wrist and upon my right ring finger, but of course I did not put on the matching necklace. Yelena's flawless diamond would continue to hang alone over my heart.

Music from stringed instruments played downstairs. I didn't recognize it and asked Mayuko if she did.

"I don't know it either. Maybe this is the older music Mirela wanted me to play."

As Mayuko helped me dress, I heard horse drawn carriages outside. I asked her to look behind the curtain and out the window. She announced there were at least a dozen carriages in the courtyard, but it was difficult to tell the exact number as the fog was so thick.

Mayuko was struggling with my black chiffon sash when I heard rapid footsteps coming down the hallway. There was a soft knock at the door. I doubted it was Mirela as I didn't think she was accustomed to knocking. Mayuko opened the door and to my surprise, it was the woman who had been watching me from the window the night before. She curtsied to me.

"May I enter?" she asked me timidly.

I nodded and she entered the room quickly.

"May I please?" she asked Mayuko, and extended her hand for the sash.

Mayuko handed it over and in an instant, this vampiric woman, who was on the shorter side and showed the very beginning of crow's feet in the corners of her eyes, wrapped the sash expertly and made other slight adjustments to my dress.

"May I ask who you are? I saw you last night through a window."

She spoke quietly and quickly, as someone who was inclined to shyness. "I am called Babette, dressmaker to the imparateasa. I have been charged with making your dresses, Mademoiselle Bialek, during your stay with us."

She finished adjusting my dress, curtsied quickly, and just as I was saying thank you, she left the room as though fleeing and hurried back down the hallway.

Mayuko and I looked at each other.

"How old do you think she is?"

"Too old to be so shy." I answered.

"She seems more nervous than I am."

"She makes beautiful dresses though," I said as I twirled in front of a full length mirror, momentarily forgetting I would soon be on display amongst the Ancients.

There was a double knock at our door, which had been left open, but all we saw was a black coat sleeve and a hand covered in a burgundy glove.

"Ladies, will you permit me to enter?" It was the voice of Alexi Pavlovich.

"Come in," I answered.

Alexi Pavlovich entered. "You look radiant, Miss Bialek," he said in a rehearsed tone. "The Ancients have arrived. You will be expected downstairs shortly."

"And Mayuko? Can she accompany me?"

"Servants are to stay out of the way but be at arms length when they are needed," Alexi Pavlovich stated. "But this is not what I have come to say. I have come to inform you that quite out of custom, the imparateasa will make her entrance into the ballroom with you on her arm."

I sensed that Alexi Pavlovich clenched his teeth after finishing that sentence.

"The Ancients, do they know I am here? Or who I am?"

"To my knowledge, they do not. You are to wait at the base of the private staircase of the imparateasa. She will come to you when she is ready."

Alexi Pavlovich bowed and departed. We stepped outside our chamber, shut the door, and headed down the hall. Alexi Pavlovich was far ahead and not waiting for us. At the staircase he descended quickly, rushing to attend to the crowd below. Mayuko and I paused at the top of the stairs.

"I guess you should probably go downstairs too," I said to Mayuko.

"Do you think it's safe? For me, I mean?"

"Of course, I'm sure they all brought mortal servants."

"Okay," Mayuko responded, but she appeared hesitant to depart alone and her eyes did not leave me for the first four steps down the staircase.

I walked on, further down the hall to where another staircase was situated—one that led to Mirela's private third floor. I waited as instructed, wondering how long it would be before she descended and resenting her making such a spectacle of me. But I didn't have to wait long, for soon enough Mirela descended the stairs slowly and regally, dressed in one of her signature violet gowns and adorned with large diamonds and amethysts and crowned with a diamond tiara.

When she reached the bottom of the staircase, she spoke. "You look ravishing, my love."

"As do you, Imparateasa," I said, curtseying to her.

"Please, Orly, do call me Mirela." She held her slender hand out for me to take and, not knowing what else I could do, I took it and we walked the length of the hall together toward the staircase where Mayuko and Alexi Pavlovich had already descended.

"I met Babette."

"Did you? That's quite out of the ordinary. She is quite shy as I am sure you noticed."

"I caught her watching me from a window."

"Don't worry about Babette. She is harmless. I am certain she was watching you only to perfect your measurements. She of course has mine memorized as she has been making my dresses for centuries."

"How many?"

"I first hired her to make a dress for me sometime in the fifteenth century. I loved it so much, I had her made immortal."

I noticed that Mirela said she had Babette made immortal, but did not say she was the one who had given her the blood.

"Immortality all because of a dress?" I asked.

"You would need to have seen the dress during the era. It is quite outdated now. But you see, Orly, you are not the only one who has been made immortal because of a talent."

I thought of Babette's crows feet and my plain looks as we descended the staircase to where the music played and the sweeping sound of long gowns told me the Ancients were dancing.

"Don't be anxious, my love, you are my special guest."

The way she adopted referring to me as her love made me feel strange. In one moment, it made me feel adored, in the next it made me want to drive a stake through her heart with Yelena's name burned into it.

Once we reached the ground floor, we turned right and continued down the main corridor until we arrived at the doors of the ballroom. Two formally dressed mortal servants pulled the doors open for us and the room beyond was now magnificently ornamented and brightly lit by the candlelight of six chandeliers. The floor was filled with pairs of unearthly dancers, pallid and appearing cheerful behind their fanged smiles. The dance occurring was not one I had seen before, and a couple of the vampiric musicians played stringed instruments I did not recognize. Most of the attendees were dressed in formal yet modern fashions, but a scattering were dressed from different ages. Though a variety of colors could be seen, mostly as accents, the majority of the Ancients tended to adorn themselves in black.

As we took our first steps into the ballroom, the dancing came to a halt and the music faded to silence. All heads turned our way. The occupants of the room all bowed and curtsied to the imparateasa, but most of their eyes remained on me. Although Mirela did not move, I was uncertain of what to do, so I let go of her hand and curtsied to the crowd. The moment I was again erect Mirela immediately snatched my hand. Her tight grip told me I was not to have curtsied to them. But special guest or not, who was I not to show respect in this room full of Ancients? I was sure they were already suspicious, if not envious of me; I didn't want them hating me at first sight as well.

The crowd parted for us as we advanced further into the room. There were many smiles, friendly or fake, I couldn't always tell, and many curious eyes, going over my face and body—the plain little girl in black. I felt the role in which I had been placed was as Mirela's daughter, and as her descendent or heir, I was to be treated with respect, whether it was meant or not. I scanned the crowd, without turning my head, searching for Mayuko. She was in the rear of the room, near the musicians, a beautiful wallflower.

As we made our way around the room, Mirela headed straight for a tall blonde man who looked out of style in his long black cloak. Being dressed in black and having such bright blonde hair, he seemed to be the male equivalent of Yelena. I could sense the many centuries of his age, without being told.

"Mirela," he said with a deep voice.

She offered him her hand and he bent forward and kissed it.

He had not called her *Imparateasa*, just as I no longer had to. He must be a favorite.

"Petru," Mirela began, "allow me to introduce you to my special guest, Orly Bialek."

I was not sure if I should offer him my hand, but as he leaned forward slightly, it signaled to me that it was expected. He kissed my hand and in his deep voice, he said, "I am delighted to meet you, Miss Bialek."

I wanted to ask him to call me Orly, but I wasn't sure if that was proper. And before I could think about it too long, he surprised me.

"Have you brought your crayons tonight?" he asked, his eyes piercing mine.

I didn't know how to answer, but Mirela cut in.

"This is a ball, Petru. Of course she has not brought crayons. It would be undignified. But perhaps I have brought them for her." Mirela laughed. I did not, as there was no humor in Petru's eyes as they remained fixed on mine.

Mirela pulled me away and I did my best to curtsey to Petru before we left. As we continued through the room, the path Mirela took seemed without direction. She headed to the far end of the room to a tall slender woman with long jet black hair, the very archetype of a vampire. She curtsied and, just like Petru had, she addressed the imparateasa as Mirela.

"Codrina," Mirela began, "it has been far too long."

"It has indeed, Mirela."

They hugged.

"Allow me to introduce you to my young guest, Orly Bialek."

I curtsied to Codrina and she bowed her head slightly.

"I won't ask about the crayons, as that subject has already been covered," Codrina said without expression. I realized then that it was likely that all the vampires in the ballroom could hear each of our conversations and thus they all knew my name by now and that there was some running joke about me and crayons. How many of them thought the joke was because of my childlike appearance and how many knew of my scribbles? Like I had with Petru, I sensed that Codrina was quite old and then it occurred to me that Mirela's pattern through the room was not random at all. She was greeting her guests in the order of their age. I therefore had to assume that both Petru and Codrina were Eternals, each over two thousand years old. I knew there were four others, and in order they were introduced—a man named Trajan, a woman named Viorica, and then two more males, Matei and Vasile. They all greeted me amiably, but I suspected Eternals, even more so than ordinary vampires, could wear many faces to hide their true feelings. Yet somehow I wanted to trust Viorica. There was something kinder about her nature, and her dark brown hair was similar in shade to my own, though far more lustrous. In my wild imagination she appeared to be the blue-eyed version of me had I also been born naturally beautiful and grown to maturity.

After I had met the Eternals, Mirela introduced me to the Ancients. I couldn't tell at that point if she was still greeting them according to their age. There were many to meet though, and had it not been for my vampiric memory, I would not have remembered a single name.

For those who desired blood, vessels, who were also formally dressed for the occasion, were selected from where they sat in a corner together to be bled.

The music and dancing resumed and I longed to go to Mayuko, but Mirela did not permit me to leave her side until Petru, the eldest of the Eternals asked me to dance. He led me by the hand to the middle of the ballroom floor. I wasn't a great dancer when it came to formal dances, and it was difficult for me to follow Petru's steps which were visibly graceful, but he didn't seem to mind, and I concluded this was because he hadn't really taken me out there to dance.

I recognize that you will have no choice when Mirela, bitch that she is, asks you to sketch us.

I was stunned that he just called the imparateasa a bitch and I glanced around the room to see who else had heard him. Many eyes were upon us, but no one seemed to have heard the remark.

Don't act so tense. My words to you are soundless. They come only from my mind. This is a skill that would serve you well to learn soon, Miss Bialek. Now say, I'm sorry, I do not know this dance.

And just as I was about to utter the words I was instructed, I stepped on Petru's foot, but it was as if he had placed it there for me to step on.

"I'm sorry, I don't know how to do this dance."

"It's okay, young Orly," he said aloud, "you'll have centuries to master it," and he smiled, his fangs white as pearls.

Let me give you some advice, Miss Bialek, he continued only in my head, if you value your life. When you sketch us, Eternals and Ancients alike, do not try to explain what you do not understand. Do not utter words for which you do not know their meaning. And most importantly, never pronounce the name Ji'Indushul.

Before I could repeat the name in my head, the song ended and Petru bowed to me and led me back to Mirela who was now seated. I sat beside her.

"You need a dance instructor," Mirela said kindly.

"Yeah, a really old one," I shot back and Mirela laughed.

"May I have this dance, Miss Bialek?"

It was Vasile, the most youthful of the Eternals. It seemed I was the belle of the ball. I stood and he too took me out onto the ballroom floor.

It was a different dance than mine had been with Petru, so I was just as lost.

Squeeze my hand if Petru has spoken to you.

I squeezed his hand.

Squeeze it again if you understand everything he has told you.

I squeezed his hand a second time.

Do you want to live, Miss Bialek? "Do you enjoy our Romanian weather?" he said aloud.

"I do," I answered, knowing that I was openly answering his previous question of wanting to live.

It was a strange ball indeed. I lost sight of Mayuko. And I didn't want to be there any longer.

The dancing continued for another hour, and as it did, it was as if the tension in the room was rising, as it would if the temperature inside had grown too hot, which it had not. I glanced at Mirela. I knew she sensed it as well, for she wore a slight smirk upon her face.

Just as the musicians began to play a new song, Codrina, the Eternal with the long jet black hair stood and with a loud voice exclaimed, "Enough of this farce! Let us come to the point. The drawings. The scribbles. However you prefer to call them. Let us witness to know their truth."

Mirela smiled at Codrina and stood. "Alyosha," she said calmly, and Alexi Pavlovich gestured to a mortal servant who left the ballroom quickly. In the servant's absence the room remained completely silent, but there was an electricity in the air that told me many conversations were taking place between the minds of those in attendance. Upon the return of the servant, who now carried a large pad of paper and a box of black crayons, the electric current of communication was grounded.

Alexi Pavlovich gestured to other servants and two chairs were brought to the center of the ballroom floor and set opposite each other with about ten feet between them. For a moment no one stirred, but then Mirela spoke.

"Orly, please sit," she said and gestured to the empty chairs.

I knew it was inconsequential which chair I chose. The choice was mine. But as I walked out to the pair of chairs alone I felt more in the spotlight than I had when I first entered the ballroom with Mirela. I chose the chair on the right and sat. Another servant quickly set the same H-frame easel down before me. The servant holding my supplies hastened to me and placed the large pad of paper onto the easel and then opened the box of black crayons and allowed me to select one, as if the selection would change things. Once equipped, the servant retreated and disappeared behind the crowd of Ancients.

In truth, I didn't want to scribble anyone because I knew everyone has secrets. Everyone has things that they don't even label a secret but they still never tell anyone about. Everyone has things they don't remember, but if recalled, they wouldn't want shared. And these piles of unspoken stories were made only more immense because of the lifespans of the subjects surrounding me. At a minimum, they had five hundred years. How many large and minuscule secrets had been buried consciously and unconsciously over so many centuries?

Who would be first? That was the question on everyone's mind but Mirela's. If Yelena were here, I wonder if she would have sat her in the seat first—to have me shame her.

Mirela spoke. "Evike, come forth."

A lithe woman with long straight brown hair stepped forward. She had been the last Ancient I was introduced to, which made me believe Mirela knew the exact age of all in her bloodline.

"It is not true that fortune favors the young," Evike said, and a din of uncertain laughter traveled through the room. Evike curtsied to Mirela and then quickly to me and then sat in the chair opposite me. I looked to Mirela, who didn't move, but I could see it in her eyes that she was telling me to draw, and thus I began. As I scribbled, I felt the crowd move in a little closer, heads moving and necks craning to get a better view of the black mess forming on my blank sheet of paper.

"You were born in the year fifteen fourteen in a city I cannot pronounce in Hungary."

"Szombathely," Evike answered quickly.

I wished she hadn't. I wanted to spell it aloud to prove my credibility and not make this look like a fake hypnosis show.

"Your mother died in labor. Your father and brother both died from yellow fever."

"The good old days," someone muttered from the crowd.

"You spent your early teen years in an orphanage but ran away. You met a woman named Jozefa who took you in and employed you as a laundress in her boarding house until you came of age and continued to work for her as a prostitute."

Evike blushed with embarrassment though there was no laughter or mockery from the crowd.

"You were made against your will by a client you had seen on two other occasions, named Gheorghe."

A murmur ran through the crowd.

I paused.

Evike looked into my eyes imploringly.

"What is it?" Mirela asked.

"When you first woke after being made a vampire, you dug yourself out of the earth, as Gheorghe had already left Szombathely," I said.

"Ha!" Viorica exclaimed. "He always was a womanizer."

"You never saw him again," I continued.

"No one ever saw him again," Matei said bitterly.

"You roamed the countryside alone for many months before meeting Marianna, who took you in."

I scanned the crowd for the face of Marianna that appeared in the scribble. She stood close by. I assumed they were still closely acquainted.

"Enough story," Mirela said sharply. "What about powers?" she asked, but it was more of a command.

I looked back at the scribble.

"She can turn to vapor and sink into the earth without leaving a trace."

"Ah, those are old tricks," Mirela said and stood up.

She gestured for Evike to rise, which she did. Mirela walked toward the youngest of the Ancients who looked wide-eyed at the imparateasa nervously. But Mirela only caressed her cheek. "Thank you for playing along, Evike." And Mirela bit into her neck and drank for a matter of seconds before releasing her in a slight swoon.

"Babette," Mirela commanded, and immediately her seamstress was at her side. From a pincushion bracelet Babette pulled a straight pin and Mirela held out her left hand and Babette used the pin to prick Mirela's ring finger. A large drop of blood surfaced upon Mirela's finger and she extended her hand. Evike opened her lips and the imparateasa inserted her bleeding finger into her mouth. Evike closed her lips upon the finger and closed her eyes, savoring the taste of the source of her bloodline. When Mirela pulled her finger from Evike's mouth, the drop of blood was gone and the wound had healed. Evike curtsied and Mirela nodded her head.

Evike went to Marianna which left me sitting alone, opposite an empty chair.

"Who shall be next?" Mirela asked with a wide smile on her face.

"Not I," Petru said disdainfully. "I shall not be subjected to such trespasses of my privacy."

Eyes in the room shifted from Mirela to Petru and back to Mirela.

Mirela laughed. "You shall be subjected, if I say you shall be subjected. But this public display was only for tonight. There, Codrina, are you satisfied? You have witnessed the child's power. Any further scribbles shall be held in private. Soon there shall be no secrets between any of us. The Cobălcescus will be more intimate than they have ever been since the time there were two, and as such we will be more powerful than ever."

The room was quiet, but there was that electricity of thoughts webbing all through the crowd again, and it was clear the sentiments were not joyous and were filled with suspicion. Clearly none of the Ancients in their thousands of years had ever seen a gift like mine. I felt like my own eternity would be cut short. With a ruler like Mirela, every single one of them would be better off with me dead and my gift forgotten like a bad memory. And if there truly were conspirators, they would have to kill me. They couldn't afford to let me live without risking their own immortalities.

Servants entered to take the pad and crayons from me and cleared the two chairs and easel from the middle of the ballroom floor. Mirela turned to the vampiric musicians who, at once, began to play. But the crowd was slow to partner with each other to dance. But dance they eventually did, and I resumed my seat beside Mirela. Petru approached again, and I expected him to ask me for another dance so he could mentally throw more warnings at me, but to my surprise, he held his hand out to Mirela, who took it. He led her to the center of the ballroom floor, and the eldest of the Eternals danced.

Sitting alone, I felt I was being watched. Mirela had referred to me as a child to the room of Ancients. As they eyed me suspiciously, did they see me as just a child even if they could sense my true age? I scanned the room and saw no sign of Mayuko before my eyes locked on the eyes of Evike. She was standing with Marianna, holding hands. They were both looking directly at me and not hiding it. Had I made enemies? I felt a pang of fear. I would soon find out as Evike released Marianna's hand and began the long approach to where I was seated.

I rose nervously when she was near and curtsied. Evike smiled and curtsied to me.

"Please sit, Miss Bialek," she said.

The fear I had felt began to subside and I resumed my seat.

"Please call me Orly," I said and Evike nodded.

I want to thank you, Orly, for not speaking of my child, Evike said to me only in my mind.

I tried to project my thoughts to communicate with her, but words escaped my lips. "It made me sad as I scribbled it."

She took my hand.

And thank you, for not telling the end, she said, again only in my mind. You show good judgment for your age.

What Evike was referring to was that she was with child the night she was made a vampire against her will by Gheorghe. She knew he was a vampire and promised to be his, but pleaded that she first be allowed to give birth. Gheorghe neglected her wishes, drank her blood, and forced her to drink his. She died and he buried her. But when she woke two nights later and Gheorghe dug her up, she screamed when she saw her baby girl had been expelled from her body as she was now a vampire. The baby was lifeless and Evike bit into her neck, attempting to drink from the corpse, and then bit open her own wrist and smeared the blood upon her baby's lips. She didn't know what to expect and she pleaded with

Gheorghe to help her, but he refused, saying there was no way to resurrect the child. He drew her out of the hole, and Evike watched as he kicked the dirt back over her dead child.

It could not have been his child as vampires are sterile. That is why he did not help, Evike said.

I thought to myself that there was probably nothing that could have been done for the baby, but I didn't contradict her as I had seen in her scribble that the memory, even after centuries had passed, still pained her. She lived with Gheorghe briefly, before she found a moment to plunge a stake through his heart and behead him. That was the ending she thanked me for not revealing, for it could have meant her life, a younger Cobălcescu killing an elder Cobălcescu. But as so much time had passed, I wondered if anyone would even care about the death of Gheorghe anymore.

"I'm sorry she did not wake," the words slipping softly from my lips.

She wasn't as lucky as you.

I promise you there is no luck in waking to a childhood that lasts forever. I can only imagine it would be worse for an infant.

Evike smiled.

I stared at her, puzzled, not understanding why she was smiling at what I said until she told me.

Orly, you just spoke without speaking.

The ball continued until just before sunrise. All retired to their chambers. Both Mirela and Alexi Pavlovich ascended to the third floor. Mayuko fell asleep quickly in her bed, but I lay in my coffin, finding it difficult to sleep. My thoughts were racing. I had learned to communicate with my mind only. That was an accomplishment for sure, but it was no time to celebrate. There were other things to think of. Was I the most hated vampire in Castle Cobălcescu? That I understood them hating me made me feel worse. Would I be able to win more of them over like I had with Evike? Why did Mirela need to exert such power over her bloodline? And what will happen when she commands me to scribble one of the Eternals? And what is this name Ji'Indushul Petru had forbidden me to speak? It had not appeared anywhere in Evike's scribble.

My questions remained unanswered when the lullaby of murmurs began again, but as much as I resisted, they put me into a deep sleep.

The next night, I woke to a scream. It was Mayuko's scream. I threw off the lid of my coffin and shot to my feet. I looked at her as she sat on her bed. She appeared unharmed, but she pointed behind me. I turned and saw what she saw. It was the lid of my coffin. A metal stake had been driven into it, but not pushed far enough through to where it would have impaled my beating heart. It was a warning. And it was left by someone whom I did not detect when in close enough proximity to kill me with an implement as rudimentary as a stake. I pulled it out with ease. It was heavy and looked like an old railroad spike. Whereas the shaft was discolored with age, its tip shined, having been recently sharpened. I gripped it angrily in my hand, determined to return it to its owner—whoever that might be.

"We need to leave here," Mayuko whispered.

I went and sat beside her on her bed and laid the stake to my side, and did my best to comfort her.

"We will, Button. We'll leave together."

And as what had transpired settled in my mind, it occurred to me that no one in Castle Cobălcescu had come rushing to our aid, even though every vampiric ear must have heard the scream that came from my chamber.

SEVENTEEN

Mayuko and I bathed together that night as we sometimes did. Mayuko was still visibly shaken by the appearance of the stake pierced into my coffin and didn't want to be separated from me for even a moment. Just as we were drying our bodies, Babette scurried into my bedchamber holding a new gown made of dark pink satin.

"I apologize for being late, Mademoiselle Bialek, I had some difficulty with the boning in the bodice."

"I'm sure it's fine, Babette, thank you."

She curtsied and turned to leave.

"Babette, wait a minute please."

Babette stopped in her tracks and turned to face me.

"Did you hear a scream tonight just after sunset?"

"Of course I did. I'm sure everyone within Castle Cobălcescu heard it quite clearly."

"The scream came from my chambers. Why did no one come to see what had happened? Or to see if we needed help?"

"Because Mademoiselle Bialek, it was only a mortal scream. They are quite common here and no cause for alarm.

Ordinarily, it means one of the guests has broken the pact made with one of the vessels. That is all." Babette curtsied and left.

Mayuko dressed first. As she had not brought more than one gown she wore her copper colored gown again. Once dressed, she helped me dress. From downstairs, we began to hear laughter, music, and the clinking of crystal glasses. I held the sharpened metal stake in my right hand and tapped it rhythmically into my left palm as Mayuko laced up my bodice. The familiar footfall of Alexi Pavlovich came down the hall and then his signature double knock on my door.

"Come in," I said, and the door opened.

Alexi Pavlovich immediately bared his fanged teeth when he stepped in and saw me holding the stake.

"What are you doing with that?"

"It was a gift."

"Give it here."

"Uh uh. It's mine."

His brow furrowed. The last thing he expected was for me, a fledgling, to defy the order of an Ancient. He stared at me for some time, before bowing slightly and departing. I heard him walk quickly down the hall and descend the staircase.

I thought of hiding the stake somewhere in the room, but as my bedchamber door did not have a key that would allow me to lock it, and even if it did, I was sure every Ancient here could open the lock mentally, I decided to hold onto it, despite the knowledge that it would make my appearance downstairs shocking if not threatening. When I was fully dressed, Mayuko shut the door and we headed down the hall, arm in arm. When we neared the staircase that led to the first floor, I felt Mayuko pulling away. She was being brave, but I held her tightly.

"Cricket," she whispered.

"I don't want you an inch away from me, Button," I whispered back and a look of relief washed over her face. We continued down the hall to Mirela's private staircase.

We had not waited long until Mirela descended the stairs clad in a strapless silk azure shaded gown. She looked beautiful.

"What is this?" she said when she reached the bottom step. I was not sure if she meant my conjoined state with Mayuko, or that I was holding a sharpened stake.

"I woke with this warning plunged into the lid of my coffin."

Mirela's expression soured. "That was unwise, as your drawings will reveal the culprit."

"You want me to scribble all thirty-eight of them?" I asked sharply. Worried I had taken too much liberty in how I spoke to the imparateasa, I softened my tone. "It would take all night. Can't you just demand that one of them step forward and admit they did it?"

Mirela smiled. "You are so young, Orly Bialek. You haven't yet learned that we are all terrific liars. Haven't you heard the term *vamp-liar* before?" she asked gleefully.

"Then use mind power to force them to tell the truth."

"There is no such power, little one."

"Please don't call me that," I said and Mirela nodded.

It wasn't the diminutive term that upset me. Had it been, I wouldn't have said "please." *Little one* was something Yelena used to call me. I only hoped Mirela didn't know that.

"And what of your servant?"

"I want Mayuko to remain with me tonight."

Again Mirela did not look happy. "As you wish, honored guest, but it would be impossible for a mortal to make our entrance with us."

"Then we'll go down now," I said, meaning me and Mayuko. Mirela's lips turned downward ever so slightly. She was jealous, but not in an angry way. She was hurt. "I need a vessel right now," I said. "I'm very hungry."

"Certainly you're not going to bring that stake with you."

"I have enemies. I want them to know I'm not afraid."

Mirela said nothing. She simply nodded her head and I took that as our cue to leave her.

As Mayuko and I turned and walked away, I thought of turning back to look at Mirela, to see if she were still visibly hurt. It was as though I cared. Having seen her feelings hurt humanized her. I was becoming confused. I was forgetting that this was the woman I had traveled so far to kill. I could feel Mayuko's pulse quickening as we descended the staircase.

The crowd in the ballroom turned to us when we appeared in the doorway, but no one parted. They were not afraid. Apparently even the stake didn't scare them. Because of my youth, it may as well have been a dandelion. Mayuko and I curtsied and slowly, one by one, they turned away and went back to their conversations.

We stepped into the ballroom and soon Alexi Pavlovich was upon us.

"Come with me, Miss Bialek," he said with a note of bitterness in his voice.

"Where are we going?"

"The imparateasa has given instructions that you are both fed."

The words were a relief to me. He led Mayuko and me out of the ballroom and down a hall into an empty sitting room. There was a platter of meats and vegetables already waiting for Mayuko on an end table, but she only picked at it, clearly not hungry as the warning of the stake in my coffin had upset her appetite.

"Wait here, if you please," Alexi Pavolvich said.

I nodded and he left, side eyeing the stake in my hands. I sat in the center of an upholstered sofa and Mayuko sat to my right, so close to me that the skin of our upper arms were touching. I looked at the paintings that hung on the wall, searching for one that looked like Marcel. None did. Mayuko placed her hand on the satin covering my knee. She was trembling.

"Don't worry, Button. I won't let anything happen to you."

"I'm worried about you too, Cricket," she said. "It feels like this whole castle is falling in on us."

I knew she was being metaphorical, but I answered, "It's been standing for thousands of years. It won't fall before we get out of here."

Alexi Pavlovich returned and to my surprise, he was escorting a boy who couldn't have been more than ten years old. Alexi Pavlovich pointed to the vacant spot on the sofa to my left and nudged the boy forward.

"Wait, what is this?" I asked. "He's a little kid."

"Yes, he is. Is that a problem?"

"I expected someone older. Like Adela. Where is she?"

"She is recovering. But Adela was once a child too."

"Well of course she was," I said indignantly.

"You misunderstand me, Miss Bialek," Alexi Pavlovich said. "Adela was once a child with us here. She is near to fulfilling her blood oath and shall be made immortal in a matter of months, I presume. This is Luca. He has taken the same oath. Much more recently, obviously."

"You mean he was kidnapped more recently."

"Either feed or do not feed. But do not judge us like a mortal. That was the undoing of your mother, I am told. You will not be the first to have fed off of Luca."

He was right. Why was I caring so much about this mortal? Just because he was a child? A kidnapped child? I was an orphaned child and who cared about me until I met Yelena? Luca was beautiful and filled with blood. That was all that mattered. And fortunately for him, his blood oath would carry him into an adult immortality, where he would most likely be radiant and beautiful for all time, whereas I would remain plain and prepubescent.

I patted the vacant spot beside me signaling for him to sit, which he did. Unlike Adela, Luca was more hesitant to offer his throat. I attributed that to his lesser experience as a vessel. I ran my fingers through his hair and then gripped it tightly and exposed his neck, parted my lips, and sunk my teeth into him. He winced, but he did not struggle or scream and his blood was delectable. As I savored his taste a thought quickly raced through my mind. Perhaps in a couple of years, Luca would reach puberty and Mirela or one of the Ancients would allow Luca's blood oath to be fulfilled early, and he too could be frozen in his immortality as a twelve or thirteen year old. Then I would wait until his mind and heart matured and then claim him as mine and I could finally be loved as appropriately as circumstances allowed.

When satiated, I released Luca from my bite. He made a move to stand, but I grabbed his hand and pulled him back onto the sofa. I held his hand and he looked at me curiously. With our palms together, I wondered if I could ever love the man that would someday be inside this boy. Upon further thought, I recalled Mirela's desire for me to be her lover. If I revealed my plan regarding Luca being turned at puberty for me, she would very likely kill him out of carefree jealousy.

"I don't think it wise for the boy to be bled anymore tonight," Alexi Pavlovich said. He too looked at me, puzzled.

I let go of Luca's hand, and with my other hand, I took Mayuko's.

"No, it would not be, and I am satisfied."

Luca rose from the sofa again and this time he lumbered, slightly off balance, to Alexi Pavlovich who led him through a doorway I had not been through myself. I figured it led to the quarters belonging to the vessels. I would like to see them. I would like to know what they ate and where they slept and how they passed their considerable time on this mountaintop.

"Shall we dance?" I asked Mayuko. I was feeling particularly energetic.

"We don't know their dances," she replied.

"And they probably don't know ours."

We left the sitting room and made our way down the hall following the music to the ballroom. The dance occurring at the moment looked quite formal. Holding the sharpened stake in one hand and Mayuko's hand in the other, I led us out onto the dance floor, where we danced undignified, lacking any grace, but full of happiness, like the silly way we used to dance together in our underwear in our apartment in Tokyo. We were completely out of place on that dance floor, and though some smiled, most looked upon us disdainfully, but I didn't care in the slightest as our dancing finally put Mayuko at ease. But holding the stake made it awkward, not to mention dangerous each time Mayuko or I tried to take each other's hand. But very quickly, Babette scuttled onto the dance floor holding a sash that matched my gown, placed it over my head and onto my shoulder and let it hang diagonally across my chest as if I were in a beauty pageant. But what made this sash extraordinary is that at the point where it hung below my waist, it was sewn into a tapered sleeve that Babette showed me would hold the stake sturdily, as if in a scabbard, while I danced. Once I placed the stake in the sleeve and saw that it fit, Babette quickly curtsied in her anxious way and made her way off the dance floor as quickly as she had come. The gesture made me feel a new affection for Babette. It was as though she were there, not only to make me look grand and glorious at these balls, but it was like she were also there to protect me.

Abruptly, the music stopped and all turned toward the ballroom entrance where Mirela now stood alone. All in the room bowed and curtsied upon her appearance. She nodded her head slightly and all relaxed. Alexi Pavlovich was soon at her side and she stood still, communicating to him mentally. He immediately left her side and headed in our direction, but to my surprise he passed us and bowed courteously to a flaxen haired beauty just past us named Mioara. Alexi Pavlovich offered his hand and she took it and he escorted her back to the imparateasa.

The music resumed and the next song played was slower and more somber. I pulled Mayuko to me, and with our bodies pressed upon each others, we danced. If I were taller,

I would have rested my head on her shoulder. As I held her and we moved to the music, I thought of how much I loved Mayuko, and how I, as an orphan who had been in and out of hospitals all my life, had never once had a girlfriend for so long. Even though, in the back of my mind, I knew we were likely in danger dancing so carefree within the walls of this castle, surrounded by so many elders, I didn't let it pervade my being. I felt happy, dancing with my best friend.

Mayuko unexpectedly, but intentionally turned us, so that while my head was still resting upon her small breasts, I faced Mirela as she drank from Mioara—a Communion of Ancients. Mioara's eyes closed in ecstasy as Mirela sucked upon her throat, and Mirela's eyes looked up, directly at me, but this time I forced a turn in our dance, turning away, like I didn't care, until I no longer saw Mirela's gaze at all.

"You should let me go, Cricket," Mayuko whispered.

"And why should I do that?"

"Because the imparateasa is watching us."

"She's watching me," I blurted out naively and egocentrically, not thinking that I could be endangering Mayuko's life by embracing her so tightly and openly in front of the antediluvian matriarch who wished to be my lover.

"She would prefer to be your dance partner."

"Then let her cut in."

"No, I must yield to her," Mayuko said, almost pleadingly.

But before we could settle upon anything, the music stopped. It didn't sound like the ending of a song. It just ended and the dancing stopped. Mirela pulled her finger from Miora's mouth, and Mioara curtsied and retreated back into the crowd. Mirela turned and left the room. Moments later Petru, Codrina, and the remaining four Eternal followed. Alexi Pavlovich rushed after them all.

And then I heard Mirela's voice in my head.

Come Orly, you are expected too. Bring your servant if you insist. It matters little to me.

I took Mayuko by the hand and made my way to the exit.

In the largest of the sitting rooms I had been shown in Castle Cobălcescu, a fire roared in the fireplace, causing ten shadows to dance upon the dim portraits that hung on its walls; however, it appeared that the sofas and chairs would only seat nine. As a mortal, I assumed Mayuko would be required to stand, and as there were two chairs set in front of the easel and pad of paper, I assumed Mirela would be sitting beside me. But she did not. Amongst everyone, Mirela took her seat first, but sat on the sofa nearest the fireplace. Petru took a chair that was most apart from the rest of the furniture. The remaining Eternal sat, with Viorica sharing the sofa with Mirela. This left me, Mayuko, and Alexi Pavlovich standing with only two chairs remaining. I was thinking of how odd it was that Alexi Pavlovich would sit with me when Mirela spoke.

"Alyosha, leave us," Mirela commanded.

I noticed the slightest curling of Codrina's lips as Alexi Pavlovich left the room angrily.

This meant that Mirela had requested a chair beside me for Mayuko—a mortal. Only moments before in the ballroom, Mayuko insisted Mirela was jealous of our relationship. I took my seat in front of the easel and Mayuko curtsied with her head bowed to Mirela before taking her seat beside me.

For some time, the only sound in the room was the crackling of burning logs in the fireplace, and besides the heat of the flames, all I could feel were seven pairs of vampiric eyes fixed upon me.

"Whom would you prefer to scribble first?" Mirela finally asked.

I looked around the room at the six Eternals and then looked at Mirela. "I don't want to scribble any of them."

"You will scribble all of them a thousand times if that is my will," Mirela replied sharply.

Say you have no preference, Orly. The voice belonged to Viorica, who sat beside Mirela, and came to me mentally. I made sure not to look in her direction as to not hint at her secret communication.

"I have no preference," I said aloud.

"Very well," Mirela countered, "I shall select for you." She turned her head toward the darkest corner in the room. "Petru, as you objected the most passionately, you shall be first."

I looked to Petru where he sat alone with a look of annoyance upon his face. "First, last, it is of no consequence to me," he sneered and then looked directly into my eyes, and then I heard his voice in my head.

As I said before, I know you have no choice, Orly. Draw us as you will, but do be mindful of what you say, and remember to never reveal the name Ji'Indushul to Mirela or to any of us.

I opened the box of black crayons and pulled six crayons out and laid five of them on the crossbar shelf of the easel. I don't know what drove me to do so, for in truth, I could have scribbled all of them with the same crayon if there was enough wax, but they didn't know how things worked and so I wanted them to think there was some purpose in using a new crayon with each new sheet and each new Eternal. The scribble of Evike from the night before was at the forefront of the pad of paper. Before I could reach to turn the page, the sheet was torn neatly from the pad, revealing the blank page beneath it. The scribble of Evike fell to my feet. I looked around the room. One of them had torn it off telekinetically. I suspected Mirela, but I wasn't sure. It could have been any of them, meaning to help or intimidate me.

I took the stake from the sheath Babette made me and also laid it on the crossbar of the easel and then looked at Petru and put crayon to paper and began to scribble. Once I saw his form begin to take shape in the scribble, I spoke. "You were born in the year seven hundred and one." I paused and corrected myself. "I'm sorry. You were born in seven hundred and one B.C., near Crişana at the foot of the Apuseni Mountains. You were turned at age twenty-five by a vampire named Mihai."

"That is enough," Mirela interrupted.

I lifted the crayon from the pad.

"No, my love," Mirela began again. "Please continue to draw, but do not recount aloud the tales of our respected elders. You will interpret for me at a later time as to not reveal any secrets that may be the cause of any humiliation."

"Come now, Mirela," Codrina interjected. "Don't treat us as fools. You care not for our humiliation. You want these drawings interpreted for you in private so that we will not know what you know of us and we will not have the advantage of knowing the secrets of our counterparts."

Mirela smiled. "The ever suspicious Codrina. How I cherish your ways."

I continued to scribble, saying no more, as the room sat in silence. I saw that Petru's maker Mihai was dead and that Mirela had set him aflame merely by looking at him. Within himself, Petru swore revenge just as I had for Yelena, but over two thousand years had passed since he made that vow. Would I too have to wait that long or longer to have my revenge if someone as old and powerful as Petru had still not made his move?

Elsewhere in his scribble I saw Mirela had also given him a relatively fresh wound three hundred years ago when Petru fell in love and turned a dark skinned Ecuadorian beauty with gray eyes. Her name was Ana Luiza. Mirela tore out her heart and beheaded her in a brief moment of rage when it crossed her mind that Ana Luiza may rival her own looks. As I scribbled him, mostly I felt bad for Petru. The majority of his existence of roughly twenty-seven hundred years was one of loneliness, and he remained isolated for the most part, often spending decades at a time in the earth.

"This isn't much of a party," I finally said aloud as I continued to scribble Petru.

"Eternity rarely is," Codrina answered listlessly.

"Mirela, I have a question," I said, pausing in my scribbling to look at her.

She raised an eyebrow and smiled without baring her teeth.

"If Petru is the eldest of the Eternal and he's just under three thousand years old, and you're over five thousand years old, how come there isn't anyone else in the two thousand plus years between the two of you?"

A chortle circulated amongst the Eternal.

"What's so funny?" I asked.

"They're all dead," Petru answered flatly.

"All of them?" I asked.

"It is true," Mirela said. "But they were mostly traitors, weren't they my children?"

Each in their own way, the Eternal assented in some slight manner.

"Wow," I said and began to scribble again.

"What wow?" Mirela asked.

"Nothing."

"Please tell us what you are thinking, Orly," Mirela said playfully, but I knew she was commanding me.

"It's just that in two thousand years, you'd think that there would have been someone you could have trusted. That you could have left one person alive."

And right then, in Petru's scribble, I saw the name I was forbidden from pronouncing—Ji'Indushul. The name was paired with the image of a sepulcher made of stone, with its doorway bricked in. Aloud, or in my mind, I wasn't sure at first, I heard the faint sound of a murmur just like the ones I had gotten so used to hearing while I lay at rest. I dropped the crayon, but it never touched the floor. Instead it sprung back into my hand. I looked around the room. It didn't appear that anyone else had heard the murmuring.

"What is it?" Viorica asked.

"Nothing," I answered. "I meant to drop it. I'm finished."

"Very well," Mirela said and then gripped Viorica's hand. "You shall go next, my dear."

EIGHTEEN

As the task of scribbling the Eternal endured under three hours, it was not nearly daylight when I finished. During those hours, I witnessed hundreds of years of passionate love affairs, all come and gone, each doomed in their own way. I saw powers I had never seen performed by Yelena or Zacharias. Powers of seduction, powers of transformation, powers of destruction, but not one had discovered a way to survive the stake or the sunlight.

Mirela was either generous or foolish by allowing me to see so much of what is possible. She did not know I already knew of the Oblivion from Konomi's guidance, but if she herself knew of it and knew any single one of the Eternal had also discovered it, she would know I now knew of it too. Be that as it may, I still I did not know how to find my own Oblivion. And as it turned out I saw that all but Vasile, the youngest of the Eternal, knew of the Oblivion.

In all six of the scribbles, the name Ji'Indushul appeared. It was present even in the scribbles of Trajan, whom I learned was fiercely loyal to Mirela, and Matei who was loyal out of fear of her. In all the scribbles I saw the same bricked in sepulcher, and discovered that within lay imprisoned a vampire of four thousand, four hundred years—a rival to Mirela and his name was Ji'Indushul.

Though the scribbles did not even elude to it, I knew with absolute certainty he was the source of the murmurs I had heard all the way back in Los Angeles. Why had he not just spoken to me with words, telepathically like the other Eternal had? Was whatever it was that was able to confine him to his tomb also able to restrict his speech? Certainly the source of such a power to restrain him had to be Mirela. But if she could imprison him, as it were, why had she not just killed him like she had with all the other Cobălcescu vampires who had grown old enough to rival her? Why was she keeping Ji'Indushul alive?

These were the questions that raced through my mind as I closed the cover of the artist's pad, dropped the sixth crayon on the floor, and picked up the stake off of the crossbar of the easel.

"Was the owner of that implement revealed?" Trajan asked, referring to the stake in my hand.

"No," I answered.

"Too bad," he replied.

"Yes. Too bad indeed," Codrina said. "It would have made the night eventful."

It was true—none of the scribbles pointed to a guilty party, though it would make the most sense to have come from one of the four who appeared to have some sort of allegiance to Ji'Indushul, as I could inform Mirela of their treachery. But it also made sense that it would have been the work of one of her two loyalists if they suspected my thirst for vengeance. The only one my heart wanted to trust was Viorica and that was because, quite to my surprise, her scribble revealed she had known Yelena and had been fond of her.

Without a word having been said aloud, servants entered the room and removed the easel and all of the art supplies. Mirela rose to her feet and the six Eternal followed suit.

"Shall we rejoin the others in the ballroom?" the imparateasa asked, and those standing assented.

"I'm exhausted," I said as I stood wearily. It was true. I hadn't scribbled so many people at once in a long time. "I would like to sleep now."

Mirela approached me. "Come, you shall sleep in my chambers."

I shook my head. "That won't be necessary."

"You will be safer with me, myshka moya."

"I have this," I said and held up the stake. "Come on, Button," I said, turning to Mayuko. I held my hand out to her.

Mayuko rose, and curtsied to Mirela and then to the room of Eternals before taking my hand. We turned and began to exit. Just as we reached the arched doorway of the sitting room, an unseen hulking strength ripped the stake from my grip. I let go of Mayuko's hand as to not throw her as I spun around in an instant, just in time to see the stake whiz through the air into Mirela's hand. All looked at me for a reaction. I looked into Mirela's face—her countenance registered at once both displeasure at being spurned, and anger for being disobeyed.

"Button, go to our room," I said quietly without turning.

Mayuko took a couple of soft steps backwards before turning and fleeing altogether. Slowly, I stepped toward Mirela, whose exasperation appeared to melt away as she received me in her arms. I slid my arms around her waist and pulled myself into her. I rested my head below her breasts and listened to her heart beating vigorously beneath her delicate silk gown. After a long moment, I pulled back from our embrace and she released me. My hands moved from her hips to her bare arms, just above her elbows. I looked up at her as she looked down at me. My fingers slipped down her immortally smooth skin, relishing her warmth, and she closed her eyes in pleasure. I reached her bejeweled wrists and then her hands. My right hand held her left, while my left hand coursed further, sliding onto the stake. She released it into my hand and opened her eyes. We stood looking at each other.

You are not fast enough to do what you are thinking, I heard Petru say in my head.

In truth, I had not yet begun to think that. I was so caught up in this moment of sensual tenderness that I forgot to kill her. I stepped back from Mirela, who said nothing. I curtsied to her and turned to leave, slowly enough to be afforded time enough to see Mirela bite her lip. It bled and began to drip rapidly upon the exposed part of her breasts above her strapless gown.

Mayuko had already undressed and was sitting on her bed wearing only a slip, with her arms wrapped around her legs and her knees pulled into her chest, when I arrived back at our room still holding the stake.

"Oh, Cricket," she said. "I had no way to know if you were coming. I couldn't bear to be left here alone."

I placed the stake upon the mattress and went to Mayuko, and wrapped my arms around her. After a moment I asked her if she felt better and, with some hesitation, she nodded her head.

"I need you to do something," I whispered softly in her ear.

"What is it?"

"I think there's catacombs under the castle. When it is day, and we are all asleep, I need you to find your way to them."

"Why? What are you looking for?"

"A tomb. One that is sealed shut with a brick wall."

"And if I find it? What do I do then?"

"See if you can break into it."

"Are you serious?"

I nodded my head.

"But how?"

"The bricks look old. Maybe they'll just fall apart or maybe you can chip away at the mortar," I said and grabbed the metal stake and held it out to her. She didn't accept it.

"And if I break through? Then what?"

"Just see what's inside it."

"Whose tomb is it?"

"I can't tell you that."

"But you can tell me anything, Cricket."

"But I can't tell you this. You just have to trust me, okay?"

Timidly, she took the stake. "I'm scared."

I hugged her again. "Nothing will hurt you as long as it's daylight," I said confidently, but I have to admit, I didn't know if that was actually true. Although I knew Mayuko needed courage, I felt ashamed lying to her.

The music downstairs died before sunrise, and those within Castle Cobălcescu retired to their places of rest. I was asleep inside my coffin as Mayuko quietly crept out of bed and got dressed. The task I had given terrified her, and what frightened her most was being caught roaming the halls of the castle during the day with a stake in her hands. She knew if she was suspected of plotting to kill a vampire while asleep, her mortal life would be taken from her immediately. Still, when she was ready, she went to the door of our chamber and opened it and looked down the hall in both directions. It was empty. She stepped out and shut the door behind her. Knowing catacombs would be beneath the castle, she had no reason to tarry on the level she was, and she quickly made her way to the staircase leading to the ground floor.

Once there, Mayuko reasoned that an entrance to the catacombs would more likely be closer to the rear of the castle than toward the front door. She walked the length of the great hall, inspecting the ballroom, then the music room, the dining room, the library, and other rooms, until she was back in the room where I had been scribbling just hours before. As this room was at the end of the great hall, Mayuko assumed she was now at the rear of the castle. There was still no sign of another staircase, but there were two closed doors on opposing walls. One was just as mysterious as another, but as the door on the right had a painted portrait hanging beside it of a man whose eyes seemed to follow her, she choose to inspect the door on the left. The doorknob turned for her. It was unlocked. Mayuko did her best to open the door noiselessly and close it behind her just as silently. A short hall led to a room enclosed in glass and filled with flowers, but the glass windows were all covered. It was the conservatory where Mirela had promised me a woman's body on the night of my arrival. Mayuko, however, had not seen it so she walked about the room admiring the flowers, wondering how they survived without sunlight. She examined the fountain closely, checking to see if she could move any of the spitting gargoyles; she could not. She inspected benches, but again she found no sign of a secret staircase, trapdoor, or any type of entrance that would lead below ground.

She left the conservatory and walked back down the short hall and took a deep breath before turning the knob, worrying that somehow it had locked behind her. But it had not. It turned as easily as when she entered, but she was startled when she looked across the sitting room and saw that the opposing door beside the painting of the man, who still watched her, was now open. She quickly scanned the room. It appeared empty, save for furniture. She quietly shut the door behind her, summoned her courage, and began to cross the room toward the newly opened door.

The eyes in the painting followed each of her steps, but Mayuko stopped watching the portrait when she neared the doorway.

"What are you doing?" a benign and youthful voice asked.

Mayuko turned quickly and saw sitting in a wing chair that had had its back to her, sat Luca, his feet not touching the floor.

"Nothing," Mayuko said quickly. "I couldn't sleep. I was told I could go anywhere on this floor."

"Oh," Luca said without interest.

"You're Luca, right?" Mayuko asked, trying to appear friendly.

"Yeah. We can't have stakes, how come you can have one?"

"Because my master is the special guest of the imparateasa. But wait, what are you doing in here?"

"I didn't sniff my dream flowers yet."

"Your dream flowers? What are those?"

"Do you want to go outside?" Luca asked, ignoring Mayuko's question. But Mayuko saw an opportunity to turn the conversation to her purpose.

"What I'd like to do is go downstairs. Do you know how to go downstairs?"

"Uh huh. But everybody is asleep."

"Can you show me anyway?"

Luca hopped off of the chair. "Okay." And he headed back down the great hall and Mayuko followed him. Luca was noticeably quiet as they made their way through the castle and Mayuko wasn't sure if that was natural for him or conditioned. Regardless, and quite to her surprise, he had led them to the double doors at the head of the castle. He placed his hand on one of the large iron rings.

"Wait," Mayuko whispered urgently.

Luca turned.

"We aren't allowed to go outside."

"This is the best way to go," Luca answered and went to pull on the iron ring again.

Mayuko placed her hand on his shoulder to stop him a second time, frustrating him.

"Luca, do you know what catacombs are?"

Luca nodded his head.

"What are catacombs?" Mayuko asked, quizzing him.

"You mean about the graves, right? You have to go under the ground."

"Yes," Mayuko said, suddenly fearful knowing he knew what the word meant and knew the way to them.

"I know what you're talking about. But we have to go this way."

And this time Mayuko did not stop him as he pulled on the iron ring and the heavy, but well oiled door slowly swung open and sunlight poured inside the great hall. The blazing sunlight hurt Mayuko's eyes as they had not seen the sun for days and she shielded her face as Luca took her hand and guided her outside. Once she was clear of the arc of the door, Luca released her and quietly pulled the door shut. As Mayuko's eyes adjusted, she was mystified and then horrified at what she saw.

NINETEEN

Luca ran out into the trees, visibly happy when the shafts of sunlight that someday he would never again know caressed his face. Mayuko stared in disbelief as she saw the forest standing so close before her, almost within arms reach, the same forest that covered the rest of the mountain she stood upon. Here and there, between the trees that had overgrown the grounds that long ago had had structure, were scant bits of rubble—all that was left of castle walls that must have fallen a thousand years earlier. She turned around and saw that even less was left of the castle she had exited only moments prior. There was no trace of the oaken doors that Luca had just closed shut behind them, and she questioned her own sanity, but concluded she was not delusional when she spotted one of the iron rings half buried in the dry dirt.

Whatever had once been here no longer stood. All that was were undiscovered ruins of a forgotten place and forgotten era. Mayuko took her first steps, still processing her observations, concluding that the castle and its walls were all an illusion—an illusion that could not withstand the sunlight. And that truth was why she was prohibited from going out of doors or looking behind the window coverings during the hours of daylight. She took her time as she walked through the woods, estimating the perimeter of the illusory Castle Cobălcescu.

At one point she knelt when she came across a rock that appeared unusually smooth. She used the metal stake to dig in the earth around it, carving away dirt, until she recognized the head of one of the gargoyles that had spit water into the fountain of Mirela's conservatory.

She continued walking, finally noticing that scattered across the ground were pockets where the earth had sunken, revealing pits of darkness. She crept up to one and peered inside and with the help of a shaft of sunlight, she caught a glimpse of a stack of human skulls, desiccated bodies covered in disintegrated shrouds, and the foot end of an old coffin. These pockets of sunken earth turned out to be the places where the ceiling of the catacombs of the castle that formerly existed had collapsed.

She wanted to run, to flee. All the way down the mountainside. She desperately wanted to put as much distance as possible between herself and this cursed place, but it was impossible for her to abandon me.

She scanned the perimeter for Luca. He was still at play, skipping through the forest. Though she felt protected by the daylight, she kept herself from calling out to him, desiring to remain as silent as she could, not wanting to tempt the danger that lay beneath her feet. And thus, as she waved for Luca to return, the only sounds to be heard were the sounds of nature—the occasional scurried movements of wildlife, and the wind whistling through the majestic pine trees.

When he saw he was being summoned, Luca lost his playful energy and no longer bounded with each step. Instead, he walked slowly back to Mayuko. Upon his return, Mayuko whispered to him as she gestured to the hole at her feet.

"These are the catacombs you meant?"

"Uh huh," he said in a loud voice.

Mayuko brought her fingers to his lips to silence him, but Luca shook her off.

"It's okay, everyone is asleep."

"Who do you mean by everyone?"

"Everyone. The vampires."

Mayuko's eyes widened. "Show me."

Luca nodded his head. "Over there it's easier," he said, pointing to an area that by Mayuko's best estimation would be the ground beneath the library.

She followed Luca to the hole he indicated. Mayuko peered into it, but a nearby tree provided too much shade so she could not get a good look inside.

"You wanna go first?" Luca asked.

"No, you can go first."

Luca smiled and then hopped into the hole, and made his way down expertly until the hole elbowed, and he disappeared from sight. Summoning her courage yet again, and with a tight grip on the stake, Mayuko entered the hole more slowly. It was made of dry and hard packed earth, with stones jutting out here and there, serving as footholds upon one's descent. When she reached the elbow, the space became more cramped, and she crab walked a short distance, with the sunlight becoming more faint with every inch of progress, until she could not see at all.

"Luca," she whispered, "where are you?"

She received no answer.

"Luca," she called again, slightly louder, but again there was no answer, and Mayuko began to panic, her breath quickening, until at last she saw firelight and she realized she was only inches away from falling through another hole.

Luca was standing on the catacomb floor, holding a lit torch. He motioned for her to come down.

Still gripping the stake, Mayuko moved the final few inches and then made the small drop to the catacomb floor below. It was noticeably frigid and she shivered, having dressed lightly. Slowly she made a full turn to inspect her surroundings. Where the circumference of firelight ended she relied on the few faint shafts of sunlight in the near distance to observe the deathly milieu. There were more stacks of human skulls, and more shrouded corpses, but most significantly, distributed throughout the room was a wide range of funerary boxes, coffins and caskets both, many of them new and highly polished and therefore out of place in this forgotten cavity of death.

Instinctively, Mayuko began tiptoeing, counting them as she went. One, two, three, four, five…

When she reached sixteen, the shafts of light lessened as the ceiling of the perimeter of the catacombs seemed more stable and thus provided more darkness. She asked Luca for the torch, as he was becoming too distracted and not keeping up with her as she counted. She switched hands with the torch and stake, and now carrying the torch in her dominant hand, she made her way through the darker expanse of the catacombs, with Luca often disappearing and reappearing in the firelight, not seeming to care when he was left behind in darkness.

She had counted to thirty-four when she stopped again, for the thirty-fourth funerary box she came upon she recognized as mine. She knelt beside it and thought of opening it to see if I was inside. But she talked herself out of it, for fear of what would happen to her down here if she woke a vampire, even if it was me.

The mere shock of seeing my coffin made Mayuko lose count, not remembering if she had ended at thirty-four or thirty-five. She decided there was no reason to start the counting over and remembered her original task of finding a bricked in tomb. So far she had not come across it. She turned full circle and saw no sign of the boy.

"Luca," she whispered, and as if he had been on her coattails all along, he immediately tapped Mayuko on the back, startling her.

"Luca, listen to me," Mayuko whispered. "Are you listening?"

The boy nodded his head.

"Good. Now, Luca, do you know what a tomb is?"

He nodded again.

"What is a tomb?" Mayuko asked.

Luca shrugged his shoulders.

"That's okay. Look, A tomb…it's like a little house. The one I'm looking for has bricks where the front door should be. Do you know if there is anything like that down here?"

Luca thought for a moment and then shook his head.

"Are you sure?"

Luca nodded.

Mayuko sighed in disappointment and resolved to keep exploring, but after a few steps a thought came to her.

"Luca. Luca, where are you?"

"I'm right here."

"Luca, do you know…" she went down on one knee to be at the boy's height and whispered even more quietly than she had been. "Luca, do you know who Mirela is?" and then she nodded her head and then shook her head, offering two choices to him.

He nodded his head enthusiastically.

"Do you know which coffin is hers?"

Mayuko was not sure what she would do with that knowledge, but she figured it was better to know than not know. Regardless, she was disappointed again when Luca shrugged his shoulders.

The catacombs were so large and contained so many alcoves that it took Mayuko over two hours to inspect it thoroughly. As there was nothing telling, no nameplates or inscriptions upon them, mine was still the only funerary box whose occupant she knew. Though she eventually came across an area of the catacombs that contained tombs, none had the bricked up doorway I had described to her. Instead, they had doorways that were blocked with iron gates, some broken off their hinges, with the skeletal remains of a long deceased mortal visible inside.

Just when she thought she had covered the entire space without success, she came across something unusual and unexpected in one of the alcoves—a wooden door that appeared new enough to not have rotted away, with stainless steel hinges, and a polished knob.

She turned around again, holding the torch away from her face, peering through the darkness, having lost Luca again. She whispered for him three times, but he never answered. With some effort, Mayuko moved the stake to her right hand and held it with the torch. She stepped toward the door and with her left hand she gripped the door knob. As quietly as she could, she turned it and gently pushed the door open. To her surprise, beyond the door was a well swept stone floor, the same type of floor that existed throughout the illusory Castle Cobălcescu. Mayuko realized it was more of a landing than a floor as a stone staircase, lighted with torch bearing sconces, ascended before her. She turned to look behind her. The door was still open, but there was no sign of Luca. She called to him repeatedly and waited, but he did not answer and did not appear. Though she worried about his well-being, Luca seemed comfortable in these surroundings, even in utter darkness, and so she decided to move forward without him, resolving to leave the door open so he would know where she had gone.

Slowly, Mayuko climbed the staircase. As the staircase spiraled upward, she could only see a few steps in front of her. She continued to climb and estimated she had wound her way up four complete circles, until she reached another landing. On the landing was an empty brazier and closed door, also with a polished doorknob. Mayuko deposited her torch in the brazier, making sure it remained lit as she did not know what was on the other side of the door. And now, having a free hand, she reached for the knob and turned it. The door pushed open smoothly.

A long corridor made of stone lay before her. Numerous closed doors were spaced evenly along both sides. Again, she turned behind her to look for Luca, but he was not there. Afraid to go on alone, she wanted to call to the boy, but resisted as she did not know who or what might be behind the doors ahead of her and might possibly hear her call. And so, as quietly as she could, Mayuko took a few steps forward into the hall alone, but then stopped abruptly. She wanted to find some way to prop the door open, as to ensure herself a means of escape and to provide a way for Luca to follow. But when she turned to look, she was met with quite a shock, seeing that both the door and doorway were no longer there.

The end of the hall, from where she had just entered, had no door, only a stone wall and painted directly upon it was a fresco depicting a scene of a vampiric gathering, full of standing figures with fanged teeth and at their feet, people on their knees with their hands outstretched toward the vampires and blood streaming from their throats. It appeared to be some sort of ritual, painted so long ago that all its pigments were dull and the figures appeared flat, lacking a third dimension. Their garments looked like things she had only seen worn in museum pieces or art history books. Mayuko stepped toward the fresco searching for faces she recognized from the Communion of the Ancients, and saw some that could have been the six remaining Eternals, most notably Petru and Codrina. But standing prominently in the center of the fresco was a woman with faded violet eyes. Undoubtedly, this woman was Mirela. With Mirela looking down on her,

Mayuko was frightened to touch the fresco but knew she must in order to see if the door leading to the catacombs would reopen. Mayuko extended the metal stake until its sharpened tip lightly touched the fresco. She was careful not to touch any of the vampiric characters with it, due to the trepidation she felt considering what the stake-to-vampire contact might produce. The surface was hard. She tapped it with the stake; it was made of solid stone. This was no exit. Mayuko stared into Mirela's dull but still piercing eyes and out of fear she took a few steps backwards to distance herself before turning again to make her way down the corridor.

The hall contained sixteen shut doors, eight on each side, and a single door at the far end of the hall. Mayuko wanted to know what was behind each of them, but was scared to turn any of their doorknobs. She put her ear to the first door on the right, but didn't hear a thing coming from the other side. She tried the same on the first door on the left, but it was similarly silent within. As she still had not located the tomb I asked her to find, Mayuko knew she needed to reclaim her courage and open each of these doors. Mayuko changed her grip on the stake, so that it would work as a blunt club, rather than a sharp piercing weapon. She felt doing so would increase her chances of survival if there were a vampire on the other side of the door and she was given enough time to explain she had no intention of plunging the stake through anyone.

Gently, she gripped the doorknob and turned it, pushing the door open as quietly as she could. To her surprise, it was lit inside, not by candlelight, but by an electric nightlight plugged into the wall. Having seen what she had just seen outside, this made no sense to Mayuko. She stepped inside the room and felt for a light switch on the wall. Just before she considered how ridiculous that was and acknowledged she had done it only out of habit, her probing fingers did in fact find a light switch mounted on the wall. She gripped the stake more tightly and flipped the light switch.

A bright ceiling light turned on. In an instant, Mayuko caught a full glimpse of the room's interior and when she saw the woman laying on the bed asleep, she quickly flipped the light switch back off. She recognized the sleeping woman as Adela, the vessel I had fed upon during our first night in Castle Cobălcescu. What was more shocking than her presence were the other contents of the room. An armoire, a chest of drawers, a writing desk and chair, a television and stereo system. On the far wall was an open doorway that led to a bathroom. Taped to the walls were posters of rock stars Mayuko only vaguely recognized. Altogether, it appeared like a dorm room belonging to a student away at college. Mayuko shut the door quietly.

She moved to the door on the right and opened it quietly. She didn't flip on the lights this time. Instead, she waited until her eyes adjusted to the night light. There were two beds in this room, and asleep in each were two more vessels, both male. Again, she shut the door quietly. This pattern continued for three more doors, until she reached a room with an empty bed.

This time, Mayuko stepped inside and shut the door behind her. Once the door was closed, she turned on the overhead light. This room had similar furniture to the others, but it was without decoration or inhabitant. What did that mean? Had the occupant been turned or killed? Mayuko walked into the bathroom. There was a tub with a shower and a toilet. Although she was hesitant to make any noise, after having come in from the catacombs below the ruins, she decided to flush the toilet to see if it worked. To her surprise, it did, just as it did in the quarters she shared with me. Everything inside Castle Cobălcescu gave the impression of a functional residence, but Mayuko remained puzzled as to how that could be when she knew what it really looked like outside in the daylight. She hit the light switch on the wall to turn the lights out, turned the doorknob, and stepped back into the hallway.

Mayuko concluded this was a hall of vessels which vampires in residence and their guests fed upon. As she contemplated whether it was worth the risk of waking a vessel by opening the remaining doors, she noticed something in the hall had changed. A door on the right, farther down the hall, was now open and the faint illumination of a nightlight glowed outward into the hall. Mayuko did her best to tiptoe silently to the open door. When she arrived, she peered inside and saw, sitting on the bed awake, was Luca. In his hands he held flowers that were of a dusky purplish hue. He was smelling them.

"Do you want some dream flowers now?" he asked meekly.

TWENTY

Mayuko did not wake me when nightfall came. Instead, I slid open the lid of my coffin myself and stepped out, and looked upon Mayuko who was still asleep in her bed. Her breathing as she slept sounded deeper than it normally did. I levitated onto the bed, not creating the slightest movement that might wake her, and lay beside her and let her sleep, even though I was anxious to know if she had found the tomb belonging to Ji'Indushul. As I snuggled next to her, I wondered what tonight would bring at the Communion of the Ancients. What would I be wearing? What would Mirela wear? Who would ask me to dance? Would I be asked to scribble again? Would I be loved or hated? But eventually all thoughts of the night before me slipped from my consciousness and my mind wandered home to Los Angeles. I missed Berthold so much, but it was hard to think of him now without coupling the thought with Kristy.

Nearly a half hour had passed when, out in the hall, I heard Babette's rapid footsteps approaching. Undoubtedly, she was bringing me a new gown to wear tonight. From out in the hall, Babette knocked gently on the door. Mentally, I asked her to enter quietly. The door opened slowly and silently and Babette crept in holding a new gown as I had expected. It was blood red.

Still in repose beside my best friend, I watched as Babette hung the gown on the dress mold and and then hung a matching sash over it, meant to hold the stake that she must have known I had no intention on relinquishing. Below the ensemble, she set a pair a red satin heels on the floor.

I hope it pleases you, Mademoiselle Orly, she said telepathically.

It does. Very much, I replied also using telepathy. And please just call me Orly.

Babette curtsied and made to leave.

I sat up slightly, careful not to wake Mayuko.

Babette, wait. I was hoping I could ask you for a favor.

I will do my best to meet your wishes, Mademoiselle Orly. Is there something about this dress that is not to your liking?

No. The dress is perfect. I was just hoping you could make a second dress for tonight.

Two dresses for the same night, Mademoiselle Orly?

The other would be for my servant. You see, she only brought one gown and has already worn it twice.

I sensed Babette wanted to sigh, but also sensed that she was not accustomed to sighing within Mirela's castle.

Any particular color?

I don't know. Red like mine?

Forgive me, Mademoiselle Orly, but I do not think it would be in good taste to wear such similar garments this same night.

Oh, alright then. Well, whatever you think is best. I trust your judgment. Should I wake her so you can measure her?

That won't be necessary. I shall have it ready before dinner, she said, and again made to leave.

Babette, I called to her again.

She turned.

Thank you, I said.

Her face hinted at a smile and she left, quietly pulling the door shut behind her.

Mayuko shifted in her sleep, perhaps at the sound of the door slipping into its latch. Gently, I ran my fingers through her silken hair.

"What time is it?" she asked sleepily.

"I have no idea. Time to feed."

Mayuko moved to rise, but I held her.

"I must get dressed for tonight."

"Not yet, Button. Babette is making you a new gown. We can lay here until she brings it."

Mayuko relaxed again, but only for a moment before she suddenly removed my arm from around her waist and sat up quickly.

"What is it? Don't you want a new dress?"

"I forgot. I need to tell you about what happened during the day."

"I know. I didn't forget. Did you find the tomb I told you about?"

"No. I couldn't find it. But Orly, there is something wickedly wrong with this place."

I sat up and faced her and Mayuko related everything that had happened during the day, how she encountered Luca, and what she saw as she explored the castle grounds. Though it took me time to comprehend, Mayuko explained how Castle Cobălcescu did not actually exist, that by day it stands in ruins, and all the opulence of its numerous rooms were only an illusion.

"That can't be true," I said. "Look at this room. Your bed. It is here. You sleep in it."

"I know it is. I don't fully understand it either, but I've seen the ruins. It is overgrown with forest. And I've seen the true resting place of your coffin. You don't sleep here, Cricket, you sleep in the catacombs with the rest of them."

"But the food. You've eaten it. I've seen the vessels eat it. If that was only an illusion, they would starve."

"I think it's only the appearance of food. Or something. I don't know. It feels powdery when I eat it. Like it's not the right texture of food, but it makes me not feel hungry. It's some kind of magic or just more of Mirela's powers. But there's more. There's something they call dream flowers, that when the scent is inhaled, it puts the vessels to sleep during the day so they may live nocturnally like the vampires."

"How did you find this out?"

"Luca. He doesn't always smell his flowers when he is supposed to because he loves the sunlight. He's the one who brought me outside."

"Button, you must not tell anyone you went out in the daylight."

"I know that. I'm more worried Luca will tell someone, you know? He's still a kid and doesn't think about consequences."

We could hear the noises of the party downstairs when Babette knocked on the door again. She entered holding a black ball gown in Mayuko's size. When I saw it, I was glad that I trusted Babette's instincts. Adorned in black, Mayuko would not be conspicuous in the gathering of Ancients.

After helping me with my dress, hair, and makeup, Mayuko got ready quickly as she knew I was hungry. I decided not to wait for Mirela and so, with the stake slung at my side, Mayuko and I headed downstairs and into the ballroom where many were already dancing in pairs. I made my way to the far end of the room where the vessels sat, in two rows of chairs, each vessel sitting quietly with an empty chair beside them. I looked them over, as I decided where to seat myself. I was curious about most as I had not fed on the majority of them. I considered tasting Adela's sweet blood again, but finally sat down beside Luca.

"Hi Luca," I said.

"Hi."

I took his hand. He turned and looked at me. I smiled and he smiled back.

"Do you remember your family, Luca?"

His smile widened and he nodded his head.

"Did you have brothers or sisters?"

"I had one brother and three sisters."

"And a mom and dad too?"

"Yeah."

"You're lucky. You must miss them a lot."

He stared forward and nodded gravely. "Yeah."

"I miss my mom too." I squeezed his hand gently.

He turned and looked at me again. I looked into his face and wondered if he would lose that innocent expression when he was finally turned.

"I like you, Luca. Do you like me?"

He smiled.

"Tell me you like me."

"I like you."

"Orly. Say it like that. 'I like you, Orly.'"

"I like you, Orly."

I leaned forward and he flinched slightly, but I only planted a kiss on his cheek.

Thank you for taking my friend Mayuko outside today and showing her the catacombs, I said telepathically.

"You're welcome, Orly."

Did you tell anyone you went outside today?

He shook his head.

Good. Do you think you can take her outside again tomorrow?

He nodded enthusiastically.

That's good. But do you know where there's a tomb that has bricks covering its door?

"Uh uh. Your friend asked me that too."

"That's fine. I was just wondering. May I feed a little now?"

Luca bent his head slightly, exposing his jugular for me. I leaned forward and lightly licked his neck before I bit into him. As I fed on his youthful blood, my eyes scanned the room before us. Musicians. Dancing. Drinking. Laughter. I thought of Berthold watching me feed, still wondering what it meant, but here, in this timeworn ballroom, no one cared enough to watch me feed. Luca's blood was flowing freely into my mouth and I felt renewed. Twice he squeezed my hand gently, then gripped it tightly, but I kept drinking. He tried to pull his throat away, but his strength was mortal and that of a child. As I bled him to death, I noticed I was now being watched. Mirela was smiling at me from the entrance of the ballroom. She had just arrived wearing a black gown with silver embroidered embellishments. All present bowed and curtsied, but she ignored them. The smile she wore grew the moment I felt Luca's heart stop. I let go of his prepubescent body and left him slumped in his chair, lifeless. By protecting Mayuko from the risk of Luca carelessly telling anyone she had been out in the daylight, I had stolen both his childhood and his immortal future. And there, standing in the doorway, seeming to view my actions as mere bloodlust, was the imparateasa who, in all her adoring smiles, couldn't have cared less for the little boy who had just died.

I scanned the room for Mayuko. She was seated at one of the round tables in the corner with other mortal servants, eating what appeared to be some sort of roasted meat with many side dishes. As she was animatedly speaking to the other mortals while eating, I could not ascertain whether or not tonight's dinner was real or felt powdery to her as well. Dancing and other merriments went on undisturbed for over an hour so that I began to think I would not be asked to scribble that night.

Finally, I rose from my seat and after taking no more than three steps, a beautiful and somewhat short vampire stepped in my path and bowed to me. He was smartly dressed and his black hair was slicked back like Bela Lugosi's. His skin was pale, but a tint more olive than most of the Cobălcescu Ancients.

"Miss Orly Bialek," he said. "Would you give me the honor of a dance?"

He offered his arm to me and I took it and he led me to the dance floor. I felt eyes following us, especially Mirela's.

As we danced I thought I was either becoming a better dancer in these time forgotten dances or he led me more expertly than the other vampires had.

"Once I was called Estero The Handsome, but for centuries I have been known only as Enrico."

"You are still quite handsome, Enrico," I said.

"I am quite touched to hear you say it, Miss Bialek." But it is my understanding that, at your young age, you have already learned to communicate telepathically. Am I correct?

I have, but it takes effort.

Well, I believe you are doing magnificently, Miss Bialek.

Call me Orly please, Enrico.

As you wish, Orly. We haven't an infinite amount of time before this song ends, so let me come to the matter I wish to discuss with you. Have you heard the name Ji'Indushul before? You may tell me truthfully.

Startled by hearing Enrico use that name, I forgot to answer in silence. "I have not," I said aloud.

Mind yourself, Orly.

I'm sorry.

You were wise to tell me you have not, but I happen to suspect that you have in fact heard that name and were told never to utter it. Am I right?

I have no idea what you're talking about. I've never heard that name before.

Well, as you have never heard it before, I also presume you have not located the tomb he is imprisoned in, have you?

How do you shrug telepathically?

Ha ha! You have quite the wit about you, Orly. I honestly could not tell you, even if I did know how. Certainly you have already learned how secretive we vampires can be, especially the Cobălcescu. But I am going to share a secret with you, Orly, if you would be so interested in hearing it.

Go ahead.

With the exception of the imparateasa, I am the only one living who knows where Ji'Indushul lies interred.

How old are you, Enrico?

I am not an Eternal if that is what you are asking. And if so, then how do I know of the name that is not to be spoken? And more importantly, how do I know where he is entombed? Is that what you would truly like to know?

I kept my thoughts to myself for a moment before finally giving in and answering.

Yes. I would like to know.

Ah, then I was right. You do know the name Ji'Indushul. But we both knew that before this dance began. Am I correct?

Yes, you are. I would still like to know though, how you know of him and where he lies.

Alas, young Orly Bialek, those are my secrets to keep. But allow me to tell you this. If your aim is treachery and you were in need of a worthy ally in that pursuit, Ji'Indushul is the only one among us who is old enough and powerful enough to challenge the imparateasa.

I had to think again. I certainly could not trust Enrico, I knew that much, but if he truly was the only one other than Mirela to know where Ji'Indushul lay, I would have to reveal that I planned to kill Mirela in order to gain that knowledge.

"If your feet are weary, you'll be relieved to know this dance is nearly concluded," Enrico said, letting me know the clock was ticking and that I had to decide whether or not to reveal my true deadly intentions.

If only there was a way to know if he too was an enemy of the imparateasa. Why hadn't luck been on my side and Mirela already ordered me to scribble Enrico? I took too long to consider my next move, for the song ended.

"The pleasure has been all mine, Orly Bialek." Enrico bowed and kissed my hand.

Just as he was about to release my hand, I spoke. "Enrico, would you please be so kind to escort me to the imparateasa?"

"As you please."

Mirela was sitting amongst a group of ladies. All, including even the typically cross Codrina, were laughing wholeheartedly. Mirela stood as she noted us coming her way. Each step toward her felt like its own eternity, and all were headed toward expiration.

The murmurs only you hear, Enrico said telepathically. *Ji'Indushul calls to you.*

With a deep breath, I decided to risk everything. *I need an ally,* I said.

We took another two steps and he still said nothing. I feared I had erred and my doom was imminent. But on the third step, which brought us within ten feet of Mirela, he finally communicated again.

The tomb of Ji'Indushul exists only in the Oblivion of the imparateasa.

"Orly, you look ravishing tonight," Mirela said as Enrico placed my hand into Mirela's, who then kissed both of my cheeks. "Leave us," Mirela said to the other vampires who, only moments ago, she had been reveling with. They all appeared displeased to have the attention of the imparateasa stolen by a child.

They left and Mirela resumed her seat and patted the seat beside her, signaling for me to sit. She took my hand and held it and we sat watching the dancers before us. I expected her to ask why I had killed Luca, but she did not.

"He's quite the smart one, that Enrico," Mirela said. "The theories he comes up with always amuse me."

Mirela had to be testing me. She must have known Enrico mentioned Ji'Indushul. But was it only theory that Ji'Indushul existed only in Mirela's Oblivion? I felt like I was being toyed with by both Mirela and Enrico.

"Look at them, all gathered here in my castle," Mirela said. "They only exist because I allow them to."

I was thinking that the castle only exists because she willed it. But instead, I said, "That goes for me too. I only exist because you let me exist."

She turned to me. "Yes, but I love you." And she squeezed my hand.

"You're only in love with my youth."

"Not only."

"And you wanna be my lover."

"Yes."

"And you think you're different than my pedophile?"

"You're not truly twelve, Orly. We both know that. But, you're also nothing like these old hags dancing before us."

"Ha!" I exclaimed. "You're the oldest hag here."

Heads turned in our direction, but Mirela only laughed.

"Yes. I am the oldest hag here. And you're the only one here who could live to say so."

"What about Alexi Pavlovich? Won't he mind losing his imparateasa?"

"Who said he would lose me?" Mirela responded.

"Oh," I said, suddenly feeling like I had grown up a little.

"Don't think of him, myshka moya. Just like the others, he only exists because I allow it."

"And if I say 'no' to you? Will I still exist?"

"Of course, my love. Until my patience wears thin. But you won't say no. Of this I am quite sure. But enough of this talk."

Mirela rose from her chair. The music died, the dancing faded, and all faced her.

"Who would like to feed the imparateasa tonight?" she asked loudly.

No one raised their hand or stepped forward.

"What selfish children I have," Mirela laughed. "I shall choose then," and her eyes scanned across her coven. "I would say for all those wearing black to step forward, but I am not that thirsty."

A cheerful laughter circulated through the crowd.

"Therefore, another color will have to do. Shall we say the color of our precious blood?"

Sitting in my red gown and red satin shoes, I was nearly certain the command to dress me entirely in red tonight came from Mirela, but did Babette know the reason? I searched the room for Babette. Our eyes met, but she looked away. She knew. Many other sets of eyes were also upon me now, but before I could stand, there was movement in the crowd.

Two Ancients stepped forward, a woman and a man. The woman wore a black gown with a necklace of large rubies. The other Ancient had long hair and it was tied back with a red ribbon that was dark enough one could argue it was closer to purple.

"Go on, knave!" A female Ancient in the rear of the crowd exclaimed and shoved her mortal servant forward who was dressed in all black save for a red necktie.

The woman wearing the rubies came forward first. Mirela ran her fingers through the woman's black hair. "Such a beauty you are, Zlata," she said softly and then pulled Zlata's head back, exposing her throat. Mirela drank and as she tasted the blood of her lineage, her eyes softly closed. Mirela released Zlata, and Babette was at her side to stick Mirela's finger with a straight pin. Zlata eagerly took Mirela's finger in her mouth and swallowed the drop of blood given her. She curtsied and stepped back into the crowd.

The man stepped forward next, smiling brightly. I remained seated and Babette still avoided eye contact with me.

"Darling Francis," Mirela said, also smiling. "Come, embrace your imparateasa."

Francis stepped up to Mirela and she hugged him tightly, her breasts swelling beneath his chin.

I watched as Alexi Pavlovich turned to the side and coughed quietly in his gloved hand.

"What century was it when I last tasted your honeyed blood?"

"The eighteenth century, my beloved Imparateasa."

Alexi Pavlovich coughed a second time.

"Time you give it me again."

Francis tilted his head to expose his throat and Mirela bit and began drinking his blood. She finished and smacked her lips. Babette approached and offered the imparateasa a pin, but Mirela waved her away. The audience gasped as Mirela offered her wrist to Francis. I watched as Alexi Pavlovich left the room, shamed. How often did he receive his lover's wrist?

Whoever this Francis was took Mirela's hand with apparent familiarity, and brought her wrist to his lips and bit into it. After perhaps only three seconds, Mirela's other hand touched his cheek and pushed his face away. Francis erected his posture, licked his lips, making sure to consume every drop, and then turned Mirela's hand over and kissed it, bowed, and from that moment, he was the man of the hour, having consumed so much of the imparateasa's blood.

Boldly, he strode back into the crowd whose eyes were again fixed upon me where I sat.

Mirela turned and looked at me and smiled but then turned back to the mortal servant who had been pushed forward by his mistress. Mirela pointed at him.

"Come," she said. "You have nothing to fear."

And a light chortle came from the crowd.

The mortal stepped forward with clear trepidation and bowed lowly to Mirela. Mirela said nothing to him before gripping the back of his head and sinking her fangs into his throat. Mirela drank longer than she had with the Ancients. The man's knees appeared to go weak. He raised his hands up to the level of Mirela's shoulders, but was careful not to touch her. The gesture made it appear he was being robbed at a bank. He was asking her to stop, but Mirela did not release her grip on his jugular. The man's gaze looked up to the ceiling, the candlelight of the chandeliers reflected in the tears that welled up in his eyes. I heard his heart stop and Mirela let the body fall to the floor and the crowd applauded their imparateasa. Even the mortal's mistress laughed and clapped her hands with delight.

Servants entered and removed the body. My eyes went to Mayuko. She struggled to remain expressionless in her black gown. I then looked to Babette. This time her eyes met mine and she didn't look away. She had saved Mayuko from the same deadly fate by dressing her in black.

For the third time all eyes moved to me. I was the only one left wearing red. And I was in all red. Mirela turned again, smiled, and waited for me to come to her, but I remained seated. It was a standoff and I could feel the electricity of silent telepathic conversations circulating through the Ancients. I made certain not to look at Mayuko in that moment, not wanting Mirela to notice her. But our deadlock finally ended as Mirela widened her smile as to not lose face as she gave in to me. She approached and resumed her seat beside me.

"My darling tragedy, what is wrong tonight? Don't you want to share your blood with your imparateasa?"

"Why would I want to do that?"

The electricity in the air surged.

"To show your fealty. You owe me tribute."

"What's fealty?" I asked, even though I knew what the word meant.

The audience laughed aloud, at the ignorance or irony, I don't know.

"It means your sworn loyalty to me, my love."

Could this be Mirela's plan all along? Was this the moment she would kill me? She had told Yelena she hoped she would choose my death over her own. But now Yelena was dead and Mirela said she wanted my love. Everyone was waiting for me to offer my throat just as Luca had offered his as I sat beside him. I had no choice. I would have to put my trust in fate.

But I did not lean toward Mirela and tilt my head. Instead, I rose to my feet, and watched her as she watched me, and I hopped onto her lap, and put my arms around her neck and she laughed. I felt the scales of fate tip in my favor. She would not kill me like this. I thought of the stake hanging at my waist but knew I would not kill her in this moment either.

No one's fangs had ever pierced my skin except while I was still in the hospital and Yelena bit into my jugular to take my life away from the cancer that had made my limbs so tired, my voice so quiet, and my eyelids so heavy.

"As you please, Mirela."

The surge in electricity again. I couldn't understand what the Ancients were saying, but I could guess. I had publicly addressed the imparateasa as Mirela, as only the Eternal did.

Darling dear! You are such the brat! Viorica said to me telepathically, laughing.

More seriously, I heard the voice of Petru in my head. That was an unnecessary risk, Orly. Mind yourself, please.

Mirela swept my dark brown hair aside, exposing my throat. I closed my eyes as I felt her soft lips press upon my skin. She kissed my neck and then bit into it. I could feel my blood pour into her mouth faster than it should have, as though my blood pressure were high, and that all of my blood wanted to be within her rather than within me. Was this a trick of my mind or an ability of hers that allowed her to drain her victims more quickly? The consumption of my blood lasted only moments, but I felt she had taken a lot, for I felt dizzy and drained of strength. I needed to sleep.

"My little mouse, your blood is sweeter than sugar," Mirela whispered into my ear, but I was sure our audience had heard every word she said.

Babette approached with her pin cushion, but again Mirela waved her away and offered her wrist to me much to the surprise of the audience before us. I quickly searched for Francis amongst their faces, to see if he was still beaming with pride, but in my weakened state I did not locate him.

I pushed Mirela's wrist away. She brought it toward my lips a second time, but again I refused it.

"But darling, you need your strength for your scribbles tonight."

I wrapped my arms around her neck again and pulled her throat toward my mouth. The audience gasped aloud and Mirela smiled hesitantly. It was the first time I had seen her unsure of herself.

Don't be reckless, Orly, Petru said.

What difference does it make where I drink from?

It's the symbolism that matters, Petru answered.

The blood will flow more quickly, Viorica chimed in.

Just bite! I heard but it was not a voice I recognized.

Be silent! Petru snapped back at whomever that was.

I moistened my lips with my tongue and leaned forward and kissed Mirela's throat, as she had kissed mine. I exhaled through my nostrils, releasing my breath over her dampened skin. I heard Mirela's eyes close. She yielded and tilted her throat toward me. The room erupted in silent exclamations as I bared my fangs and bit into the jugular of the imparateasa. Her blood was thick, and though I could not see it, by its taste, I felt it must have been of the darkest shade. Mirela let out a soft moan of pleasure. She shuddered in my arms. How many centuries had it been since someone pierced her throat? Something told me Alexi Pavlovich had never drunk from his lover's neck. How close could they possibly be? Is it possible that it had not happened with anyone since Marcel? The Marcel who existed before falling in love with Yelena? These were the thoughts that traveled through my mind, as I felt her blood filling my veins, giving me more power than I had ever felt. But just as I was beginning to recognize and relish in the ecstasy of this newfound vigor and energy, I was torn from her throat, by Mirela herself, and tossed to the floor like a rag doll. My eyes widened as I looked up at her.

"Greedy child!" she screamed down at me and then raised her head and began speaking quickly and harshly in Romanian, and what she said escaped my understanding until servants rushed into the room, carrying two chairs, the easel, large pads of paper, and an excessive supply of black crayons. After all were set in place, Mirela stormed out of the room with her personal mortal servants following quickly upon her heels, and the Ancients I had not yet scribbled solemnly lined up in single file behind the chair not meant for me. And it was clear then that I was to scribble them all that very night.

TWENTY-ONE

I was weary when I dropped the last black crayon on the floor, having just scribbled the portrait of the Ancient who was only thirteen years older than Evike. It was nearly sunrise, and most of the Ancients had already retired to their coffins. I had long since asked Mayuko to go upstairs to bed and she offered little resistance. But in the hours I spent with the Ancients, I became privy to thousands of years of their secrets. Mirela would want to know them all, and though I knew I'd never give her that much, I also knew I'd have to reveal enough to make it appear I wasn't hiding anything. And since Mirela was certain there were always traitors, I would have to hand some over to her by handpicking hidden memories that could be construed as treacherous from the histories of the Ancients I liked least. It felt like I was reliving my own short history—selecting victims, innocent or guilty, for Yelena to feed upon with a clear conscience.

I wondered how many of the Ancients understood this was the way it would work. I wondered if they realized just how much of them I could see in the black wax scratched onto the cotton cellulose sheets of paper provided me. I wondered if they were scared. I wondered how many of them were thinking of killing me. I wondered if the next stake delivered would be driven all the way through my coffin and pushed right through my heart.

And would Mirela take me at my word and act ruthlessly at any suggestion I made of disloyalty in her bloodline? And what about the Eternals? Would I have to accuse any of them to satisfy her? And if I did, shouldn't I choose the Eternal who, in truth, was the most loyal to her? That would mean Trajan. I already knew he didn't like me, so fuck him, right? But I knew it wasn't that simple. Mirela might trust him completely and then discover I had been lying and cherry-picking all along.

I didn't know what to do. I only knew I was tired.

I picked up the stake and rose from my chair. The few Ancients who remained watched me as I stretched, holding the stake above my head. A couple of them gave me a slight bow as I retired. I had either gained their respect or they were aware, after all, that their lives were in my hands. I left the ballroom and headed upstairs.

As I opened the door to my chamber, I could feel the warmth emanating from Mayuko's body and that comforted me and I became even more sleepy. But my hard won somnolence didn't last very long before my eyes snapped wide awake when I realized my coffin was not there.

"Button," I said, and placed my hand on Mayuko's cheek. She woke slowly.

"You're back."

"My coffin is gone."

Mayuko sat up and looked where my coffin had been. She appeared as surprised as I was.

"I'm sorry, Orly. I didn't hear anything."

I nodded my head. I wasn't mad at her. I knew who had taken it or at least who had ordered it to be taken away.

I didn't care about the house rules anymore and so I didn't hesitate to ascend the staircase to the third floor with the stake sheathed at my side. I knew Mirela was waiting for me there—her greedy child.

Thick curtains, the shade of dark red wine, were drawn shut along one wall. Judging by their size, the windows behind them must have been enormous. Again, I thought of Yelena, and the thick window coverings in her home that automatically lowered on a timer before each sunrise and how she had raised them via a remote control while lying in bed the morning she perished as the first rays of sunlight seared her skin, forcing her to cry out as she was reduced to a pile of motherly ash. I can still hear her screams when I think of it, and thought perhaps very soon, I would be tearing down all the curtains hanging here and watching Mirela go up in flames even if it meant the same agonizing and permanently destructive fate for me.

There were only three sets of double doors on the entire third floor, suggesting that the rooms, like the windows opposite them, must also be enormous. I wondered which I should try first, in order to confront Mirela about my missing coffin, but before I could make a choice, the set of double doors at the far end of the hall opened, seemingly of their own accord, for no one stood in the open doorway.

I traveled the length of the hall with an even and determined gait, but my determination and irritation began to falter as I neared the end. As I approached confrontation with the imparateasa I realized, despite what I thought earlier, that I was afraid of her after all. Her anger toward me when she threw me in the ballroom had engendered that fear. By the time I reached the doorway, I was the little mouse she affectionately called me.

I peered into the room. It was lit faintly by candlelight. The same thick, wine colored curtains covered windows that were as immense as those in the hall. A vanity table and bench sat before a large mirror. I recalled sitting on a similar bench beside Yelena at her own vanity table, but I was certain Mirela spent far more time looking at herself in the mirror than Yelena ever had. There was a pair of wing chairs and a round table on which a large vase of violets and a candelabra rested. Further from the candlelight, in the recesses of darkness, I saw Mirela's mammoth four poster bed. Above it was a canopy, from which sheer drapes, again the color of wine, hung.

Behind the drapery and atop the bed, Mirela lay in repose, wearing only a black slip that contrasted sharply against her ivory skin. She was alone.

"Come in, myshka moya," she said gently.

Her recent fury toward me seemed to have softened. I stepped into the room and the double doors gradually crept shut behind me.

"Where is Alexi Pavlovich?" I asked.

Mirela crossed one bare leg over the other without saying anything, yet in my mind, I had a clear depiction of her servants undressing her from tonight's ball gown while Alexi Pavlovich remained in the room. At first I thought it was my imagination, but as the scene played out, I realized it was not.

"Alexi Pavlovich," Mirela said listlessly.

"Yes, ma chère," he answered affectionately with a smile.

"You must retire to your own quarters. I shall sleep in my chambers alone at daylight."

Alexi Pavlovich's expression soured. "Because of that little chit of a girl?" he asked nastily.

And the image faded from my mind. Somehow, Mirela had mentally shown me what had transpired hours earlier, while I was still downstairs with my crayons and a ballroom full of Ancients.

Without moving a muscle, the drapery hanging from the canopy parted.

"Come, Orly, you must be tired," she said, wearing a gentle smile.

"I'm very tired. Where is my coffin?"

"Your coffin?"

"Don't pretend you didn't take it. Or have somebody take it."

"Maybe Luca took it. Oh, wait. That won't do. Luca is dead."

Her smile widened. She wasn't going to tell me. I was too weary to play games and her smile infuriated me enough that some of my courage returned.

"Bitch! Stop fucking around!"

And without seeing anything coming, I was struck across the face hard, and my feet left the floor as the force of the blow sent me flying back through the air. I landed hard on the plush, carpeted floor.

"That is no way to speak to your imparateasa, young lady. Now get up this instant."

I rose to my feet, nearly more angry than exhausted.

"As it seems you have no coffin in which to rest your weary soul, you have no other choice but to sleep with me as the sun passes overhead. Consider it a favor, my dear, for you will find that in my arms, you will regain your strength faster than you would in any coffin."

So this was her ploy. I would be forced to sleep with her. I remembered I still had the stake hanging from my sash.

"Shall you undress yourself, or would you prefer that I undress you?"

I was taken aback. Though I was wearing undergarments, I hadn't expected to undress. I must have taken too long to answer, for soon I noticed a glimmering at my feet. A small flame caught fire at the hem of my dress, as though someone had placed a single candle on the floor below me. Once the flame caught, it began to rise and spread across my gown. I knew we were not immune to the pains of fire and so I tore the dress from my body quickly, let it fall to the floor, and stamped out the flames with my red satin high-heeled shoes. The fire went out easily, but it had definitely been real and no illusion for the gown was scorched into ruin.

As I stood motionless in my undergarments, I noticed another feeling sweeping over me, one I had not experienced since I had been turned—I felt cold. As a vampire, my skin was naturally as frigid as a dead man's, but I didn't feel it unpleasantly, until now. Mirela was causing me to feel it, and I began to shiver. The heavy blankets on her bed suddenly looked welcoming. I knew I had no choice. I would have to go to her.

I stepped out of the pile of ruined clothing at my feet, removed my shoes, and began to approach her bed.

"Don't forget your toy," she said, and, from the discarded and charred garments now behind me, the stake tore from the sash and flew up into my hand. This surprised me. She put the item I needed to kill her right in my hand. But I didn't interpret the gesture as making it easy for me to kill her; I could just tell she wasn't the least bit afraid of me. But would she sleep even if I were able to force myself to remain awake?

I could kill her then. And after I did, I knew everyone on the floor below us would kill me, even the conspirators, but I would have avenged Yelena. I gripped the stake firmly and continued to advance toward her bed.

Mirela finally moved as she pulled the covers back, inviting me in.

I stepped up into the bed and lay upon the sheets. Mirela covered me in the blankets and then crawled under them herself. My body began to warm immediately, so much so, that I could tell that not all of it was due to the warmth of the bedding. Mirela had simply withdrawn the benumbing chill she had cast over me.

As I lay there covered, I clutched the stake in both hands like a deadly teddy bear, and struggled to keep my eyes awake.

"If you sleep holding onto that thing, you're liable to pierce your own heart."

I gave that some thought and realized she was right. As she let me bring it to bed, I also concluded she had no intention of taking it from me. So I rolled over onto my stomach and slipped the stake beneath my pillow, keeping it within easy reach. I looked at her as she lay beside me beneath the blankets.

"That's better," she said. "So tell me, did you find any traitors?"

I yawned. "You know I'm tired, do we have to do this now?"

Mirela moved closer and wrapped her arms around my body, pulling me into her warm embrace. I could not believe

I was now cuddling with the woman who killed my mother. But as we lay there in silence for what felt like an hour, I noticed that it was true what she had said—in her arms, I was quickly regaining my strength and mentally, I was becoming more awake as if I had already rested a full day in my coffin.

I looked into her violet eyes, and she must have seen my gaze had become more keenly alert, for she asked me again, "Did you find any traitors?"

"Of course I did," I replied.

"Tell me."

"Many of them are traitors to themselves."

"How so?"

"Most of them are bored and don't live the lives they want."

"They betray their true desires."

"That's right," I responded.

Mirela pouted. "Is that all? I don't care about that."

"No, of course that's not all. But I can't remember everything. I'd need to have the portraits in front of me."

"Agrapina!" Mirela shouted, and immediately I heard footsteps rushing down the hall. Soon there was a soft knocking at the door and a female servant entered.

"No," I said pleadingly, "I don't want to look at them now. I'm so sick of looking at them. Can't we wait till tomorrow?"

The servant stood waiting for orders.

"Leave us," Mirela said sharply to her and the servant promptly left.

I rolled over and, unexpectedly, Mirela spooned me.

My weariness continued to dissipate. I felt I would never have to sleep again if I remained in her arms. I thought about what Mayuko said about the castle being nothing more than an illusion and wondered if I were truly in this luxurious bed with Mirela or if I were actually buried somewhere in the catacombs, sharing her coffin. But my thoughts quickly turned as, in my spooned position, my orientation of the room had changed and I saw a portrait of a blonde man with a serious expression hanging on the far wall. I recognized him from Yelena's scribbles.

"Marcel," I said.

"I wasn't sure you knew what he looked like."

I rolled over and faced her again. We lay in silence for some minutes. I expected her to say something, but when she didn't, I finally asked, "What are you thinking?"

"I'm thinking about the past. That's mostly all there is to think about when you're immortal. If you haven't learned that yet, you will." She clutched me tighter. "And what are you thinking, darling Orly?"

"Don't you know?" I replied.

"Perhaps I do. But perhaps I want to hear you say it."

"I'm wondering why you loved him so much."

"That talk will have to wait for some other century. Do you know why Yelena loved him so much?"

"Of course I do. I scribbled her often. He was always there."

"Tell me," she said disappointedly.

"No. I think you're right. It'd be better to tell in some other century."

She went quiet again. Eventually I broke the silence.

"Do you love me like you loved him?"

"No. Not yet."

"But you could?"

"I am hoping to."

"But even though you don't know yet, you want me to be your lover?"

"Yes. For only lovers can achieve that kind of love."

"Are you sure you're not a pedophile?"

"Not in the slightest. For as much as I love your youth, Orly, I know you are no child. You are immortal. I told you this the night you arrived."

"But my body."

"In the five thousand years I have lived, I have witnessed marriages involving boys and girls even younger than the twelve-year-old body you currently possess. Though in some ages that was the norm amongst mortals, I myself have never participated in such a relationship. Regardless, as I told you I will give you a new body. Do you doubt me?"

"But until then."

"Until then will be just like after then. I will love you for you, the you beneath whatever skin you are wearing."

She wasn't like Joe. I could feel it in the way she gazed at me. There was a difference. She did not see me as a child.

Despite that I still wanted desperately to be rid of my childish form.

"Whose skin will I be wearing?" I asked.

"I planned to leave that up to you. Do you have an idea of the type of woman you'd like to look like?"

I rolled over in the bed and faced away from her.

"Ah. You know more than the type of woman. You already know who the woman is," Mirela said. "Tell me, who is she? Some celebrity?"

"No. She's no one."

"And what is this no one's name?"

I don't know why I said it. I knew I shouldn't have. But I did, because I was jealous. "Kristy," I said.

"Kristy," Mirela repeated. "And will I be fond of this Kristy's appearance?"

"Yes. She's very beautiful," I said with resignation in my voice, again revealing too much.

We lay speechless for a short while until Mirela asked another question.

"Do I have any rivals for your love, Orly?"

"Like who?"

"Like your servant."

My heart jumped, and I was worried Mirela had felt it. I knew she wouldn't hesitate to kill Mayuko. And even though I generally thought of Mayuko as a sister, I knew deep down that sometimes I had felt desire for her. It was difficult not to considering how close we were. But I lied anyway.

"No. I don't have feelings for her like that."

"And Berthold Leitz?"

That surprised me. I didn't expect her to mention Berthold. Until that moment, I wasn't even sure she knew who he was. And this worried me as my feelings for him had been far less buried than those for Mayuko. But again, I lied.

"No. He's like a father to me."

"Yet you are his elder."

"Only as a vampire."

"That is all that matters now, Orly. Your human lives do not."

"Well whatever, he's not your rival."

"And is this Kristy your rival?"

Again, I was surprised by what she knew. "What do you mean?"

"She is Berthold's lover, is she not?"

I didn't answer.

"You want the body of Berthold's lover, yet you say Berthold is no rival of mine."

In that moment, I truly feared for Berthold's life. I should have said something to downplay his significance to me, but I was at a loss for words.

"Do you know what five thousand years has taught me more than anything else?"

"What?"

"You must kill all potential rivals."

Thoughts came like flashes of lightning. She will kill Berthold. I had come to kill her for killing Yelena. Protect him and avenge her. My moment had come unexpectedly soon. Now! I must kill her now!

With all my concentration focused on vampiric speed, I thrust my right hand under the pillow, grabbed the stake, rolled atop Mirela, and with both hands and using all my might, I plunged the stake down to her chest. I saw her eyes alight as the sharpened point made contact with the surface of her skin.

A pain surged through my forearms as the metal stake vibrated so terribly in my hands as it deflected off Mirela's chest, not leaving the slightest blemish on her skin. It was as though her soft flesh were made of iron and I had just struck it with an aluminum baseball bat. She was impenetrable.

Enraged and defeated, I threw the useless stake across the room and it bounced off the stone wall with a loud clanging before falling to the carpeted floor. I had played my hand and lost, and though I was certain I would now die, I still had to fight. I raised my hand to strike the imparateasa, hoping to smash her fanged smile to bits, but before my hand could come close to making contact with her teeth, she caught my fist and with the greatest of ease rolled me off of her and instantly, it was I who was on my back, with her on top of me. I saw her open her mouth, fangs extended, her violet eyes gleaming as she thrust her face forward and tore into my jugular. As she drank, I struggled beneath her, my slip riding up my thighs, my naked legs kicking. But my efforts were fruitless. She was the imparateasa, the source of our bloodline—I could not escape her bite.

As my blood was drained from me, I began to feel my senses dim. I tried to think of Yelena, wanting my last thoughts to be of her, as that was all I could give her now that I had failed to avenge her. My struggles lost their spirit just as they had in the hospital when my leukemia had finally closed in on me. Resigned to my fate, I tried to relax as death took me again. Shadows from the candlelight swayed gently upon the ceiling. The wine colored drapes hanging from the canopy fluttered faintly. I felt her sharp canine teeth in my artery, but also her soft lips upon my throat. I was slipping into sleep. In the back of my brain I smelled the rubbing alcohol again. Memories of the hospital were washing back ashore. The stiff sheets. My numb legs. Staring at the patterns in the ceiling tiles. Waiting for nightfall. Waiting for Yelena. The faint pulsing of the heart monitor. It was slowing. I was dying. I allowed my eyes to close. And in the dream between life and death, I felt Mirela's teeth lightly pull themselves from my skin.

I had little energy to wonder what it meant that she released me. She had to know I was not dead. My heart had not yet stopped. However little, I still had blood in me.

"Little one," she whispered in my ear, "why do you hurt me so?"

I had hurt her heart by trying to kill her.

"Forgive me, Orly. Forgive me for Yelena, and I will forgive this."

I heard her words but had trouble reasoning them. She brought me to the brink of death and asked for my forgiveness. I was too weak to forgive or not forgive. It was too late. She had drank too much.

But then there was taste. Mirela had opened my mouth, and I felt blood spilling on my tongue. Her blood. Her thick and dark blood that had coursed through her for thousands of years. With her fingernails she had opened her jugular for me. She lowered her throat over my mouth, still bleeding, and steadily I felt all my senses returning. Her blood was life. In that moment, I wanted nothing else than the blood of the imparateasa. I felt my canines extend, and then felt Mirela's hand slip behind my neck. She pulled my mouth to her throat tighter. I bit, and the blood flowed faster and more freely between my greedy lips.

I don't know how much time passed or how much she allowed me to drink before she pulled herself from my mouth, but it was enough for me to feel renewed and stronger than I had ever been. With my blood still upon her lips and her blood upon mine, she leaned forward and kissed me ardently. Overcome with an ecstasy of an intensity unknown to me, I responded to her kisses vigorously. My hand, which only moments before had been wielding a stake, slipped behind her head, my childish fingers weaving their way into her hair, and pulled her face forcefully into mine.

As we kissed, our tongues commingling, somehow I began to understand that this vehement passion I was feeling was not due to the strength of the imparateasa, but rather that so much of her blood was circulating through me and my blood through her. We were bonded in a way I had never been bonded with anyone else. We truly were vampiric lovers, a state of being that could only exist between immortals.

She sat up, and a strap of her slip fell from her shoulder. She pulled her arm through, allowing the slip to fall enough to expose one of her breasts. I trembled. I was nervous. I knew this experience would be different than my experience with Joe. Mirela reached for my left hand, took it, and placed it upon her right breast. I touched it gently. She let the other side of her slip fall, revealing her other breast and her stomach to me. She placed my other hand on her left breast. I caressed them both, and my eyes looked to Mirela's for a sign that I could go further. Diffidently, I began to explore her body using both hands. I was enthralled by her perfection and bewildered as to how her incredibly soft skin had repelled the stake I had just tried to kill her with. She took me by the shoulders and lifted me toward her and kissed me sweetly before sliding my slip over my head, uncovering my underdeveloped breasts. I saw her glance at the diamond in the asymmetrical heart pendant hanging over my heart.

She didn't remove it. She didn't touch it. She said nothing. Did she know what the necklace meant to me? Did she know that the diamond was made from Yelena's ashes? I hoped not. I couldn't bear the thought of it being scorned, let alone being touched.

Yet with Yelena on my mind, I didn't feel guilty for what was about to happen between me and Mirela. Did that make me deplorable? Wasn't this act the supreme betrayal of someone I loved so much? Was I so overruled by my want of love or sex or affection that I could accept my willingness to forget Yelena in the moment and lay with the woman who had killed her? It seemed so and I didn't know how to feel about myself. I was twenty-two and only knew I wanted. I wanted it all.

Mirela eased me down gently, and I lay back as her fingertips glided from my shoulders to my ribs and then down my waist until they hooked onto my panties and she slid them off my girlishly skinny legs.

She lay beside me and her bright violet eyes stared into my own as she reached forward and ran her fingers through my hair. Her fangs were still out and she bit into her own lip deeply, causing it to bleed profusely. And with her lips, she lightly placed bloodied kisses on my neck and chest. The warmth of her wet blood upon my skin followed by the icy chill of her breath, as her lips moved over my flesh, caused my eyes to slowly close, enraptured by the opposing sensations. Her legs entwined with mine, and her mouth again found my lips. I was unsure of myself. Unsure of what I was feeling. But I knew I wanted to give myself to her as she was giving herself to me, and so with my fingernail, I slit my own throat, and my blood began to spill upon her uncovered flesh and soaked into the silken sheets beneath us. I raised my fingertips to my throat, coating them with my youthful blood, and then ran my fingers along her face, smearing her cheek, before placing my fingers, one after the other, to her lips. Patiently, her tongue lapped the fresh sanguine liquid from each of my fingers.

I was not certain what was expected of me as a lover and so I did my best not to think too much about it and let the moment take over. I rolled on top of her, enjoying the sensation of my naked flesh sliding upon her flawless skin. My throat, though already healing slowly, was still open, and my blood rained down on Mirela's breasts in large drops. I reached for her hands, slipping my fingers between hers, and then gripped them tightly. I extended her arms above her head and slid forward until my pelvis was up against the bottom of her ribcage, and allowed my bleeding throat to drip into her open mouth.

My self inflicted wound eventually closed, and I slid back down Mirela's body and sat on my heels with her legs under me. I leaned forward and rested my right ear over her heart. It thundered rhythmically in her chest. My hands explored her body—the pits of her arms, her collarbone, each rib that pushed against her skin. I lifted my head and continued down her body, until my thumbs were at her navel. I was trepidatious as to where I was going, but I felt myself being led, not by her, but by what was natural. My hands slid down her porcelain thighs until they reached her perfectly formed knees. I lifted my hands from her skin and extended my fingers until they were like talons. I ran them along the length of her thighs a second time, this time cutting into her flesh, creating ten rivers of dark blood. Mirela inhaled deeply at the pleasure of the pain I had just inflicted. With my right hand, I placed my fingers between her legs, and began to lightly massage her in the way I had learned to massage myself. But as I rubbed her gently, and though she was wet, my inexperience made it difficult for me to distinguish what was pleasurable to her and what was not.

Mirela's hands reached for me and she ran her fingers up the sides of my legs, her middle fingers sliding into the crevice between my thighs and calves. Was she trying to signal something to me about how to touch her? I wasn't sure and began to worry I wasn't pleasing her. I removed my hand and instead took her by each wrist as I slid further down her body, until I was laying between her legs. I kissed her pelvis slowly and then licked the blood upon her thighs from where my fingernails had cut her. The blood was still wet, but the wounds were already closed. I licked it all until her pale thighs retained only the slightest reddish hue, as if washed with a rosy watercolor. Mirela reached forward again and her long fingers weaved their way into my hair. I took this as a sign and responded by lowering my face between her legs and began to lick her clitoris. But as I did this, Mirela's fingers closed and she pulled my hair toward her, and I realized she was asking me to travel back up her body until my face was again with hers.

Our mouths found each other again, but this time, with our fangs still fully extended, we nibbled on each other, first upon lips, then necks, and then upon our breasts and nipples. In our nibbling we often pierced skin, causing rivulets of blood to surface. In each other's arms we tumbled in the bed, kissing and biting harder and harder all the while, until we were bleeding from countless perforations, and our blood-soaked limbs and torsos became nearly indistinguishable if it weren't for the difference in the size of our body parts.

"I want to taste you," Mirela whispered in my ear.

I turned my head and offered her my throat. Mirela bit into it, but only to make it bleed. To my surprise she didn't drink. Her open mouth moved down my body and I was overcome with a nervous excitement as I realized what she had truly meant.

She kissed me softly upon the smooth, prepubescent area between my legs. My eyes closed and my body tensed as she began to tease me lightly with her tongue. I responded, my body beginning to writhe slightly, and she reacted with a faint increase in pressure and rapidity. I thought the muscles in my legs were as tight as they could be, but they tightened even more. This felt nothing like it had with Joe when he had buried his pedophiliac face into me poolside. This was more than that sex had been, but how, I couldn't place words on. Was this love?

My skinny thighs gripped her head firmly. She was taking me further than I had ever been able to take myself. Mirela rose to her knees and sat back.

"Don't stop," I whispered, pleadingly.

Gently, she took me by the hips and lowered my pelvis to hers. With her fingers, she gently massaged me, before slowly entering me with only a single finger. She explored my insides without hurry. Her touch was soft as she penetrated me, venturing deeper and deeper within me. With her one finger still inside me, Mirela used her thumb to massage my clitoris. With her free hand, she pressed down on my lower abdomen, causing a sensation I had never experienced. My body twitched and I felt myself tighten. She continued, the rhythm of her slight movements ever increasing.

I gasped and inhaled intensely. Our eyes locked and she smiled faintly, and without meaning to, I bit my lip until it began to bleed. Mirela's lips parted. She wanted that blood. But instead of moving back to my mouth, she slowly slid me off of her, laid me back on the blood-soaked sheets and lowered her head again between my legs. The sensation of her tongue was now more than I could handle. I felt my blood rush to the tip of my clitoris and in my struggle to keep from writhing away from her mouth, I tried gripping the sheets, gripping for anything. Mirela slipped her fingers between my fingers, and closed them, holding my hands tightly, so that I was restrained just as my back began to arch.

A series of unfamiliar violent eruptions surged through my body. The flood of sensations felt like they had pushed me over a cliff and I was falling through the air. The bliss and the ecstasy I was experiencing rivaled the first night I fed on human blood.

Then a warmth washed over me and I felt disoriented. My body, still shaking, and covered in sweat, collapsed back on the bed, and all the energy was drained from me through a joyful transcendence I had not known was possible. What Mirela had given me was something I could not yet reason, but I knew in that moment I felt loved.

As our naked bodies were still coated in blood, I realized our blood did not evaporate as it did upon mortal skin. Upon our vampiric skin, it behaved naturally—it smeared, stained, and dried. I lay in Mirela's arms facing her, running my fingers along her imbrued skin as she embraced me. Filled with blood and having satiated something beyond love and lust, I had never felt so satisfied, but I also had never felt so confused. I was still duty bound to kill this woman who inspired feelings inside me that my heart could not interpret.

Were my feelings for Mirela real? Were they pure? Or was it only the exchange of our blood that lent me this amorous exaltation that left me stranded, overcome with joy? Though I wanted to resist my feelings, I knew in that moment, still in her embrace, I couldn't. And thus, in my struggle between love and hate, I felt love winning out. I could only hope that the mingling of our vampiric blood would not lead me into a fool's paradise.

I wondered what she was feeling. Fear of disappointment kept me from asking.

"What time do you think it is?" I asked.

"Just past noon," she replied.

In my undead existence, I had never felt so awake during the day.

"Why did you let me drink so much? Downstairs you called me a greedy child."

"Darling, that was only for show. You will drink again. I will give you power, Orly, through blood and knowledge."

"And the others will know? How much you've given me?"

"They will sense it. And they will fear you."

"And Alexi Pavlovich?"

"I don't love him. I never have. I love you."

"That's why you let me live? Even though I tried to kill you?"

"It's your youth that drives you to do the things you do. The lies you tell. I will continue to look past it until you mature as a vampire, if…"

She didn't finish her sentence.

"If what?" I asked.

"If you forgive me."

"And if I can't forgive you?"

"Then, in the plainest terms, with your new strength, you will be a rival, my love."

TWENTY-TWO

I must have fallen asleep at last. For when my eyes opened, Mirela was still spooning me, but the table with the wing chairs had the stack of scribbles laid upon it. A servant could not have brought them. Their footsteps would have awakened me. Had another vampire come with them and seen us in bed together? Had it been Alexi Pavlovich? If so, he must be enraged with jealousy. Perhaps it was Babette, for when I sat up, I noticed there were two white silk robes placed at the edge of the bed. The curtains were drawn and the sky outside was black.

"It's night," I said.

"Your vampiric powers are really growing," Mirela responded sarcastically.

"Shut up, your majesty. They'll be waiting for us. Well, they'll be waiting for you, is what I mean."

Mirela smiled when I told her to shut up. I got the sense the novelty of being spoken to like that excited her. But I also figured it was too soon to try calling her a bitch again.

"They can wait all night, for all I care. I wish to talk to you alone."

Though I could hear the vampiric festivities beginning two floors below us, I knew it was time to talk about the stack of scribbles. I slipped out of bed fully nude, my skin caked with our dried blood, and put on the smaller of the two silk robes. Babette surely made it, as it fit perfectly. With her skin similarly bloodstained, Mirela too got out of bed, covered herself and then took me by the hand.

Wearing our silk robes, we sat opposite each other at the table. Agrapina entered, bringing us both tea. Mirela laughed when I asked for scotch instead. It was brought to me. I drank a tumbler full quickly, poured another and began to sip it more slowly.

Mirela held up one of the scribbles. "Who is this one?" she asked.

"Catina," I answered.

Mirela studied the scribble before moving to the next.

"And this one?"

"That's Kronid."

She studied Kronid's scribble too.

"And this?"

"Terika."

Again she studied. And it went on like this until we had gone through the entire stack of Ancients I scribbled the night before. The stack also included all of the Eternal, Evike, and Babette. The scribble of Alexi Pavlovich no longer existed as it had been burned to cinders when I had tried to scribble

Mirela. When we were done, Mirela laid the scribbles on the table and began to mix them up, sliding one over the other, rearranging their order, like she were shuffling cards in a game of go fish.

She pulled one from the scatter and held it up to me. "Who is this?"

"Veaceslav."

Mirela glanced at it and nodded her head.

"And this one?"

"That's Byni."

Again she nodded her head.

Though I was certain she could not interpret the scribbles, she had memorized their shapes, patterns, and gestures, and put the proper names to them. She was making sure that each unique scribble was truly distinguishable to me and belonged to an individual in her brood.

"Are you done testing me or are we going to go through all of them again?" I asked after she tested me on four more.

"No. I am convinced. They are all recognizable to you. Tell me what powers you have discovered amongst them."

"Really? That list is really long. And you've probably heard them all before."

"We have until forever. Tell me."

"Well, like I said before, Evike can turn herself into vapor and plunge into the earth without disturbing the soil, leaving no trace. But many of them can do that."

"Yes. Many."

"All of them can turn into bats. But Simeon can also turn into a crow. They are all fast and physically strong. They can all read and learn quickly. They can all move objects."

Mirela stopped me. "I'm only interested in the powers you didn't know to exist amongst vampires."

I had to be careful. There were things I already knew about that I didn't want Mirela to know I was aware of, so I just continued, feigning ignorance at every turn.

"Many can disappear in their own shadow. Some can dissolve into seawater if they walk into the ocean. All can make candles extinguish or lightbulbs explode. All can communicate telepathically."

She interrupted me there. "Can any of them read thoughts?"

"Only the thoughts of mortals. None can read vampiric thoughts."

This answer seemed to please her.

"Can you read vampiric thoughts?" I asked.

"What do you think?"

"I think you can," I answered, but Mirela didn't respond. I continued.

"They're all unaffected by crosses, garlic, the cold, and poisons. They can make their voices come from other locations. All can fly. Not as high as you though."

Mirela smiled, but her smile quickly turned to a frown when there was a soft knocking at the door.

"My heart, may I come in?" It was Alexi Pavlovich.

The door opened without anyone touching it. Alexi Pavlovich entered. His gaze soured at once when he saw me sitting with Mirela, in our robes, covered in blood. It was obvious we were post-coitus.

"What is it?" Mirela asked sharply.

"The Ancients, they have gathered downstairs and await your appearance."

"Let them wait. I am under no obligation to any of them."

"Yes, of course. I understand, but they are in attendance at your pleasure. Many have traveled great…"

Mirela interrupted him. "I am speaking with Orly now. Tell them that."

"My heart, I beg you reconsider. That will only create unease amongst them."

Mirela looked at me. "He is tiresome, is he not?"

I looked at Alexi Pavlovich, but did not answer her.

"Send him away," Mirela said. It was a command, and I was the only other person in the room.

"Go away," I said flatly, not taking my eyes off of him.

Alexi Pavlovich huffed, turned, and stormed out of the room. The door slammed shut behind him. Again, no one had touched it.

Mirela laughed and it was infectious. Soon we were both laughing wildly like childhood friends. When it finally passed, Mirela asked that I continue. I emptied my tumbler first.

"All can charm mortals through gaze or voice or through touch. Some can pass through walls."

"Who can pass through walls?" Mirela asked.

The fact that this skill interested her told me it was not common and was probably very difficult to accomplish. I had to go through the stack of scribbles and I set aside ten—all six of the Eternal and four Ancients. Mirela simply nodded.

"All can hold those weaker than them in place, making it impossible for them to move their limbs."

"Have you learned that skill yet?" she asked me.

"No. But I haven't tried."

"Now, with my blood in your veins, it should come to you more easily. Go on."

"You're the only one impenetrable by a stake. No one can withstand fire or sunlight."

"How many can create fire just by willing it?"

"Almost all of them can do it like you did with my dress or light candles. But only a few can make something like a person burst into flames."

"That's only the Eternal, correct?" Mirela asked, again seeming concerned.

"Yes. But only the four oldest of the Eternal."

Mirela nodded again, a grave expression passing over her face.

"Petru and Codrina can make a mortal or a vampire bleed out through their facial orifices just by looking at them."

"Interesting," Mirela said listlessly.

"Trajan can slit someone's throat just by willing it."

Mirela nodded.

Did that nod and her being unimpressed by all the feats I described mean she could accomplish all of them as well?

"Some have killed other vampires. Terika, Neculai, and Rasvan killed their makers."

"I did not know about Rasvan," Mirela mused.

I wondered if Rasvan would be killed.

"Some of the Ancients have gone more than ten years without drinking human blood. With the Eternal, the longest seems to be about a hundred and twenty years. Not all of the Ancients have gone to ground before. Every single one of them has had their heart broken. And Viorica can make a mortal's heart burst. That's about it."

"That's about it?" she asked.

I couldn't tell if she was testing me.

"Well, except some of them think of something they call the Oblivion. I feel like it's a place they go to. Do you know where that is?"

Mirela didn't answer me. She changed the subject.

"Did you find out who drove the stake into your coffin?"

"No, I didn't. You didn't have me draw any mortals, but it couldn't have been one of them anyway, because they would have woken me. And you won't let me draw you. That means you did it, doesn't it?"

"No, Orly. It does not mean that. It was not me, I promise you."

"But I drew everyone else."

"Think on it, Orly. You'll figure it out," Mirela said and sipped her tea.

I heard those downstairs erupt into laughter. I wondered what was so funny. I wondered if Mayuko was safe. I poured another scotch and drank it in a single swallow.

"Before the stake appeared," I said, "I already drew Evike and Alexi Pavlovich."

"Precisely. Draw them again and you will find your culprit."

I filled my tumbler again.

"It wasn't Evike," I said.

"How are you so sure?"

"I just know. That means it was Alexi Pavlovich or you."

"Then you do not believe the promise I just made to you that it was not me."

"I would be stupid to take someone's word for it, especially yours."

"You are wiser than I knew, myshka moya."

"Let me draw you then," I asked.

"Never."

A moment of silence passed between us. Mirela crossed her legs the other way.

"None of the Ancients or the Eternal were made by you. How come?" I asked.

"My blood is too powerful. Any vampire I made would eventually grow strong enough to rival me."

"You gave me a lot."

"What does that tell you?"

I knew what she wanted me to say. I didn't want to say it, but I didn't know how not to say it in that moment.

"That you love me," I said.

Her lips curled into a smile and her fangs slipped out.

"So tell me, who are the traitors?" she asked.

Though her changing the subject left me wondering if it were she or Alexi Pavlovich who thrust the stake into the lid of my coffin, it also allowed me to feel successful in not telling her all of the powers I witnessed, such as Petru being able to make his blood gelatinous so it was difficult for him to bleed or be bled, or Codrina being able to turn to ash as though she had been swallowed by the sunlight. Despite those successes, I knew the moment I dreaded was finally here. I would now have to accuse and sentence immortals who had lived for hundreds of years to what I imagined would be horrible deaths. Though it felt hopeless, I would at least try to evade answering.

"How am I supposed to know who are traitors? It's not like they have secret meetings to talk about how to kill you."

"Who does want to kill me?"

I lied. "None of them, as far as I can tell. They're too afraid of you."

"I don't believe you, Orly. There are traitors and if you protect them, you are a traitor yourself."

"I don't think you know how this works. When I look at the scribbles I see years and years of things that have happened to them. A lot of it I don't even understand. And it's not like any of them have the word 'traitor' written on their foreheads when I draw them. You have to tell me what I'm looking for and then I'll be able to tell you if it shows up in their scribble."

I drank again.

"I see. That is helpful to know. Then let's try this another way, Orly, my dear."

The way she said, "Orly, my dear" had a weird tone to it, something close to annoyance. It felt odd since we had just been saying how she loved me.

"After me, who is the oldest of the Cobălcescu?"

"Petru," I answered.

"No one older?"

"Well, there is one named Ji'Indushul, but I think he's dead."

"What makes you think that?"

"Because all I see is a tomb and he is not here for the Communion of the Ancients."

"You see the tomb in the scribbles. Whose scribbles, Orly?"

"I'd have to look through them again."

"Then look," Mirela answered firmly.

But I didn't have to look, and I was pretty sure she knew I was stalling. How could I lie my way out of this and keep any potential allies safe by saying they were ignorant of Ji'Indushul? I couldn't think of a way in which she would believe me, so I told the truth, which I reasoned wouldn't cause too much harm, since it included those loyal to her and those not.

"All six of the Eternal know who he is. Nobody else."

"You're forgetting one person," she answered.

"Who?"

"You. I suspect you had already heard the name before you drew any of the Eternal."

She suspected. She couldn't read my mind. She either wanted me to know that or she wasn't as smart as Berthold insisted or she was truly the most deceitful person I ever encountered.

"Then why did you play games with me through Enrico?" I asked defensively. "I saw when I drew him you told him to mention the Oblivion and Ji'Indushul to me, even though he doesn't know what either one means. You did that just to test me. Are you going to have to kill Enrico now that he knows the name Ji'Indushul?"

"Maybe I should. And yes, you're right. I did tell him to say what he said to you. But when he told you Ji'Indushul only exists in my Oblivion, you understood what he meant even if he didn't. So who told you, Orly?"

"Tell me you love me," I deflected.

"I love you," Mirela answered without hesitation.

"Then if you love me, don't make me do this."

"If you loved me, Orly, you should want to do it."

I drank again, just for the sake of pause.

"I see then that you do not," Mirela said softly, sadly.

I almost blurted out that it wasn't true. That I did love her. But then I didn't know if I really did or if some part of me just didn't want to hurt her. With her blood pumping through my heart I didn't know what my true feelings were. I didn't know how to separate my heart from her blood.

"I already knew about the Oblivion before I came here. Konomi told me about it," I said, hoping to satisfy her.

"Konomi told you. The Ketsuen cunt."

"She's my friend."

"I'm older than she is, by thousands of years."

"I know. But she was made by Hisashi, one of the original eleven. That makes her powerful. Maybe even more powerful than you."

"Not likely," Mirela answered, dismissively.

"You know, there is someone all of the Eternal and Ancients know about who is older than you and Ji'Indushul— your maker, Mikonost. And everyone knows you beheaded him yourself. How come?"

"He was weak."

"But he was your maker. He had to be stronger."

"Not weak like that. He was weak in heart. He could not lead us. I wouldn't expect you to know this, but long ago there were more bloodlines than eleven. Many more. The eleven is just what was left after the great war. Had I not killed him and ruled in his place, there would only be ten bloodlines today and the Cobălcescu would not be amongst them."

"Did you love him?"

"Only for a few hundred years. When I saw the war coming and saw he was weak, I began to despise him."

"Did he make Ji'Indushul?"

"No."

"Then did you?"

She exhaled out the side of her mouth as if she was exhaling cigarette smoke and not wanting to blow it in my face.

"Who wants to set Ji'Indushul free?" she asked, not answering my question.

"Free him? Nobody. They all think he's dead."

"You're lying."

"Tell me who he is, Mirela, and I'll tell you who."

"He's a traitor. Punished for eternity."

"Punished by you?"

"Yes.

"Why didn't you just kill him? 'Kill all rivals' you said."

"It pleases me to let him wallow in pain."

"How long has he been in pain?"

"Over three thousand years."

How is she like this? I wondered. Was she always so cruel? Would I even want Mirela to linger in pain that long? Especially now with the way my feelings had shifted. No. That wasn't accurate. My feelings hadn't shifted. My original feelings for vengeance remained, but now I had new feelings to set beside them.

"Don't ever betray me, Orly," Mirela said with the utmost seriousness and I feared her more than ever.

Quietly, for fear of her answer, I asked, "How did he betray you?"

"He stopped serving his imparateasa."

"That's it?" I asked incredulously. "I don't even want to serve you. I'm not ever gonna serve anyone."

"Like it or not, Miss Bialek, you are part of my bloodline, and all those in my bloodline owe their allegiance to me, and live only at my pleasure."

"Fuck you," I said, but she didn't react angrily as I expected.

She moved on and said flatly, "Now it's your turn. Who wants to free him?"

"I do," I said, annoyed at her supremacy.

A warmth began to spill over my face. I soon noticed I was bleeding—through my ears, eyes, and mouth. She was exhibiting the power I had seen only in Petru and Codrina.

In my most brattish voice, I said defiantly, "Let it all run out. See if I give a shit."

We sat looking at each other and she let me continue to bleed out.

I shut my mouth and let it fill and then spit blood across the scattered scribbles on the table. "There, I just spit on the ones who wanna let Ji'Indushul out. Is that loyal enough for you?"

But of course my blood had only stained those who, by chance alone, happened to be at the top of the piles. They weren't even the Eternal, so of course it couldn't be true.

"I want to love you," I said with still more blood in my mouth. "But I don't want to spend an eternity telling you which friends to kill."

A sadness passed over her face and moments later I felt my blood begin to coagulate. She wouldn't bleed me to death.

My little body fit comfortably between her comely legs as I sat with my back upon her breasts. The bathwater, which never grew cold, was tinged red with the blood she washed from our bodies.

The castle was finally quiet. Daylight had certainly come, but I was still awake, and unfatigued in her embrace. In our relaxed state, we spoke in hushed tones.

"We missed the party," I said.

"I care little about that."

"But some of them were probably hoping to taste your blood."

"I care even less about that. I enjoy your company far more."

"Think they're scared I betrayed them with all the scribbles?"

"I wish you would betray them, Orly. I would give you everything for that."

"Would you even bring me to your Oblivion?"

"I said everything, didn't I?"

"Yeah, that's what you said, but I could kill you there if I wanted to. Because you'd be mortal."

"Then I shall have to wait, until I actually believe you love me. Right now, I suppose I only lie to myself, pretending that you do."

"But maybe I already do," I said. And in that moment, I meant that much. It wasn't for sure, but it was at least a maybe.

She kissed my right ear.

"What is the Oblivion like?" I asked.

"Didn't Konomi show you?"

Yes, of course she knew Konomi showed me.

"Yeah, she did. But I meant, what is yours like?"

"It's a very old place. A lonely place. The world looked much different then."

I remembered night being darker despite there being more stars in the sky in Konomi's Oblivion.

"Remember when I tried to draw you? Before you set the paper on fire? I saw your eyes in the scribble. I knew they were yours because they were violet. There was fire reflected in them."

"Yes. I remember it quite well."

I didn't know if she meant she remembered me trying to draw her or if she remembered the fire in her eyes.

"What do you think my Oblivion is like?" I asked.

"I could only guess," she answered, and again there was a sadness in her voice.

"But you do have a guess?"

"I'll tell you a secret, Orly. Not everyone has a way to the Oblivion."

That revelation disappointed me. If I had an Oblivion, I wanted a way to get there.

She kissed my right ear again and then nibbled on it. Hours earlier, Agrapina replaced the bedding that had been drenched in our blood. I longed for the moment Mirela would lift me out of the tub, lay me on her bed, and make love to me again. My tongue felt the sharpness of my fangs. I wanted more of her blood and I was dying to give her more of mine.

TWENTY-THREE

Kristy pulled herself closer to Berthold as they lay in her bed together. Though he had been sweating only moments earlier, Kristy had grown accustomed to the frigidity of her lover's vampiric body. Her feelings for him continued to swell. And even though she recognized Berthold truly loved her, Kristy slipped into a postcoital dysphoria as she knew their love would not last forever. He could not turn her. If she took his blood it would only kill her with no hope of resurrection. She would quell this feeling by asking herself why she felt entitled to more than the lifetime she had been born with. But despite her best efforts, the feeling would always return when she felt his love for her.

"You're quiet tonight. What are you thinking?" Berthold asked her.

"You're quiet every night," Kristy responded and they both uttered a stifled laugh.

"Something is on your mind though. What is it? You can tell me."

"I'm thinking about getting older while you don't."

"Ah, I see. I think of that myself, quite often actually."

"What are we going to do?"

"What can be done?"

Kristy hesitated, and though Berthold could guess what she was going to say, he waited for her to say it.

"You could ask Zacharias. He's old enough to turn me."

He held her more tightly.

"Kristy, would you really want this life? Living in eternal darkness?"

"I want you is what I want. And I don't want to be old by the time I get it."

"You have me, but I understand your meaning. But you have to understand, it also means you will be turned into a murderer. And you will murder every night."

"You told me the guilt leaves you when you are turned."

"But you're not turned. You're making the choice right now with your own conscience to murder."

Kristy grew silent.

Berthold kissed her full lips. "Believe me. I don't want to lose you either. But it's also not easy asking another vampire for their blood. Not for the purpose of turning a mortal. There's no explanation for that sentiment, but instinctually, there's an impropriety in such a request."

"But he's your friend."

He turned his head away from her on the pillow they were sharing, faced forward, and stared at the ceiling. "I'll think about it, but I can't give it my full attention right now, not until Orly is home safe. I hope you understand."

"I do," Kristy responded and then reached for his face to make him look at her. "She's lucky to have you."

They lay in silence until Kristy fell asleep, and while she was dreaming, Berthold slipped out from under the covers and climbed inside the casket they had shopped for together and placed beside her bed.

Zacharias Underland sat on the wooden fence that lined the large pen, watching pigs feast on the naked corpse of the street hustler he had picked up on Melrose earlier that night. He stared at the pigs blankly, lost in thought, as they tore away at the flesh, disfiguring the young man's face until his skull was all that was left of his humanity.

His thoughts went to me—not in regard to my safety and quick return, the way Berthold fixated. He was thinking of my pain and hoping Mirela would make my death a quick one, for Zacharias knew how pleasurable cruelty could be within our race and did not expect me to survive. He knew when the invitation arrived it was a death sentence. It was for this reason he did not tell me he loved me when we said our goodbyes, as he had never told me those words before. He suspected if he suddenly said it in that moment, his expectation of my demise would have been made clear. Still staring at that skull in the mud, he wished Alexi Pavlovich had never come to Los Angeles with that deadly invitation.

"Who made you?" he had asked me so many years ago, when he encountered me just off the Hollywood Walk of Fame, on the second night of my vampiric existence. I had just killed a man for the first time on my own, and I had not planned ahead on what to do with the corpse. I didn't answer him.

"I could make you tell me."

"Then make me," I had said, trying to appear fearless.

A wistful smile passed upon Zacharias' lips as he remembered the posture I took as I stood before him defiantly.

Immortality is painful, he thought, as he looked upon two pigs fighting for a femur. *What a brave little girl.*

Zacharias was certain he would never see me again.

"Do you want more?"

Hisato shook his head and Grace pushed the five inch mirror off the table of the crescent shaped booth where they both sat. It fell onto the floor of the nightclub, smashing to bits, a snowfall of cocaine blanketing the slivered reflections of the spinning lights overhead in the aftermath.

"O what can ail thee, knight-at-arms, so haggard and so woe-begone?" Grace recited.

"Your fascination with Keats, that's what," Hisato answered dejectedly.

"Okay. I'm being serious, Poo Boo," Grace responded. "Tell me."

Hisato downed the rest of his drink and pushed the glass away from him. "I'm just thinking about Yelena."

Grace leaned over and kissed his face. "I know how much you miss her. But it's okay Poo Boo. When I think of Yelena, knowing her as I did, some part of me thinks she's happier no longer having this immortality of ours and all the things that come with it."

"I know. But it's not that that I'm thinking about. I just wonder what she would have done if she were still alive."

"About Orly?"

"Yeah, about Orly. Who else?"

"What could she have done?"

"I don't know. She always seemed to come up with something."

"She probably would have tried to sacrifice herself."

"Yeah, I've had that thought too. She would die a million times over for that little brat. Still, I wish she hadn't fucking gone."

"We talking about Orly?" Darcy asked, as she and Corinne slid into the booth.

"Yeah," Grace answered.

"She's going to be alright," Darcy replied. "That girl is smarter than everyone thinks."

"Yeah, but she's reckless. She doesn't think before she acts," Corrine said phlegmatically.

"Cheers to that," Hisato said, raising Grace's champagne glass before downing it. "Let's get out of here. Come on, let me out."

"Where to?" Darcy asked.

"Let's go drive off a cliff," he replied.

"Oh fun!" Grace giggled, clapping her hands in approval.

The following night, when Berthold opened the lid to his casket and rose, he looked to the bed. It was unmade, but Kristy was not there. She having long since adjusted to his nocturnal lifestyle, he thought nothing of it and expected to find her in the kitchen, having breakfast while reading the news on her iPad. But there was no aroma of toast or scrambled eggs, not even coffee. The shower was not running. As he stepped out of his casket he focused his senses, narrowing them for any sounds of life or her scent but she was not in the house.

He exited her bedroom and walked down the hall into the living room and then stopped abruptly when he saw them.

"Berthold Leitz. It is an honor," one of the three vampires he did not recognize said, bowing courteously.

Two men and a woman. They were all much older than he was and he had not detected their presence. Confused by their appearance within Kristy's house, he said nothing, courteous or otherwise, and he was right not to trust their smiles. Fangs bared, the three flew at him. They were faster than he was and soon Berthold was in their grasp, slammed to the floor, his back smashing the Spanish tiles below him. While wondering who they were and whether they were here to kill him, Berthold quickly reasoned that by their age, one of them would have been sufficient to subdue him, but three made it impossible for him to move in the slightest, so he didn't bother to expend his energies in a wasted struggle. His own fate was sealed to whatever their whim, but he wondered where Kristy was and whether she was still alive.

Zacharias stood in the barn before one of the meat grinders, occupied with the pulverization of the bones of the hustler he had killed the night before, when he turned about suddenly and faced the barn door, sensing their arrival. He heard them land just outside. There were five of them and by the scent of their blood he knew they were Cobălcescu. The doors to the barn flew open and he saw them. Though they were all part of the same bloodline, unannounced visits were never a good sign amongst vampires who were not also friends.

With all his speed and all his might, Zacharias rushed at them. He struck one in the face, leveling him to the ground. But just as he grabbed the throat of another, he was struck on the back of the head and soon the brood held him firmly in place.

The one who appeared to be the eldest gestured to the meat grinder. "I wonder, if you wonder, would that contraption kill you were we to grind you through it?"

The others snickered.

The vampire he had struck was already back on his feet. He took his turn and made a fist and punched Zacharias in the jaw, throwing his head back.

"Let's try it, shall we?" the leader said teasingly.

Zacharias, in fact, did not wonder. He was of the opinion that being put through the grinder would indeed kill him as his head would certainly be severed from his body. What he did wonder was, if they really meant to do it, how slowly they would turn the crank.

Uncharacteristically, Hisato stayed home that night. He and the girls had all bathed together in their large and deep soaking tub, but they had since gone out dancing in search of hot men to fuck and kill. Hisato remained behind, sitting naked in the steaming hot water. His head was reclined and a warm washcloth covered his eyes. He was still thinking about me, his little brat, wondering what the hell I was doing at that moment in Romania.

When he sensed their presence inside his mansion, he didn't move. He waited for them to find him in the bath. Without removing the washcloth from his eyes, he made an X with his forearms in the Japanese fashion to convey to someone that something is prohibited. He said haughtily, "Haven't you assholes heard? Soaplands are for Japanese only. You'll have to find some other high-priced whore to suck you Eurotrash off!"

TWENTY-FOUR

A noise woke me, but Mirela, who had remained awake throughout the day, rotating between spooning me and rising to stare at the piles of scribbles, didn't hear it at all. It sounded only in my head. It was Ji'Indushul, or it was at least what I concluded to be Ji'Indushul. I had not heard the murmurs for nights and thought perhaps they had gone quiet because I had grown so close to Mirela. But here I was, in her bed, again covered in blood from our lovemaking, listening to the anguished moans of the most eternal of the Eternal subjects of Mirela Cobălcescu. Enrico, ignorant as he was, was still correct in what he said. Ji'Indushul was calling to me. That Enrico told me so meant Mirela knew this to be the case. This one-way conversation, if you could call it that, couldn't go on. I had to find some way to answer him.

"What time is it?" I asked Mirela.

"Dusk," she answered dully from the table.

"Come back to be bed," I said softly.

"No, my love, we must rise soon."

"Will we be attending the ball tonight?"

"There will be no ball tonight," she said, not looking at me but at one of the drawings instead. She seemed distant, like a friend who talks to you while staring at their smartphone.

It worried me that there would be no ball as I thought it my best way to check on Mayuko without openly showing concern for a mortal to someone as jealous as Mirela. I sat up and rested my back on the headboard.

"When will you give me my new body?" I asked.

"When will you deliver my traitors?"

"I told you already. They're all too scared of you to try to kill you."

"Petru is not too scared."

As I already liked Petru and considered him to be my most valuable ally, I panicked and spoke stupidly. "No, not Petru. I promise, he's not one of them."

I closed my eyes, and I knew Mirela saw that I recognized my misspoken mistake.

"'He's not one of them,'" Mirela repeated my words slowly. "Who is 'them,' Orly?"

I had backed myself into a corner. I would have to give her names. Though I truly believed none would try, the scribbles showed me there were Eternal and Ancients who wished they could kill Mirela. And as I understood their feelings, I felt a kinship with them. Even if I removed my need to avenge Yelena, I could see how unlikable Mirela was to her bloodline. She was not generous. She was arrogant and a bully.

"Tell me their names, Orly."

I thought the smartest thing I could do was to only name the youngest of them, the weakest, those who would be the least useful in a coup d'etat, but I knew Mirela wasn't stupid enough fall for that. I took a deep breath and sighed.

"Neculai," I said, naming one of the eldest of the Ancients.

"And why do you accuse Neculai?"

"He speaks to others of being democratic. Leaderless."

Mirela's jaw tightened. "Who have gone to his side?"

I sighed again and then answered. "Uta. Valeriu. Daciana. Liviu. Ioana. Anghel."

"Daciana," Mirela repeated wistfully.

I couldn't interpret what it meant.

"Who else?"

"No one. The others think the Cobălcescu will die without a leader."

"And there are others, for reasons other than democracy?"

"You killed Spiridon's lover and Wodeleah believes she would be the most beautiful if you were dead."

"Wodeleah is right. But I will overlook her jealousy as she is still weak. But they are all weak and you know this. Tell me what I really want to know, Orly. Tell me the Eternal who wish to see me dead."

"There is only one."

She stared at me, saying nothing, waiting for me to speak.

"Trajan," I said at last.

"You lie to me, Orly Bialek."

"I promise, my love."

"Then your promises are worth nothing. Trajan is my most loyal. You accuse him to protect the true traitors amongst the Eternal. But you will tell me. I will make certain of that."

There was a knock at the door. Mirela opened it without rising.

Babette curtsied in the doorway before entering. She carried two silver gowns. The smaller gown included a sash to sheathe my stake.

"Imparateasa, I thought these would glimmer most strikingly in the full moon tonight. I hope they please you and Mademoiselle Orly."

Mirela was comparing two scribbles and didn't reply.

I sat up in the bed. "Thank you, Babette," I said. "They are just perfect."

Babette laid the dresses over a chair in the corner, bowed her head and left, closing the doors with her hands.

I looked at Mirela, but she just kept staring at the scribbles.

"You were rude to her," I said.

"She is only a servant," she replied without looking up.

"It bothers you that you cannot see what I see in them, doesn't it?"

"Of course it does."

"Did you hope you would gain the ability by drinking my blood?"

She looked at me at last. "Yes, but that is not why we exchanged blood, Orly. You should know that."

I looked down at my hands. They were clutching the duvet. I hoped she was being truthful. "You said there wasn't going to be a ball tonight."

"Yes. And I still say that."

"Then what'd we need gowns for?"

Mirela picked up another scribble. "We have another tradition to partake in tonight," she said at last.

"What's that?"

"We shall race down the mountainside. You will enjoy it."

"A race? Are you serious? Why would we race each other? And even if we do, I'll never be able to keep up with the Ancients."

She finally put the drawing down.

"You don't know that, love, now that you have my blood in you. But that is beside the point. We won't be racing each other, Orly. Not in the sense you mean, at least. We will be racing after those we kidnapped."

"Kidnapped? But we didn't kidnap anybody."

"I sent out parties of Cobălcescu who are not yet Ancients. The captives are within the castle at this very moment, awaiting their fate."

"Their fate? What is their fate?"

Mirela smiled.

"It's an old and simple game. You set the captives free. If they can make it to the base of the mountain before being caught, or remain hidden well enough until daylight, they will be let go. If not, and they are caught, they will die."

"You're right," I said. "I will like that game."

"Yes. I thought you would, my dear."

"Were the vessels all kidnapped?"

"Of course they were."

"You never said anything about me killing Luca."

She went back to the pile of scribbles, again speaking to me dully without looking at me.

"What was there to say? He was mortal. I care not at all for mortals. Besides, if he were still around, I'd have to worry about you making him your everlasting little boyfriend."

"What do you mean, everlasting?" I asked, hoping to hear the answer I wanted.

"You've had much of my blood, my love. Enough blood that you could have turned him," she answered, now comparing three scribbles.

It was indeed the answer I wanted. If what she said was true, only ten years a vampire, I was far ahead of my age. I could already turn a mortal into a vampire.

The Eternal and the Ancients were already assembled outside in the courtyard, audibly animated in anticipation of tonight's planned activities when Mirela and I descended the staircase in our matching silver gowns. We made our way through the house and exited through the front doors to join them. They were seated at large garden tables, drinking various wines and liquors in the light of the full moon. When they saw us, they went silent, rose to their feet and bowed and curtsied. I knew they were being deferential to Mirela, but I noticed that some of them were looking at me as they showed their respect. Were they now being deferential to me as well?

I curtsied to the crowd. Mirela did not. I quickly looked for Mayuko, and saw her off to the side with the other mortal servants, wearing the black gown Babette had made for her.

"Where are the captives?" I asked.

"Bring them!" Mirela commanded, and I was relieved that there really was a group of captives that didn't include Mayuko.

I heard another door open from around the castle and with it came the whimpering of mortals—women, men, and the distinct cries of children. They were marched into the main courtyard surrounded by vampiric faces I did not recognize. These were Cobălcescu who were old, but not yet Ancients. There were over thirty captives. They were terrified and shaking. A vampire carrying a sack that was filled with something that sounded wooden, like a bundle of sticks, followed the captives into the courtyard. Fangs flashed all across the Ancients.

The captives were lined up and the vampire carrying the sack went to each one, reached into the sack and pulled out a wooden stake and handed it to them. Some understood, some appeared confused, some shook their heads pleading not to take one but just to be let go. All were forced to take one.

The last man in the line was burly and wore a face that looked more angry than afraid. He grabbed the stake offered him and as quickly as he could, he tried to plunge it into the heart of the vampire who had given it to him. But of course he was not quick enough. The vampire easily stepped aside, disarmed him and tossed the wooden stake onto the dirt before tearing into the man's neck and drinking from him until he died.

The other captives screamed in horror. The portcullis was raised and the smartest made a run for it. Quickly the other mortals followed, clutching their stakes, sprinting in sheer terror out of the castle grounds.

The Ancients resumed their seats and again began to drink, many of them already full of intoxicated festivity.

"How long do we give them to run?" I asked Mirela, but in a voice loud enough that it was as though I were speaking to the entire group.

"At least an hour," Mirela answered.

"It is a tall mountain after all," Valeriu chuckled and raised his glass to me. "To your health, Young Eternal," he said and drank.

I nodded to him, gratefully.

The term was an oxymoron, but it was clear he meant it out of respect. It was the first open recognition I had seen acknowledging my quickening. At my very young age among them, I was seen as powerful. Was he trying to be my friend? If so I felt bad, for little did he know that before Mirela and

I made our appearance I had named him as a conspirator to kill the imparateasa.

The tall and exceedingly good looking Caturix offered me a tumbler of scotch, which I accepted. He raised his own tumbler to me and we touched glasses before taking a drink. It was clear I had gained respect among the Ancients, but I still presumed it was mostly out of fear of my scribbles and what Mirela would do with them.

"If we have an entire hour in the moonlight, I would like to draw," I said and then turned to Mirela and added, "If it pleases our imparateasa."

I felt the electricity of silent conversations rapidly circulating through the Ancients.

What are you doing? I heard Petru ask me mentally.

Haven't we had enough of that? Matei, the two thousand, two-hundred-year-old Eternal asked.

But I had my own plans and didn't answer either of them.

"You have drawn everyone, Orly. Have you not?" Mirela asked.

"I would like to draw someone again," I answered.

You dare? Mirela said indignantly, now also speaking to me telepathically.

What dare? I asked. You said you don't love him.

Very well, Mirela answered. There was a hint of resignation in her words. Mirela gave commands in Romanian and quickly her mortal servants reentered the castle to fetch my crayons, paper, and easel. When they returned the items were set before me. The electricity amongst the Ancients continued.

Who are you drawing? Petru asked and I presumed that is what they were all wondering.

I'm drawing my enemy, I answered.

"Well, Orly, please tell us all, whom would you like to draw a second time?" Mirela asked politely and feigning ignorance, for she already knew the answer.

I answered differently than I had answered Petru, calling my suspected enemy by name. "Alexi Pavlovich, will you please do me the honor of sitting for me once more?"

Alexi Pavlovich tilted his head, perplexed. He looked to Mirela who looked indifferent. He looked back at me.

"Young Orly, why would you ask me to sit a second time?"

"Because time has passed since the first time I drew you," I answered.

"Only a matter of nights, surely nothing significant has changed."

"Are you refusing?" I asked plainly and all eyes were upon him, wondering what he might be hiding.

"Not at all," he said cooly. "But had I known I'd be having my portrait sketched instead of participating in a foot race, I would have dressed appropriately. I hope you will pardon me."

He hoped I would pardon him. He knew what I would see.

He took a seat before me and sat with an erect posture. "Does this meet your liking?"

"It's fine," I answered as I brought a black crayon to paper and began to scribble.

The Ancients again moved in to watch the mess of black lines and curves form on the blank page. I put the crayon down. I saw in the scribble what I needed.

"That didn't take long," Alexi Pavlovich commented, and I sensed his nervousness.

I rose to my feet as did he and we stared at each other. I pulled the metal stake from its sheath.

"I believe this is yours and I would like to return it to you."

Mentally, I tried to hold him in place, but upon his next word, he gestured, waving me off, and I knew I had not succeeded. "Nonsense!" Alexi Pavlovich exclaimed haughtily.

I felt the stake being pulled from my hand, by whom I did not know, but I was strong enough to keep my grip upon it, or rather, they were not strong enough to take it from me, now that so much of Mirela's blood coursed through me.

"Who dares bind me?" Alexi Pavlovich spat, and I could tell he was struggling to move but couldn't.

He inhaled deeply, as I took a step toward him, holding the stake, but then I too could no longer move. Someone was binding me as well, holding me back from killing my enemy.

"Release her!" Mirela commanded firmly to no one in particular, but at once I could move again and I took another step toward Alexi Pavlovich.

"Ma chère!" Alexi Pavlovich exclaimed to Mirela. "I loved you."

But Mirela didn't answer him. Instead she spoke to me. "Remember what I told you, Orly. You must kill all rivals."

She addressed me by name, but I knew it was a threat to the crowd.

Deliberately I stepped up to Alexi Pavlovich, lifted the metal stake, and plunged it right into his chest and left it there. His eyes bulged from their sockets and began to bleed. Whoever had been holding him in place for me released him, and to my surprise, Alexi Pavlovich remained standing. He closed his eyes. He was in extreme anguish and, with both hands, gripped the stake, but he was unable to wrench it from his heart. Dying by the stake took longer than I expected, but I supposed extinguishing one's eternity should take a long time, and I recalled how long Yelena continued to scream as the sunlight engulfed her.

Alexi Pavlovich opened his eyes and stared at me with pure hatred. He bared his fangs and I saw his own blood spilling from his mouth. Just before his body crumpled, he spat blood upon me. It splashed across my face and my new gown. He fell to his knees first and then toppled over. Splayed upon the ground, I watched my enemy die.

I turned to Mirela. All eyes were on her now. Her gaze was fixed on the corpse of Alexi Pavlovich and I could not interpret her expression. Was she wounded? Had she loved him more than she had led me to believe?

You savage brat! I heard Viorica laugh inside my head.

A multitude of voices sounded in my head. The speed of telepathic conversations far outpaced spoken words.

You did right, Orly.

He deserved to die.

I never liked him anyway.

Great pompous ass he was.

Trying to remove the stake. What a coward!

Ha ha! The look on his face!

And then I heard Petru speak inside my head. Learn from this, Orly Bialek. Do not get carried away now that you are consort. Alexi Pavlovich was hated by many, for he treated few with respect.

Why do you give me your guidance, Petru? Why favor me like you do? I asked telepathically.

Because we have the same goal, Orly, he replied.

I know. But now things are different. It's her blood or her love. I don't know which. But whatever it is, it's changing me. The closer I become to her the less I feel capable of revenge. Surely you must have expected this. Oh! I am young and foolish! Shouldn't that frighten you? Doesn't that make you not trust me?

He replied, It tells me we must move forward with great haste even if it forgoes caution. Have you found the tomb of Ji'Indushul?

No. But I was told it only exists in Mirela's Oblivion. She won't let me in.

You must get in, Orly. You must make her trust you so that you might free Ji'Indushul and unleash him upon her. Condemn us, even me, to gain her trust. Give her her traitors.

I wanted to tell him that I had already given Mirela a short list of names, but didn't know if she believed me, but Mirela interrupted our conversation.

"I say they have had long enough!" Mirela shouted and the crowd of Ancients cheered. Her violet eyes no longer lay upon the corpse. It appeared no one mourned Alexi Pavlovich.

Mirela took my hand and in our matching gowns, mine stained with the blood of her former lover, we exited the castle grounds in pursuit of the captives. The Ancients, with great enthusiasm raced out of the castle, passing us, heading in all directions down the mountainsides. I wanted to look over my shoulder, to get a glimpse of Mayuko for I missed her dearly and longed to speak with her, but with Mirela gripping my hand, I didn't dare look back.

The mountain was so expansive that quickly Mirela and I were completely alone as we traversed the declivity together, pursuing our prey easily and swiftly by following their scent.

"When we catch one, are you gonna feed with me?" I asked.

"To be honest, my love, I'd rather only taste your blood tonight. But you should feed to your heart's content."

"Let's walk," I said. "This is too easy. We've already caught up to one. I don't want it to be over so soon."

Mirela laughed, "Relish in the hunt all you like, love. I remember the delight it gave me when I was young."

We slowed down knowing we would still catch our prey. It was a woman. I could smell her fear and the salt of her sweat and tears.

"I have a question for you," I said.

"And what would that be, my darling Orly?"

"No listen. It's serious. I want you to answer me and I want you to tell me the truth."

"Oh, this does sound serious. Ask me then."

I thought for a moment on how to begin.

"When Konomi took me into her Oblivion, we still existed here on Earth. Our bodies did at least. So how can Ji'Indushul only exist in your Oblivion? I don't believe you."

"Are you so eager to betray me that you wish to find Ji'Indushul here on Earth?"

"It's not about betrayal. It just doesn't make sense. You said someone has to find their way to the Oblivion. That doesn't mean they leave here completely. The Oblivion is a place only in the mind."

"Did one of the Eternal reason that out for you?"

"No. I thought of it all by myself."

"Now, I don't know if I should believe you."

"Fine, don't believe me. I don't care. I knew you wouldn't answer me straight," I said, separating from her, heading in a different direction. As the distance between us grew, I spoke more loudly, purposely not using telepathy, knowing the vampires on the mountain nearest us could hear me. "You told Alexi Pavlovich to threaten me with the stake. To drive it into my coffin. I saw it in his scribble."

Mirela was instantly at my side. "Hush with that now. You know that's not true." And then telepathically she said, You're right. I did have him do that. I wanted to see how easily you were frightened. Obviously, though foolishly, you were not frightened at all. You turned the stake into an accessory.

She laughed, but I did not.

What do you care if I'm frightened?

I needed to know if you would be too afraid to reveal the names of the traitors in my coven.

You're too paranoid, Mirela. There aren't even any real traitors. The names I gave you, they're not traitors. They just wish things were different but they're never going to do anything about it. And do you know why they wish things were different?

Tell me.

"Because you're a bully and a bitch," I said aloud.

I expected her to strike me, but she didn't.

"You like being a tyrant. No one will ever love you. They'll only be afraid."

Mirela laughed.

"What the fuck is so funny about that?" I asked indignantly.

"Nothing. I'm laughing because we're already bickering like an old couple." She composed herself and reached for me.

She took me by both hands and had me face her. "Don't you love me, Orly?"

I looked at her, into her eyes, the wide moon reflected in them. I was searching her face for the truth. Did she truly love me? The way she looked at me told me she did, but I knew there was no one in the world more deceptive than she was, and so I didn't know how to believe in her love.

"I want my new body tonight," I said.

The hope in her face diminished. She shook her head slowly. "I cannot give you your body tonight."

"Why not?" I asked sharply.

"Because Kristy is not yet here for me to give to you."

"Kristy? You're really bringing her? You're going to give me her body?"

"It's what you wanted. I told you I would give you anything, Orly. Anything you wanted. And you were right. I was told she is quite beautiful."

I was in disbelief. I didn't think she'd really give me Kristy's body. My mind immediately went to Berthold and how I betrayed him. If she truly had been stolen from him because of my stupid and jealous wish, I had broken his heart, and that made my own heart hurt. I had to keep that sentiment off my face so Mirela wouldn't detect it and perceive Berthold as her true rival. I tried instead to appear excited about the prospect of having Kristy's body. But in my heart I was wondering where Berthold was now. Did he fight for her? Was he still alive? Or had Kristy's abductors killed him? Though I wanted to, I didn't ask Mirela. It would only ensure she killed him if he were not already dead.

I went to my tiptoes and kissed Mirela on her lips. "Thank you," I said.

"For what are you thanking me?"

"For keeping your promise. For giving me Kristy," I said though I was still aching over Berthold's death or despair.

I kissed her again, this time more deeply. I began to lower myself to the ground and pulled her gently down with me.

She looked at me quizzically. "But the woman. You haven't fed yet and she is near."

"Someone else will kill her," I said and kissed Mirela again. "I guess it's the same for me. I only want your blood tonight."

The mountain was so large and we vampires so few that it was unlikely any would come upon us. We undressed each other, drank from each others' throats, and made love in the forest, the blood of our lust spilling over the fallen pine needles.

We held each other, unclothed and unseen, as the night went on, not caring at all if all the captives survived and all the vampires starved for the night. Through vampiric powers I had not yet gained, she gave me human warmth that I, undead and inhuman as I was, did not naturally posses. Her fingers delicately traveled along my left arm and when they reached my hand, she slipped an unseen ring upon my finger. It was an elegant platinum setting, gracefully cradling two perfect amethysts, the color of her eyes. I extended my hand and stared at it. How perfectly it fit my finger.

"I love you, Mirela," I whispered. And though touched as I was by the gesture, I again had Berthold at the forefront of my mind. But my words moved her and she held me more tightly and radiated even more of her loving warmth and I nestled in the clutches of my lover.

Daylight was less than an hour away and Mirela sensed the others had already returned to Castle Cobălcescu and retired. We rose and dressed and before we began our ascent, I kissed her lovingly once more.

To my surprise our path back to the castle was not direct, and I began to worry about the approaching sunlight even though the forest was dense.

"Where are we going?" I asked.

"Earth," she answered.

And within a couple of steps, there before me, dug into the mountainside, was the bricked in tomb I had seen in the scribbles of each of the Eternal. My seduction had worked. Misguided by love, Mirela had brought me to the resting place of Ji'Indushul.

TWENTY-FIVE

I knew daylight was approaching and we would have to flee to the safety of the castle, but I couldn't take my eyes off of the tomb that rested on the slope of the mountainside.

"Is this your Oblivion?" I asked my lover.

"No."

"Is this really the tomb of Ji'Indushul?"

"It is his earthly tomb."

"I don't understand. It's not even hidden. How come no one else—none of your traitors or not even mortals have found it and dug him out?"

"It *is* hidden, Orly. You can't see its concealment because I am choosing to show the tomb to you. All who walk past here, vampires and humans, see only forest."

"How is that possible?"

"How is it possible that your carriage carried you over the fog? This mountain is my domain. I rule everything on it."

"Not the daylight. Because your castle doesn't exist during the day."

"Your servant has broken the rules."

Worry must have flashed upon my face.

"Don't distress, myshka moya. You are mine. I won't harm your mortal. But yes, in the sunlight my castle is in ruins, but the tomb of Ji'Indushul is buried in the earth and covered with boulders and is overlooked during the day. At night even his concealed resting place is hidden by magic."

"You have magic?"

"You have magic. What else would you call our powers?"

"I don't know. I never thought of it as magic though. I thought magic was for witches."

"Magic is just a word. A very old word. You can call it whatever you like. But I keep the tomb hidden. Not even you, with all the blood I have given you, will be able to find your way back to it."

"There's no heartbeat."

"It beats only in the Oblivion now."

I turned to her. "I want to open it."

She shook her head.

"If he's trapped in the Oblivion, what difference does it make if I open it?" I asked.

"There's nothing to see."

"Then let me see nothing."

"Okay then, look at nothing."

I turned from her and looked back to the tomb, but it was no longer there. I saw only forest upon earth that appeared undisturbed.

"I could dig it back up," I said, thinking I could excavate deep enough to find the tomb.

"You would find nothing. What I showed you was a doorway to his resting place. Without that doorway, you'll never find him. His tomb could be anywhere on this mountain."

I shook my head. She had so many secrets.

She smiled and held her hand out to me. I took it and we hurried back to Castle Cobălcescu ahead of the approaching dawn.

I woke in Mirela's arms, fully rested, although I had only slept for a couple hours. The bedding was again covered in our blood. Though she was spooning me, I could sense she was awake.

"What are you thinking about?" I asked.

"I'm thinking about you."

"What about me?"

"What you would do if you were to see Ji'Indushul. Would you betray me, Orly?"

"I wouldn't even know how to betray you."

"You could set him free."

"Could I really do that even if I wanted to?"

"I won't tell you if you could, but I would like to know if you would want to."

"When Konomi shared her Oblivion with me, she said she could leave me trapped there, just as I think you left Ji'Indushul trapped. I should be the one who's worried. If you brought me to your Oblivion, you could leave me there forever."

"But I wouldn't. It would end our love."

"You would stop loving me?"

"Never. But our love is what it is because as vampires we have shared so much blood. But in the Oblivion, I would again be mortal and my bond to you would be limited to that of mortal heartstrings which, though substantial, would still pale beside the bond of shared vampiric blood."

"I think you're worried I'd kill you there, since you would be mortal and I wouldn't."

"In my Oblivion, as you would still be a vampire, you would still be bound by the blood we share here. If you truly love me you would have to conquer the bond of our shared blood. It is not as easy to do as you might think."

"How do you know? Who did you try to betray in the Oblivion? Marcel?"

She didn't answer with words. She sighed.

"Will you take me there anyway?"

"After what I've just said, why would you still want to go?"

"Because I'm hoping it would help me find my way to my own Oblivion."

"It won't. If there is a way to it, you must find it on your own. Through your own senses."

I felt defeated. She would not bring me to her Oblivion. I decided not to push any further in the moment. I changed the subject.

"Will there be a ball tonight?"

"Yes. Have you grown weary of them?"

"I just think I need some time to myself. I wanna go outside. Into the forest."

"To look for Ji'Indushul, you mean."

"No. I just want to walk and think. This stuff with us is all going so fast. Can you still understand that?"

"I can. And you'll come back to me before daybreak?"

I nodded my head. From behind me, she kissed my hair.

"Just know, you won't find the tomb, Orly."

"I told you I wasn't going to look for it. But I'm gonna bring my servant with me. I need to have girl talk."

"You can't you have that with me?"

"I need to talk about my relationship problems."

"Do we have relationship problems?"

"I need to learn how to trust you. To believe you really do love me and will keep your promises."

"Go then, but come back."

With her arms wrapped around me, I nestled into her deeper and kissed her hands.

Though we were both dressed in evening gowns, Mayuko was happy to leave the ball with me. We exited the house and stepped out into the moonlight, and with the portcullis raised, we walked outside of the castle walls and headed into the forest. Though the blood in my veins kept my heart feeling fervidly drawn to Mirela, my mind felt overwhelmed by how quickly things had developed between us. Though in reality there was probably no escaping her, my instincts told me I needed to put distance between us and so I decided to flee and leave the ball taking place in her honor far behind me. Since Mayuko could not keep up with my vampiric speed, I lifted her over my shoulder and descended halfway down the mountainside in a preternatural rush until the sounds of the ball were no longer audible.

I set Mayuko down, and we walked at a leisurely place. I examined our surroundings with each step we took.

"Cricket, how much longer do we need to remain here?"

"I don't know. Until Mirela says we can leave."

"I hope it's soon. Every night that passes the less safe I feel."

"I won't let anything happen to you, Button," I said in a rote manner, while still looking at the grounds around us as we walked.

"Are you looking for something?" Mayuko asked, noticing my attentions were diverted.

"I'm looking for a place to dig," I said.

"Dig for what?"

"I have a surprise for you. It's like a really good gift."

"And you buried it?"

"Here is good," I said, not answering. I went to my knees and began to dig as quickly as I could into the earth.

Mayuko tried to help me, but I waved her off. Her mortal speed was not worth getting dirt beneath her fingernails. Within moments I had dug a hole that was deeper than I was tall and I had to levitate out of it.

"And now what, Cricket?"

"Now I'm going to bury you," I said with a smile on my face.

My expression hardly matched Mayuko's. She looked at me in terror.

"Bury me? Why?"

"To protect you," I said, continuing to play with her.

"But I'll die. I'll suffocate."

"You'll die, but you won't suffocate."

"I don't understand, Cricket."

"I'm going to make you immortal. Right now."

"Oh my god. Can you do that? You're still too young."

"I am young, but my blood is not. I can already turn mortals."

"But how do you know that?"

"Mirela told me I could have turned Luca."

"But you didn't turn him. She could be lying or be wrong."

"No. I can feel it inside me. I know I can do it."

Mayuko still looked reluctant. Understandably, she wasn't hasty to experiment with her life.

"You have to trust me, Button," I said.

"I do trust you. But I wish you had already done it on someone else. Maybe I won't wake up. I could die."

"Even with an Eternal, you might not wake up. There's always that chance. Yes, I've never turned a mortal, but you'll be over seventy years old if we wait until I was an age you'd feel safe with. I'm trying to let you keep your beauty."

Mayuko inhaled deeply. She was thinking.

"Button, I would never play with your life. I'm sure I can do it."

And in my heart and mind, I was sure. I took her hands and looked into her eyes, until she returned my gaze. She looked at me for some time and then nodded her head. I smiled and we hugged warmly. She continued to hold me as I began to let go.

"This isn't goodbye, Button," I said. "I'm gonna love spending eternity with you."

Softly, she said, "Me too."

Taking her hands once more, I lowered her to her knees, lessening our height difference.

"Are you ready?" I asked.

She bit her lip and nodded her head. With my thumb, I pulled her bottom lip out from her teeth and leaned forward and kissed her lightly on the lips.

"Wait, Cricket."

"What is it?"

"If I don't wake up, don't leave me here. Bring me back to LA or even Japan, but don't leave me on this mountain. Promise me."

I nodded my head. "I promise. But don't worry, Button. You're going to wake up and we're gonna have a forever."

She smiled slightly, still hesitant, and I smiled back wider, trying my best to reassure her. I kissed her lips again, and then looking deeply into her eyes, I began to charm her, knowing it would palliate the pain of the bite. When I could tell by her gaze she was under my spell, I moved her hair aside, lowered my mouth to her throat and bit into the jugular of my best friend.

Her body tensed at the bite, but relaxed as I began to drink. Her blood was rich and less metallic than most blood I had tasted, and I drank enough to bring her near death without stopping her heart. I laid her on the forest floor and bit into my own wrist, allowing it to bleed generously. I brought the blood to her lips. She opened her mouth weakly to receive it. With my blood now being so powerful, she had to swallow relatively little before the poisoning effects became apparent. Her body stiffened and she began gasping for air. I closed her mouth and covered it so that she would not spit out the blood. In moments, my best friend Mayuko was dead.

Gently, I lifted her body and levitated to the bottom of the hole I had dug and laid her to rest. I levitated out of the hole and landed atop the mound of earth that resulted from the digging of the grave. Choosing to use mortal speed, as if doing so would acknowledge the solemnity of the deed I had just committed, I pushed the dirt back into the hole covering Mayuko. As I did, my thoughts returned to my own awakening. Yelena had waited nearly an entire week before my eyes finally opened and I screamed inside my casket. It was my understanding that taking a week to wake was excessive, and I hoped I would not have to wait in agony for so many nights for Mayuko to be reborn as a vampire. The other strange thing about my awakening was that it had occurred during the hours of daylight. This was so rare amongst our kind that it was considered good luck. But I imagined it was the kind of good luck that a bride has on a rainy day. It was only labeled good luck out of consolation and nothing else. So far, I hadn't seen what luck it had brought me.

Once the hole was filled in, I said a little prayer to no one in particular, hoping Mayuko would wake and be reborn. I didn't doubt my blood was powerful enough to turn her, I just knew it was never a guarantee that a mortal would reawaken regardless of who turned them.

Ascending the mountain, I took my time heading back to Castle Cobălcescu, but when I arrived the ball was still in full swing, and I learned Mirela had given many drops of her blood to Trajan, her most loyal of the Eternal.

Since my dress was soiled with earth, I received many strange looks as I stood in the ballroom. Mirela was smiling as she danced with Trajan. She looked happy, like someone in love, and yet I was sure the love she exhibited was not for Trajan, but for me. She stopped mid-dance once she saw me. She said something to Trajan, who bowed to her, and Mirela left the dance floor and came to me.

"What have you been up to?" she asked. "Were you mud wrestling with your servant?"

"No. I buried her."

A quizzical expression swept over her face.

"You killed her?" she asked.

"No. I turned her."

The quizzical expression turned to one of displeasure.

"And why did you do that?"

"You said I could."

"I said you had the ability to turn mortals, which you do, but I did not tell you to turn her. Has she even served you for ten years?"

"No."

"Then why would you turn her early?"

"I just wanted to," I answered flippantly. "I need to get out of this dress and take a bath. Will you come with me?"

"Yes. Of course I will. But one thing more first," she answered.

Before I could ask what that one thing was, she turned to the crowd. The dancing stopped and the music died in anticipation of the imparateasa speaking.

In a harsh voice, Mirela said, "Neculai, Uta, Valeriu, Daciana, Liviu, Ioana, Anghel, Spiridon, come forward!"

The electricity swept through the Ancients. Mirela had called for those I named as traitors. The tone of Mirela's voice caused them to step forward most quickly. They bowed and curtsied to the imparateasa, each wearing an expression of fear upon their face as they looked at her.

"Orly's drawings have named you all traitors. Conspirators to kill your imparateasa."

The group before her began to deny their guilt and plead their innocence, all in great earnest, and the electricity amongst those who stood behind them swelled.

"Silence!" Mirela commanded, and the conspirators went silent, and even the electricity of private conversations became dull, as all waited anxiously to see how this would play out.

"Spiridon," she began harshly. "It is no secret I killed your beloved Danaë. Do you seek revenge?"

"No my liege," Spiridon spoke firmly. "I do not. I have forgotten her to the past."

"Your sketch says otherwise," Mirela answered.

Knowing his fate was sealed, Spiridon rushed with lightning speed toward Mirela, hands outstretched for her throat. Before he reached her, he burst into flames and screamed in ear shattering agony as he burned from fire that roared unnaturally hot, seeming to rival the sun. He crumpled to the floor still screaming and then poof! He went silent, turning into a pile of black ash, with only a scattering of embers of the fire that had extinguished his life, still glowing.

The remaining Ancients who stood accused went to their knees protesting their innocence. Mirela looked down upon them.

"Let it be known," Mirela said sharply, "that these seven groveling before me believe the Cobălcescu would fare better without an imparateasa. They believe in democracy," she said and then laughed haughtily.

The seven seemed to know it was pointless to refute the accusation, so instead they all screamed for mercy.

"I will not show you mercy like I did for Spiridon," Mirela answered their pleas. "You will all face the slicing."

Immediately, they cried out, again begging for mercy, some bursting into tears, blood running from their eyes. But Mirela remained stoic.

"Trajan, Matei, and Petru," Mirela said, "You shall hold them until dawn and then administer the pain. I must go bathe my lover."

The crying continued and all eyes turned to me. Upon the faces it seemed the respect I had won when I killed Alexi Pavlovich had turned to a spectrum of other expressions, ranging between fear and hatred.

Even though I did not know what the slicing was, I wanted to plead upon their behalf.

Don't you utter a word, Orly, Mirela said telepathically. You might wake Mayuko prematurely.

It was clearly a threat. Mirela was angered I had turned my best friend who I now knew was seen as a rival. She took my hand roughly and dragged me out of the ballroom toward the staircase leading upstairs.

TWENTY-SIX

I sat in the tub with Mirela, but this time the water did not feel warm. She washed the dirt from my arms and hands. If I listened closely I could still hear the wailing and weeping below.

"They all hate me now," I said flatly.

"They all fear you now," Mirela answered.

"I told you they weren't really going to do anything. I told you they're too afraid of you."

"A treacherous thought is still an act of treachery."

Her voice was without emotion. I knew I would not reach her. I knew I could not save them.

I tried to focus my hearing on the water dripping from my arms, rather than the cries of the condemned.

"What is the slicing?" I finally asked.

In a matter-of-fact tone, again lacking any emotion, Mirela answered me. "A tunnel for each of them will be dug from the catacombs up to the surface. They will be inserted into these tunnels, and held in place, unable to move. When the sun rises, their bodies will be pushed out of the holes, telekinetically, feet first, centimeter by centimeter, so that the sunlight slices them slowly into ash. It will be very painful for them as you should remember from Yelena's screams. We will hear them scream well into the afternoon. They will live through it until the sunlight burns through their pumping hearts."

I lowered my head and stared into the bathwater. I hated what I had done, giving Mirela names. Furthermore, I hated that she referred to Yelena's death.

"Please, Mirela," I said softly. "Spare them. For me. Because you love me."

"I do love you, Orly, even when I'm angry at you. But spare them I cannot. I have already condemned them openly. Showing mercy shows weakness. Do not ask me a second time."

I wanted to ask her again anyway, but didn't as I didn't think she would appreciate my brattish and rebellious nature in the moment. So instead I said, "Spare Mayuko then. You haven't condemned her."

"You think I plan to kill your servant?"

"She won't be my servant anymore," I said. "But she'll only be my friend. I promise."

"'But she'll only be my friend,'" Mirela repeated slowly and contemplatively.

"That's the reason you got so mad, isn't it? Because I turned her?"

"I am a jealous woman, Orly. I have been for over five thousand years. That should be plain to you by now."

"She'll only be my friend," I said again.

"Fine. Stop asking. I will let your friend live as long as she is nothing more to you than a friend."

"Thank you," I said feeling I had just saved my best friend's life, but still felt horrible about the painful and lingering deaths I had caused others in my bloodline. "I'm clean already. Take me to your bed."

We wore camisoles of silk and lace—mine black, hers violet— as we lay entwined upon the bed gently bleeding into each other's mouths. In the back of my mind, I knew sunrise was approaching. I wanted to plead for the condemned again, hoping this current exchange of love and blood had softened Mirela's feelings, but I asked nothing. I was scared of angering her and fearful she would take back her promise to spare Mayuko's life.

I was on top of her, fondling her and spitting her own blood back into her mouth, when the screaming began.

"Don't stop," Mirela said.

But I couldn't continue and got off of her. I pitied them, despised myself, and heard Yelena in their cries.

"Make it stop!" I screamed in turn.

"Ignore it if you cannot cherish it."

"I can't ignore it," I said and the blood tears began to spill from my eyes.

"You're crying for those who would see your lover dead?"

"I'm crying because it's all my fault! I have to get out of here."

"There's nowhere to go. It's daylight, Orly. You need to grow up and hear them die."

"I can't. I can't," I said, still crying. "Take me away from here. Please. Take me to the Oblivion. I can't live with this."

"The Oblivion," Mirela repeated calmly. "You would see me vulnerable. You could kill me there."

"You can kill me here. I'm vulnerable to you everywhere."

"Not in my Oblivion."

"Then leave me there forever, trapped like Ji'Indushul. Don't show me the way out."

The screaming downstairs continued all the while and I could tell she was thinking. I continued, sniffling and softening my words. "If you truly want my love, you must make yourself vulnerable to me, Mirela. We have to be equal. Otherwise you'll never know if I truly love you or if I'm just afraid of the consequences if I don't pretend to."

I had given her more to think about and in the meantime the screams were shattering my soul. She grabbed me and pinned me down upon the bed and brought her face close to mine and looked into my eyes.

"Forgive me for killing Yelena," she said.

I was caught off-guard and needed to think but couldn't as the wailing echoed all around me. I couldn't bear it.

Looking into her eyes, I said, "I forgive you."

"What are you forgiving?"

"I forgive you for killing Yelena. I forgive you for killing my mother."

I had finally said it. I said what she wanted to hear all along. I said the words that betrayed my mother, but before I could regret it or change my mind I saw that Mirela's expression had changed and I was captivated by it. Moments before she had been phlegmatic but now a wave of contentment washed over her face. She kept me pinned with her face close to mine while the screams continued to reign over Castle Cobălcescu. I waited for her to do something, but she didn't move. My stomach sickened as I began to smell smoke. I thought it was the smoke of slowly burning bodies, but then, in her violet eyes, I saw the flames again. The flames I had seen in the beginning of her scribble.

"Watch the fire," she said.

And I stared into her eyes watching the flames dance, each swaying and rising like disappearing phantoms that were continually reimagined in the core of the inferno below. My head began to spin, and I could no longer tell if I were lying or standing. In my peripheral vision, the world around us began to darken as if the candles in the bedroom were being snuffed out, one by one. And at last, in my ears the cries of torment grew softer and softer until I could hear them no more. In their place I heard the wind. It whistled lowly all around us. Though I knew we were in the hours of daylight, we were enveloped by the darkness of night.

My fingertips felt cold earth below me and I discovered I was sitting on a dirt floor. I looked up at Mirela; she was standing. The fire had vanished from her eyes and from behind her head I saw a sky full of stars. I knew we were now in her Oblivion. I stood up and looked at my surroundings. There were definitely more stars in the sky than I was accustomed to, like there had been in Konomi's Oblivion. This must have been how the night sky looked thousands of years ago. But other than the sky above I saw nothing else but four dirt walls surrounding us, and I realized we were at the bottom of a pit that was too deep for a mortal to climb out of.

I still had blood upon my lips from the start of our lovemaking in the real world, but Mirela did not. Her face was dirty, not with blood, but with earth. As I licked vampiric blood from my lips, I realized that here I could smell mortal blood, and it belonged to Mirela.

Though I was still dressed in a black camisole, Mirela stood fully naked, most of her skin was smudged with earth, and she was shivering. I went to her and wrapped my arms around her, but the frigidity of my vampiric skin caused her to gently push me away. Though shivering, she still felt warmer than I did.

"I'm okay," she said. "When I come here, I can feel the cold of night again."

"What is this place?"

"It is where I was put when I was condemned for being a witch."

"Before you were a vampire, you were a witch?" I asked, unable to keep myself from smiling.

"You find that funny?"

"It just sounds like Halloween."

"Yes. You would find that funny, wouldn't you? Perhaps it would be even more humorous if I said, 'trick or treat.' Forgive me for not laughing with you, but you have to understand, Orly, that in the Oblivion, if you ever find it, inside yourself you will feel as you did before you died."

She was being so serious that the smile faded from my face. I looked around again. It was truly a miserable place at the bottom of that pit. I changed the subject. "Konomi felt excited I think. It was the night before a big battle."

"Lucky her," Mirela said bitterly.

"But they were really outnumbered. That's why she died."

Mirela put her back to the wall and lowered herself to a seated position. "My Oblivion is a place of despair. This pit they put me in is where I awaited my execution."

"Who's 'they'?"

"The Creacs. The tribe I had been enslaved to as a handmaid to the chieftain's fourth and youngest wife, the one with the violet eyes."

"She had violet eyes too?"

"You misunderstand. She had violet eyes. But I did not. Not until I stole her body."

"So you did steal your body."

"You doubted me?"

"I don't know. Maybe? I thought you did it as a vampire, not when you were still a mortal."

"I learned how to do it under the tutelage of a shaman before I was enslaved. It is an old magic that has been lost to the world but was known to the tribe I was born into."

"And you still know how to do it?"

"Of course."

"What was your tribe called?"

"The Cobalshik."

"That's where you got Cobălcescu from."

"Yes. But that was many centuries later."

"I didn't go to school much as an orphan. But I never heard of Cobalshiks or Creacs."

"Most of history no longer exists, Orly. But in that time the Cobalshik were known to be body stealers and were feared for it. That is why we were eventually slaughtered and enslaved by the larger tribe of Creacs."

"And you got revenge by stealing the body of the beautiful woman you served."

"Yes. I killed her by taking possession of her body and they found my corpse instead. As I had only been a slave, nothing was thought of my death. And with my new body

I now had a position of power as the most beautiful wife of the chieftain. I almost got away with it except the chieftain noticed the personality of his fourth wife had changed. Apparently, his real wife had been a very sweet and good-natured girl," she said wryly.

I smiled again, but I was not laughing at her. I was admiring her instead. And I felt excited knowing she truly could give me a new body.

"By coincidence members of the tribe began to die nightly, their corpses bearing bite marks upon their throats. They did not know of vampires then and thought a witch had cursed them. Because of the personality change of the wife who had been served by a Cobalshik, I was accused of not only stealing the body of the fourth wife, but also of the deaths of the tribesmen. It was then I was condemned to die in this pit. They left me here for six days and nights, until the mourning rituals of the real wife had been completed. On the sixth night, they came and threw bundles of sticks collected from the forest into the pit and set fire to them. I backed up against this same wall I am backed upon now waiting to be burned alive."

This was the fire I had seen in her eyes in her scribble and in her bedroom before she brought me to her Oblivion.

"But you didn't die?"

"No. That is when the vampire Mikonost saved me. Always wandering, Mikonost had recently traveled into the domain of the Creacs, feeding on them and watching me from afar in the body of the fourth wife. He fell in love with my beauty and had planned to kidnap me and take me as his own until they threw me in the pit. I knew nothing of him, and he knew nothing of the body stealing, and so he didn't understand why I had been condemned."

"Why didn't he save you before the sixth night?"

"Yes. Why didn't he? I was angry with him about that for a very long time. His answer was that he was curious to see what would happen—what the customs of the Creacs were and whether or not I would beg for my life. When the sixth night came and I didn't beg for my life even as the fire drew near and I could feel it beginning to burn my skin, he loved me even more and finally took action. He swooped in over the tribesmen, striking and scattering them. His rage, his eyes—which were entirely black—and his ability to fly made them believe he was an angry god. At great risk to himself, he leapt into the flaming pit and lifted me out. Though they were armed, no one dared touch us, and we disappeared into the night."

"And he didn't know he was running off with a stolen body?"

"No. I only told him the truth after he turned me."

"And eventually you killed him."

"That too was centuries later."

"And so in your Oblivion, do the tribesmen always come to burn you to death and you get to see Mikonost again?"

"Never. I'm assuming you already know, but the sun never rises in the Oblivion. So I can only guess that the night of my Oblivion is one of the first five nights, but not the sixth."

"So you never see anyone here?"

"No. But listen, you can hear the Creacs in the distance."

"Yes. I can hear them easily. I can go kill them all, if you want."

"It would be a waste of time. Even if you killed each and every one of them, they will always be here the next time I come. But, Orly, that's not what you really want. What you really want is to find Ji'Indushul."

"Is he really here?"

"Yes. He is entombed near enough that when he moans in sorrow, my mortal ears can hear him. It comforts me. It is the main reason I visit this wretched place."

Cruelty flashed across her face. She loved that she had damned him here.

"But he's so stubborn now that he rarely makes a peep."

I took her hand and she looked at me. "Mirela, hasn't he been punished long enough? Why don't you just kill him already?"

"Yes indeed. Three thousand years of confinement in this place may be punishment enough but I keep him alive because he can still be of use to me."

"Hearing him suffer, you mean?"

"No. I keep him alive because perhaps one day he will come to his senses and agree to serve me again. If he did, I would release him in a heartbeat."

"Wait a minute," I said. "If Ji'Indushul is really here in your Oblivion, that means he's still a vampire. Why doesn't he break out of his tomb and come here and kill you? Wouldn't that get him out of here?"

"Just as he is bound to his tomb in reality, so he is bound here."

"But how? Here you're mortal. How can you bind him?"

"I hope that is something you will never figure out, my love."

"So you will always have secrets from me then."

"Of course. I am your lover Orly, but first I am imparateasa. But come now, lift me out of this pit and I will take you to him."

You need her not to find me, Orly Bialek, a voice said in my head. *Come out of there now and I will guide you in silence so she will not hear.*

I shuddered at the sound of his voice. It did not sound like I expected. The pitch was higher than the low murmurs I had grown so accustomed to, yet he sounded weary and sad.

"He's talking to you, isn't he?" Mirela asked.

I knew there was no point in lying to her.

"Yes," I answered tonelessly, waiting for Ji'Indushul to speak inside my mind again.

"Does he ever talk to you?"

"In the beginning he used to torment my thoughts with his, but I learned to just laugh them away. He hasn't tried again for centuries."

Mirela sighed. I don't know why she did, but I got the sense the weight of centuries upon centuries pressed heavily upon her.

"Before you go, tell me you love me, Orly."

She knew I would not take her with me. That I would meet Ji'Indushul alone. That she accepted that and probably even anticipated it before bringing me into her Oblivion surprised me.

"I love you," I answered.

"Then go now. Go to him. Free him from his tomb if you can. But know he will never leave my Oblivion."

I rose to my feet and Mirela rose with me. She leaned forward and kissed my lips. I thought of killing her right then but wasn't sure I wanted to, and wasn't confident I would be able to escape her Oblivion if I did. I thought it better to find Ji'Indushul. I kissed her back and she returned to sitting with her back to the dirt wall, wearing the sad expression of a condemned woman.

TWENTY-SEVEN

I levitated out of the pit, leaving Mirela, my lover, behind. I studied my surroundings. The pit was dug in a clearing. The area around it was mountainous and forested. It looked similar to the region where Castle Cobălcescu had been erected in the real world.

Hurry, Orly Bialek, Ji'Indushul said telepathically. We haven't much time.

As he spoke to me inside my head, instead of using an audible voice, I couldn't gauge where he was by sound. He was everywhere.

"Where are you?" I said softly.

This is the Oblivion. I am where I am supposed to be.

"That doesn't help much."

Walk in whatever direction you think I should be and you will find me there.

It made little sense but I chose a direction following a star in the night sky that glowed green. Walking about sixty yards, I left the clearing and headed into the forest. Very quickly the ground began to slope and I was ascending. Trees towered over me.

"All that moaning I heard, even when I was still in Los Angeles, that was you, wasn't it?"

I called to you, yes. I can sense the outside world, but my telepathic communication cannot penetrate Mirela's Oblivion. Only the sounds of my suffering escapes. She allows that because it pleases her to hear it.

"Then every time you called to me she could hear it."

Yes, it is her Oblivion after all.

"Then why did she let me come here? Why is she allowing me to find you?"

I have been trapped here for over three thousand years. She knows there is no way for you to free me.

"Even if I killed her?"

You failed to do that.

"But if I did kill her, would you be free?"

Yes, the death of the imparateasa is the only way I will ever leave this place alive.

"Am I still walking the right way?"

You are here.

"Where? I don't see anything."

Turn around.

I turned and looked behind me. To my amazement, I saw the bricked in tomb I had seen so many times before. It was as though I had walked right past it without noticing. The sides and the roof were made of large gray stone slabs. Where the doorway should have been were smaller, unmatched bricks and mortar. I ran my finger along the mortar, feeling its rough texture.

"When was the last time this doorway was opened?"

It has never been opened once it had been shut.

I made a fist and pounded on it. I expected it to be difficult to break, but the mortar crumbled easily.

"Do you mind me breaking it?"

For three thousand years I have longed for it to fall.

I continued to pound on the bricks and within moments, the entirety of the door had fallen away, most spilling into the tomb.

"You couldn't have done that yourself?" I asked.

It is not the tomb that binds me. It is my sarcophagus.

Inside the tomb was empty, except for the fallen bricks and a single sarcophagus covered in dust. The foot of it rested nearest the doorway I had just smashed in. I thought the perspective of it lying flat on the stone floor was playing tricks with my eyes, but when I stepped inside the tomb and knelt beside it, I gasped. I knew then I had seen the truth. The sarcophagus was small—too small for the mighty Ji'Indushul.

"Are you a child?" I asked in disbelief.

Are you?

"No. I mean, were you when you were turned?

Yes. As were you. We have a lot in common, Orly Bialek.

I used my hand to sweep the layers of dust off the top of the sarcophagus. It was made of wood, sanded smooth and stained black. It was covered in symbols, painted in blood or at least the color of blood, in a language I did not understand or even recognize. At the head of the sarcophagus was the carved and painted face of a child, and I presumed it to be the likeness of Ji'Indushul. He did not have an angelic face as did most vampires. Like mine, his face was quite ordinary. I ran my hands over the the entirety of the sarcophagus, but was unable to find any hinges or latches that might open it. I could not even find a seam in the wood that would indicate there was a lid to lift off.

"How do you open it?"

You cannot open it. It is cursed.

"Then what am I supposed to do?"

Place your fingers over the eyes.

I did so.

Now press down.

I pressed down and the painted eyes receded a few centimeters into the sarcophagus.

Now push them up, like you were opening eyelids.

I slid them up, expecting to see Ji'Indushul's real eyes behind them. But I did not see eyes that were brown, blue, or green. There were no eyes at all, only blackened eye sockets recessed deep into a skull.

Press down on the lips and then part them as though you were opening my mouth.

I did as instructed, and to my horror, when the lips of the sarcophagus lid parted, I saw only teeth, including the fangs of a very old vampire. All around his white teeth his gums were blackened, his lips burned off.

The mouth of teeth moved.

"My voice has not escaped this box in over three thousand years," he said. "I am quite hideous, am I not?"

"No," I answered.

"You need to become a better liar if you expect to live long as a vampire, Orly Bialek."

All I could see beneath the surface of the sarcophagus was the blackness of the cavities of his eyes and mouth, and the whiteness of his intact teeth.

"You were burned by the sun, weren't you?"

"Yes. The night my punishment was mete, I was confined to this box and placed out of doors. Later, when the sun was high above, mortal servants of Mirela's—may they be dead—opened the eyes and mouth of the sarcophagus long enough for my eyes and mouth to be burned off my face. Once they were again closed, I was entombed on the mountainside and have been there ever since."

"You remain unconscious there, in the real world?"

"Yes. My mind and everything else that is me remains trapped here."

"When was the last time you had blood?" I asked.

"Since before I was confined."

"That's thousands of years. How come you haven't died?"

"Time moves differently in the Oblivion. But who says I'm not already dead on the side of that mountain in the true world?"

I bit into my wrist and let the blood flow. It spilled onto the sarcophagus as I brought my wrist to his lipless mouth. He drank fervently until the wound closed. I opened it a second time and let him drink again until it healed over once more.

"I thank you," he said.

"I can't keep talking to a box," I said. "I have to get you out."

I made a fist and pounded it hard onto the sarcophagus, expecting my vampiric strength to splinter it, but nothing happened. I hit it harder. Again, nothing. I tried pulling it apart.

"Don't waste your strength, Orly Bialek. It is hopeless. But come. As I said, we have little time to say what needs to be said. She can withdraw at any time. Now please place your fingers where my eyes once were."

"Inside the holes?"

"Yes. Do not be afraid. Insert your fingers, and tell me what you feel."

I placed an index finger into each eye socket. I expected it to feel like dry charcoal, but I was wrong. In the depths of each cavity I felt something gritty.

"It feels like sand," I said.

"Close your eyes and listen to the wind of the desert. It is different than the wind of the forest."

I shut my eyes and listened closely. Eventually I noticed a change in the sound of the air passing outside the tomb. Or perhaps the change occurred only in my mind. But somehow the breathing wind exhaled longer, each breath traveling a greater distance unimpeded. With my eyes closed, I massaged the grains of sand with my fingertips in the depths of his eye sockets until I felt them no more. Sensing I was being watched, I opened my eyes. I turned and looked out through the doorway of the tomb, and quickly ascertained I was no longer inside the tomb, but instead, inside a large circular tent. A small fire in the center of the sandy floor lit the interior. It had a slit for a doorway that the wind would lightly blow open, revealing sand dunes below a crescent moon. On a rough, woven carpet stood a young boy, about the age I looked. He wore loose fitting clothing, the color of sand. He was thinly built and had short dark hair, a caramel complexion and hazel eyes. I approached him. He was exactly my height.

"This is your Oblivion, Ji'Indushul, isn't it?" I asked.

"Yes. I live much of my existence in my own Oblivion. It is my only escape. But bringing you here is not for comfort's sake. An Oblivion within an Oblivion will buy us more time. You have many questions, but we must concentrate on what is essential. You mean to kill her, is that correct?"

"Yeah. That's what I intended when I came here. To her castle, I mean."

"Is it not your intention now?"

"It is. But…but I don't know."

"What don't you know?"

"Things have changed. She's changed."

"She killed your mother, did she not?"

"I know she did. But I have forgiven her," I said, acknowledging I had said the words in the real world shortly before entering Mirela's Oblivion.

"But did you mean it when you forgave her?" he asked.

I thought about whether or not I meant it. Though I had said it in haste, to escape the wails of the slicing, I had said it nonetheless. Perhaps I only wanted to forgive her because I loved her. But did I love her? Or was that sentiment only a manifestation resulting from the exchange of our vampiric blood? Both love and vengeance grappled in my mind.

"You have allied yourself with others—Petru, Codrina, Viorica, Vasile. They too seek her death."

"I wouldn't say the word allied. I didn't promise them anything. But Petru told me to find you. They need you to kill her."

"Alas, you must tell them, Orly Bialek, I cannot kill the imparateasa."

"You can't? Why not?" I asked incredulously. "I thought that was the whole point of finding you!"

"I am quite impotent confined in that cursed box, trapped in her Oblivion. Tell them, it is you who must kill her."

"Me? Why me? I can't kill her."

"You must."

"I mean, even when I want to kill her I can't. I already failed once with the stake."

"You will not kill her with the stake. You will kill her within your Oblivion."

"My Oblivion? I haven't even found my Oblivion. And even if I did, I would be mortal there, and she would still be the oldest vampire in the bloodline. How could I possibly kill her like that?"

"When you were turned, you awoke in the ground during daylight. I have never encountered one who could say the same. It is why I sought you out. I have been waiting for someone like you for centuries."

"I don't understand."

"They say the sun never rises in the Oblivion. That it is forever night here. And for all of us that is true. But you are different, Orly Bialek. You were reborn when the sun was in the sky. I believe the sun will rise in your Oblivion. And that is how you will kill her."

"You believe it will, or you know it will?"

"Find your Oblivion, Orly Bialek. Lead her there and don't let her out. Let the sun rise and burn her to cinders. The sunlight will not harm you in your Oblivion, for you will be mortal."

Without thinking, I struck him in the face. My vampiric strength sent him flying into the fabric of the tent, tearing it, his body landing halfway outside. His mouth bled mortal blood. Slowly, he rose from the sand to his feet, his legs wobbling, and reentered the circular tent. I had just defended

Mirela, my mother's killer, from this four-thousand-year-old boy who would plot to murder my lover. I stormed toward the opening of the tent, intending to leave him and walk out into the dunes, but to my surprise, as hard as I tugged I could not part the opening wide enough for me to fit through. He was keeping me within.

I turned to him. Slowly he walked to one of the carpets and sat. He beckoned me to sit with him. I calmed myself and then took a seat before him.

"You are wondering how Mirela brought me into her Oblivion while inside my sarcophagus and tomb," he said.

He was right, but I didn't answer him.

"I assume what you wear now is what you wore in the true world before you came here."

It wasn't a question so I didn't answer. But I wondered if Ji'Indushul seeing me in my camisole with so much of my skin exposed would make Mirela jealous. It was fortunate that we had not been fully undressed and covered in blood when the slicing began.

"And when Konomi took you to the Bokyaku, as she called it, her clothes changed, while yours remained the same."

"How do you know about me and Konomi?"

He didn't answer my question, but continued in his train of thought.

"I was already inside my sarcophagus and interred in my tomb. Perhaps that is why I remain confined within them while in Mirela's Oblivion. And if not that, then as I said, my sarcophagus is cursed. It is possible that curse allowed my resting place to penetrate her Oblivion."

"So you don't really know anything, is what you're saying?"

"I am only putting things together in this moment based on what you've shared with me. I've never had a visitor before."

"But I haven't shared anything."

"But you have. I can read your thoughts. I do not desire to see you naked."

"That's not possible for you to read my thoughts. I'm a vampire."

"It should not be possible, but it is. Just like your drawings that show the pasts of your subjects. I too was made immortal for my talent."

I was stunned. We truly did have a lot in common.

"My people were called the Shul'Mara," Ji'Indushul continued. "You will not have heard of us. We are a forgotten nomadic people of the desert. As a boy, I thought everyone could read the thoughts of others, but eventually I learned that was not the case. News of my great ability spread until one night my people were visited by pale visitors from across the sea. That was the first time I laid eyes on Mirela's beauty. She charmed me and had me read the thoughts of her brood and then tested me to see if I could read her thoughts as well.

I could read the thoughts of each of them, including Mirela's. But unlike your drawings, where you can see a person's entire past, I can only read the present thoughts that come to mind in the moment. Your gift, Orly Bialek, is greater than mine.

"The vampires killed many of our people and kidnapped me. Mirela was overjoyed that I could read the thoughts of other vampires, but was also furious that I could read hers as well. She did her best not to think revealing thoughts, but was still unpracticed at doing so. She decided to turn me herself, to see how her blood would affect me. If it didn't have the desired effect and I could still read her mind, I knew from her thoughts she would kill me immediately. I received her blood and died, and when I woke as a vampire she unearthed me.

"With her blood in me, all her thoughts vanished from my awareness. She tested me in a number of ways, most often thinking of horrific ways to kill or torture me. As I never exhibited fear or concern when she thought such things, remaining ignorant of my imagined fates until she spoke of them, she eventually she became convinced I could no longer read her mind. I thought it was a blessing at the time, that I had been spared and made immortal. But as I could still read the thoughts of her descendants, she used that to her advantage. For twelve centuries I read the passing thoughts of those in her bloodline and accused those who might betray her. Out of fear, I even sent friends to their deaths. Remorse eventually overcame me and I refused to serve her any longer. And that refusal was the cause of my confinement."

Mirela had used him for the same purpose she now used me.

"Yes, our usefulness to her is quite the same," Ji'Indushul said.

"Do you still talk to her?"

"No. There is no point in it. And she comes here little. The pit brings her great sadness. In it she relives feeling abandoned and doomed. Though intellectually she knows Mikonost will ultimately save her, she also knows that in her Oblivion the night of her rescue will never come. Thus while here she can feel no hope of liberation. Plus as a mortal, she knows I can read her present thoughts again, so she thinks of very little that can be of use to me. She mostly sleeps and never dreams. But inadvertently her thoughts twice went to you, and that is how I learned your name and of your artistic talent."

Ji'Indushul took me by the hands. "I warn thee, Orly Bialek. If you will not kill her, you must never feel remorse for those you send to their deaths. Never stop serving her, or you will end up here beside me."

The thought of being similarly condemned for eternity frightened me, but as I knew this ancient boy's goal was to kill my lover, I remained defensive. "She couldn't have dragged you here though. She could only show you the way."

"Yes, you are correct. I went with her willingly."

"But why? You would have been better off trying to break free in the real world."

"At the time, I did not know what the Oblivion was, or that it even existed. After three hundred years entombed on that mountainside, Mirela finally visited my resting place. In whispers she described a peaceful place called Rauerk. It's the Cobalshik word for oblivion. She said there both my eyes and mouth would be restored. I would still be her prisoner in this mysterious place, but I would be allowed to roam freely again and feed as much as I liked. As you now know it was a lie, but remember I could no longer read her vampiric thoughts. After three hundred years, I thought she was finally taking pity on me, or at the very least, trying to employ my services again. When she said she'd guide me to Rauerk, I allowed her to take me there even though I was still confined within my sarcophagus."

I didn't want to hear anymore about Mirela's misdeeds.

"I want to leave," I said.

"Are you going to kill her?"

"After Mirela, you are the oldest Cobălcescu, right?"

"I am."

"And you're also the only one left who was turned with her blood. Is that right too?"

"It is."

I realized that with Mirela's blood inside him, perhaps even more than was now inside me, that if I killed her, he would be free, the eldest, and the most powerful. He would rule the Cobălcescu.

"I promise that is not my aim," he said, having read my thoughts.

"How do I know that? Maybe you want her dead just for power."

"Believe that if you must," he said. "But allow me to tell you one more thing, Orly Bialek. Mirela promised me a man's body just as she promised you a woman's. As you can see, she never gave it to me, not after twelve centuries of service. I have come to doubt that she truly has the power to steal the body from another."

"But her own body. She stole it."

"Yes. She told you that, didn't she?"

I felt angry. I felt stupid. I didn't want to believe him. I wanted to believe Mirela stole her perfect body and would steal one for me.

"The hands we were dealt, as they say, are so very similar. Are they not?" Ji'Indushul asked.

His words felt like daggers, but I could not deny them. Our lives paralleled in such crucial ways. But instead of acknowledging that aloud, out of jealousy I asked instead, "Were you ever her lover?"

"Never," he replied, and I was relieved.

I rose and moved again toward the exit of the tent. Ji'Indushul leapt to his feet, as if to stop me.

"Before you go, Orly Bialek, I beg a favor of you," he said beseechingly.

"I can't kill her," I said, "I love her."

"Yes, I understand that now. But I am asking you for this favor whether you intend to kill her or not."

"What is it?"

"Kill me," he answered solemnly.

"What?" I asked, startled.

"Take pity on me. I have lived too long as her prisoner. I am weary beyond all comparison. I am enervated with no vitality left for living. You are the first to visit my Oblivion, the first to see me mortal in over four thousand years. I may never have this opportunity again. It is not possible to kill yourself in the Oblivion. I have tried. There is only pain, but no death. You must do it for me."

The anger I had felt toward him only moments before for wanting to kill Mirela, and for making me believe she would never give me or could never give me a woman's body, quelled inside me as he implored me to kill him. Could I do it? Should I do it? Was it a mistake? Was it a trick? Should I not pity him? What would Mirela do if I killed him? I didn't know the answers to anything.

"Don't think of it. Any of it. We haven't time," he said desperately. "Please, free me from my fate."

I looked into his eyes. "If you know you can't kill yourself here, how do you know I can kill you?"

"Because I know Mirela has killed those in her brood while in their Oblivion."

"So what you know is someone can be killed in their own Oblivion while they're mortal. But you don't really know a vampire can be killed the same way. You don't actually know Mirela can be killed in my Oblivion."

He stepped toward me and took my hand. "No. You are right, I do not know and will never know if you kill me now as I am asking you to do. But I believe one day you will discover it to be true when you kill the imparateasa, as the sun will rise in your Oblivion."

For a reason unknown to me, I did not think of striking him again as he mentioned killing Mirela. Instead, I closed my eyes, searching my mind for an answer. Do I kill Ji'Indushul or leave him to his infinite fate?

"Please," he implored. "Let the compassion you feel for immortals compel you. I know you hated damning those to the affliction of the slicing. Show me mercy. Release me from this eternal suffering."

I opened my eyes and looked at him. Saline tears streamed from his eyes. I nodded in assent. I would kill him.

He took my hands and kissed them. "I thank you, Orly Bialek. You have saved my life." He then tilted his head, offering me his throat.

"Good bye, Ji'Indushul," I said, feeling the significance and permanence in ending the life of someone who had lived so long. I swallowed the lump in my throat and then bared my fangs. I leaned forward and bit into his jugular. I could feel his cheeks stretch. He was smiling at his own death. He embraced me, forgiving me as his savior. I drank the mortal blood of Ji'Indushul until he grew weak and I had to hold him up. I drank until his heart stopped. And when it beat no more, the fire in the center of the sandy floor extinguished. In the darkness I felt him slip from my arms but never heard his body hit the floor. When my eyes adjusted from the absence of firelight, I saw I was back where I had been—beside the sarcophagus inside the tomb I had broken into. But as I peered into the eye holes of the sarcophagus, I saw it was empty. Ji'Indushul was gone.

TWENTY-EIGHT

I felt the invisible insides of myself, what I thought to be my soul, pulled violently from Ji'Indushul's empty tomb, and through a blur of night, I was sucked back into the pit with Mirela, who stood grabbing me by the hair. Her grip on my hair felt hostile and as a reflex I bared my fangs. I thought of killing her as it would be easy to accomplish with her being mortal. Did I truly love her? Did she truly love me? Had I really forgiven her for killing Yelena or had I only said that to escape the cries of the condemned I blamed myself for back in the real world? These thoughts raced through my mind in the fraction of a second. And just as I opened my mouth a little more, the walls of earth around us fell. The illusion of their falling made it appear as if the walls had stood above us from the ground up, rather than having been the boundaries of a sunken burial pit. Behind their fallen masses I saw an abundance of candlelight and with it returned the shrieks of those slowly being put to death.

"They're still screaming!" I screamed myself. In vain, I attempted to drown out the noise by covering my ears.

Time had certainly moved slowly here while we were away in the Oblivion.

The world that existed over five thousand years ago had completely vanished and we were once more in Mirela's bedroom, and Mirela was again the eldest of vampires in my bloodline. Mirela was no longer nude. Again she wore her violet camisole. She licked my blood—still wet—from her lips as she got out of bed and covered herself in a robe.

"Yes, they are still screaming," she said flatly. "I am delighted we have not missed it entirely. At best I imagine they have only reached their ankles."

Their suffering did not matter to her at all.

"I wanna go back!" I shouted, meaning back to her Oblivion.

"No," Mirela answered, devoid of any emotion.

She finally came to life when I stormed out of the room, wearing only my camisole.

"Where are you going?" she asked desperately.

But I didn't answer. And as she was not properly dressed, she did not follow.

I made my way downstairs, but did not know how to get to the catacombs without walking out the front door into the daylight as Mayuko had done with Luca. That the castle was still standing during the day stupefied me momentarily, but I concluded I was merely under Mirela's spell. As such, the illusion of the castle remained a reality during the day as it had all the days I had spent awake in bed with her. If what Mayuko had told me was true, I was already in the catacombs, and always had been, but I needed a way to see through the illusion of Castle Cobălcescu. But with all the screams tearing through my brain, it was difficult to combat the false image in my mind.

Orly, don't try to come here. Seeing these deaths are far worse than hearing them.

It was the voice of Viorica in my head. I spoke back to her telepathically.

I must see what I've done. Please, Viorica, show me how to get there. I'm begging you.

There was a pause. She didn't speak.

Please, I said again.

And then she spoke.

Very well. Close your eyes and imagine yourself at rest inside your coffin. Feel the satin beneath you. Inhale the dead air trapped within. You want to sleep.

It took time and great concentration, but eventually, I could smell the wood polish of my coffin. I could feel the familiar satin upon my fingertips. But once more, I also smelled the distinct scent of rubbing alcohol.

Open your eyes. Are you there? Viorica asked.

I opened my eyes and to my surprise and utter confusion, I realized I was indeed inside my coffin.

Wasn't that easy? The truth is often more simple to find than it might otherwise seem. Open your lid, Orly, Viorica said. Come and witness the end of eternity.

I slid open the lid of my coffin and stepped out into the darkness of catacombs that were scarcely lit by torchlight. To my amazement, the catacombs were heavily populated. The Ancients and Eternals were all awake, their funerary boxes empty. The cries of the condemned were louder and more pronounced here. I saw Petru, Trajan, and Matei across the large expanse of the catacombs, administering the pain of the slicing. Ignoring my self-consciousness regarding my state of dress, I walked toward them. The cold stares of the Ancients never left me as they parted, making way for me to pass.

I reached the shafts that were burrowed to the surface for the purpose of the executions. The condemned hung upside down within them. The parts of them that protruded the earthen floor above the sunlight scorched, searing flesh until the ash of their remains showered below ground. Much of the white ash clung to the hair of the condemned, discoloring it, making them appear elderly. Some stuck to the blood that dripped from their eyes and mouths. Judging by the visible lengths of their hanging bodies, Mirela had been right, it seemed they were only burned down to their ankles. The faces of the damned became aware of me and stared with hatred in their bloody eyes as they continued to screech in anguish.

"Stop it!" I screamed at their executioners. "Stop them from suffering!"

"You would be wise to shut up, little girl," Trajan said to me disdainfully. "This is the will of the imparateasa."

With vampiric speed, I rushed at Trajan, hoping to throw him off balance and free those he was slowly pushing into the sunlight above. But I was not fast enough. As I got within reach of him, he struck me in the face with the back of his hand and I went flying, hitting the dusty floor of the catacombs and rolling into empty coffins.

"Stupid girl," he spat.

As I lay on the ground, recovering my senses, voices of Ancients spoke to me telepathically over the screaming of the vampires being tortured to death.

This is your doing, Orly Bialek!

Stop acting like a baby! You must live with this!

You have much to learn about loyalty and betrayal, little girl.

You cursed child! You will bring upon all our deaths!

Do not think being Mirela's favorite will keep you safe. You saw how easily she let Alexi Pavlovich die.

I rose to my feet, all eyes still upon me. Of the three Eternal administering the slicing, I knew Petru was the only one I could appeal to.

Petru, I said telepathically. Which of them are you holding in place?

I hold both women, Daciana and Ioana. I also hold Valeriu.

I again walked past the Ancients until I reached Petru. I placed my hand upon his arm.

"Please, don't fight me," I said.

"You cannot save them, Orly. They are doomed."

"I know I can't save them. But please, at least let me hold them."

Petru nodded solemnly. "As you wish," he said aloud, and telepathically he said, I know what you intend to do.

With that he slowly released them to my care. Daciana, Ioana, and Valeriu began to slip from the holes burrowed for them, falling slightly into the catacombs, until I was able to concentrate my efforts enough to hold them and prevent them from falling all the way to the the floor. They still groaned from the pain they had already experienced, but managed to stop shrieking as loudly as the others as their limbs were no longer exposed to the sunlight. I touched their faces.

"I am so sorry," I said, as blood tears fell from my eyes. "Forgive me for what I have done. This is all I can do for you now."

And with all my mental faculties, I used the strength gained by Mirela's blood to telekinetically eject all three of them instantly through their holes, up into the sunlight above, where they again screamed in agony as they incinerated. Their suffering as they burned to death was lengthy, but still far shorter than it would have been had they faced the full extent of the slicing.

Many of the Ancients gasped in surprise at what I had done.

The screams of those still being sliced continued at full volume.

"You fool, Petru" Trajan said angrily. "Mercy is not the way of the imparateasa. If I were imparat, you would face the slicing next."

"But you are not imparat," a firm feminine voice said.

All turned. It was Mirela. She was now dressed in a dark gray gown and tiara and had joined her coven in the catacombs. The crowd, except for me, bowed and curtsied to her with great reverence. It was as though I were the only one unable to ignore the torturous cries of those still being burned alive.

The Ancients parted for their imparateasa as she walked slowly to me. She placed her hand upon my cheek, and with her thumb she wiped midstream the blood running from my left eye, and then placed her thumb between her lips, tasting me. The Ancients remained silent; I did not even feel the electricity of their telepathic communication. Mirela's gentleness toward me must have been quite an astonishing spectacle for them.

Finally, Viorica's voice echoed in my head.

She has not shown such affection since Marcel Bousquet.

"Merciful Orly," Mirela said sweetly. "You are still too gentle for our kind. And how you love to defy me. I would punish you if I did not love you so much," she smiled, her fangs shining brightly in the darkness. She then turned to Trajan and Matei. "End my lover's misery. Follow her example."

"Mirela," Trajan began. "It is precisely an example we are trying to set."

"No. It is an example I set. However, in this moment I am overruled by Orly's tender heart. Now close your mouth and do as I command this instant."

Immediately, Anghel, Neculai, Uta, and Liviu were ejected above ground and met their excruciating deaths in the sunlight. Nearly ten minutes passed before we heard nothing more from above than the wind, blowing their ashes into nothingness.

"It is still daylight," Mirela began. "We should all take our rest."

Upon those words, Ancients and Eternals alike returned to their funerary boxes. Mirela walked me to my coffin and laid me to rest. With the lid closed over me, I did not see where she herself went. As I slowly fell into a slumber, my thoughts drifted between the Ancients who had just met their deaths, the unborn Mayuko buried in the earth, and the realization that whilst in my coffin I would never hear the sorrowful murmurs of Ji'Indushul ever again.

I hadn't slept long before I noticed I was no longer lying upon the satin cushions of my coffin, but instead was wrapped in the silken sheets of Mirela's bed. She lay at my side, again wearing only a camisole, spooning me.

"You're awake," Mirela said softly.

"Is it night?"

"Not for a few more hours. You showed weakness today, Orly. That will not serve you well."

"I know."

"It will not serve me well either."

"What do you mean?"

"Well, beyond defying my decrees, the coven will see you as the one they can use to undermine me because of the favor I show you."

"You didn't have to make Trajan and Matei end their lives quickly. You said you did it for your love for me, so you showed weakness too."

"That is precisely what I mean. In their eyes, you've placed a satin pillow beneath my iron fist. You should have let them suffer. You don't care about the lives of mortals, so why do you care about them?"

"Because they aren't mortals. They're like us."

"Ah yes, but before you became a vampire, you fed Yelena many mortals. Why did you not care about them as they were mortal like you?"

"A lot of them were bad people. But mostly it was because I was gonna die as a little kid. It made me really bitter and so I couldn't pity people who'd already outlived me."

"And now you shall outlive them all."

I thought about that for a moment and saw the faces belonging to all my foster families, the nurses and doctors in the hospital I died in, and the face of my social worker Sigrid Paz. I would outlive them all, if the Cobălcescu Ancients didn't kill me soon.

I kissed Mirela's wrist. "Can I have some?" I asked.

"Whatever pleases you, my love."

I bit into her wrist and drank slowly, savoring the taste of the imparateasa's blood and feeling her strength flow into me until her wound closed.

"You killed Ji'Indushul," she said calmly.

I sensed no anger or hostility in her voice and wondered how she knew, but I didn't ask.

"That was weakness too, Orly. You took pity on his suffering and have stolen thousands of years of pleasure for me."

"It wasn't pleasure for him."

"Whom do you love, Orly? Me or Ji'Indushul?"

"I just don't know why you like to see people suffer so much."

"I don't like to see people suffer so much, only my enemies."

"But he was your enemy just because he didn't want to read minds for you anymore. What happens if I tell you that I don't want to draw for you anymore? Will you tell me I'm your enemy?"

"You don't really love me, do you, Orly?"

I kissed her wrist where the wound closed. "I do love you. I promise."

"Then why would you stop drawing for me if doing so keeps me alive?"

"If you love me why do you make me do something you know I hate doing? And why would you trap me in your Oblivion if I stopped drawing for you?"

"Who said I would trap you in my Oblivion?"

"That's what Ji'Indushul said you would do."

"But I didn't love Ji'Indushul," Mirela answered. "I would kill you before doing to you what I did to Ji'Indushul. And that's because I love you."

"Some love," I said sarcastically.

"You know you did not gain any of Ji'Indushul's strength when you killed him. The blood you drank was mortal, not vampiric."

I didn't know if she was lying to me or not. It's not lying if she really believed it to be true. But I didn't know it wasn't true. For I had felt something, some essence of Ji'Indushul pass through me as I drank every ounce of his blood.

"When are you gonna give me my new body?"

"When I believe you've truly forgiven me."

"I told you I did."

"Yet you thought of killing me in my Oblivion."

"No. It wasn't like that. I saw you as a mortal for a second and it was just an instinct. That's all."

"I don't believe lies, Orly, so don't ever tell me any."

"And so now you don't even believe I love you?"

"I no longer want to think about that. Not in this moment," Mirela said. "In this moment, I just want to have you here with me."

"You're showing weakness again," I said.

"Yes, I am. Aren't I?"

I loved her for admitting her vulnerability. I rolled over in her arms and faced her. I brought my face to hers and moved to kiss her, but she turned her face away. Though I felt rebuffed, I tried again, kissing her bare shoulder instead.

"Stop," she whispered, and gently pushed me away.

"What's wrong?" I asked. "Don't you want to make love to me?"

"Leave me. Go back downstairs. Back to your room. You'll find your coffin there."

"I don't get it. What did I do?"

She didn't answer. She rolled over, turning away from me. I was confused, but also frustrated. I wanted her to touch me and I wanted to touch her and I wanted more of her blood, but she had utterly rejected me. I got out of bed, picked up the gown smeared with Mayuko's grave soil off the floor and dressed myself, watching her as I did, hoping she would turn back over to look at me and relent in my expulsion, or at the very least to watch me go. But she didn't do either.

I opened the bedroom doors without touching them, and after I had exited and walked a few paces down the hall, I slammed them as hard as I could.

When I returned to my room, my coffin with its punctured lid was indeed there, but I didn't lay in it as I had already rested more than enough in Mirela's arms. I removed the filthy gown instead and drew a bath. As I lay in the hot water wondering why my lover had turned me away, I noticed blood had dried upon Yelena's diamond. Was it my blood or Mirela's? I submerged deeper into the water so that the diamond was below the surface. I watched as the hot water slowly began to lift the blood from the diamond in wispy sanguine threads. I felt guilty that the traces of my love for Mirela had smeared something so sacred to me as my remembrance of Yelena and her love for me.

TWENTY-NINE

When nightfall came, I dressed myself in a green satin gown Babette had made for me. I sensed the Ancients already gathered downstairs. Though I could hear liquors being poured and the clinking of crystal glasses, the merriment was diminished from what it had been over the preceding nights. The executions I had caused during the day had clearly ruined the nighttime festivities of the Communion of the Ancients.

Once dressed and adorned in my diamonds, I opened my chamber door and stepped out into the empty hall. I dreaded going downstairs to face everyone. Still feeling rejected by Mirela, I decided to wait for her at the base of her private staircase rather than ascend to the third floor uninvited. I sat on the stairs in my gown and as I waited I thought of Mayuko, wondering how many nights would pass before she would awaken. A quarter of an hour passed when I heard Mirela's voice, but it had not come from her bedroom. It had come from the ballroom below. She had gone downstairs without me. Perhaps she no longer desired my attendance, and that wounded me. I thought of going back to my coffin, but I thirsted for blood and wanted a vessel.

I rose to my feet and summoned the courage to go down alone. I descended the staircase and walked the great hall as silently as I could, but when I appeared in the doorway of the ballroom, all eyes were upon me, including Mirela's. No one smiled, not even my lover. I felt outcast by all and would have retreated to my chamber if I didn't need blood.

They are simpleminded fools who cannot see the position you've been placed in by the imparateasa, Petru said.

Ignore their dirty looks, Orly. Come and feed, Viorica said.

Quite unexpectedly, even Codrina addressed me.

Spit on them if you like. They know nothing of what it is truly like to deal with her.

I stepped into the room and scanned the room for vessels. They were not seated in their usual corner so I kept looking until I saw three sitting at a single table. To my surprise, by their sides sat Berthold, Zacharias, and Hisato, all wearing black tailored evening wear. And with a vessel to Berthold's right, Kristy sat at his left. She was dressed in a peach colored strapless gown that accentuated her breasts. I wondered if Babette had made it for her and at the thought I felt a slight and momentary bitterness. Kristy appeared relaxed which either showed how brave she was or how unaware she was of the danger she was in. I was, of course, not delighted to see her. But that wasn't only because of jealousy. I felt that way mostly because Mirela had truly delivered her body to me which meant I would soon break Berthold's heart.

Still, I was excited to see my three friends and hurried to their table. Berthold stood tall and smiled when he saw me approaching. With vampiric ease, I sprang over the table, landed in his arms and embraced him tightly.

The room had grown quiet. Everyone was watching the table of non-Ancients. Berthold put me down. I glanced at Mirela. She too was watching me and I hoped I had not displayed anything in my interaction with Berthold she would find threatening. But she turned to the musicians, waved her hand, and they began to play. Slowly and with some reservation, the ancient vampires partnered and began to dance.

Zacharias, Hisato, and Kristy were now also standing.

"Hi Zacharias," I said, hugging him. "How are our pigs?"

"They were well fed, Orly, but now I do not know."

"We'll see them again soon. I don't think this Communion can go on for much longer. I'm so sick of it already."

I turned to Hisato and after I hugged him he held me by the hands and looked at me.

"There's something different about you, my impish brat," he said.

"She's more powerful," Zacharias answered.

"Maybe a just little," I said, smiling until I turned to Kristy.

"We haven't been introduced. My name is Orly."

"It is a pleasure to meet you Orly. Berthold has told me a lot about you," she said pleasantly.

I forced a smile, making sure my fangs were showing.

No. She had no idea of the danger she was in.

"Let's sit. You don't know how happy I am to see you," I said to my friends. "When did you get here?"

"We arrived last night. We were brought here by force," Berthold whispered, not knowing everyone in the room could hear him distinctly.

Continuing in hushed voices, my friends described to me their abductions. The violence that had been employed to arrest them disturbed me but I did my best to hide my displeasure as to not encourage their consternation.

"We were locked in rooms we could not open, essentially imprisoned," Berthold said at the close of their retellings. "We heard terrible screaming and thought the worst. I'm relieved to see you alive."

"I'm fine," I said. "You don't need to worry about the screaming."

"It was awful," Kristy said.

"Well it's over now," I answered abruptly. I didn't like her talking to me when I could be talking to my friends instead.

"Even so, it does not explain why we were brought here, especially Kristy," Berthold said quietly.

The *especially Kristy* part of his sentence annoyed me.

"You don't have to worry. I'm sure everything's fine," I said not knowing how much of that was true, but I wanted to put them at ease as I knew there was nothing that could be done at the moment to remedy their unwilling presence. "Mirela knew I missed my friends, that's all."

"A simple fucking invitation would've done the trick," Hisato said spitefully.

"I see they gave you vessels. Have you fed yet?" I asked, excluding Kristy.

"Not yet," Berthold answered. "We were just about to when we saw you enter."

I scanned the room again and made eye contact with a mortal vessel across the room. I signaled for her to come to me.

"Where is Mayuko?" Berthold asked.

"She's in the ground right now. I turned her."

"You have grown more powerful indeed," Zacharias said.

I held up my hand and separated my thumb and forefinger a few centimeters to indicate how much power I had gained.

"How did you accomplish that?" Zacharias asked curiously.

I brought my forefinger to my lips. "It's a secret," I said playfully.

"When will we be able to talk privately?" Berthold again whispered.

"Don't whisper," I said. "It looks suspicious. Everyone here can hear you even when you do. But I'll ask Mirela if we can talk alone."

Berthold looked around the room warily.

The vessel I summoned arrived and I offered her the seat beside me.

"Cheers to you being here," I said happily and bit into the throat of my vessel.

Berthold, Zacharias, and Hisato all bit into the throats of their vessels. Kristy watched Berthold as he drank, as did I.

Have you tasted her blood yet? I asked Berthold telepathically. Kristy's I mean. Don't answer out loud, just open your eyes if you have.

Berthold opened his eyes.

Disappointed, I released my vessel early. I had had enough.

As I waited for them to finish feeding, I looked over at Kristy, going over the curves of her breasts and the beauty of her face. She finally noticed me watching her, but when I didn't break eye contact she looked away. That pleased me as I wanted her to fear me.

"Does anyone wanna dance?" I asked when they finished feeding, but none readily accepted my offer.

"She's coming," Berthold said suddenly.

I turned and saw Mirela approaching our table. Zacharias rose to his feet immediately and I and the others followed suit. The three men bowed to her, Hisato slightly less deferential, which I'm sure had not escaped Mirela's notice. Kristy and I curtsied.

"I would like to dance with you, my love, if they will not," Mirela said to me.

Her use of *my love* sparked curiosity in the faces of my friends.

"But first, you should introduce me to your companions."

Mirela smiled warmly as I introduced each of them. To the three men she said, "You were all friends of Yelena Solodnikova, I believe." They all seemed to gulp at the same time and then acknowledged it was true.

To Kristy, she said, "Orly was not lying when she described to me your beauty."

Kristy smiled. I wished Mirela had not said that.

Mirela excused us and took me by the hand and led me to the dance floor.

I didn't think you wanted to talk to me, I said to her.

We held each other as we danced.

I must apologize for my behavior. I am a deceitful woman, Orly.

What do you mean?

I've told you I loved you when I knew it would serve me even when I truly didn't, or rather, when I didn't fully mean it. I wanted your love more than I wanted to love you. But now I do love you, Orly. And that is the truth. There is no escaping you. There is nowhere I can hide my heart to keep myself from giving it to you.

Then why did you get so mad at me?

I wasn't mad at you. Orly, you make my heart overjoyed and woeful at the same time, and it makes me weak. Weaker than I have ever been. Weaker than I was with Marcel. I cannot resolve how to love you and still rule and it frightens me.

As fragile as you have made me I need your scribbles more now than ever. But as you refuse to draw for me any further, I know I must refuse you as my lover.

My heart panicked.

I didn't say I refuse. I said I don't like doing it, I said desperately.

One day you will refuse. We must end before that time comes, she replied sadly.

I had gotten what I had wanted—her vulnerability— vulnerability to match my own, and I was going to lose her because of it.

Had I really made her weaker than she was with Marcel or was that just another lie? If it were true, I lamented over the thought that she hadn't discovered her love for me when we first met so that she might have abandoned her vendetta against Yelena and let her live. Perhaps we could have all existed in some weirdly harmonious way. But I supposed it would not have been possible for Mirela to have loved me back then as I had not yet become a woman.

The song ended and the couples who shared the floor with us parted, but I stood holding Mirela, not wanting to let go. Her hands gently gripped my arms and she separated our bodies but did not release me entirely.

"You have already fed. Would you like to retire early?" she asked.

"With you?"

"Yes, with me."

"I would," I answered, "but my friends are here. And I haven't seen them in so long."

She bit her lip and looked over my head toward the table where my friends sat.

"Just give me a couple hours more with them," I said.

"Very well. You know where I will be waiting." She released me and then left the floor and exited the ballroom altogether.

I looked around the room and saw all eyes were on me as I stood alone in the center of the ballroom floor. My friends appeared bewildered by my closeness to the woman I left them intending to kill. Though the stares of the Ancients were expressionless, I didn't feel safe without Mirela by my side.

I walked back to the table and resumed my seat. All the vessels had already left to recover in their quarters, and my friends were drinking cognacs.

"Pour me one of those," I said, and Zacharias poured a glass and slid it in front of me. I drank.

"I didn't know you were so intimate," Berthold said.

I took another large swallow of the cognac. "She is my lover," I replied.

Berthold and Zacharias quickly made eye contact with each other, both confused at what I had just revealed.

"And what about Yelena?" Hisato said sharply. "Have you forgotten her so easily?"

"Of course I haven't," I spit out hastily. I calmed myself, took another drink and more softly began again, "It's just that…" but I hesitated to finish.

Hisato raised an eyebrow. "It's just that what?"

"Things changed since I got here."

"Changed?" he repeated, eyeing me suspiciously.

"Eternity is a long time to live with hate in your heart," I said, repeating the words Mirela said to me the night I arrived.

Hisato was visibly displeased. "You don't have to hate for eternity once the person you hate is dead," he said as he lifted a snifter of cognac to his lips.

I recalled having come to that conclusion myself, yet I cautioned him. "Be careful, Hisato," I warned.

"Like I care what they hear."

"Yelena would want me to move on and live," I countered, again retelling what Mirela had told me.

Hisato swallowed his entire drink and slammed the snifter down hard on the table, breaking it at the stem.

"She's doing the right thing. The smart thing," Berthold said. "And she's right, Yelena would want her to move on, especially if her life depended on it."

Zacharias nodded. "I agree."

"Me too," Kristy said.

"No one asked you," I shot back.

"Orly," Berthold said, quickly coming to Kristy's defense, who appeared startled at my hostility.

"Well, she didn't even know Yelena," I said sharply.

"Everyone calm down," Zacharias counseled.

"Yes. Everyone calm down," Berthold concurred. "The most important thing is that we get out of here alive. All of us."

Hisato exhaled dismissively. "Well why don't you ask your lover for some first class one-way tickets outta here?"

"And find out the real reason she brought us here," Berthold said in a serious tone.

"Yes, please do. We are all scared out of our wits here!" Kristy exclaimed.

I was wrong about her. She just hid her fear well.

"I'll tell her to let you all go home," I said, knowing it might not be possible and least likely for Kristy.

"And to let you go as well," Berthold continued.

My lips shifted slightly.

"What's wrong? Don't you want to go?" Berthold asked.

I smiled. "Of course I do. I told you I'm sick of it here."

The conversation after that was largely disjointed when it existed. We passed the next few hours pouring more drinks, with me drinking the fastest, until I was quite drunk. I rose from my seat too quickly and had to grab the table to keep from falling over.

"Where are you going?" Berthold asked.

"I told her I wouldn't be long and it's been long. Don't worry. I know you'll be safe."

I regained my balance and slowly stumbled out of the room, no longer caring who was watching me. I was stopped by Petru.

Have you found the tomb, Orly?

Ji'Indushul is dead.

What? How?

I killed him.

So you betrayed us after all.

If you wanna think that. But he asked me to kill him.

He asked you?

He asked me for mercy. He told me to tell you all that he couldn't kill Mirela anyway. That I had to do it.

You have to do it? Don't be ridiculous. I know you have gained strength from her blood, but believe me, you are not nearly strong enough to overcome her.

Ji'Indushul told me how to do it. He had it all figured out. I just don't know if I want to anymore. Sorry.

I patted Petru on the chest and used the solidness of his stature to push off of him and propel me toward the doorway. Gradually, I made my way to the staircase and, overwhelmed by the amount of stairs before me, I levitated up them to the second floor instead. Once there, I continued to levitate down the hall until I reached the base of Mirela's private staircase. Still not wanting to traverse the steps in my drunken state, I took to the air again, but much too quickly as I hit my head on the ceiling. I continued floating the length of the hall, sometimes bouncing off the wall, until I finally collided with Mirela's bedroom door and fell to the floor, landing on my bottom.

The double doors opened. To my surprise, Mirela had actually opened them by hand and stood in the doorway, wearing only a white slip, looking down at me where I sat.

She smiled. "Someone has had much too much to drink."

I looked up at her, laughed and then keeled over and vomited on the carpet.

"Agrapina!" Mirela shouted.

Mentally, she lifted me off the floor and lowered my body gently across her arms. Agrapina came down the hall in a hurry and bowed.

"Clean this," Mirela said, and then carried me into her bedroom. She willed the doors shut behind us.

Mirela undressed me, pulled a slip over my head, and put me to bed. She got in and lay beside me. She ran her fingers through my hair tenderly and I struggled to stay awake. Eventually she spooned me and caressed my body with her right hand. But her caresses stopped when her fingers touched the diamond pendant.

"You never take this off," she said.

"Uh uh," I answered sleepily and still drunk.

"It's associated with Yelena, isn't it?"

"Mmm."

"Did it belong to her? Or did she give it to you as a gift?"

"Shhhhh," I said and removed her hand from the pendant and held it myself over my heart until I fell asleep.

I was no longer intoxicated when my eyes opened. Mirela's arms were still around me and I rolled over and faced her. For the first time I saw Mirela asleep. At last she looked peaceful. I wondered if it were true what Ji'Indushul had said—that Mirela didn't dream. Her sleeping was so beautiful to behold that I longed to kiss her, but didn't want to wake her. I wanted the moment to last as long as it could.

Nearly an hour passed before she finally opened her eyes and found me looking at her. She smiled softly and blinked her eyes.

"What time is it?" she asked.

"That's always my question for you. I can't tell. I feel so rested that it feels like midnight."

"No, it is definitely close to noon. The sun is high above us. You were watching me. What were you thinking?"

"I was thinking I love you."

"That's a nice thing to wake to."

"Let's lie here all day. We can pretend we need the rest and just be lazy."

She leaned forward and we kissed gently at first and then more passionately. But I pulled away and she looked at me, perplexed.

"What is it?"

"That's not being lazy enough," I answered and she smiled. I looked at her fangs and tried to imagine how many lives they must have taken over the thousands of years she'd been alive.

"You were pretty drunk last night."

"I should never drink cognac. It always fucks me up."

"Why did you drink so much?"

"I don't know. I guess I just didn't want to think about stuff."

"You didn't want to think about what stuff?"

"Everything. Me killing those Ancients. You telling me I make you weak. Wondering how much longer this Communion of the Ancients thing is gonna last, and why you kidnapped my friends."

"That is a lot to think about indeed. Would you like another drink?"

"That's not funny."

But I realized she wasn't joking. She bit into her wrist and offered it, bleeding, to me. I took her hand and brought her wrist to my lips and drank as much as I could before the wound closed. I licked her skin clean.

"Better?" she asked.

I nodded my head. She caressed my cheek and then let her hand rest on the bedsheet in the small space between us.

"You didn't kill those Ancients. I did. And you making me weak is the truth, but I don't want to lose your love, Orly. So I've decided I will only ask you to draw someone when I have reason to suspect them and only need proof. Can you do that much for me?"

I bit my lip and felt pressured to say yes. But instead, I said, "I can't answer that so fast. I need to think about it. But I don't want to lose you either."

"I understand. You are wise to think about it, because once you answer, I'll expect you to hold true to your word. And the Communion of the Ancients can end tonight if you like. I'll send them all home if you promise to stay."

"And you'll let my friends go too?"

"Yes. All except Kristy of course."

"I get why you brought her. You brought her so you could give me her body, but why did you bring everyone else?"

"I thought if they were here, you wouldn't want to leave."

"Would your scribble say the same thing?"

She paused a moment before shaking her head.

"It would say that, but there's more. It would say I'd use them as leverage if you chose not to draw for me anymore."

"Meaning you'd kill them if I didn't?"

"One by one. Until it broke you."

"How can I love you when you're so evil?"

"It's not a question of being evil, Orly. It's about being ruthless. To survive as the head of this coven, it requires me to be ruthless. Luckily, you will never have to bear that burden."

I felt compassion for her in that moment as I finally understood her ruthlessness as a burden for her to bear. It reminded me of Yelena's guilt. I was glad it was not mine to carry and felt relieved to be living relatively carefree. But I wondered if I truly could stay here with her and say goodbye to my friends. Most significantly, could I say goodbye to Berthold?

"Would I ever see my friends again if I stayed here with you?"

"You would not be my prisoner here. You could see them as often as you liked, but know it would break my heart if you no longer wished to return."

As much as I loved her, it crossed my mind as to whether or not I could believe her. I knew she was full of lies and overflowing with motivations. But perhaps this time was different. Was it possible this was purely love for me and nothing more? I decided to test her.

"When you send them home, send Kristy with them."

"What?"

"Send her home untouched."

"But her body? Do you no longer want it?"

"It would break Berthold's heart to lose her."

"Ah, Berthold. How deeply you care for him. It makes me suspicious."

"I told you. I love him as a friend. Besides, do you even need me to have a woman's body anymore?"

"I thought it was what you wanted."

"It is. Or it was. I don't know. I feel like I don't need it as much since I have your love. Unless you would fall out of love with me without it."

"That won't happen."

"Maybe it won't. But what if I changed bodies and you loved me more?"

"I'll always want to love you more."

"That's not what I mean. It would be like you loved me more because I wasn't me anymore."

"If you no longer want a new body, you don't have to have one. I told you. I know you are no child and I love you as you are. Keep your body. You have all the time in the world to change your mind."

"You'll send them home tomorrow then?"

"Will you stay with me?"

I thought a moment, taking longer than I probably needed just to show her it was not a simple decision for me to make. But eventually, I nodded my head.

"And you will draw for me when I need you to?"

"Only when you need proof of someone you suspect. That's what you said."

"That is what I said."

"Then you have to tell me what you suspect and I'll tell you if it's true or not. That's all I'm gonna do. You're too paranoid for me to do more."

"I agree," she answered.

"Okay," I said. "I'll stay."

She caressed my cheek again and then leaned forward and kissed me on the lips. In turn, I kissed her eyelids closed.

"Lazy time," I whispered.

We slept the rest of the day.

THIRTY

The straps to my black slip were thin and I woke to Mirela kissing my bare shoulder.

"It's after sunset," she said.

"On the last night of the Communion?"

"If it still pleases you."

"I just want my friends to be safe. I know they're not comfortable being here. And I'm so tired of having so many people around us."

She kissed the back of my neck and then placed three kisses down my spine.

"Are you seducing me?" I asked.

"Only if it's working," she answered mischievously.

"It's working."

She kissed me more and then rolled me over so that I faced her and pressed my hand to her heart. I felt it throb beneath her ribs. I kept my hand over her heart as she released her gentle grip and reached for the chain that hung from my neck. When she took hold of it, the asymmetrical heart shape pendant that held Yelena's diamond fell out from beneath my slip. Mirela held it between her fingers, looking at it curiously. I didn't stop her from holding it even when her thumb rubbed the surface of the diamond.

"Will you do something for me?" she asked.

I already dreaded her response when I asked, "What is it?"

"Take this off before we make love."

"But why?"

"Because I want to know that I have you all to myself. I know it's important to you, but you can put it back on afterward."

"I can't take it off."

"I can do it for you, if it will help you feel like you weren't betraying her in some way."

"It would be the same thing. But it shouldn't matter. You have me all to yourself."

"Do I? Is that the truth, Orly?"

I nodded my head but wondered. She felt Yelena between us, and symbolically she was between us. But even if I convinced her to overlook it and make love to me anyway, we had a whole eternity before us, and certainly the subject and the meaning of the pendant would come up over and over throughout the centuries ahead of us. I thought perhaps I should just remove it during our lovemaking but then considered how Yelena might feel if she were still alive and knew of its removal. And then I wondered if I gave in now, would Mirela later ask me not to wear it in other moments until someday I never wore it at all?

"Let me think about it," I said. "But right now, just kiss me, please."

Mirela smiled and I felt she was satisfied. She ran her long fingers through my straight hair as our lips pressed firmly together.

She separated her mouth from mine just long enough to tell me, "I love you, Orly."

She rolled on top of me and I smiled as I looked into her eyes as she removed the straps of my slip. I bared my fangs and watched as she closed her eyes in anticipation of what was to come. I reached up and placed my right hand behind her neck and pulled her throat to my mouth. I bit into her and began to drink, this time sweetly instead of savagely, not allowing any of her precious blood to escape my lips. Mirela let out a soft pleasurable moan, and I was overcome with bliss and ecstasy as I tasted and swallowed her potent blood.

The rapturous sensations were increased as I felt Mirela's hands slowly roam my body, sensually gliding over my bare skin, her fingers eventually finding their way between my legs. My soul swooned slowly as she touched my most sensitive areas and I continued to satiate my carnal and emotional desires with her blood flowing between my lips.

But then it came—a scream inside my head. My body stiffened and I released my bite.

"What's wrong?" Mirela asked. She sounded not only perplexed, but concerned.

"It's Mayuko. She's awake. She's screaming."

"Let her scream. Stay with me. She's immortal now—she won't die."

"I know. But I remember how scared I was when I woke inside my casket the first time. She needs me. I'm sorry, I have to go."

Mirela rolled off of me, visibly annoyed.

"I really am sorry. I mean it. I promise I'll be back and I'll give you everything I have in me."

I kissed her lips quickly and pulled the straps of my slip back over my shoulders and left her bed. She sighed heavily. I exited her bedchamber in a hurry and, once out in the hall, I heard a loud crash. A candelabra hitting the wall, I guessed.

I didn't even bother to put anything on over my slip. I flew down the mountainside headed directly to where I had buried my best friend. I could hear her screams in my head the entire way. I'm coming, Button, I called to her mentally. I was confident she could hear me as I remember hearing Yelena's voice comforting me when I first woke in the earth. But as I had awakened during the day Yelena was forced to wait until nightfall to dig me out of my grave. Fortunately, Mayuko woke at night, as it is supposed to be with vampires, and would not have to wait so long to be unearthed.

Once I arrived at her burial spot, I hit the earth and began to dig as quickly as I could. I was ecstatic she was awake. I had turned my first mortal and she was my best friend. What an eternity we would share together. Dirt flew everywhere as the hole deepened and I dreamed of us journeying the world, hand in hand, leaving innumerable love-filled affairs in our wake.

But then I remembered Mirela. I had asked her to spare Kristy and allow her to keep her body in order to not hurt Berthold. I would need an adult body again for my new life with Mayuko. But that was the easy part to fix—I could kidnap any other adult whose beauty enthralled me and take her body as my own. The hard part would come after my transformation was complete. Once I had my adult body, I would then have to break the promise I made to Mirela to stay with her as her lover. But when I thought of doing that, my heart ached. I wasn't sure I wanted to break my promise to Mirela, and I could only guess how harsh the consequences would be if I did.

I wanted everything without giving up anything, and felt myself torn between two futures as I began to brush the cold moist grave soil from Mayuko's face. Her eyes were open, and as I wiped the dirt from her lips she opened her mouth and inhaled deeply out of habit. I saw her fangs for the first time. They were long, sharp, and beautifully deadly.

I hadn't thought about Mayuko when I told Mirela I would stay with her, even though Mayuko was my best friend. Looking back, I may have loved Mayuko more than I loved Mirela, but in a much different way. Unfortunately, for the inexperienced, romantic love is always amplified and thereby overrules all other loves.

Mayuko blinked her eyes and stared at me dumbfounded as I unearthed the rest of her. She shook fearfully. I pulled her into my arms and held her tightly. I felt her blood tears spill upon my shoulders.

"I'm here," I said. "You're safe, love."

It took a few sobs before she could speak. But I understood completely as I recalled my own terror when I first woke. She finally caught her breath and spoke in a frightened whisper.

"Oh, Cricket, I didn't know where I was. It was so dark and cold. I was so scared. It felt like I was suffocating."

"I know, but it's alright now. I promise. Everything's gonna be okay."

She hugged me back firmly. After a long moment, I pushed back and looked into her beautiful face. Her hair fell across it. It had lost its artificial milk tea brown shade and was now her natural color—pure black.

"Welcome to eternity," I said, and kissed her lips.

I rose and, still weak, Mayuko struggled to stand with me, so I lifted her and levitated out of the grave. I sat her down as I refilled the grave with earth. I picked her up again and walked with her in my arms, unhurriedly back to the castle.

"We did it," I said. "You're a vampire now. We can see the world together like we always said we would."

She nodded upon my chest and said softly, "I'm so happy."

"I am too, Button. Think of how much we're gonna do! Think of how much we're gonna travel! And we'll have tons of romances! We'll live forever together," I said, giving in to the moment, swept up in fantasy.

But then I realized I had forgotten Mirela again. Why was it so easy for me to forget her if I loved her as much as I felt I did?

As I continued to ascend the mountainside carrying Mayuko in my arms, it occurred to me I had also forgotten Mirela's promise to me. In exchange for staying with her she would send my friends home safely. Those friends certainly included Mayuko. I looked into Mayuko's face and felt myself flush. Though in Mirela's presence I had taken time to answer when she asked me to stay with her, I now felt I had answered hastily and regretted it sorely. Fanciful notions of freedom as a beautiful adult woman wandering the world with Mayuko thrilled my entire being despite my love for Mirela. I knew the two lives couldn't coexist and I didn't know which I wanted more.

I dreamed of living my life moment to moment, spending it happily in Mayuko's company, having meaningless romances when I wanted and returning to Mirela when I longed to be in her arms and truly loved. But with each uphill step we gained on Castle Cobălcescu the more resigned I felt, convinced Mirela would not be so giving.

We returned to the castle, visibly unnoticed. Everyone was already partaking in the night's carousing. In our private chamber, Mayuko and I bathed together. With the water hot, I sat behind Mayuko and washed the soil from her skin and hair, the way Mirela washed the blood from mine. The intimacy of the act was stark and after all that had happened between me and Mirela, it felt strange, perhaps even wrong to be sharing such a moment with someone else.

"I need to feed," Mayuko said.

I bit into my wrist and let the blood flow, and then wrapped my arm around my best friend and brought my wrist to her mouth. She drank eagerly until the wound closed.

"Come," I said, rising to my feet in the tub. "You need more. We'll get dressed and find you a vessel."

My blood had given Mayuko the strength to rise and step out of the bathtub unassisted. But with thick towels, I dried Mayuko's skin, caring for her like my child, before drying myself.

When we stepped out of the bathroom it was clear our return was noticed after all. Two dress molds stood in the center of the bedchamber, each adorned with new gowns. The smaller was black velvet, Mayuko's was white lace.

I sat Mayuko down on the bed, helped her with her undergarments and then went to the dress mold and removed her gown.

"When are we leaving here, Orly?"

She rose and stepped into the gown and I zipped up its back.

"Mirela promised me tonight would be the last night of the Communion."

The white lace gown cascaded down her lithe body all the way to her feet.

"I'm so glad. We can finally go home," she said.

"Button, I have something to tell you. Berthold, Hisato, Zacharias, and even Kristy are here."

"They're here?" she asked, surprised.

"They were kidnapped and brought here."

She gasped. "Kidnapped? But why?"

"It doesn't really matter now since Mirela said she'd let them all go, but they brought Kristy because Mirela was going to give me her body."

"She *was* going to give you her body? She's not now?"

"No. I asked her to even let Kristy go back home with Berthold."

"But your adult body."

"I'll have to pick someone else. Or maybe I won't at all."

She looked at me confused as I dressed myself.

"Mirela already loves me like I am."

"You really think she loves you?"

I answered quickly to prevent Mayuko from saying more. "I know she does. In my heart, I can feel her love for me. But Button, listen. She wants me to stay here with her."

"Stay here? No! You can't stay here! This place is a prison. It's cursed! Remember what I told you. None of it's real!"

"I know. But we've become close. And I think I love her back."

"I don't want you to love her. She's evil. And she doesn't love anyone or anything but herself."

I changed the subject, not wanting to listen.

"Do you still remember the day you found out the castle wasn't real? The day you went outside and found the catacombs?"

"Of course I remember it."

"That's good," I said, forcing a smile. "Remember it as long as you can. It was the last time you saw the sunlight."

"You can't stay here, Orly."

I looked away. "But I love her," I said softly.

"Do you really? Just a second ago you said you think you love her. I don't think you really know. And a week ago you were all in love with Berthold. Do you really even know what love is?"

It was a good question. What I had with Mirela, it felt like love, but I knew I was young and unseasoned. Regardless, I knew I didn't want whatever it was to end.

"And what about me?" Mayuko continued. "I won't stay here. I'm going back to Los Angeles, or anywhere else. You have to come with me."

I wanted to nod my head and agree to leave with Mayuko, but I didn't. I had already made one promise that was tearing at my insides. I didn't want to foolishly make another in the spur of the moment.

To our surprise, the room stood and applauded when Mayuko and I entered. Mayuko could not help but smile and the applause grew when her fangs showed. Our friends from Los Angeles, again at their own table, followed by example in their welcoming of Mayuko.

Mirela approached. Mayuko curtsied with her head bowed reverently before she arrived. Mirela took her by the hand and asked her to rise.

"You are one of us now," she said, "a Cobălcescu, made by my own beloved. You must be thirsty. Come."

As we walked, Mirela said to me, "This is also a celebration for you. You have turned your first mortal. May she be your last."

I looked at her, puzzled.

"Don't fret, my love," she said. "It is only a saying. It means, *May you never again be lonely*."

Mirela led us to a table and waved its current occupants away. They bowed and curtsied to Mirela and left. Mirela instructed us to sit, and she sat between us. The rest of the room resumed their seats.

A beautiful young man was brought to our table. I'm certain Mayuko could smell his mortal blood. He was a vessel and took his seat beside Mayuko.

"Drink," Mirela said.

The young man offered his throat and cautiously Mayuko leaned forward and took him in her arms and bit into his throat. The room watched her, but Berthold watched me. He turned away though when Mirela noticed and looked directly at him.

She turned to me and placed her hand on my thigh.

"The last night of the Communion of the Ancients. I hope you enjoy yourself tonight, my love, even though you will be saying goodbye to your friends."

I looked over at the table where Berthold, Zacharias, and Hisato sat.

"I will miss them very much," I said softly.

"You sound sad."

"I'm sorry but I am. I feel so confused."

"Tell me, what confuses you? Don't you still love me?"

I took her hand that rested on my thigh and squeezed it softly.

"Of course I do. But I'm so young. I want to be with you, but I also want the life I envisioned before coming here and receiving your love."

"I see," Mirela answered without expression.

"I'm sorry."

"Yes. You've said you are sorry. So you would trade our love for an endless series of affairs?"

"I don't think of it as trading. I just want to experience life."

"Ah. Life."

I had betrayed myself. I had revealed my uncertainty of staying with Mirela before she had given me the adult body I might travel the world with in Mayuko's company. I loathed myself for having the need to spill my secret feelings so readily instead of keeping them to myself.

We both turned to our right as the young man in Mayuko's arms began to struggle, but Mayuko did not release him. We looked on as he died and fell to the ballroom floor.

With blood dripping from her chin, Mayuko turned to Mirela and said, "Forgive me, Imparateasa. I could not let him go."

Mirela noticed the room was still watching. She tilted her head and looked at the ceiling and laughed heartily. She turned back to Mayuko. "It's okay my dear, it's your first night. Kill another if you like. Actually, kill them all!" She laughed again though her laugh was clearly forced. Truly, she was hurting inside from what I had revealed to her.

She looked at the room. All were silent.

"You heard me! Kill them all! All the vessels. This is the last night of the Communion. You have no further use of them."

Mortal screams came from around the room. Vessels sprang to their feet and tried to run, but it was futile. They were devoured despite their screams and thrashing. Even Adela, with her sweet blood, Adela who had been so close to being made immortal, perished in the mayhem.

My friends appeared rattled by the confusion. They looked to me and I raised my hand slightly trying to tell them to remain seated and that they had nothing to fear.

"You need not worry about them. I told you I would send them home safely," Mirela said, but I felt her assurance was in truth a reminder of my promise to stay with her.

Simeon, the vampire who could turn himself into a crow approached, holding a teenage boy in his arms who was kicking and screaming, fighting for his life.

"For you," he said to Mayuko and thrust the teen into her arms.

In his struggles, the teen slapped Mayuko in the face, but she was unfazed and tore into his throat. Mirela looked at me again.

"Forgive me, but I cannot bear the thought of you leaving me."

Just then a vampire placed his hand on Kristy and Berthold stood up immediately and began to struggle with the elder vampire.

Mirela sprang to her feet. "No! Not her! She is for my lover!"

The elder vampire released Kristy, bowed to Berthold and stepped away. Berthold and the entire table looked to me, perplexed.

"I told you, no," I said under my breath to Mirela, but she ignored me.

"Kristy Amare," she said, staring into Kristy's puzzled expression. "You are quite beautiful. My lover desires to have your body as her own and I promised to give it to her. You will die in the process, but be satisfied knowing your body will live forever as Orly's."

"Orly, what are you doing?" Berthold asked desperately.

I swallowed. I had hoped he would never have known of the plan to steal Kristy's body.

"I told her not to do it, Berthold! I told her I changed my mind!"

"But perhaps I have not changed mine," Mirela said flatly.

"You said you loved me as I am!"

"And you said I might love you more were you in her body."

"You're twisting my words! Berthold, she's twisting my words!"

Neither Mirela nor Berthold spoke.

Petru, help me, I said.

I fear there is nothing I can do to prevent this, Petru replied.

Viorica, please help me. Help my friends.

What can be done, Orly? She is mortal, was Viorica's response.

"Bring her to me," Mirela said.

In an instant, Ancient vampires were upon Kristy. She screamed but there was nothing Berthold or Zacharias could do to help her, as they too were grabbed by Ancients and were subdued. Only Hisato did not try to help. He did not even stand. He likely knew it was futile, but it was also likely he simply didn't care enough about a mortal like Kristy.

I watched as Kristy was brought toward us. I looked at Berthold, but quickly looked away, ashamed, when he returned my gaze with fear for Kristy in his eyes.

"Lay her on the table," Mirela said.

Hurriedly, glasses and bottles were wiped from the table. They shattered on the stone floor. Kristy was laid on her back atop the table. The Ancients who had placed her there released their grips, but it was clear Kristy still could not move. Someone, if not someones, were mentally holding her in place.

Mirela looked to the table of my friends. "We had agreements, you see. Orly would forgive me for killing Yelena and become my lover. In exchange, I would give her any adult body she desired and she chose this one," she said, waving her hand over Kristy's prone body.

My friends looked at me in amazement, especially Hisato. At the very least they all wondered how I had forgiven Yelena's death.

"It is true she later changed her mind. Consequently, our agreement changed. All of you, her friends and this mortal would be allowed to go home safely, provided Orly remained here with me."

"Stop it. You said enough," I said. "I said I'll stay with you. Just let them go."

Mirela turned to me. There was no sign of affection in her expression.

"I'm sorry, my love, I don't know that I want you to stay any longer. If you stayed, it appears your heart will always be someplace else."

"It won't be. I promise."

"Do you promise? Well, if you stayed you also promised me something else. Do you remember? You promised to draw for me whenever I needed you to."

"Of course I remember. But I promised to draw only when you suspected someone."

"And if I suspected someone? What then?"

"Then you'd tell me what you suspected and I would tell you if it was true or not."

"Yes. That was our agreement precisely. Let us see how it works. Shall we?"

"You want to do this right now?"

"You puzzle me, Orly. I believe there is a traitor in our midst this very moment. That puts the life of your lover in danger. How can that not concern you?"

"Fine then. Tell me who it is and what you think they did."

Mirela spoke harshly in Romanian. Servants quickly entered and set up the two chairs and placed the easel before one of them and equipped it with paper and black crayons. I looked at her, anxiously awaiting the name of her traitor and what treachery he or she might have committed, but she took her time. She gestured toward the chair for me to sit and I sat wondering who would be seated across from me.

The room was silent. Not a single telepathic conversation occurred. My friends at the table looked on at the scene with the gravest expressions on their faces. Mayuko, with blood still on her lips, looked frightened for me.

Finally, Mirela spoke.

"Petru. I command you to sit and be drawn."

My heart dropped into my stomach. Not Petru.

Petru remained stoic. "What do you accuse me of?"

Mirela answered just as stoically. "I accuse you of conspiring with my lover to free Ji'Indushul and overthrow me. Do you deny it?"

"Of course I deny it," Petru answered indignantly.

"Very well. Orly, you may begin to fulfill your promise to me now. Please be truthful and do not test me. The lives of your friends depend on it."

THIRTY-ONE

Everyone looked on in silence as I put crayon to paper and began to scribble the eldest of the Eternal. Petru looked back at me sternly. The electricity in the air felt soft, as if the telepathic conversations occurring in the room were being whispered.

Don't worry, Petru, I said. I won't betray you. She doesn't know for sure about anything we said about Ji'Indushul, right?

Not unless you made a slip. Think hard now, did you?

I thought for a while, not even paying attention to what I was scribbling.

I don't think so. I really don't.

Among the Eternal, there is only Codrina, Viorica, and Vasile. They are all loyal and would not have made such a mistake. Trajan and Matei are pissants who belong to Mirela. Certainly you did not reveal anything to them.

No. For sure I didn't. Trajan scares me and I never trusted Matei.

If all that is true, you should be safe to lie.

I scribbled slowly, trying to make it appear that my drawing was thorough so my lie would be more convincing. I glanced at Berthold and then turned my head toward Kristy. She was still lying on the table, being held in place by whom I did not know. I stopped scribbling and brought my hands to my lap.

"Are you finished?" Mirela asked.

"No," I replied. "I can't concentrate with her lying there. Let her go or tell whoever to let her go."

It was the first kindness I had shown Kristy, but I really did it for Berthold's sake. It was risky though. Mirela could have simply killed her. But without warning, and quite immediately Kristy could move her arms and legs. She quickly climbed off the table and rushed to Berthold, who held her.

"Thank you," I said to no one in particular and brought the crayon to the paper once more. After what felt like fifteen minutes, I placed the crayon back on the easel.

"Are you finished now?" Mirela asked.

"Yeah. I'm done. But this is pointless. Even if Petru tried to get me to get Ji'Indushul to kill you, why would I admit to that? I'd be in just as much trouble as him."

"That is not true," Mirela answered plainly. "I would fault your youth for allowing you to be mislead by him and therefore punish you less severely. But that is beside the point. Your task is to tell me if Petru's drawing shows him conspiring with you to set Ji'Indushul free. Does it? Answer me now."

I looked directly in Mirela's face for emphasis and said, "No. It doesn't show anything like that at all."

The telepathy in the room reignited until finally Francis, the favorite of Mirela's who had been given so much of her blood during his communion with her, spoke. "Forgive me for interrupting, Imparateasa, but all within this room are wondering, who is Ji'Indushul?"

Mirela turned to Francis. "Perhaps Petru could answer that question for you," she said and then turned to Petru. "Well? What are you waiting for, Petru? Tell them. Who is Ji'Indushul?"

Petru did not turn to Francis, Mirela, or to the room. He looked straight at me and said in the calmest voice, "Ji'Indushul is a vampire who, like Orly Bialek, was made as a child, but over four thousand years ago, making him the eldest of the Eternal. That is, until Orly killed him."

What are you doing? I asked Petru silently.

He didn't answer me but continued to look me in the eye as he continued. "Ji'Indushul was a traitor, and as such was imprisoned by our imparateasa for thousands of years. In order to protect the imparateasa, I tested Orly's loyalty by asking her to help me set him free."

"So you have lied to me, Orly," Mirela said tonelessly. "Your drawings are worthless to me if you will not commit to telling the truth of what you see in them."

You betrayed me, Petru.

I did.

Viorica, did you betray me too? I thought you were my friend.

No, Orly. I most certainly did not. Petru has betrayed you on his own. Codrina, Vasile, and I had no knowledge of his treachery. He might very easily betray us as well. I am sorry for this, but at this moment, I see no way to help you.

"It appears it was wise to kidnap your friends after all," Mirela said. "I told you I would use them as leverage if I had to. That I would kill them one by one until it broke you."

I looked at my friends and then looked at Mirela. I was terrified for them.

I slid off my chair and went to my knees. "Imparateasa, please. I'm begging you not to kill them. I am broken already and promise I will always tell you the truth."

My words did not move her. Outside I heard the sky thunder and a hard rain began to fall.

"You are not broken, my love. For you have not suffered. One of your friends must die. I will let you choose who it shall be, but it shall not be the mortal woman, for her death would not pain you."

"No. Please. Don't do this. You can kill me, but let them go. They haven't done anything wrong."

But again she was unmoved.

"I would not kill you over one of them. They are of no use to me as you are. If you do not choose, I will choose for you."

I felt the blood begin to stream from my eyes. I crawled to her and held the hem of her wine colored gown. Some amongst the onlooking Ancients snickered.

"Please. Forgive me. Because you love me," I said to Mirela, clutching the fabric of her gown tightly.

Voices of Ancients echoed in my head.

She will not love you now. Your reign was short-lived you little bitch!

She shall not forgive you child! And nor should she!

You have brought upon your own ruin, Orly Bialek! Ha ha!

Maybe now you and your friends will face the slicing as my friends did.

Mirela looked down at me, "Choose."

I looked up at her pleadingly and shook my head. "Please. I love you."

"Very well," Mirela said, "I choose the insolent one." She pointed to Hisato and he was immediately grabbed by the Ancients Francis and Enrico, and driven to his knees. "I know you are vain," she said to Hisato. "I recognize your vanity as I recognize it in myself. I have the perfect death for someone like you."

"No!" I screamed.

"Go to hell you ugly cunt," Hisato said spitefully.

Mirela looked up at the ceiling. Above rain began to fall, uncloaking a hole in the illusion of the ceiling, and revealing a storm-filled sky outdoors. The rain showered over Hisato.

I looked on frightfully, not knowing what his fate would be. But suddenly among the Ancients, fangs were bared and many of the vampires hissed. In the falling rain, which seemed to take a step forward, the gentle figure of Konomi appeared. Her kimono was nearly white, having a slight jade hue, and she held her sword, still in its scabbard, in her left hand. She wore a pleasant look upon her face. As her form solidified, the rain ceased to fall, and she remained completely dry. Though I was glad to see her and hoped she would save us all, I was astonished by her appearance.

How did you know? I asked Konomi.

I have been watching over you, my blood sister, she replied to me silently. She then spoke openly and peacefully to Mirela. "Forgive me, Empress, but I cannot allow you to kill this one."

"Konomi," Mirela replied cooly, "You would be wise to leave before you get hurt."

Konomi stepped toward Mirela and answered more firmly, "What you do amongst the Cobălcescu is your own affair, but he is Ketsuen and will not die by your hand."

Just then, Francis released his grip on Hisato and rushed at Konomi, attempting to attack her from behind. In an instant, Konomi spun, unsheathing her sword and swung, beheading Francis. Her spin ended with her again facing Mirela, but this time her sword was extended toward the imparateasa.

No one else moved. Mirela looked at Francis' severed head on the floor. His beheaded body continued to gush his ancient honeyed blood. Mirela was visibly displeased.

"That was in self defense. That is undeniable," Konomi said.

"Even so," Mirela replied, "You cannot fight us all. Least of all me."

"Certainly Empress you do not believe I am here alone. My lover is with me. Undoubtedly you sense Hisashi's presence in the storm. We do not wish a war with the Cobălcescu; however, if you desire one you shall have it. But you know very well the Ketsuen have far more elders than the Cobălcescu as your history of paranoia has diminished your coven."

There was a standoff until Mirela finally moved. She grabbed one of my hands that still clutched her gown and jerked me to my feet. She clutched my hand tightly.

"Take your little rat then, and leave us," Mirela said bitterly.

Konomi looked at me. "Orly, come with me," she said.

"That is not possible," Mirela said. "She is Cobălcescu. She stays."

"She is also my blood sister."

"I cannot go with you Konomi," I said, "not unless you take my friends. All of them."

"I cannot take them, Orly. Hisashi will not risk a war for them, not even for you. I am venturing to take you on my own."

"Then I have to stay," I said meekly.

Konomi nodded her head slightly in assent. Tell me, Orly. Have you found your Oblivion?

No. I still can't find it.

I hope to see you again my sister.

It thundered outside. Inside, the rain began to fall again, showering over Konomi. She stepped toward Hisato, who rose to his feet, and slapped Enrico's hand off his shoulder. The rain enveloped them both, falling harder and harder until their shapes were obscured and they eventually vanished in the cascade. The rain stopped once they were gone and the floor remained dry except for the blood that had spilled across it from Francis' headless corpse.

Humiliated, Mirela let out an ear-piercing scream of anger, causing even the eldest of the coven to shudder. She threw me across the room and I landed at Zacharias' feet. As I looked up at him, into his emerald eyes, he gently moved to help me up but then, in an instant, he burst into flames. A cry leapt from his lips as he burned alive, his limbs flailing. And in an instant his body shot back into the stone wall, the illusion of the castle again solid, and poof! His screams went silent. All that was left of Zacharias was a large smear of black ash on the facade. Our dear friend Zacharias, Yelena's friend Zacharias, Zacharias who had been made by Marcel, was dead forever.

I grabbed myself by the hair and screamed. Blood ran from my eyes.

Mirela shouted something in Romanian I did not understand and immediately servants exited the room.

I looked over at Berthold and Mayuko, making sure they were still there. And then I looked at Petru, still seated where he had been when he betrayed me. I closed my eyes and tried to will him to go up in flames, as Zacharias had, but nothing happened. Did I not possess the power or was he able to resist me? I heard the servants return and opened my eyes. I rose slowly from the floor when I saw what they were carrying. It was a small sarcophagus—painted black and covered in red writing I did not understand. As I got to my feet, I could see it had a carved and painted face that resembled my own likeness. I turned to Mirela in disbelief. She looked back at me expressionless. I screamed at her hatefully.

"You had this made for me already? Before I did anything wrong? When you were telling me you loved me? You're evil!"

"No, Orly. As I told you, I am ruthless," she answered flatly.

I felt far more betrayed by my lover than I did by Petru. My heart hurt in a way I had never experienced. "You promised you would kill me before doing to me what you did to Ji'Indushul."

Mirela spoke in Romanian once more and the servants placed the box at my feet. They opened it. There were no hinges. The expert craftsmanship simply fitted the top to the bottom, but I knew whatever curse had held it shut for Ji'Indushul would hold it closed over me. I wondered if the box were equipped to allow the sunlight to burn my eyes out of their sockets and sear my lips off, and whether Mirela would have such punishment meted out to me, the girl she said she loved. Mirela looked into my eyes and with her hand gestured to the box.

"Please, Mirela, don't put me in there. I still love you. Forgive me. I know you want to."

"You are right, Orly. I do want to forgive you, but I will not. One way or another, I will make you loyal."

"I can't scribble for you without my eyes," I said, hoping to save myself from the pains of sunlight.

"Get yourself in the box, before I kill the rest of your friends."

"And when you shut me in, what will you do with them?"

"As I told you, I will send them home."

I didn't believe her, but felt I had no choice but to hope she wasn't lying.

"If you ever loved me, please don't break that promise."

"I did love you and I love you now. I shall love you forever. And to prove my love to you, I shall keep you with me for all time."

I had lost. I knew it. To save those I loved, I had to doom myself. I had to step into the sarcophagus and face condemnation. I looked to Berthold. He was looking back at me. I tried to smile so he would remember me that way. "Goodbye, Berthold," I whispered, but he said nothing.

I turned to Mayuko. Before I could say anything, she ran to me and wrapped her arms around me.

I hugged her tightly.

"Orly," Mirela said harshly, "I command you to get into the box now."

I let Mayuko go. I looked into her face one last time. Blood tears spilled from her eyes.

"Don't do it, Button. Don't get inside." Mayuko said, reaching for me again, but I gently pushed her hands away. "No, Orly! She'll never let you out!" Mayuko cried. Blood began to drip from her nose. She noticed the sensation and brought her right hand to her face and wiped below her nose and looked at the blood on her fingers. In the next moment, blood began to drip from her ears. "What's happening to me, Button? I feel…." She fell to her knees and I went to my knees with her. The amount of blood coming from her ears and nose began to flow more quickly.

"No, don't!" I said, looking up at Mirela, who towered over us. "Please! Leave her alone!" I screamed.

As I looked back at my best friend, I noticed below her face, across her throat, a thin red line began to form. It widened and began to spill blood.

"Stop it!" I screamed.

"Button," Mayuko said, coughing up blood.

The blood from her throat spilled even faster until her white lace gown was soaked in blood. Mayuko's head tilted to the right. She was losing consciousness, and I noticed at the place where her throat bled her head began to separate from her body. I gripped her head, trying to hold it in place while also trying to hold her up. "No! Please!" I screamed to Mirela in desperation.

Mayuko's bleeding eyes closed. I held her face in my hands as her body fell away to the floor, her head completely severed. My own blood tears were falling again as I quickly tried to place her head back upon her prone body. I bit into my wrist and let my blood spill upon her wound. I smeared it over her throat, but her wound wouldn't heal and shortly thereafter I sensed when her heart stopped. My best friend, who had been so loving and loyal to me, was dead. We would never have our forever.

I fell across her body and wept. The black velvet of my gown became wet with her spilled blood.

Hands were suddenly upon me, gripping me by the shoulders, trying to pull me away from Mayuko's body. They were the hands of Ancients. I screamed and without much effort, I threw them from me—my vampiric strength stronger than theirs. But their grips were soon replaced by more powerful hands—the hands of Eternals—Trajan and Matei. They lifted me to my feet, but even they had to struggle to hold me. I freed myself successfully and struck Trajan in the face hard and he fell away from me. I turned to Matei and looked him in the eye. For an instant I saw fear in his face and as my rage increased he soon went up in flames. He writhed in the inferno, and with all my will, not knowing if it was possible, I tried to concentrate on the fire, willing it to grow hotter and hotter. He eventually fell to his knees and then fell over completely, disintegrating into a pile of black ash on the stone floor. I had done it. I had killed an Eternal. They had underestimated how strong Mirela's blood had made me.

Trajan, who was about to approach me again, stopped in his tracks. I looked at him, concentrating my anger to unleash the same fiery death upon him. I would burn them all to death if I had to. But just then, from a force unseen, I was lifted off my feet and thrown into the wall, my head hitting stone. Each time I fell an arm's length away from the wall I was thrown into it again and again until I was weary and dizzy. I finally fell to the floor and, beginning with my limbs, I felt my body petrify. This was not the same as mentally holding someone in place. It was as though my whole body had progressively turned to stone. Only my eyes could move, and I saw Mirela looking down at me, devoid of all emotion. As I had not seen such a power in any of the scribbles, I knew only she could have done it.

"Put her into the box," she said coldly.

I don't know who lifted me in, or how many, for I felt no hands upon me in my hardened state, and I had closed my eyes, feeling conquered and overwhelmed, anticipating the endless fate that awaited me. I heard my body hit solid wood beneath me, but I didn't feel it. Still petrified, my body felt nothing.

I heard the hollowness of the lid being lifted and reopened my eyes. I caught a glimpse of Mirela, my lover, just as the lid was shut upon me and everything went black. From without, I could hear Mirela chanting in a language that did not seem of this world. I guessed it was in the lost language of the forgotten people of the Cobalshik.

The feeling of petrification receded slowly, my fingers first being able to move. Then my toes. My arms and legs, and soon I could move my head, but only scarcely as the confinement of the sarcophagus was so tight. I felt my chest rise and fall as I breathed the air that smelled like timber. I tried to lift my arms. My wrists pressed upon the lid of the sarcophagus. I knew that even without enough leverage, my vampiric strength should enable me to push open any funerary box, but the lid didn't budge. I lifted my head the couple of centimeters allowable and hit it on the lid as hard as I could, but the box did not open. I tried to remove the lid telekinetically, and when that didn't work, I mentally tried to make the box explode into splinters, but that too was fruitless. My final attempt came when I thought of Matei perishing in fire—I tried to will the box to burst into flames, knowing that doing so endangered my own life. But as much as I willed it, it never ignited. The ancient Cobalshik curse was too powerful for my vampiric magic. I was doomed, and after losing Zacharias and then Mayuko, I was also broken. Slowly, thoughts of my personal fate escaped me and I prayed to I don't know whom—maybe Yelena—for Berthold's safety.

THIRTY-TWO

I lay wondering what it would feel like to have my eyes burned out of my head. And then my lips, if that is what Mirela had in mind for me.

I sensed when the box I was trapped in was lifted from the floor and knew it was carried by servants. I knew they were servants because the box wobbled to and fro with each step, and would have glided evenly had it been carried by vampires. I did my best to determine whether the box was being turned right or left, but it was abundantly clear when it began to ascend. The ascent shook, which told me we were going upstairs, and with the amount of steps that had occurred before the shaking stopped, I presumed I was on the third floor of Castle Cobălcescu—Mirela's private floor.

If I were to be alone again with Mirela in her chambers, I deeply hoped my confinement to this cursed sarcophagus was another ruse—a show to put on before the Ancients. But even harboring that hope did not assuage my despair at losing both Mayuko and Zacharias and I felt the warmth of blood streaming from my eyes. Within the sarcophagus, I began to mourn the deaths of friends who were so dear to me, and began to cry in earnest. My wailing came from deep within my soul. From outside the box I imagined my lamentations resounded louder than Ji'Indushul's tortured murmurs.

Zacharias had been my friend since the second night of my vampiric existence. Though he was two hundred years older than I, he never patronized me. Yet I always sensed he was looking out for me and tried to guide me as best as he could, especially after Yelena died. The bright green eyes I saw as he looked at me tenderly for the last time before bursting into flames seared into my memory and pierced my heart so sharply that it felt as if it were now struggling to beat with any regularity.

With the unbearable agony I felt thinking of Zacharias' death, I didn't expect my pain to deepen. Yet when I thought of Mayuko, I felt my heart impaled even further. It was being rutted, as if whatever torturous spike mourning had pushed through it was now being brutally dragged within, carving out bleeding crevices and hollowing out my heart. Mayuko had not even lived an entire night in the immortality I had promised her. All our dreams of spending eternity hand in hand were lost. She had accompanied me here trusting I would keep her safe, yet more than once I had carelessly placed her life in danger and finally I lost her forever. The irony of it pained me—had I not turned her and made her immortal, she might still be alive. Some part of me knew turning her would anger Mirela. Yet I still acted recklessly with Mayuko's life, trusting Mirela's love for me would forgive all my brattish and wayward behaviors. But all along Mirela knew she would kill Mayuko once she was unearthed. And I should have known that. I had only myself to blame for my best friend's death.

In fact I blamed myself for the deaths of both Mayuko and Zacharias. They were both dead because I did not betray Petru who had planned to betray me all along. I hated myself for being so young and gullible. I trusted when I shouldn't have, even though I had been warned what terrific liars we vampires were. If I were ever freed from this cursed sarcophagus, even if it took four thousand years, I would kill Petru.

And where was Berthold now? Would Mirela keep her promise to me and send him home? Of course she wouldn't. I felt foolish for ever believing she would. Would I even know the moment of his death and how he perished? I had no faith I would, and that ignorance wounded me still further. I, headstrong and impetuous Orly Bialek, had brought upon the deaths of so many people I loved. The sarcophagus was so cramped I could not even wipe the tears of blood that spilled from my eyes.

Hours passed in grief as I lay in what I expected was Mirela's bedchamber. Where was she? I expected her to say something to me—either audibly or mentally—but she didn't. As the night went on I listened to the hubbub of the vampires downstairs—they sounded happier than they had after the slicing. Many spoke of me with callousness and all spoke of Ji'Indushul in wonderment. But I heard nothing of Mirela's voice. Perhaps she was not even with them. Perhaps she was in this very room, sitting beside me.

As I waited for any sign of her I hated myself even more. I wanted her to talk to me as one yearns to be spoken to by a lover they have quarreled with. Why did I want that? Why did I want anything more from her? Why wasn't my only thought of her how to bring about her demise? How could I possibly still love her, if that was in fact what I was feeling? Was it that we had exchanged so much vampiric blood or was there more to it than that? The more I reflected the more certain I was I still held her within my scarred heart. I tried to shut off my ardor as one would a spigot. I was deplorable and despised myself for feeling anything other than hatred for the woman who had now killed three people I loved—Mayuko, Zacharias, and Yelena.

I closed my eyes and, for want of the slightest comfort, I tried to stop thinking at all. It was after many minutes in that forced thoughtlessness that my senses quickened. I smelled the rubbing alcohol again, just as I had while lying in my own coffin. I inhaled its distinct scent and tried to absorb it within me. As I breathed it in, each time more deeply than the last, I began to hear something—a familiar sound from my past that I knew was not really present. It was the noise made by a ventilator. It aligned itself to the inhaling and exhaling of my lungs. Soon the smoothly sanded wooden texture of the sarcophagus upon my fingertips changed, and instead my sense of touch recalled the stiff fabric of inexpensive and over-laundered bedsheets. And then, faintly at first and then more pronounced, I heard the steady and rhythmic beeping of a heart monitor. From beneath my closed eyelids, I sensed a soft light and slowly opened my eyes. In low light, I stared at memorable patterns in ceiling tiles overhead. The fluorescent lights that the tiles bordered were turned out; the dim lighting I had sensed came from out in the hall. It poured faintly into my dark room. I was back in the hospital, lying in bed, in the room I had spent so much of my dwindling and deteriorating youth. The single table in the room once more stood bedside and held my pad of paper and crayons. The curtains were open and out the window, beneath the night sky, I saw the scattered lights of other hospital rooms and the glow rising from the lamps in the parking lot below. Though everything about my surroundings was familiar, I knew where I truly was—I had finally found my Oblivion.

Though it was startling to be back in the place where I spent so much time dying and eventually died, it was also painful to be there. I was as I had been—before Yelena, before Berthold, Hisato, Zacharias, and Mayuko. It was me alone—orphan Orly—before I had any true family at all. The tears I felt fall from my eyes felt thinner than blood. They were real saline tears. Mortal tears. With my right hand, I reached for the top of my head. My hair was no longer full and thick. It grew thinly, and I had many bald spots. In my mouth, I realized my teeth were no longer sharp. I looked at my wrist. It was no longer scarred by where the sunlight painfully singed it the morning Yelena died. My hand went to my chest. The asymmetrical heart pendant was in absentia. And with the weakness I felt, I not only knew I was no longer a vampire, I knew my leukemia was my own again and that cancerous blood cells flowed freely through my body. I would die soon. I didn't know how I knew, but I could feel it. The cancer of my blood was ready to take me.

"Good evening, little one," said a voice I had never forgotten.

With effort, I turned my head slightly toward the doorway, and immediately a renewed flood of tears rushed from my eyes as I beheld the unmistakable silhouette of Yelena Solodnikova—my mother who had given her life to save mine. She had come to visit me in the hospital as she always had.

"Mommy," I said. "You're here."

"I promised I would come."

"I mean, you're alive."

"Of course I'm alive."

Her platinum hair she wore up, held in place with diamond-studded black chopsticks, with wisps of hair escaping only at her temples. She was dressed in a strapped black dress that accentuated her curves and the porcelain skin of her bare arms. In black high heels, she stepped into my hospital room and shut the door behind her.

It was undoubtedly Yelena, but was it truly her? Was this her spirit in an afterlife I did not know existed for vampires? Or just a shadow of her that existed only in my Oblivion? I loved and missed her so much that I didn't care. Gathering my strength, I extended my arms to her, beckoning for her to hug me. More than ever, I needed to be held. Yelena smiled and came to my bedside, leaned forward and embraced me firmly. I again felt the coldness of her skin. She kissed my face.

Though vampiric memory is inhumanly accurate, the feelings those memories could engender still did not compare to how I felt with her standing before me again in the present. My heart melted as I studied her eyes, her skin, and her pearly fanged smile.

"Move me over, Mommy. Get in bed and hold me like you used to."

"Like I used to?" she asked quizzically. "Like I did just last night?" She looked at me lovingly and pulled me toward her, near the edge of the bed. She walked around the bed, to the side near the window, and climbed in and lay beside me. She wrapped her arms around me and with slow movements I turned toward her and buried my face in her breasts and sobbed.

"There, there, Orly," she said, gripping me tighter. "Don't cry. You'll be well soon."

"No. It's not about that. I killed my friends, Mommy. Zacharias is dead. Berthold is probably dead. And my best friend, Mayuko. I killed them all with my stupidity. I trusted Mirela. I believed she loved me and I loved her back even though she killed you. I've been so stupid. I'm so sorry. I'm so sorry for loving her. Please don't hate me."

"I will never hate you, Orly. It's quite the opposite. I will always love you and don't blame you for loving Mirela. I know what life I gave you. I knew you would need love and would only find it in another vampire. But yours is a young love. An innocent love. You've fallen so quickly and completely for her because that is what young love is."

Was this really Yelena forgiving me or was I forgiving myself?

"But remember Orly, Mirela is not young. Her age complicates her love. For her it's too late for love to be innocent or pure. She's far too old and experienced to be head over heels for anyone. She may love you, but there will always be designs lurking beneath her affection."

And was this really Yelena advising me or was it only me admitting what I always knew to be true? Was Yelena real and independent of my Oblivion or was she merely a character within it? Was I even sincerely questioning the authenticity of her being? No. Not really. For as real as she felt and as much as her presence touched my heart, I felt she was only what I needed her to be—my comfort in this place we called the Oblivion. In that moment I felt I could lie in that hospital bed with Yelena forever. My confinement within that sarcophagus adorned with its strange lettered curse and my painted face was very far removed from my mind. I only wanted to be here—in the arms of the woman who loved me more than anyone ever had.

"Even though it will break your heart, you must kill her, Orly," Yelena said.

When she said that, I knew with absolute certainty she was not real in my Oblivion, for the words she spoke were my own. They were the words I hid from myself and would never allow to escape my lips.

I lifted my head from her breasts and looked into her face. As Yelena looked back at me I saw the pure adoration she had always looked at me with when she was alive. Her countenance warmly soothed my soul and though I never wanted to look away, the cancer that was again killing me made me lethargic and I soon closed my eyes, tranquil and consoled in her embrace.

"You're the dearest thing to me, Orly. The dearest thing I ever had," she whispered just as I fell asleep.

I don't know how much time had passed in the real world, maybe only seconds, but here in the Oblivion I knew I had slept for hours when I felt the warmth of sunlight on my face. Slowly I opened my eyes and immediately shut them again when I beheld the horror lying beside me.

I would have expected Yelena to have left before daylight as she always had, the rising sun marking the end of her visiting hours. But here, in my Oblivion, she had not gone home to her coffin—she still shared my hospital bed.

Yelena had been turned to ash once more. Her mouth was open as if she had been screaming. But I had heard nothing. If the sunlight that killed her still hurt her in my Oblivion had she been able to remain silent as to not wake me to witness her suffering? Or was it possible that my Oblivion could assuage my grief by making mute the screams I could not bear to ever hear again? I did not know.

What I did know was that Ji'Indushul was right. The sun did rise in my Oblivion.

Still facing Yelena, I reached for her face. The white ash was much more delicate than dry sand. Her ashen form fell apart at first touch. Instantly, there was no likeness of her at all, only a formless pile of her dusty remains upon hospital bedsheets.

Had this been my one chance to see my mother again? Or would Yelena appear each time I reentered my Oblivion? I didn't know that either, but in that moment I felt like my mourning for her had been freshly renewed with her lying dead and disintegrated beside me. I closed my eyes and shut out the sound of the ventilator and the beeping of the heart monitor. Upon my fingertips, the stiff bedsheets slowly regained the tactile feel of sanded wood. The scent of rubbing alcohol gave way to the smell of fallen pine trees. I opened my eyes into complete darkness. My consciousness was inside the cursed sarcophagus once more.

I lay there thinking of Yelena, trying to retain my hold on the happiness I had felt in her presence, but it slipped from my grasp quickly as the knowledge of my whereabouts and the recent events in the real world regained its grip upon my being. Mayuko was dead. Zacharias was dead. Berthold's fate was unknown. Petru had betrayed me. Mirela was out there. And I was doomed for eternity.

THIRTY-THREE

The din downstairs had died away hours ago. Castle Cobălcescu was quiet. Morning must have arrived. As far as I knew, the sarcophagus I was trapped within had been deposited inside Mirela's bedchamber. I tried using my vampiric powers to sense her whereabouts, but my mental faculties could not locate her.

As daylight had come, I was naturally inclined to sleep, but instead I considered trying to regain my Oblivion, if only so I could see if Yelena would come again. I inhaled through my nostrils. I smelled the pine of the sarcophagus, and to my relief, it was not difficult for me to also distinguish the scent of the rubbing alcohol beneath it. I closed my eyes and listened—not of the outside world—but within my mind. Again I heard the ventilator and expected I would soon hear the heart monitor, when my eyes suddenly opened. A hand had been placed on the outside of the sarcophagus, much in the way Mayuko used to place her hand on the lid of my casket to wake me. The friction of the touch pulled me back from the sensations leading me to my Oblivion.

Are you awake, my love? Mirela asked me mentally.

My love? After killing my friends and condemning me to this box, she still referred to me as her love. I wanted to tear her eyes out, but at the same time I also wanted her to open this box and wrap her arms around me.

I abandoned both desires and asked, Is Berthold alive?

Just then, a faint light entered the sarcophagus as the carved eye holes were pressed down and slid open like eyelids. I saw Mirela's face close to the sarcophagus lid. She moved slightly and the lips of the carved mouth parted.

"Berthold is alive," she said aloud. "His purpose to me is not yet lost as his life still remains in your hands."

With Mayuko and Zacharias dead, I should have learned my lesson and remained servile, but the way she dangled Berthold's life before me angered me. I bit my tongue until it bled, and with the mouth of the sarcophagus open, I spit blood in Mirela's face. I expected her to close the mouth of the sarcophagus so I couldn't spit again but she only smiled and wiped the blood from her cheek and chin and placed her fingers in her mouth and tasted my blood.

"What am I going to do with you, Orly?"

"You already decided. You're gonna keep me in this box and make me your new Ji'Indushul."

"If only it were that simple, for I do love you so."

I thought of what Yelena had told me in the Oblivion—that Mirela's love would always have designs behind it.

"If you really loved me, you wouldn't have killed my friends and locked me in here."

"And if you loved me, you would have told the truth when I accused Petru."

Maybe she was right. Maybe I didn't love her even if it felt like I did. Maybe what felt like love was actually hate. I marveled how my true feelings could remain a mystery even to me. But whatever they were, in that moment, I felt at my most simple level, I wanted her lips upon mine.

"Kiss me," I said.

Mirela smiled gently and leaned forward and placed her lips into the opening of the sarcophagus and kissed my lips. Her lips were warm. She did still have feelings for me and though I knew that was the advantage I needed, my entire being felt torn. The version of myself that wanted Mirela's love wrestled with the version that wanted to avenge those I loved and wanted out of this box.

"You're wrong. I do love you," I said. "I just thought I'd get away with lying about Petru."

"But you promised me truth, Orly."

"I know but, before he stabbed me in the back, I liked Petru and knew he couldn't really hurt you without Ji'Indushul. And I already killed Ji'Indushul."

"It still wasn't the truth."

"I don't want to live in this box forever."

"Then tell me how I can ever trust you not to protect or even join the conspirators."

I knew what I needed to say, but my feelings for her made it difficult for me to begin. I hated her and I loved her. I wanted to kill her but didn't want her dead. But I only had a moment to chose between love and hate, forgiveness and revenge.

"You don't have to trust me," I said. "You don't even need me to get what you want."

"I don't understand."

"There is something I never told you about Yelena."

"Ah, Yelena. How I detest hearing you say her name. And what would that be about your Yelena that you haven't told me?"

I swallowed before speaking. "After Yelena drank my blood to turn me she could see all the things I see in my scribbles."

"I don't believe you, Orly. You had been giving Yelena scribbles of innocent people for her to feed on. Had she been able to read the scribbles she would have known."

"She did know. She stopped caring."

"Again, I don't believe you. What could have made her suddenly forget the conscience she was plagued with?"

"Her love for me. She was happy again. Remember? That's why you killed her. Because she was happy again."

"But I've drunk your blood and I still see nothing."

"You drank my vampiric blood, not my mortal blood," I replied.

"You have no mortal blood to drink."

"I do in my Oblivion."

"And have you found your Oblivion?"

"Yes. I have." Could I really do this to her? I wondered and felt like crying.

"When did you find it?" she asked.

"When you shut me in this box."

"No. That would be too sudden."

"You bringing me to yours and Konomi bringing me to hers made it easier for me to know how to find it. My Oblivion is my hospital. I'm back there again, dying from my cancer."

She paused. I think she believed me.

"I drank Ji'Indushul's mortal blood," she said. "I didn't gain his ability to read minds, nor did you."

"I can't say what happens with Ji'Indushul's power. I can only tell you what happened with Yelena."

It was all a lie. Yelena could never see what I saw in my scribbles, before or after she drank my blood. But I was fighting to avoid an eternity in this sarcophagus and fighting to finally get my revenge and would say anything I needed to.

"Take me to your Oblivion then," she said.

"Let me out of this fucking box and I will."

"How do I know you're telling the truth, Orly?"

"How do I know you're not gonna just kill me once you drink my mortal blood?"

"Because I love you," she answered.

"And I want you to love me. I want you to be able to read the scribbles yourself because then when you tell me you love me, I'll know it's not just because of the scribbles."

I wanted her to say that she loved me and that it never had anything to do with the scribbles, but she didn't.

"Even if I could read the scribbles," she said, "you'd still have to draw them for me."

"No. I taught Yelena how to draw them herself. It took her a while to get it but she did."

"You better not be lying to me, Orly."

"I'm not. I promise. I never told you before because I thought you wouldn't want me anymore."

"You were wrong," she said, and I wanted to believe her, even though the die was already cast, and I was leading her to her end.

Mirela spoke an incantation in the language of the Cobalshik and I knew she was letting me out. And though it was what I had hoped for and what was necessary for me to kill her, I felt my heart retreat, and wondered if in this quick conversation I had gone further than I was willing to follow through.

Slowly, the sarcophagus separated at its invisible seam that ran lengthwise around the perimeter of the box and the top half lifted off like a lid. As I suspected, we were in her bedchamber. I lay there looking at her, searching for love in her eyes. The way she looked at me differed so much from the way Yelena looked at me.

Still wearing the bloodstained black velvet gown Babette made for me, I rose and stepped out of the bisected sarcophagus. I extended my hand to Mirela. She took it and I guided her toward the bed.

"Is this the way to your Oblivion?"

"I want you to make love to me one more time," I answered.

"One more time before what?"

"Before you don't need me anymore."

"I'll always need you," Mirela said demonstratively.

I turned my back to her and she unzipped my gown. It fell to the floor. I turned to her and stepped out of my shoes. Mirela turned and I unlaced her corset and she removed the rest of her gown herself. She stepped out of her shoes and we removed each other's undergarments and, completely undressed, save for the diamond that hung over my heart and the two amethysts on my finger, we climbed into bed.

She kissed me gently. I stopped her.

"What is it?" she asked.

"Once you know how to read the scribbles yourself I want you to promise me something."

"And what would that promise be?"

"I want you to kill Petru."

"I was going to kill him anyway. I do not trust his betrayal of you was entirely innocent. I believe he conspires."

She planned to kill him anyway. Though that surprised me, it didn't bother me, as I hated Petru now.

"Kill in the most painful way you know," I said.

She thought only briefly and then said, "As you desire," and she kissed me again.

I rolled on top of her and kissed her more vigorously. She offered her throat and I drank and then offered mine to her. Our lovemaking, though heightened by the ecstasy from the exchange of blood remained graceful and quiet as the rest of the coven slept beneath us, many perhaps dreaming of my damnation within that painted sarcophagus. In the sensual bliss shared between us, my love for Mirela surged and I struggled to ignore the image of her being burnt to cinders in the sunlight of my Oblivion.

Our lovemaking lasted hours and when we were finally finished, we lay covered in blood, completely spent. We allowed ourselves to sleep in each other's arms. When we woke, it was nearly nightfall.

"We should bathe," I said. "Have Agrapina change the bedding."

Mirela called for Agrapina as we climbed out of the bed and headed to the bath.

I sat between her legs, with my back to her, as she washed the blood from my skin. I looked at my left hand, at the ring with the two amethysts she had slipped on my finger. I submerged it below the water's surface and watched as the amethysts stared back at me, quivering as the bathwater rippled.

Wouldn't this be the last time she bathed me? Would Yelena be alive again in my Oblivion? What would Mirela do when she saw Yelena? Would the sun certainly rise again in my hospital room? Could I really go through with damning her to the sunlight? Is it possible Mirela is impervious to the sunlight? I had failed to penetrate her breast when I tried to kill her with the stake. And even if she is subject to the pains of the sun, did I have the power to keep her trapped within my Oblivion? Would I be able to endure watching my lover die?

I turned in the tub and faced her. She looked at me as if waiting for me to speak, but I didn't. I took the sponge from her and dipped it in the hot, soapy and bloodstained water and brought it to her skin.

When we finally left the bath and dried each other and reentered the bedchamber, Mirela's bedding had been changed and made up with fresh blankets and pillows. Undergarments had also been laid out for us and we began to dress.

"Put on a gown and wear your tiara," I said.

"Why?"

"Because it feels like my wedding day. I want the first time you see my Oblivion to be special. I'll put on a gown too, but it won't really matter because I'll end up being in pajamas."

She stopped and looked at me. "My instincts tell me to fear your Oblivion, Orly."

"Why? I told you it's just my hospital. You'll still be a vampire and I won't just be mortal, I'll be a mortal dying of leukemia."

"Something Ji'Indushul told you."

What made her guess that? Was it her endless suspicions or did thousands of years give her a wisdom that told her everything?

"The only thing Ji'Indushul said was to never stop serving you or I'd end up like him, and it seems like he was right."

"Tell me you love me, Orly."

"I love you. With all my heart."

"Tell me you forgive me. For Yelena."

"I already forgave you for Yelena."

"Tell me you forgive me for your friends. For Mayuko and Zacharias."

I felt this was a test. If I forgave her for them already she would know I was lying.

"I'm sorry. I'm still too hurt. I can't forgive you for them yet."

She nodded her head and went to her expansive wardrobe to select a gown.

"Wear white for me, my love," I said.

She turned to me, suspiciously and I thought I had gone too far. "What?" I asked.

"The way you called me your love. It felt different. It felt like you had grown up a little more."

With nothing to say, I merely shrugged.

A new gown, one of black satin, had been laid over a chair for me.

I finished dressing first and, in my new gown, I climbed back onto the bed, lying atop the new bedding, and rested my head on the pillows. I watched as Mirela put her hair up and fitted her tiara—the tiara of the imparateasa—upon her head. I felt my heart pounding with love as I stared at her in all her radiant and sublime beauty, and I was overcome, believing she loved me. Once her tiara was properly fastened, she spoke.

"How do I look?" she asked.

"You look angelic. No. You look seraphic," I said.

She smiled gently but enough that I saw her fangs. She approached the bed. I moved over and she lay beside me. We lay in silence like a virginal couple waiting to make love for the first time.

Finally Mirela spoke. "So how do we get there, Orly? Through sound? Through touch?"

"I haven't the slightest idea," I said. "I just wanted to get out of that box."

She turned and looked at me quizzically and I laughed.

"I'm only kidding," I said and turned on my side to face her and felt Yelena's diamond slip into my armpit. She in turn faced me. "Give me your hand," I said. She offered her left hand and I took it and placed it upon my heart. I felt the warmth of her touch upon my chest. "Do you feel it beating?" I asked.

"Yes."

"Close your eyes. Do you hear it beating?"

"Yes."

"Listen closer," I whispered. "Do you hear the beeping?"

No. I hear no beeping, she said telepathically.

I heard it already.

It's my heart monitor. Keep listening, you'll hear it.

A few seconds passed.

I hear it now, she said.

Inhale. Can you smell the rubbing alcohol?

I listened as she inhaled.

Yes. It's slight, she answered.

I opened my eyes. I was already in my hospital room, in my bed, in my pajamas, feeling weary and sick. Things looked as they did during my first visit except for two things. The first was that Mirela lay beside me in her white gown and tiara with her eyes closed. The second, and much to my surprise and dismay, the curtains over the window were drawn shut. As they had not been shut during my first visit to my Oblivion, I was confused as to why they were shut now. And as I knew I was too weak to get out of bed to open them myself, I felt my plans had been thwarted and I wondered if there were any way possible that this circumstance could be by Mirela's doing. Did she know the sun rose in my Oblivion?

"Your fingertips on your right hand. Feel the bedding. Is it not soft anymore?" I asked.

"The sheets feel rough. Cheap," she spoke aloud.

"Open your eyes," I said.

Mirela's eyes opened slowly. She smiled faintly. "So you really did find it," she said. She looked at me and touched my face and then touched my hair, undoubtedly feeling the bald spots, and I felt myself blush.

"You poor thing," she said. "How do you feel?"

"Tired. Like I'm dying again."

I still had the buttons on the rail of my hospital bed memorized and I pressed one to make the top half of the mattress rise and we were brought to an inclined position so that it was easier to look about the room.

"This is where I lived," I said.

Mirela sat to my left, away from the window, on the opposite side of the bed Yelena had lain when I first visited my Oblivion. I watched as she took in the surroundings. There wasn't much to see. Her eyes moved over the hospital equipment, the generic framed art print on the far wall, the closed door that led into the hall, the lone visitor chair in the room. Her eyes finally settled on the table. Upon it was my pad of paper and crayons and a couple of completed scribbles.

"If you go and get my stuff, I can finally draw you," I said.

"Not on your life," Mirela said with a smile. "It looks like you've already drawn some people. Who are they?"

"I don't remember. I can't tell from here. Get them for me and I'll tell you."

Mirela climbed out of the hospital bed and stood before the table and picked up the scribbles and stared at them. As

I watched her, I recognized that even here I still held her tenderly within my slowly beating heart. I hadn't been sure I would still love her once I was again mortal. And I hadn't wanted to love her in my Oblivion because this was where I knew I had to kill her. I had counted on my mortality to unbind me, as her blood no longer flowed through me here. But it was unmistakable—I did still love her and killing her would try my already weakened heart.

She brought the two scribbles to me. I could see the one on top.

"Yeah, I remember him. I hated him so much."

"Shhh," she said. "Don't tell me any more of what you see. I want to be the one telling you."

I knew she wanted my blood because she thought it would unlock the scribbles to her, but I didn't know how long it would be until sunrise.

She laid the scribbles on the blanket covering my legs and climbed back in bed beside me. Her face moved close to my throat.

"Wait," I said.

"What is it?"

"If I give you this, can you really give me an adult body?"

"Do you want an adult body?"

"I don't know. But I'm asking if you really can do it if I wanted it."

But before she could answer, there was a knock at the door and it began to open.

"You have visitors here?"

"Only nurses," I replied.

A soft voice greeted me.

"Good evening, little one," Yelena said as she entered the room.

Mirela sat up quickly. She looked at Yelena and then looked at me.

"Mommy?" I said, puzzled as if I had not expected to see her.

Yelena came around the bed, bent forward and kissed my forehead. I reached up for her and she hugged me affectionately. "I've missed you so much," she said softly into my ear. She then stood and curtsied politely to Mirela.

"Hello, Imparateasa."

"You still call me your imparateasa even though I killed you," Mirela said plainly.

"Here you have not yet killed me," she said to Mirela kindly without any trace of bitterness. She then looked at me. "I didn't realize you already had a visitor tonight, my sweet girl. I'll just straighten up a bit and let you be."

Yelena picked up the scribbles off the bed and placed them neatly back on the table. She then walked to the window and opened the curtains.

"The stars are out tonight," she remarked as she stared out the window, but her tone was distant as if she were not speaking to anyone in particular.

Yelena turned to us, but no one said anything, not even Mirela, who seemed passive and out of character. The silence quickly made the moment uncomfortable.

"I'll leave you now," Yelena said and stepped to my bedside and leaned forward and kissed me again. This time she kissed me on the lips.

"Will I see you again?" I asked.

"Of course you will." She smiled with adoration in her eyes as she looked at me. And then she turned to Mirela. "Goodbye, Imparateasa," she said.

Mirela did not say goodbye. She only nodded as she would to any of her subjects. Yelena walked to the door, turned back, and smiled at me lovingly, her fangs bright. She left and shut the door behind her. Mirela and I were again alone.

"Has she ever come before?" Mirela asked me.

"No. But I've only been here once."

"I don't know that I believe you."

"Why would I lie about that?"

"I'm not sure, but I don't think you would have let her go so readily," Mirela said suspiciously.

"I promise I'm telling you the truth. I wouldn't have even let you come here if I knew she'd be here too. I don't want to see you kill her again."

"Give me your blood," she said, seeming to ignore what I just said.

"You're mad," I said, trying to buy time.

"I'm not mad. I'm just finding it difficult to trust you."

"Kiss me first."

"Your mother just did."

Mirela had been jealous of Yelena because of Marcel. Was she now jealous of Yelena because of me?

"I can't help it that she loves me too," I said. "And you know she's not even real anymore. She's dead."

Mirela pondered that momentarily and seemed to soften. She leaned toward me and placed her lips upon mine and kissed me gently.

"I'm sorry," she said. "You know how jealous I am."

"I know. Thank you for kissing me." I turned my head toward the window as if offering my throat. I wasn't sure if the sky outside had gotten any brighter. "Drink," I said.

I felt her icy breath on my neck. She bit and my blood began to flow into her mouth. Though she had drunk relatively little, it was enough for me to feel lightheaded.

"That's more than Yelena drank," I lied.

Mirela pulled her face away from my neck.

"Heal the wound," I said softly, turning to her.

Mirela bit her lip and a drop of blood surfaced. She leaned forward again and kissed my throat where she had bitten, using her lips to smear the blood. Soon, the wound was no more and her blood on my mortal skin evaporated.

Mirela's mood seemed to brighten even though I was still dying before her eyes.

"Should I get the scribbles?" she asked.

I reached over and took her hand and squeezed it.

"Not now," I said. "I feel so weak. I need to rest. Just hold me for a while."

Mirela nestled closer and wrapped her arms around me. I closed my eyes in resignation and sorrow. Though hours away, I sensed the approaching dawn. The time was coming for her to burn. I knew I had orchestrated her death well. And though I tried to harness my need for revenge for Yelena and my recently killed friends, my heart was still breaking for my lover. I still had time to let her go.

She whispered in my ear. "I'd like it if yours was the first scribble I read. It would make me feel closer to you than ever."

Of course she wanted to scribble me. She wanted to know everything, all my secrets, all my lies, just as I wanted to know all of hers.

Lethargically, I replied. "The first scribble Yelena read was her own. I think it made it easier for her to learn how to do it, looking at herself. And it brought back so many memories for her."

"I told you. I won't allow you to scribble me, Orly."

I squeezed her hand again. "Shhh," I said softly. "Let me rest a bit more."

She held me tighter and I struggled not to cry and give myself away.

"Tell her to leave. Tell her to leave now!" my soul shrieked.

But I said nothing. I let the lassitude of my cancer put me to sleep.

THIRTY-FOUR

I woke with a start when Mirela screamed. With great sadness I ascertained she had allowed herself to fall asleep while holding me in my hospital bed. Though the warmth of sunlight was hardly perceptible upon my face, I saw out the window that daybreak had come and the sky had grown lighter than it had been before I fell asleep. The sun was definitely rising in my Oblivion.

I quickly noticed the smell of her smoldering flesh. Still screaming and with a look of terror I had never seen in her, Mirela jumped out of the bed and rushed to the curtains, but she could not pull them closed. It was as though they had become an immovable prop on the set of a television show. She rushed to the door and pulled down on the handle, and though the handle gave way, the door would not pull open for her. Something instinctive told me I had to will the ability for the door to be opened for someone foreign to my Oblivion. She slammed into it, still screaming, but she could not break the door down. She could not escape my Oblivion. I was the master here.

As the room continued to brighten, her skin sizzled, and she began to burn slowly. She leapt to the floor, trying to take cover in the shadow of my bed, but it wasn't enough. She continued to burn.

"Orly, let me out!" she cried, but I didn't answer.

I could hear her thrashing on the linoleum floor. The smell of her searing and smoking flesh sickened my stomach.

"Please, Orly!"

Warm tears began to slip from my eyes, but still I did nothing but lay in my bed.

She groaned on the floor in agony.

"I'll kill you, you traitorous bitch!" she spit out in a voice that did not sound like her own. It had taken on a tone I can only describe as demonic. Her right hand reached the top of the bed, clutching at the sheets. As she gripped it, her hand and arm became increasingly exposed to the sunlight and her skin ignited. Her left hand, similarly alight, gained hold of the sheets and Mirela struggled to pull herself up. It was then I saw her face—all of her flawless beauty was being torched, her perfect skin deteriorating and sinking into her skull.

I could see it in her eyes, which remained violet, that she meant to murder me.

With the strength she still possessed, and despite the steadily rising sun setting her ablaze even more furiously, Mirela climbed back onto the bed and straddled me. She placed her withering hands around my throat and tried to strangle me the way a mortal would. That she didn't kill me mentally—that I didn't explode into flames, bleed out of my facial orifices, or have my head sever itself from my body—told me she was powerless in the sunlight. But as she was now completely aflame, wherever her body touched me, my human skin burned upon contact and it was painful. I thought I might die in the inferno she was sharing with me, but I didn't fear it. Some part of me wanted to perish with her so that the feeling of loss after loss after loss in my heart would cease to exist.

She finally bared her fangs and I waited calmly for her to tear into my throat and kill me, bleeding me dry, but the morning sunlight in the hospital room of my Oblivion continued to grow brighter and the sun's luminosity quickly overpowered Mirela so that she lost her grip on me and fell off the bed. I could smell she was still burning, but with her skin no longer in contact with mine, most strangely, I did not feel the aftereffects of being burned. My skin appeared and felt completely unharmed.

On the linoleum she kicked and flailed and began to weep. She whimpered in despair. "My love. My love."

I gripped the sheets tightly. How long her death was taking. It lasted far longer than Yelena's death had or the deaths of those I had expelled from the slicing. My heart ached, but I resisted my love for her and tried to see only the faces of those she had killed and taken from me.

"I love you, Orly. Don't let me die," she said, now gasping for breath.

I was breaking inside because, despite her wanting to kill me only moments before, I still felt she loved me. I wanted to go to her and take her in my arms. My saline tears now streamed ceaselessly and unabatedly. I needed her. Who else would ever love me the way she did? In allowing her to die, I was resigning myself to an eternity without love.

I gathered what stamina I had and slowly climbed out of bed. Standing beside the bedside table, I swept the scribbles and all the blank sheets of paper and crayons to the floor. Then, losing the strength to stand, I collapsed beside her. Lying on the floor, I struggled to gather my wits. I saw Mirela, curled in a fetal position and covering her face. Her once porcelain skin had blackened to charcoal and resembled the cracked underside of a burning log after it is flipped over.

A clean sheet of paper lay beside me. Mercilessly, I looked for and found a crayon and reached for it. I had to see what was true and what were lies. I had to know if she truly did love me. And so most cruelly, with her painfully burning to death before me and unable to resist, I began to scribble my lover—the imparateasa—as quickly as I could.

Though still aflame she lay motionless upon the floor. Though completely charred she was still recognizable as Mirela. Though she had been so long exposed she still had not turned to ash. The strength of all her vampiric centuries continued to sustain her in the certain death of the sunlight.

"Orly, make it stop," Mirela gasped. "There's still time to let me live."

I had seen enough. I dropped the crayon and pushed her scribble away. I crawled to the door, and reaching up as far as I could, I grabbed its handle and pulled the door open.

I was no longer in my pajamas. I lay in Mirela's bed wearing my black gown. I was again strong. I was again a vampire.

I turned to my left. Mirela's burned body lay beside me in a white dress that remained scorched by the fire of my Oblivion. The tiara barely clung to the head of the imparateasa.

"Put me in my coffin," she whispered. "I can still recover."

Mirela had escaped my Oblivion. I had allowed her to escape so that she might continue to live, though it was clear she was still dying from the injuries she had sustained there. Could her coffin really save her? Would it allow her to reverse the harm of my Oblivion and regain her strength now that she was here, in the real world? Was it possible that she would even reclaim her beauty? My wrist still bore the sunlit scar I received the morning Yelena died. Had Mirela's unrivaled age made her so powerful that she could even overcome the damage daylight had so savagely wreaked upon her flesh?

"My coffin," she said again.

I didn't move. I'd never even seen her coffin. "I don't know where it is," I said.

"Any coffin," she said.

I rose slightly and rested on one elbow. I looked down at her, searching her face for traces of her former self. I reached forward and stroked her hair.

She looked at me, directly into my eyes. I could see she understood I would not bring her to any coffin. I thought she might cry, but no tears fell from her eyes. They still glistened violet.

I cried though. My blood tears dripped onto the bed where we had made love so many times.

"Don't cry, my love," Mirela said softly. "Do what you mean to do, for that is why you permitted my escape. You are a vampire, so drink. Drink it all."

In that moment I felt ashamed knowing she understood why I had brought her back from the Oblivion. In her weakened state it took effort, but she smiled at me and in her eyes I saw love. I took her in my arms, drew her face close and kissed her one last time. Her lips, though burned, were still soft. My face slid below her chin. She gasped as I placed my lips upon her throat. I felt her grip upon me tighten. I opened my mouth and plunged my teeth into her.

"Be ruthless, my love. Be ruthless."

Her breathing quickened momentarily but slowed the more I drank. It was as though she were relaxing into her death. I felt the strength of all her murderous years entering my body as each remaining gush of her blood spurted into my mouth. My heart screamed at me to stop, but I didn't. My blood tears ran down her neck. Eventually the propulsion and the intensity of her bleeding began to diminish, and I began to suck upon her wounded throat until there was nothing left. At last she was empty. She was dead. Mirela died in my embrace as would a lover.

Just as the walls of the pit of Mirela's Oblivion had fallen away as we departed, everything in the room—the bed, the furniture, the candles, the tapestries—even the painted portrait of Marcel Bousquet fell away, crumbling like a sandcastle that had stood on the shore too long.

The illusion of Castle Cobălcescu faded away, and I found myself on the floor of the catacombs, surrounded by funerary boxes. My body was still entwined with the charred and desiccated corpse of the imparateasa.

One by one, the coffins and caskets began to open. Ancients and Eternals alike stepped out of them. All gathered round to view the body of the imparateasa—tyrant of thousands of years and the source of the Cobălcescu bloodline—dead in the arms of a child.

THIRTY-FIVE

I unlocked my arms from Mirela and rose to my feet. I looked into the faces of the coven. Some showed anger, some repressed excitement, but most registered a look of uncertainty. As I scanned the crowd, I made eye contact with a number of them. Trajan looked at me with hatred. Viorica looked upon me warmly. Petru, whom I vowed to kill, confused me as he wore a gentle smile upon his face. My eyes finally found Berthold's. To my relief, he was still alive and he looked back at me tenderly and sympathetically, clearly relieved I had survived. Kristy was not with him.

From the crowd an Ancient rushed at me. My thoughts were now quicker than ever, and I looked upon the outcome of what was about to happen with sadness. It was Babette flying toward me. In her hands she gripped the metal stake that had slain Alexi Pavlovich. I stood still, knowing by intuition that I was stronger than ever. Babette thrust the stake at my heart, but it failed to puncture my skin. It vibrated so fiercely in Babette's hands that she dropped it. She burst into flames before me and an instant later exploded into a cloud of black ash. I had not wanted to kill her. She had been so kind to me. I knew she had acted out of loyalty to her mistress.

The coven looked on with amazement. Not because Babette was dead. Not even because Mirela was dead. They were amazed that I was impenetrable by the stake. That power had not appeared in any of their scribbles. It was mine alone, now that all of Mirela's blood was inside me.

"You would be fools to challenge her," Petru said firmly.

"She will die another time then," Trajan replied, spitting on the dusty floor, before retreating to one of the holes in the ceiling, created by the sunken earth above. He shot out of the hole into the night. Others quickly followed, but I was not certain if they were following him, or simply fleeing from me.

Most of the Ancients remained, as did the rest of the Eternal, including Petru. I knew he knew I wanted to kill him. That, in all his wisdom, he remained confounded me.

"How come you stay?" I asked him. "You know I'm going to kill you for betraying me."

Viorica placed her hand upon my shoulder. "Be gentle, Orly. It was not Petru's fault any more than it was mine. We knew your love for Mirela caused you to abandon the revenge we all along intended to assist you with. We, the Eternal who remain here tonight, agreed to betray you in order to force you to act. Petru risked his own life to ensure Mirela's death."

Vasile nodded in assent.

"It is true, Orly," Codrina said in a solemn voice, uncharacteristic of her.

I looked at Petru.

"I am deeply sorry for the friends you lost, Orly Bialek," he said. "But it was the only way conceivable. Some of us had to die in order to kill Mirela. As Viorica said, it could have just as easily been me."

"How could it have been you?" I asked. "You proved to her I was a liar."

"Mirela's love for you changed her. For once in her life she became capable of forgiveness. I knew if she forgave you, she would kill me."

He was right. Mirela had forgiven me, and when I asked, she had agreed to kill Petru in the most painful way she knew. My legs felt as if they were about to buckle and I lowered myself to the the flagstones and sat upon the floor of the ruined catacombs.

"I've lost so much. Even her," I said quietly, looking at Mirela's body.

Petru knelt beside me. "Eternal life means eternal loss. The older you become the more you will realize that truth." He extended his hand toward Mirela. Her tiara lifted from her head gently and drifted into his waiting hand. "Filled with her blood, you are the strongest of us now, Orly Bialek," he said and placed the tiara upon my head. "You are imparateasa."

I was shocked by his last sentence. I was shocked to be wearing Mirela's tiara. I had no will to be imparateasa. Yet as I looked around the catacombs, all remaining bowed and curtsied before me. It was undeniable. It was inescapable. I was imparateasa. Though my legs still felt weak in the contemplation of all I had lost, I knew I had to stand and slowly I rose to my feet. The entire coven, even the Eternal, lowered their heads in reverence.

"Please rise. All of you," I said. "The Communion of Ancients is over."

The coven rose, and standing beneath the low ceiling of the ruins, they towered over me. I looked up into their faces and then again upon Berthold's.

"Where is Kristy?" I asked.

"I told her to flee when daylight came. I am sure she is still making her way down this mountain."

"Find her then and bring her home," I said before turning to the others. "Each of you find your way home safely. I wish to be alone with my love."

I lowered myself before Mirela's body and lifted her. I carried her across my arms to my coffin—the one which was too large for me alone and had been damaged by the metal stake. I laid her inside it and then climbed in with her and shut the lid. From without I could hear the coven departing one by one. I sensed Petru was the last to leave.

"This will be our last day together," I whispered into her ear as I lay my arm over her and pulled her into me.

The next night, I knelt beside my coffin and looked down at Mirela's charred corpse for the last time. I ran my fingers through her brittle hair, touched her cheek, and then fitted the coffin lid over her.

From the floor I lifted crumbling flagstones and dug an excessively deep hole. I laid my coffin that held Mirela's body at the bottom of the grave.

"Sleep now, my love. I will live and I will try to be ruthless," I said quietly before throwing the first handful of earth upon the coffin that was now hers for eternity.

Once the grave was completely filled, I replaced the flagstones over it and said a prayer that no one would ever find it.

Though I took my time descending the mountainside, knowing I had hours until daybreak, my path was deliberate. I headed back to where Mirela had shown me the earthly tomb of Ji'Indushul. She said she had only shown me a doorway to his tomb and that his true resting place could be anywhere on the mountain, but I suspected it was a lie and that with Mirela gone, her magic would no longer conceal it.

But it was not a lie. When I arrived at the spot, the boulders that were supposed to cover the burial place were not there. I went to my knees anyway and began to dig. Quickly, I found myself at the bottom of a hole, twenty feet deep, but there was no tomb. Resigned, I levitated back upon solid ground and replaced the earth I had excavated. I didn't have to refill it but chose to as I didn't want to suggest to anyone who might come this way that there was anything on this mountain worth digging for.

I wiped the freshly turned earth from my dress the best I could.

I sailed through the forested mountainside, scanning the ground for piles of boulders that might be covering Ji'Indushul's buried tomb. I smelled the sap of the pine trees, heard the the chilled night wind rushing between them, and sensed the burrowing of animals below the forest floor. After over an hour of searching I finally landed when I came upon something completely unnatural in these natural surroundings. My feet touched down at the edge of a crater that looked like it had been created by a fallen bomb or meteor. It was significantly deeper than the hole I had dug in my earlier searching. Large stones were littered around its rim. Trees had been uprooted and lay fallen. Inside the crater were the remains of the tomb, now nothing more than a scattering of broken bricks. It was as if an explosion had gone off from within. At the very base of the crater was the cursed wooden sarcophagus. It lay in splinters and was empty. In what had been his earthly resting place, the body of Ji'Indushul was nowhere to be found.

At the foot of the gravestone that bore my name, I excavated the earth until I found the empty and broken casket I had once been buried in after I had died my mortal death in the hospital and had awakened within after Yelena's vampiric blood had made me immortal. Upon the grass above me laid a new, highly polished black casket. Within it was the body of my best friend. I had kept my promise not to leave her behind in Mirela's domain. Mayuko would remain close to me—buried in my own grave.

"I'm sorry, Button," I whispered as I laid her to rest.

As I departed the cemetery, I passed a small group of goths sitting amongst the graves. They were passing around a bottle of vodka and having a good time. They didn't hear me coming, but were startled when I came into view. They stared at me bewildered as I looked back at them. And then, wanting nothing of them, I disappeared. And when I did, they didn't scream, they didn't run. They had forgotten me. They had forgotten they had seen me at all.

I had been back in Los Angeles for over a month before I saw Berthold. I hadn't fed once since I returned. I lay the entire time inside my casket where it rested in the secret chamber beneath Yelena's house. From within my casket I repeatedly visited my Oblivion.

"Good evening, little one," Yelena always said when she arrived. She would climb in bed with me and hold me as I mourned the entire night. When dawn approached, I would send her home so that I would never again see her turned to ash. Sometimes, before she'd leave, I'd ask her to bring me the scribble of Mirela. That scribble, far from complete and not filling the entire sheet, existed only in my Oblivion. Yelena would pick it up without bitterness and lay it upon the blanket that covered me and then kiss me goodbye.

I learned from Mirela's scribble that she had lived throughout the centuries deeply troubled by the thought of being overthrown and killed. As a result she had killed hundreds of vampires who were not Cobălcescu, and many more who were. I also learned that though the Cobalshik had the legendary reputation of being body stealers, Mirela had not stolen her own body, and did not know how to steal one for me. It had been a lie. Mirela had been born that beautiful and with her arresting violet eyes. But the thing I learned that caused me to suffer the greatest was that in Mirela's heart—despite her words, her affection, and her forgiveness—it wasn't beyond doubt that she had truly loved me. Rather, what appeared in her scribble was that she loved me only as much as she was still capable. Living through so many centuries had blurred her ability to love anyone wholly and purely.

I wondered had they both lived, would Yelena have eventually lost her ability to love Marcel as completely as she had? And as Marcel was so much older than she, had his ability to love her back in the same unfaltering way already begun to recede while they were together?

Had I not killed Mirela and become empress, would I someday have stopped loving her inasmuch as I still did? Certainly the intensity of new love would have faded and the overwhelming madness of limerence would have gone with it, but would the night have ever come where what I felt for Mirela would only be recognizable as a ghost of love past?

Having survived, I still had eternity before me. In that eternity I hoped to love again, but wondered if my years in their endless compounding would inevitably prevent me from truly loving anyone—even when they truly loved me. The answer seemed to be yes and this foreshadowed emptiness filled me with a despondency I had never known.

I was in my casket when I heard the front door open. I heard two sets of footsteps. I recognized Berthold's and concluded the softer steps had to belong to Kristy. I pushed the lid of my casket open and stepped out. I climbed the stairs, passed through the empty closet, and headed to the living room to find Berthold standing with Kristy. Berthold looked slightly ill at ease, but Kristy was definitely anxious.

"Empress," Berthold said, and he bowed as Kristy curtsied.

"Please don't do that, Berthold," I said.

He straightened himself, but Kristy remained curtseying until Berthold reached for her elbow and nudged her to stand.

"Does Hisato know I'm back?" I asked.

"I haven't seen him."

"Why did you take so long to see me?" I asked looking straight at Berthold, doing my best to ignore Kristy. "Were you avoiding me?"

"Of course not. In the catacombs…the way you asked to be alone, I knew you loved her, Orly. I wanted to give you time to grieve before I came back."

Kristy sat closely to Berthold on the sofa, as if counting on his protection. We sat mostly in silence, me looking at Berthold and him looking at me. Where was my love for him now? Had it been buried beneath my love for Mirela? Could it ever resurface and bloom once more?

During our fifth round of scotches, Berthold asked, "Why did you ask to have Kristy's body?"

I did not let him know it was not possible to steal her body. I emptied my tumbler and placed it back on the table. "I wanted to be grown and beautiful," I said.

"You are beautiful, Orly," he answered.

I finally looked at Kristy. "Do you think I'm beautiful?" I asked.

She hesitated but then meekly said, "I do think you are beautiful."

I was glad she didn't say "very beautiful" because I would know for sure she was lying.

I rose to my feet, still looking at Kristy. "Come with me."

They both stood.

"No. Not you, Berthold. Just her."

They looked at each other warily.

"I said come with me."

I headed toward the back of the house and the French doors that led out onto the terrace were thrown open as I approached. I heard Kristy following me hesitantly. I went out and stood at the balustrade. Kristy stood behind me. I said nothing and waited until she finally came closer and stood beside me.

"The stars are out tonight," I said.

"They are," she replied apprehensively.

"Have you ever loved someone so deeply as him?"

Without pause, she said, "No. Never."

I knew I would never have Berthold to myself as I did when we were in Tokyo. Not as long as Kristy was in his life. I thought of Mirela's last words to me, *Be ruthless, my love. Be ruthless.*

I extended my hand to her and cautiously she took it. I felt her shudder at my touch though my skin now possessed humanly warmth. I pulled her down to me, her face near mine, and startled, she let out a subdued cry as I bit into her throat. It was as if she were too afraid of me to scream in earnest. I heard Berthold's rapid footsteps approaching as I drank. When he reached the doorway of the terrace he exclaimed, "Orly, please! No!"

Her blood was sweet and I savored it. I relaxed my jaw and released my bite. She was still alive. I brought my wrist to my mouth and bit into it and then thrust it to Kristy's mouth.

She didn't open her lips readily, and I had to press my wrist upon them to get my blood to spill into her mouth. Quickly, I pulled my wrist away. I had given her enough.

"Swallow it, or I will kill you," I said.

Her eyes widened, and I watched her swallow the little I had given her. The strength of my blood caused her to begin trembling and gasping for air immediately. She died swiftly thereafter and her body went limp in my arms. By now, Berthold was out on the terrace with us, but he still kept his distance. It was true—even Berthold was afraid of me, afraid of my power, afraid of me as empress. In a nostalgic way, I missed the old us. I knew we would never be the same. I had lost him. I had lost the Berthold who had once been mine.

Eternal life means eternal loss. The older you become the more you will realize that truth.

I carried Kristy's lifeless body to him and placed her in his arms. With my hand whose ring finger was bejeweled with two amethysts, I reached for my heart and slipped it beneath the pendant that held Yelena's diamond. My heartbeat was faint.

Berthold looked into my eyes. In them he recognized that after all that had happened between me and Mirela, he had lost me too. He nodded slightly and then carried Kristy off into the night. He would bury her somewhere, and when she woke, they would experience forever together.

THANK YOU FROM THE AUTHOR

I would like to thank my beta readers: Paul Burt, Rosemary Giese, Kristy King, Aaron Marshall, Amirah Schwartz, Holly Vernola-Angelopoulos, and Christine Wu, for their tireless commitment to the writing of this novel. Your sincere feedback has made it a better book. I appreciate your patience and endurance when answering my many, many questions.

I would like to thank my editor, Carol Jean Tomoguchi-Perez, for her expertise and precision which have made this book printable. Your affection toward the text is invaluable.

I would like to thank the employees of Starbucks Store #20537 for all the coffee drinks they made me and for allowing me to sit there for so many months as I wrote this novel. You're my favorite barista crew ever.

Finally, I would like to thank my readers for staying with me on my journey as an author. This book would not exist were it not for you. My gratitude for your support and continued readership is beyond words.